NOTHING
HUMAN

NOTHING HUMAN

RONALD MUNSON

S I M O N   &   S C H U S T E R

LONDON·SYDNEY·NEW YORK·TOKYO·SINGAPORE·TORONTO

First published in Great Britain
by Simon & Schuster Ltd in 1992
A Paramount Communications Company

Copyright © Ronald Munson, 1992

Simon & Schuster Ltd
West Garden Place
Kendal Street
London W2 2AQ

A CIP catalogue record for this book is
available from the British Library
ISBN 0-671-71754-5

Printed and bound in Great Britain by
Butler & Tanner Ltd, Frome and London

To Miriam

"Ring-bright and subtle of mind"

I am grateful to Miriam Grove Munson,
Marian Young, Jane Rosenman, and Stephen
Selesnick for help in making this a better book.

I am human: nothing human is alien to me.

Terence

Contents

PART ONE

PROLOGUE

April 8
Friday

1

Friday 9:30 A.M.

The body had no head.

The head had been severed high up on the neck, and a stump of pale, mangled flesh stuck out from the torso. The butchery had been neatly done, and when viewed directly, the neck seemed to be a cross section of an anatomical display. Anyone looking closely could pick out the whitish strands of connective tissue and nerve sheaths embedded in the dark red flesh of the muscle. The ragged hole of the trachea gaped open in what appeared to be almost the exact center of the raw stump, and white glimpses of bone and cartilage showed through the crust of dried blood.

Lieutenant Eric Firecaster found himself staring at the grisly display longer than he needed to or wanted to. His mind was playing a trick on him and making it impossible for him to simultaneously see the body both as human and as headless.

The body was like a grotesque gestalt figure: viewed one way, it looked ordinary and familiar, but viewed another way, it looked alien and obscene. His mind simply refused to accept as real the combination headless–human. He suspected it was too threatening to his own sense of security and integrity. The combination was a contradiction that made the dominion of death undeniable.

The corpse was female and nude. It lay front down, and in addition to being headless, it had been mutilated in other ways. A pattern of five parallel cuts ran from the right shoulder to the waist on the left side, and another set of five ran from the left shoulder to the right side. It was as though the body had been marked with a large X. The cuts were narrowly spaced, about an inch apart, and obviously had been made with some sort of instrument. Whatever it was had been very sharp, for the flesh was sliced to the bone along most of the length of the slashes. The small amount of dried blood surrounding them suggested they had been made after death, maybe after the head had been severed.

The same instrument had clearly been used on the buttocks, but

3

even more destructively. Both sides had been ripped and torn, as though the instrument had been sunk into the flesh with great force, then ripped out again. The mutilation seemed to have been thought out, rather than impulsive.

Firecaster knew that when the body was turned over, he would see much the same thing, only worse. The breasts would be cut to shreds, and the vaginal labia would be torn apart. Slashes in the abdomen would be as deep and destructive as those on the buttocks, and the slick reddish purple of the stomach and intestines would bulge through the mutilated tissues.

He refused to force himself to look at any of that. It would only make him feel sick and angry, and he would learn nothing useful. The pathologist's report would tell him everything he needed to know about the condition of the body.

He had needed only to glance at the body to realize he had seen the same methods and patterns of destruction three weeks earlier. The similarities were too obvious to miss. This realization brought with it the sickening awareness that if two young women had been killed in the same bizarre way, he wasn't dealing with independent homicides. Another headless, mutilated corpse would turn up before long, unless he could do something to stop it. Sensing his responsibility was like throwing a switch on a pump, and he immediately felt the pressure in the left side of his head start to build.

Mauve jogging shorts, a sweatshirt of the same color, white Nike running shoes, a white sports bra, and thick gray socks lay in a heap beside the body. The clothes were not folded, but they were piled all together in a neat stack. Everything seemed to have been done in an unhurried, carefully planned way. Firecaster felt certain an inventory of the clothes would show that the underpants were missing.

The body lay sprawled on the ground, with its legs together and its arms stretched out in a sacrificial position. A screen of yew bushes blocked off the scene, even though it was no more than thirty feet from the frozen mud of the jogging path that ran alongside the Charles River. Harvard students and local residents ran along the path at all hours, so it was possible that someone had seen or heard something.

The young male runner who had found the body was seated on an aluminum equipment box talking with Detective Sergeant Don Renuzi. Renuzi was sitting on a box beside the man, and the two were leaning toward one another in earnest conversation.

Firecaster suspected they would learn little from him. The man was on the scene too late to see more than Firecaster could see for himself. Still, during the four years he had worked with Renuzi, he

4

had come to respect his imagination and skill as an interviewer. Renuzi's ordinary, friendly approach won people's confidence in a way his own subdued, distant manner never did. If the man knew anything useful, Renuzi would find it out.

The area was cordoned off with white plastic flagging tied to iron rods driven into the frozen ground. Red and white "Crime Scene: Do Not Enter" placards hung from the plastic tapes, and the forensic crew was ready to go to work in the area as soon as he gave them the word. Three members of the team, two men and a woman, all dressed in uniform-blue down jackets, hovered just outside the rectangle, waiting impatiently for him to be finished with whatever it was he was doing.

He knew they wanted to get on with their jobs, but he had to study the scene until he was certain he had absorbed the details. Only in that way could he feel sure his unconscious might be able to tell him things about it his conscious mind had missed. He had to incorporate the scene, make it a part of himself. Although his body wanted to turn from the horror, his mind forced him to immerse himself in its most repellent features.

At least he was not holding up the work of the sketch artist. She was squatted down outside the tape barrier, a pad of quadrille paper clipped to her drawing board. She was already busy making a diagram of the general area, and as she sketched, she repeatedly glanced up to check details. The photographer was also busy. He was circling the area, snapping shots of the scene with Firecaster in it for scale. The detailed pictures he would do later with a meter rod in place.

Detective Karen Chase had enlisted the aid of two uniformed officers, and they were searching the scene. While Chase spiraled out from the location of the body, one of the officers spiraled in. The other officer walked a looping pattern that intersected with the spirals. It was all being done by the book, but Firecaster doubted the search would produce any results.

He decided he had seen as much as he could stand. The pressure in his head was worse, and he was beginning to feel the tug of tense muscles on the left side of his face. If he pushed himself, he would develop blurred vision and a dull nagging headache that was never helped by the aspirin he ate like candy. If he kept pushing, he would end up feeling he was outside of himself looking down on the scene, in some dead space cut off from everything. "Panic attacks," his internist had told him. "Anxiety reactions caused by sustained stress."

He had lived with these reactions for the last three years. They began as periods of agitation and nervousness during the worrying

5

months his wife was in and out of treatment at the Rush Psychiatric Institute. In the beginning, the reactions were relatively mild and occurred only episodically, but after Alice left him, they became severe. His mind felt fogged. Even getting through the day was a struggle.

After a few months, he came to realize that at least his intelligence and judgment didn't seem affected. He could still do his job, and strangely enough, it was during this period of concentrated misery that he became a better police officer. His own painful experiences extended his sympathy, and he found he could better understand people's aims and motives. With Alice gone, work became the focus of his life, and his accomplishments began to match his aims.

He studied the body in front of him. The crime was brutal and ugly, but more than that, it was morally repulsive. The killer had treated this unknown woman as a mere object, a trinket that he might do anything with he wished. He hadn't just taken her life, he had denied her humanity. This was the true crime. The mutilations were only its visible sign.

Firecaster's own body was now telling him it was time to leave.

He ducked under the ribbon of white tape and walked over to where Ed Murphy, the Deputy Chief Investigator of the forensics unit, was standing with the two others in his crew.

Firecaster nodded to Murphy. "Sorry to hold you up, but I wanted to get a sense of the scene."

"No problem," Murphy said.

"So far as I can tell, the perpetrator left a clean scene." Firecaster gave a slight shrug. "Maybe your group can turn up something I missed, at least some fibers or hairs. But don't worry about embarrassing me if you find something I should have seen."

Murphy shook his head, then pushed his red hair back from his forehead. "I don't go to church enough to believe in miracles," he said. He didn't smile.

Murphy was a tall man, well above average, but very thin and frail-looking. His pale, lightly freckled face always seemed to mirror an inner exhaustion ordinary rest couldn't remedy. Firecaster was aware that he and others working homicides asked more of Murphy than it was humanly possible to deliver. When you have no witnesses and no suspects, you always hope the lab people will tell you a little about who you should be looking for.

"I don't want to jinx us with a bad attitude," Murphy said. "Still, I'm afraid this scene is going to be just as bare as the last one."

"Me too," Firecaster admitted.

The crowd gathered on the path below the roped-off crime scene was not particularly large. Between fifteen and twenty people stood almost silently, watching the police go about their business. Fire-caster scanned the whole group carefully. He was not so much looking for familiar faces as he was familiarizing himself with the ones that were there. If he encountered any of the people again, he wanted to make sure he would recognize them. He would have a chance to study the faces later, since the photographer would get some shots of the crowd as part of his standard workup.

Taking crowd shots was a departmental requirement he had pushed through himself. He had gotten the idea a year earlier when a chain of investigation in a rape-murder case led to a man Firecaster vaguely remembered seeing before. It was the man's short curly hair that stuck in his mind, and when he finally associated the man with the crime scene, he was able to confront him and make him believe the police knew everything and he might as well confess.

As best Firecaster could tell, this crowd was made up mostly of students, professors, retirees, and people without jobs—just the cross section of citizens he would expect to find walking along the Charles on a chill but sunny weekday morning.

As he passed through the crowd, everyone looked at him with open curiosity, but as he turned his gaze toward them, they glanced away. Most seemed vaguely embarrassed about being there, and they had the same lowered eyes and slightly furtive look he had seen on the faces of men coming out of pornographic movies. The eight or ten women in the group seemed as uncomfortable at being noticed as the men.

Firecaster walked toward the collection of police vehicles parked on the side of Boylston Street, hardly more than three hundred feet away. He walked slowly, his eyes focused on the hard-packed dirt of the jogging path.

He looked up, then glanced over his shoulder. Detective Karen Chase and the two uniformed officers were still walking their intricate patterns in the wooded area outside the roped-off rectangle, still trying to find anything at all that might be connected with the headless human lying inside. Their heads down, their steps slow and deliberate, the three might be performance artists enacting a contemporary *danse macabre* for the gathered crowd of spectators.

He thought Murphy was right. The crime was too much like the Marie Thomas murder to make it likely they were going to learn anything. But they had to try, no matter how frustrating the effort. When he assimilated the facts about a homicide, he seemed incapable of keeping distance between himself and the victim. Along with the facts, he also seemed to assimilate the victim's anger, outrage, and sense of betrayal.

The only way he had discovered to relieve himself of this painful burden was to make sure that the killer not remain anonymous. He had learned that reparation was impossible and justice couldn't be guaranteed. The most that was obtainable was for the killer to learn that someone else knew what he had done to his victim and condemned him for it.

He had been carrying the burden of Marie Thomas for almost three weeks. She had been a twenty-six-year-old day-care teacher killed near MIT, in the parking garage of the Executive Inn, where she had been visiting friends staying at the motel. Although it had been a Friday night, she was going to hold parent conferences the next day. She had left her friends around eleven o'clock and was returning to her car when someone jumped her.

She must have been knocked out immediately and then dragged behind the elevator housing where the actual killing took place. No one had heard any sounds of a struggle, and particles of grease and dust from her clothes and scuff marks on her shoes indicated that at some point she had been pulled across the garage floor.

A study of the crime scene produced virtually no physical evidence. No weapon, no fingerprints, no semen, no hair, no fibers. All the blood seemed to belong to the victim, although there was so much of it that it would be impossible to detect a small quantity of anyone else's mixed with it. Even if the killer's blood type was different, it would take a lot of luck to get a sample containing it. Thomas's body showed no bruises, no defensive wounds, no skin under the fingernails. She might have been murdered by a ghost.

A microscopic examination of the edges of the wounds by Dr. Benson, the pathologist who did the autopsy, revealed traces of metal particles. Murphy's tests of the particles showed them to be low-quality carbon steel, much lower than the kind used in the manufacture of garden tools or cutting instruments.

Murphy had suggested that the killer might be using some sort of homemade device. "They don't use such poor-quality metal even in crap imported from Taiwan," he said. "There's no need for us to bother to look for manufacturers, because there just ain't going to be any."

The head had been relatively neatly severed, but as Benson pointed out, not much could be made of that fact. "Everybody knows you can't cut through bone," he said. "You've got to avoid the cervical vertebrae and the bony covering of the larynx. As long as you've got a fairly sharp, long-bladed knife and stick to the soft tissue, you're home free. That's what this guy did. You can tell by the nicks he made that he had to redirect his knife, whereas somebody like me would just cut through the neck without hitting anything."

Firecaster had been hoping for at least something useful from Benson, because he had gotten nothing from any other source. As this hope faded, he felt his frustration giving way to anger, but he knew Benson had done everything possible.

"Thanks," Firecaster said to him, trying to turn his anger into irony. "Now we know we don't have to waste time looking for a pathologist. Nothing special about the knife?"

"A heavy kitchen knife would have done it, the same kind all serious cooks use. Julia Child probably has a dozen of them."

"I don't think I'll bother asking her to see them," Firecaster said.

Interviews hadn't been any more helpful. They had turned up no jilted lovers or jealous boyfriends, no feuds or quarrels. Marie Thomas had been just an ordinary young woman who lived a very regular, ordinary sort of life. She had liked her job, was engaged to a social worker, and was happy to stay home and watch TV most nights. She and her fiancé had shared an apartment near Davis Square; both of them were science fiction fans whose idea of a good time was to attend science fiction conventions anyplace on the east coast.

No one appeared to have any reason to kill Marie Thomas. But then Firecaster hadn't thought she had been killed for anything like an ordinary and understandable reason.

Firecaster was nearly to his car when he turned around and walked back to talk to the uniformed sergeant in charge of crowd control. The man was sipping coffee from the gray lid of a stainless steel thermos bottle. The radio in his other hand crackled with distorted voices, and from time to time the sergeant said something into the condenser microphone. His eyes were in constant motion, watching civilians and keeping track of his own officers. His heavy face was reddened with the cold.

When he saw Firecaster coming toward him, he smiled and gestured with the plastic cup. "How about a little warm-up, Lieutenant? But I warn you, it's just coffee."

Firecaster smiled and shook his head. "Thanks, Teddy, but I'm going back to the shop anyway. I just want to ask you a favor. As soon as Murphy's team is finished and they move the body, will you call the fire department and ask them to send out a pumper and wash away as much blood as they can?"

The sergeant nodded, his smile gone. "I know the man to talk to," he said.

"I appreciate it," Firecaster said.

He gave a little fly-chasing wave of good-bye and walked toward the dark blue Saab sedan parked behind the patrol cars. Just as he was slamming the door of the Saab, a white station wagon with the Channel 5 logo painted on the doors pulled up to the curb. For a moment he wondered whether he had an obligation to be interviewed. He decided he didn't.

He started the engine and drove toward the station house. He tried to forget the way a small flap of pale skin had hung loose from the stump of her neck, like the skin hanging from the neck of a chicken.

2

Friday 3:30 P.M.

Firecaster sat in the partitioned cubicle that constituted his office. He was hunched over his desk and turning through the stack of color photographs in Murphy's preliminary forensic report. His guess had been right; the front of the victim's body looked just like Thomas's.

The muscles of his stomach and throat tightened, and he had trouble breathing as he made himself study the two dozen detailed prints of the body. He hadn't wanted to look at the mutilations, and he didn't want to look at photographs of them, but it was a part of his job he couldn't ignore. It was quite possible that something not apparent at the time would show up in a picture.

At least the photographs gave him some distance, and he didn't have to force himself to bear the awful stench of blood and the foul odors of death. He was embarrassed by his reaction to the displays of death. Anyone forced to deal with death should become hardened to its physical manifestations, yet he had not and probably never would.

With great relief he finally set aside the photographs and turned to a list of all the items recovered from the scene. Working carefully through the two pages, he discovered he had also been right about the underpants. None had been found. It was possible the victim hadn't been wearing any, but that was unlikely.

He had realized at a glance that the woman was killed by the same person who killed Thomas. Still, it was reassuring to find his judgment supported by the last section of the report. Dr. Benson had retrieved from the wound edges the same sort of microscopic metal particles taken from Thomas's cuts. Murphy confirmed that the particles were from the same source by using a scanning electron microscope to determine the orientation of the ferrous oxide molecules.

Firecaster looked at the electron micrographs, but they meant nothing to him. They reminded him of pictures he had seen in *Life* magazine when he was growing up—photographs of familiar objects so highly magnified they took on an alien appearance.

Dr. Benson hadn't completed his report, but Murphy had included a page of handwritten notes based on his conversations with the pathologist. Dr. Benson had found no evidence of strangulation. The cause of death was probably decapitation, but without the head to examine, it was difficult to be sure. Death might have come from an insult to the brain and consequent hemorrhaging. The mutilations took place after death, but only very shortly after.

Firecaster suddenly couldn't stand to go on reading. He threw down the report and stood up. "Goddamn it, goddamn it," he said out loud. He crossed his arms over his chest and took a deep breath. He made himself sit back down and pick up the report once more. He would start again from the beginning.

The case seemed to be an exact replay of Thomas, and as with Thomas, nothing of any real help had turned up. He had hoped for at least some bite-marks. Fingerprints were too much to expect, but with clear bite-marks they would be able to make a positive identification if they ever got a suspect. They might even get a blood type from the saliva. Or if they had semen residue or even stains. Murphy could do a lot with those.

But they had nothing. Absolutely nothing. Not even a place to start. That's what made him feel so helpless and frustrated. He could sense the killer gloating about his cleverness.

What did happen? He could visualize the killer stalking his victim, sneaking up behind her, then . . . what? Did he hit her over the head or choke her until she became unconscious? Or did he do something else to control her? Did she know what was happening to her? Is that something he wanted? Did he want to feed on her fear and watch her eyes fill with horror? Or did he just want to destroy her body? What was he after? Why the mutilations? Was he acting out some shadowy childhood memory or some infantile fantasy?

Firecaster felt angry at his inadequacy in trying to answer such questions. He was too rational, too controlled. He should be able to enter the mind of the killer, think his thoughts and feel his desires.

He should be able to use his own imagination to grasp the logic of this insane act, because he knew the sense must be there for the killer. The action was the expression of some coherent pattern, some way of thinking.

Yet when he wasn't so frustrated, he had to admit he didn't really want to try to think that way. He didn't want to take the chance that the effort to identify with the feelings of a distorted mind would trigger something in his own mind, something that would bring back his feelings of being shrouded in dark fog, shut off from the world. Sometimes he wasn't sure he was the right person for his own job.

In an abstract way, he realized he was being too hard on himself. He knew from experience that the intuitive understanding he needed to get a sense of the killer would come later. Good investigative methods and clear thinking were more likely to lead to results than inspired guesses.

That homicide investigations required a vast amount of dogged and detailed work was a lesson he had learned during his six years of investigating homicides. In the first year after his promotion to the rank of Detective, he had expected to be able to apply his mind to the evidence and come up with a solution to a crime in the way he used to be able to solve problems in formal logic. Even the previous two years of working the street in uniform had done nothing to change this expectation. He still thought he could reason his way through to the end of an investigation, with little more to go on than a few shreds of evidence.

His background gave him confidence in that way of thinking. He came from an academic family that believed in the power of the mind. His father had been a medical historian at Harvard, and his mother was still a professor of pediatrics at Tufts. Firecaster had graduated from Harvard and gone on to Columbia with the intention of getting a Ph.D. in philosophy.

Within six months he knew that the academic life wasn't for him. He had always had a problem-solving attitude, and the discipline of philosophy suited him perfectly. What he didn't like was that nobody's solutions stayed nailed down. A proposal to resolve a problem like the conflict between causal determinism and personal responsibility would sound plausible, then somebody would devastate it with a set of objections that also sounded totally convincing. This would signal the start of another round of response and criticism.

He couldn't face the idea of spending the rest of his life engaged in these endless, unresolved debates. He wanted definitive solutions

12

with practical results. The faculty agreed to let him write an M.A. thesis and drop out honorably.

By the time he had finished, he had a job offer. A college friend asked him to move to Washington and join the staff of Paul Simmons, a Congressman from the Fifth District.

The position consisted mostly of attending committee meetings and writing digests of pending legislation. The job turned out to be too bureaucratic for his liking, but it had one important result. While he was serving as a liaison between the House Committee on Domestic Terrorism and the Justice Department, Congressman Simmons's Chevrolet convertible was rigged with a bomb. Simmons escaped with facial injuries, but his secretary was killed.

Firecaster had never been so close to violence before, and it shocked him. But he had been fascinated by the investigation the bombing set in motion. The FBI, CIA, DEA, and the local police all cooperated in developing the evidence that finally led them to the killer.

Firecaster became friendly with Steven Allison, the FBI agent in charge of the case, and Allison gave him a running commentary on their aims and procedures. Firecaster had a chance to see from the inside how professionals worked, and he gradually realized that criminal investigation would let him fuse his abilities and his interests. He could satisfy his penchant for problem-solving, but he could also be sure of a practical result and not feel he was squandering his life in arid disputes.

At the age of twenty-five, Firecaster became a trainee in the Cambridge Police Department. Even with Steve Allison's support, it was the only department of the fifteen he contacted willing to give him a chance. The others considered him too old and too educated. But then they hadn't bothered to talk to him. Chief Collier Bryant had spent an hour with him, asking him questions about his views on police work, challenging his ideas on social responsibility, and making sure Firecaster wasn't in the grip of some romantic fantasy.

"I think we can find a place for somebody like you," Bryant had said at the end of the interview. "We would be a piss-poor department if we couldn't."

Alice was a recognized presence in the art world of Washington, but she surprised him when he asked her to move to Cambridge with him. "If I can make prints at all, I can make them in Boston," she told him. She even suggested they get married. "We fit together like two halves of an apple," she said.

Now Alice was gone, and for the last two years he had been the head of the Major Homicide Squad. "Life gives, and life takes away," his father used to tell him. "Those who see the glass as half full are happier than those who see it as half empty." Firecaster knew his father was right. Still, it was the taking away, the loss of what couldn't be replaced, that always affected him most.

Firecaster closed the red plastic cover of the report folder and pushed it aside. He had pulled a yellow pad of paper toward him to make notes for his own report when Detective Sergeant Donatello Renuzi rapped on the door and stepped inside without waiting for a response.

Renuzi said nothing as he sat down in one of the two gray steel chairs in front of the desk. Although he looked tired, he sat up very straight. He might have been a loan officer at a suburban bank at the end of a long day of politely turning down applications.

Renuzi was thirty-two years old with dark brown hair, brown eyes, regular features, and a slightly olive complexion. He was a wiry five-eight and compensated for his lack of height by maintaining perfect posture and dressing in well-tailored three-piece suits.

Renuzi had a memory for detail that constantly astounded anyone who worked with him. When talking to a witness, the only notes he ever took were for numbers. He had a hard time remembering even his own badge or social security number, but for anything else he seemed to have absolute recall. Even after a lengthy interview, it was only later when forced to write a report that he would transfer the contents of his memory to paper.

More than anything else, working with Renuzi was what had helped Firecaster pull through the dark period when he was losing Alice. When Chief Bryant made him head of the Major Homicide Squad, he had unhesitatingly chosen Renuzi as his second-in-command. During that first year, they had cleared more cases than ever before in the history of the department.

Firecaster was good at putting together puzzle pieces, but Renuzi was usually the one who supplied them. Renuzi could dig out information the way a pig could sniff out truffles.

He also owed Renuzi a more personal debt. The first year they worked together in Homicide, two years before Bryant started the MHS, they went to a nice middle-class condominium to investigate a woman they suspected of killing her retarded eight-year-old son for insurance money. She had gone into the kitchen, and when Firecaster started after her, she had rushed him with a stiletto-thin boning knife. Before she could get to him, Renuzi grabbed her and threw her to the floor. Only she was very fast, and the knife sliced the palm of Renuzi's left hand, leaving a slash that became a raised white scar. Firecaster rarely saw the scar, but he never forgot it was there.

"They're calling him Crazy Cat, you know," Renuzi said abruptly. "I mean the uniformed guys and the people who've been working with Chase and me."

"I hadn't heard it, but it fits," Firecaster said. "I predict we're going to get a lot more publicity now."

"Why?" Renuzi asked.

"Because once you hang a name on a perpetrator, it's like turning a generic product into a brand-name. Soon it's going to be 'Crazy Cat Killer Spotted Buying Milk at 7-Eleven Store' and 'Woman Says Ex-Boyfriend Is Crazy Cat Killer.' "

Firecaster paused, then shrugged his shoulders. "But maybe it will do some good," he said. "Maybe somebody knows who the guy is and will tell us about it."

"Maybe," Renuzi agreed. "But I gave an interview to Chris Carter of Channel Five News, and I didn't get the impression they intend to start any kind of crusade."

"We didn't hear a lot about Thomas," Firecaster admitted.

"Exactly," Renuzi said. "I doubt the new homicide is going to make the publicity level go up. This isn't California, and besides, for most people murder is just a fact of life nowadays. Part of the price we pay for living in the big city."

"You're right," Firecaster said. "A killer has to hit the double digits now before anybody pays much attention. Then if he ever gets caught, he becomes famous, gets big book contracts, and sells his story to the movies."

Renuzi nodded in agreement. "When we catch this guy, maybe we can do our own book. Buy houses on the Cape, retire, and watch the tide come in."

Firecaster tapped the red-covered report lying in front of him on the desk. "We're not going to catch shit unless you've come up with more than Murphy has so far."

"I've got a little something," Renuzi said. He sounded smug. "Not much, but a little."

"Brief me, and I'll save the questions," Firecaster said.

"Her name is Anna Louise Hamilton," Renuzi said. "She used both first names, like a Southerner. She lived on Mass Ave in a second-floor apartment in a two-story building next door to Brewester Funeral Home."

"A pretty ratty building," Firecaster said.

"She apparently didn't have much money," Renuzi went on. "She worked part-time as a waitress at the Coffee Corner, and the rest of the time she either worked as a dancer or tried to find work as a dancer. She's been in a number of shows, some of them even professionally done." He glanced at Firecaster with an inquisitive

15

look. "I could give you some of the names, if you want to know," he said.

Firecaster shook his head. "Let's stick to the basics for the moment. We'll need to know if we decide we have to check out the people who've been in productions with her, but let's save that."

"Hamilton was twenty-seven, and she shared the apartment with her lover, a woman named Janet Quick. The two have lived together for the last three years." Renuzi's trick memory let him reel off the facts as if he were reading from a reference book.

"Is she also a dancer?"

"She's some kind of editor at Harvard University Press, but I don't think she gets paid much. I got the impression she paid most of the bills so Anna Louise could try to make it as a dancer." Renuzi shook his head. "She was so broken up I could hardly get her to talk."

"How did you locate her?"

"It was easy," Renuzi said. "The victim had a shoe wallet with a key and an ID card inside, and Janet Quick was listed as the person to notify in case of accident."

"Some accident," Firecaster said. "Did you talk to anybody else?"

"Janet Quick broke the news to the parents," Renuzi said. "They live in West Newton, and Chase went out to talk to both of them. Her father came home from work. Then I sent somebody to talk to the manager and a couple of waitresses at the Coffee Corner."

"Did you learn anything worth knowing?" Firecaster asked.

"Not for the most part," Renuzi said. "Mostly it was just like Thomas. A young woman living an ordinary life, minding her own business, not involved with drugs or anything else illegal. Just another good citizen."

"But you said you had something," Firecaster pressed.

Renuzi didn't smile, but it was clear that he was taking pleasure in the dramatic buildup, holding the best until last. That was one of the rewards of tedious and frustrating hours of interviews. Sometimes the only one.

"She got a telephone call," Renuzi said. "Exactly one week ago yesterday. Late at night, maybe midnight or close to it. Janet Quick answered the phone, and the caller asked for Anna Louise by name. When she came to the phone, he said, 'Beware, the jaguar is on the prowl.' Then he hung up."

"It was definitely a male voice?" Firecaster asked.

"No doubt," Renuzi said. "Both of them heard it. Quick described it as a deep voice, almost like the voice of an actor, but he sounded tight, strained."

"Neither of them recognized it?"

"No, and they talked about it," Renuzi said. "It didn't sound like anybody they knew. And a couple of lesbians aren't likely to know all that many men to start with."

"He asked for Anna Louise by her full name?"

"He only asked to speak to Anna," Renuzi said. "Of course they figured that meant he wasn't somebody who really knew her."

Firecaster glanced at Renuzi. "What did they make of it?"

"They were upset at first, Janet more than Anna Louise. They talked about all kinds of possibilities. Somebody trying to put the make on Anna Louise, somebody who didn't like gay women, somebody who mistook her for somebody else, somebody playing a practical joke."

Renuzi threw up his hands in an expansive gesture. "Just the sort of stuff you would expect them to think of," he said. "Just the sort of stuff we would think of. But neither of them thought it was a death threat."

"And he never called back?"

Renuzi shook his head. "After a couple of days, they stopped talking about it. Anna Louise started out being more cautious than usual. Not going out by herself, getting Janet to meet her after work. Then when nothing happened, they pretty much went back to their usual life."

"And that meant Anna Louise went jogging by herself down by the river?" Firecaster said.

"Sometimes Janet went, but not often. Anna Louise tried to go every night."

"Always at the same time?"

"Not always," Renuzi said. "If it seemed too late to her, she wouldn't go."

"What about last night?"

"As bad luck would have it, we don't know," Renuzi said. "Janet went to Amherst for her brother's birthday party. She spent the night and didn't get back to Cambridge until late this morning. She assumed that Anna Louise had gone to work on an early shift and wasn't even worried about her."

Renuzi glanced away, then back again. "I was the one who had to tell her," he said.

Firecaster said nothing, but he nodded at Renuzi. They shared the knowledge that the worst part of a homicide investigation was often having to inform people that somebody they cared about had been suddenly and pointlessly slaughtered by another person.

"The preliminary estimate is that she had been dead from twelve to fourteen hours by the time we arrived," Firecaster said. "That means she was jogging somewhere around six or eight o'clock last night."

"I'll get some people out there at five tonight and question anybody who comes by," Renuzi said. "Joggers tend to be regular, and there's a good chance that a lot of the people who show up tonight were there last night. Somebody might have seen or heard something."

"We've got something else to do now, too," Firecaster said. "We need to go back and reinterview Thomas's fiancé and see if she ever mentioned getting any strange phone calls."

"I've already asked Karen Chase to do that," Renuzi said. "She's also supposed to let Ed Murphy know when Hamilton's body is released to her parents so Ed can arrange to have a photographer at the funeral."

"You're still going to handle the metro area coordination?"

"Right," Renuzi said. "I've already sent out preliminaries saying we think we're dealing with the same perpetrator. I also told the contacts that we're interested in people who say anything about jaguars or make threatening phone calls mentioning jaguars."

"Have somebody check with the telephone company and make them run through their records of crank calls," Firecaster said.

"That's probably going to take that somebody a couple of days." Renuzi's tone questioned the wisdom of taking the time away from more pressing tasks.

"We've got the power," Firecaster said. "I talked with the Chief, and he said give the Thomas and Hamilton cases top priority. He also said we can call on the Division Commanders for what we need."

"What about the other cases we're working?"

"If they can wait, let them wait," Firecaster said. "If they can't, turn them over to Clarence Cowart and ask him to reassign them. The same goes for Chase. We're going to stick with Thomas and Hamilton exclusively."

"That's the way I like it," Renuzi said.

He stood up and tugged at the bottom of his vest to remove the wrinkles. He then checked to make sure the bottom button was undone. He had once read an article about vests in *GQ* and come to Firecaster to ask whether it was really true that he should leave the bottom button unfastened. Firecaster had never seen him in a more serious mood. Since then, checking to see if the button was undone had become almost a compulsion for Renuzi.

"Sit back down a minute," Firecaster said. "I was just thinking about something when you came in, and I want to try it out on you. When was Thomas?"

"About three weeks ago."

"I mean exactly."

Renuzi sat down on the metal chair and took a small black notebook from his coat pocket. He flipped it open and ran his finger down a page. "March eighteenth," he said.

"Let me check to be sure I didn't miscount," Firecaster said. He swiveled his chair around and counted days on the calendar pinned to the partition behind him. He turned back around to face Renuzi. "I'm right," he said. "Twenty days from yesterday."

"You think there's a pattern?"

Firecaster shrugged and tossed his pencil down on the desk. "It could just be an arbitrary time," he admitted. "The guy gets an urge to kill somebody and just goes out and does it. If we had three or four victims, we would know for sure."

"Let's hope we don't have to find out that way," Renuzi said. "It sounds like a reasonable hypothesis, but of course that may be just because the number turned out to be twenty. And after all, it's got to be some number."

"You're right." Firecaster nodded. "But let me see if I can make it fly." He leaned back, put his feet on his desk, and stared at the top of the gray metal partition that separated his office from the main room.

"Here's a guy who committed two murders in exactly the same way," Firecaster said. "We're not talking about a simple signature, like using the same weapon. We're talking about carbon copies."

"Agreed," Renuzi said.

"That suggests that whatever he does, he does systematically. It's all thought out in advance. He follows a method, and if he does that, he might also follow a timetable."

"It's possible," Renuzi said.

"Twenty days also just happens to constitute a month in some calendar systems," Firecaster said. "Put that together with the sacrificial position of the body, and we might be dealing with some kind of cult killer."

"Or maybe just with some guy who gets a day off every twenty days," Renuzi suggested. "It could be as simple as that."

Firecaster swung his feet down from the desk and looked at Renuzi. "He's killed two women, and it's possible he won't kill any more. We might never hear from him again, and we might never catch him. But I'm not betting on that. Everything has gone so smoothly for him that I'm certain he's going to do another unless we can nail him first."

"So what can we do that we aren't doing?" Renuzi asked.

"Let's start taking a close look at any threat or complaint that involves anything out of the ordinary," Firecaster said. "If the Jaguar always gives a warning growl before he pounces, then we may have a chance. So set up a screen for all complaints."

"Do you want me to draw up the criteria?" Renuzi asked.

"I'll do it," Firecaster said. "I'll make them fairly broad, because we can commandeer enough people now to help do the sifting. We don't want to exclude anybody who seems weird."

"Suppose your guess is right," Renuzi said. "If there is a schedule, then we've got nineteen days from today before we can expect to hear from the creep again."

"Even if I'm wrong and there isn't any schedule, we should start looking for a warning right now," Firecaster said. "If he telegraphed his intentions once, he'll probably do it again. Tell Chase everything we've talked about, but let her know it's important for her not to leak anything to the media. If we make him feel threatened, he may drop the warning. If he's on a schedule, he may even strike early to throw us off."

"Let's also get a psych profile," Renuzi said. "You can't really trust them, but they do make you think. I also don't like to be turning over the woodpile without having any idea at all of just what kind of insect I'm supposed to be looking for."

"I agree," Firecaster said. "When we just had one victim, I thought maybe we had a fluke killing. But things have changed now. I think I can get Ted Castle at Rush to help us."

"There's nobody better," Renuzi said.

"I'll send him the reports and see what he can come up with," Firecaster said.

Renuzi stood up again, let out a long sigh, and looked at Firecaster with a direct gaze. "You know, Eric, it's entirely possible we will never catch this creep. We've got shit for physical evidence, and so far we've got nobody who saw anything."

"The odds are against us," Firecaster agreed. "We need a motive or something to connect the victims with the killer. Otherwise we don't have a clue about who we're looking for."

"If he stops now, chances are good that he's home free."

"Then I guess we'd better hope he tries again," Firecaster said.

"I guess we'd better," Renuzi said. "But God help somebody if he does."

PART TWO

April 25
Monday

3

Monday 7:15 A.M.

He didn't want to steal the green Nissan wagon.

Its diminutive size made it look like an oversized toy, and that made it conspicuous. And that made it dangerous. Of course, danger was part of the game. Without risks, there would be no thrills, and being willing to take the risks was one of the ways he was different from ordinary people.

He had always known he was different. Only the nature of the difference was a relatively recent discovery. Compared to others, he was a visitor from a more highly evolved planet, a wolf in a world of sheep. The images crossing his mind caused him to smile with satisfaction. The wolf's fangs were very white and as pointed as knives. Its eyes glittered with intelligence as it watched the sheep grazing in a smooth field of green grass. Their heads were down, their eyes dull. Oblivious to any threat, the sheep munched the grass contentedly. They were aware of nothing until it was too late.

The Nissan might be dangerous, but there was no other obvious choice in the parking lot. He needed something that could pass for a service vehicle. A pickup truck or a van would be best, but nobody in the apartment building seemed to own one.

He considered going somewhere else, but it was already past seven. People would be getting ready to go to work, and soon every parking lot of every building would be filled with commuters climbing into their cars. Knowing how to calculate risks was crucial. Stealing a car in broad daylight was an acceptable risk, but stealing one with witnesses around, maybe even the owner himself, was plain stupidity. The Nissan would do just fine.

The sun was already bright on the horizon, but it was early enough in the spring for the weather still to be brisk. It was sufficiently cool that nobody would think it strange for him to be wearing his loose, hip-length blue corduroy coat. No one on the bus he caught at Harvard Square had given him a second glance throughout the trip. So far as anybody could see, he was just another poor sucker on a

23

cold gray morning who had to be at work a couple of hours earlier than the rest of the world.

Without the coat, it would have been hard to hide the tools. He had started to bring a toolbox, then decided against it. It would have been fine on the bus, but anybody walking around a parking lot with a toolbox would be likely to attract attention, if not suspicion.

He walked directly to the driver's side of the Nissan, without any hesitation. He would act as though the car were his. He wasn't stealing it; he was just getting into his own car and driving off. People don't look over their shoulders when they walk up to their cars, so he kept his head still. Yet he didn't keep his eyes still. He let them sweep back and forth across the whole area.

Nobody was around. A few cars passed along the suburban street behind the parking lot, but nothing else moved. The windows of the four-story brick apartment building were either still dark, or lighted and covered by curtains. He trusted probabilities, and it was highly unlikely that anyone would just happen to glance down at the parking lot that early in the morning.

Taking a flat piece of steel curved and tapered at one end out of his coat pocket, he inserted the point between the door and the body of the car. His thin black leather gloves kept the dew that wet the surface of the car off his hands.

Poised to act, he could feel the rush of fear and pleasure that came whenever he was about to do something there could be no pulling back from. The feeling was comparatively mild now, yet it was real and he liked it. In all his life he couldn't remember experiencing anything else so satisfying.

This pleasure he had discovered so recently had shocked him into realizing how emotionally dead he had been during the previous twenty-five years of his life. The emotions described in books had seemed no more than elaborate ways of talking, and his own experiences of sex only a pale counterfeit of the pleasures people boasted about.

He wondered what had happened to make him so different. He felt vaguely that his mother was somehow to blame, the way she ignored him and even seemed to resent his existence. Yet he never let himself dwell on such thoughts; the past was dead, and he was alive. What was important was that he had discovered a new and intense feeling. He would risk a lot to experience even a little of it.

With a single hard shove, he levered the metal strip toward the right. At the same time, he jerked the door toward him with his left hand. The door opened with no difficulty at all and with virtually no noise. Without pausing to congratulate himself, he slid into the tan velour-covered seat and closed the door behind him. The door clicked into place with a satisfying sound that indicated he hadn't broken the latch.

Using heavy Vise-grip pliers, he twisted off the chrome key guide surrounding the ignition lock. He pressed the lever on the inside leg of the pliers. The jaws broke their grip, allowing the chrome guide to fall softly to the carpeted floor.

From the inside of his coat, he then removed an ignition puller and screwed the corkscrew-shaped end of it into the exposed key-hole. Working carefully, he turned the handle at the top of the tool and slowly extracted the cylinder lock from its metal housing. Without taking time to unscrew the wires, he took out a pair of cutters and snipped them off. Using the built-in stripper on the side of the wire cutters, he exposed the ends of the wires. He twisted two of the bare ends together, and when he touched the ground wire to them, the engine turned over once, then jumped to life. The cold and damp made it run rough until the automatic choke kicked in and established a high, smooth idle.

He left the tools on the passenger seat and put the Nissan in reverse. Barely three minutes had passed since he inserted the flat piece of steel and popped open the door. Now he was on his way, already out of the parking lot and on the neighborhood street leading to the main artery feeding into Boston. He felt the tension that knotted his body relax a little. He was still floating from the rush of anticipation and fear, still high on his own feelings. He smiled deliberately for his own benefit. He was pleased with himself. Good planning and good organization helped guarantee success. Yet there were always enough wild cards in every hand to make the game interesting.

Earlier that morning, when the harsh buzzing of the alarm on his clock-radio had awakened him at five, he had seriously considered postponing the action portion of his plan. He had slept so poorly he simply hadn't felt capable of carrying out everything the plan required. He felt dull and wasted, exhausted by another long night of restless struggle that took place in the same dark dream that had tormented him intermittently since he was eleven years old.

He called it his hard dream.

It was always the same. In the dream he is eleven and in his bed, the white laminate bed with the bookcase headboard that took up most of the space in his narrow third-floor bedroom. The room is in his mother's brownstone on Charles Street in New York, and he can hear the muted sounds of traffic outside—horns honking, cars accelerating to a shift point, and the occasional drawn-out wail of a siren. The room is the only place he feels secure, for his mother never comes there.

When he was younger, perhaps five or six, he would beg his mother to come to his room and let him display the treasures he had accumulated during the day. He would want her to see the broken wing from a red plastic airplane he found in the park or the white marble fragment splashed with asphalt he picked up on the walk home with his nursemaid.

She would always refuse. "I'm not interested in your garbage," she would say, hardly glancing up from the papers on her desk. "Now go tell Mrs. Sanders to give you your bath." The words would strike him like a slap across the face, and he would hurry from her study with tears burning in his eyes. He would wish then with a passion he couldn't admit to anyone, especially not to her, that he had a father to run to.

His mother never came after him when he cried. Even Mrs. Sanders, the housekeeper, would offer him no word of comfort. She was the one who supervised him during the endless time his mother was at the medical school performing surgery, seeing patients, or doing her research. A nursemaid might be hired to take him on walks, but even then, it was Mrs. Sanders who was in charge. She was his mother's ally, and she treated him with the same impersonal efficiency she gave to cleaning the kitchen or ordering groceries. He might have been just another household appliance, and like his mother, she was moved neither by his tears nor by his loneliness. Eventually he learned not to ask his mother to come to his room, and at some point, he found that he was glad she never did.

In his dream, the room is as it had been then. Two tall bookcases take up most of the wall space. In the area between them is a poster of the interior of the spaceship in *2001*, the movie he loves above all others. Above his bed is another poster. Not a poster, really, but a computer printout in several sections that fit together to form a portrait of Mr. Spock.

Spock is the character he identifies with most closely, the one who is unemotional, totally logical, and highly intelligent. Spock never becomes angry, and he is never upset when others become angry at him or yell at him, because he can just shrug off their response as "illogical."

The top shelves of the bookcases are filled with science fiction and fantasy and with books about the Mayas, Aztecs, and Central American archaeology. The lower shelves are taken up by stacks of fantasy fan magazines—fanzines. Robert Howard is his favorite fantasy author and Conan the Barbarian his favorite character. Conan is courageous to the point of recklessness, and his powerful body guarantees he will always win the crucial battles. The difference between Conan and the strange creatures he fights lies not so much in intelligence as in cunning and lack of fear.

He has been able to find many of the pulp magazines in which the Conan stories originally appeared. They nestle by the fanzines on the lower shelves and help make him feel that the room is really his.

That's what makes the dream so terrible. The room is lost to him. He can no longer sleep there safely, and even during the day, the room makes him uneasy. He's haunted by the sense that something terrible and frightening has happened to him there, but he doesn't know what it could be. He has lost all security.

He is in his bed, floating in the peculiar liquid twilight between sleeping and waking. He becomes aware of one figure, then another. Both are coming toward him. They are ambiguous, amorphous shapes surrounded by diffuse bright lights. They are coming to steal his brain.

He knows this and feels panic clawing at his chest, yet he is helpless to prevent what is happening. He struggles to wake, to resist, to run. But his arms and legs feel paralyzed, immovable. As the figures come closer, he has trouble getting his breath. The faces are above him now, peering down. He looks up, prepared to gaze on something horrible, but he sees only empty blanks where the faces should be. He gasps and heaves, desperate for air, then feels himself falling endlessly into darkness.

Now he hears the voices. Mostly they are indistinct mutterings that seem to be spoken in some other language, but sometimes a familiar word emerges with clarity. He hears "blood . . . pain . . . punishment"—and all through the rest, like a litany, "jaguar . . . jaguar . . . jaguar."

Eventually there is nothing but the blackness. He wonders if his brain will end up across the hall in his mother's study. There, arranged on shelves at the end of the room, are more than a dozen brains. Some are whole brains and some are thick slices, but all are embedded in blocks of Lucite.

"Why do you have them?" he asked once.

"I use them in my work," his mother told him. "But you are never to touch them and never to go into my study without my permission."

The bright, hard plastic sparkles, but the yellowish white stuff inside looks as disgusting as a bundle of dead worms. Is that what his brain will look like when it is taken out and mounted?

Throughout his childhood, fascination had made him unable to obey his mother's command to stay out of her study. Whenever he could avoid detection by her or Mrs. Sanders, he would go in, sit on the floor in front of the shelves, and look up at the rows of specimens. It was as though by being close to them and studying them he could become closer to his mother.

The only picture of her he ever had was one stolen during one of those forbidden visits. He took it from a black cardboard box full of photographs from her life before he had been born. She had never shown them to him, so he wasn't sure who all the people were. He recognized his mother's sister, Emily, who was married to Uncle Dick, and their parents. His grandmother had died long before his birth, and his grandfather before his second birthday. He knew who they were only because his mother kept a picture of them on the living room mantel. It was her only concession to family sentiment.

The picture of his mother was a color snapshot. The colors were faded to a peculiar bluish green tinge, but the image was still clear. The photo showed her in jeans and a heavy gray fisherman's-knit-sweater, standing with her hands on her hips and smiling directly at the camera.

Her black hair was long and tied back to show off her face. She looked beautiful and happy. She was at the bottom of a long flight of steps leading to a building he recognized as Colton Hospital. According to the developer's date stamped on the back, she must have been in the final year of her neurosurgical fellowship. He had been born less than a year later, but if she was pregnant at the time, the picture didn't reveal it.

He had fallen in love with the photograph, because it showed his mother the way he wanted her to be—smiling, joyful, and full of warmth. He wanted her to be that way so much that he would turn his head to the wall and pray to the god he believed was living inside it to give him the power to make his mother pleased with him. If he could only please her, he was sure the smiles would follow.

The photograph revealed nothing of the seething rage that she controlled with a cold iron will. If the rage had been there when the photo was taken, he was certain he could detect it. He could have read it in the set of her mouth, the shape of the lines around her eyes, and the immobility of her face. He knew the signs.

But the rage wasn't there, and that meant she actually had once been the way he wanted her to be. Something had made her change, and even before he ever found the photograph, he realized he was in some way responsible for it. Something about him was disgusting and awful to have done such a terrible thing to his mother.

28

He kept the picture hidden at first because he had stolen it. When he was fourteen and was sent to a boys' boarding school in Pennsylvania, he took the photograph with him. He still kept it out of sight, though, and even now, after her death, he kept the picture in a drawer by his bed. He wanted it hidden, because it was proof of his own guilt. It showed how he had ruined his mother's life.

During his time at prep school, the hard dream had almost disappeared, coming no more than once or twice a year. He had found it difficult to leave home, with all its routines, but he soon learned that school provided its own form of security. He enjoyed the discipline of study, the organized games, the chance to play music, and the special interest clubs.

His grades put him near the top of his class every year, and for the first time in his life, he even became popular. He was elected president of the Debate Union and founded a science fiction club he named "The Galactic Alliance." Even kids who weren't science fiction fans joined, just because they wanted to associate themselves with him.

"Let's go to Miami," his friend Jack suggested to him at spring break when they were seniors. Jack's parents were more often in Europe than at home, and Jack had his own car that he garaged at his family's house in Philadelphia.

He told his mother he would be staying with Jack's parents, but instead they drove to Miami in a single day and night. They hit the beach exhausted, but before the day was over they had met two girls who were willing to take a boat to Bimini with them. It wasn't his first time smoking marijuana, but it was his first time having sex. Long before the end of the three days they spent on Bimini, he was bored with it.

Susan and Rachel worked out the pairing between them. Rachel had chosen him, and Susan had agreed to accept Jack. Rachel had told him about the discussion, because Susan had wanted him as well. "I had to promise her I'd buy the bus tickets back home, if she'd give me first pick," Rachel said.

Rachel was a freshman from some small college in North Carolina. She wasn't very interesting to talk to, but he had no complaints about her looks. She had long blond hair, and a tanned, lanky body she covered with only the scantiest bathing suit. He realized he ought to be attracted to her. He was, but the attraction lacked the kind of passion he had expected to experience. Everything he did with her was almost mechanical.

Rachel noticed it. "You don't really seem to be into sex," she said to him the second day as they were lying together in bed. "You

29

never start anything, and I feel like I'm almost raping you every time I put the moves on you."

"I'm sorry," he told her, feeling embarrassed.

"I'm not complaining," she said. "You're better than a lot of guys, because you've got real staying power. That I like."

"I'm just a little shy," he said.

She shook her head. "It's more than that," she said. "I think your heart's not really into screwing."

"You think I'm gay, don't you?" he said in an accusing tone.

"I didn't say that," she told him. "Maybe there are just some things we haven't done that you'd get a kick out of." She rubbed a hand along the inside of his thigh. "I know a lot of tricks. Want to give them a try?"

They began by trying her tricks, but he experienced only mild satisfaction, until the time he let himself go. Then Rachel refused to have sex with him again. "You're real sexy, but you scare me too much," she told him.

"I know I got a little rough," he admitted.

"I guess you did," she said. She was wearing a long-sleeved shirt to hide the bite-marks and bruises. "I was scared you were going to kill me. You didn't seem to be able to hear me talking to you, telling you to stop."

He realized then that ordinary sex couldn't do for him what it did for ordinary people. He knew better than to reveal that to anyone. It would make him seem too different, too alien.

Harvard was different from prep school. The structures that had supported his life were jerked away, and he found himself with time he didn't know how to organize. The academic competition was brutal, but he seemed to have lost his knack for studying. He was a stranger among hundreds of strangers, and everyone else seemed so much more confident and able. Some days he wouldn't even leave his room. He would watch TV and eat the sandwiches from Elsie's he stored in his rented refrigerator.

His first year was representative of all the others. He passed like a shadow through the university, making no friends but being regarded by dozens of acquaintances as friendly. He managed to get a degree in anthropology, and at that point his mother told him she would no longer support him. He was suddenly desperate for a job.

Even though he couldn't speak Spanish, Exotic Travel hired him as a guide for twelve two-week tours to the archaeological sites of the Yucatan. The pay was pitiful, and although he could make handsome tips by being charming to the elderly customers, he quit when his contract expired at the end of two years.

Working at the Anthropology Library was better, although it paid barely enough to live on and the hours were long. Even worse, the work was boring. So when the Allen Agency advertised in the *Globe* for security officer trainees, he realized it was a job that offered the possibility of excitement. He had been right.

In the years of working after college, he had almost forgotten about the hard dream. During the last year, though, since his mother's death, the dream had increased in frequency and intensity. It now came several times a week. He dreads sleep, and during the day, he feels both on edge and driven. Something always seems about to happen, and although constantly tired, he can never sit still. Only the excitement of action and planning for action bring him any peace.

This morning, it took all his effort to overcome his exhaustion, but now that he is at work, he realizes he did the right thing. Now he feels alive. His mind is sharp, his senses attuned to the world around him.

He is in control.

Because of the earliness of the hour, the traffic from Fresh Pond into Harvard Square was light. The Square itself was almost empty of people. Students and professors started the day late, and the shoppers and tourists wouldn't begin pouring in until the stores opened.

He parked on Church Street and pulled the ignition wires apart. The engine shut off as abruptly as if he had turned a key. He picked up the tools from the seat and hid them under his coat again. After getting out of the wagon, he checked to make sure he was legally parked. He was always shocked at the way people he thought of as significant criminals called attention to themselves by ignoring minor laws or acting suspiciously. Most who got caught were found to have been questioned or even arrested earlier. That was true even of Bundy and Bono, who in their different ways were both models of caution.

Not exactly hurrying but also not wasting time, he made his way along Church Street to Massachusetts Avenue and then down the stairs of the MBTA subway station. The soft rubber soles of his work shoes made hardly a sound as they hit the metal edges of the concrete steps. He kept his head down, and passengers who had just gotten off the subway passed by him on the stairs without a glance.

He took a key from his pocket and opened one of the gray metal rental lockers set against the wall opposite the platform. A train was just leaving in the Park Street direction, and the people rushing to climb on were too distracted to pay any attention to him.

The locker was a large one, large enough to hold the oversized brown vinyl suitcase he had stored inside it. Kneeling on the gray-tiled floor, he opened the clasps of the suitcase and took out a rolled-up sheet of white plastic. Then he removed a small metal toolbox that had once been painted olive drab but had since faded to a color even duller. In addition, the box was scuffed and greasy and looked as if it had seen hard use for a long time.

With his coat spread wide to provide a degree of concealment, he emptied his pockets of the wire cutters, pry bar, ignition puller, and a few other small tools that he had carried with him but not needed. He put the tools in one of the side pockets of the suitcase. From another side pocket, he took a small, flat case of gray suede with compartments filled with bright metal instruments that looked like something a dentist might use. They were lockpicks.

He slipped the case into the back pocket of his gray work pants. Into a front pocket, he put a narrow metal case that resembled an oversized pocketknife. It was a set of skeleton keys. Each key was hinged to the case, and like the blade of a pocketknife, it could be opened out for use. Attached to the case as they were, the keys could not rattle together.

He braced the locker door with his knee to keep the powerful spring from slamming it shut, then wedged in the large suitcase. When the suitcase was in place, he used a free hand to ease the locker door closed. Without any noise, there would be no curious glances. He fed quarters into the money slot, turned the key to the left, then pulled it out and dropped it into his pocket.

The quarters made a metallic rattle as they fell into the coin box. He would be back later, at his leisure, to retrieve the suitcase. He picked up the rolled cylinder of white plastic and the scruffy toolbox and walked out of the subway station. He attracted no more attention going out than he had coming in.

As soon as he got back to the Nissan wagon, he untied the string that kept the cylinder rolled and unfurled the sheet. It was an embossed sign with a flexible strip magnet molded into the plastic along the edges. He smoothed out the sheet against the left door panel and pressed the magnetic strips until they made good contact. He gave the left corner of the sign a slight tug, then another, until the whole sign was level across the top.

He nodded to express his satisfaction with the result. *Expert Plumbers* the sign read. Below the name, on two separate lines, was a street address on Comstock in Belmont. He had checked the Yellow Pages for the Boston area to make sure there was no such firm. It wouldn't do to have somebody calling up a real company and asking why one of its vehicles was parked in the neighborhood.

It was getting close to eight o'clock now. That was about what he had estimated. It wouldn't be a good idea to get on the scene too early, because that would just call attention to himself.

He put the toolbox on the floor of the passenger side and twisted the ignition wires together. The warm engine caught smoothly, and he pulled out of the parking space. He knew exactly where the house was. The only problem would be to find the location of her apartment or room, whichever she had. That would take some looking around. Of course he had anticipated that. That was why he was dressed in gray pants and gray shirt, carrying a toolbox, and driving a station wagon with a plastic sign on it.

He drove down Church Street, turned right on Appian Way, and went past the Radcliffe buildings and the Cambridge Common. He turned right off Garden Street and onto Oliver. The house was in the middle of the block. Both sides of the narrow, tree-lined street were parked full with cars. Yet his luck was good, and opposite the house, there was just enough space between a driveway and a white Volvo for him to park the small wagon. Having to steal the Nissan, rather than something larger, turned out to have been another piece of luck.

The house was a two-and-a-half-story Victorian frame, painted pale yellow with chocolate brown gingerbread decoration above the doors and windows. A wide front porch ran the length of the house, and a row of bushy evergreen shrubs all but obscured the coarse native-stone foundation. Oak trees taller than the house stood on either side of the concrete sidewalk leading up to the front door.

The flanking houses were similar in size and style. The one on the left was white and had no porch, while the one on the right was gray and had a shorter, narrower porch. A ragged screen of spirea bushes separated the backyard of the gray house from its pale yellow neighbor. On the opposite side, a waist-high wire fence with a cathedral top ran between the two properties. The fence was rusty and sagging slightly, its bottom portion matted with dead grass bleached almost white by the weather. The fence didn't constitute much of a barrier, but it didn't offer much cover either.

He sat in the green station wagon for a few minutes, carefully scanning both sides of the street. He then got out of the car and closed the door forcefully. He didn't slam it, but he made no effort to be quiet or unobtrusive. He didn't want to call attention to himself, but he didn't care if he was noticed. He hefted the toolbox, switched it to his left hand, and pulled the bill of a blue and white cap down to shield his eyes. The cap said *Rowland Raiders* on the front. He had no idea where or what Rowland was. The cap, like the rest of his clothes and the toolbox, had come from a Salvation Army store in south Boston.

He walked across the street. Then without hesitation, he turned into the paved driveway of the pale yellow house. Without slowing his deliberate pace, he glanced into the windows along the driveway as he passed them. Through the first, he saw a darkened dining room with a heavy table surrounded by chairs with high, curved backs.

The second window was higher up and, he guessed, was probably set above the kitchen sink. A hanging light fixture illuminated yellow walls paler than the color of the house, and at the edge of the window, he glimpsed the boxy shape of a dark brown refrigerator. A round, white bowl piled high with apples and bananas sat on top.

The windows at the rear of the house were all dark, except for one at the far corner of the second floor. He turned off the driveway and walked along the paved sidewalk that intersected with it at a right angle. He noticed with interest the stairwell entrance to the basement, just below the stairs to the kitchen, and the white-painted entrance door at the back of the house.

During the two weeks he had put her under surveillance as a part of his plan, he had watched her walk down the driveway, never using the front door, so the chances were good that this was where she lived. Maybe she shared the house, but probably she just rented a room or small apartment in it. That would be a typical Cambridge arrangement.

From the direction of the upstairs window, he could hear the faint tapping sounds of a typewriter. Someone was obviously awake, but he wasn't worried. He hadn't done anything. On the opposite side of the house, the ground rose in a gentle slope from the flat, grassy lawn to the screen of spirea. Moving quietly but without appearing to hurry, he walked up the slope and turned the corner.

The blinds were open on a wide, rectangular window near the ground. He put down the toolbox near the corner of the house and dropped to his knees. If he lay prone on the grass, the rough stone foundation was high enough to hide him from the view of anyone looking out the window.

He stretched out on the ground with his body parallel to the house. The grass felt cold through the legs of his trousers, and almost immediately he could feel the dampness soaking through the fabric. Using his elbows to provide leverage, he crawled along, snake fashion, until he reached the edge of the window. He raised his head slowly, looking in at the corner of the window so that he would run the least risk of being seen by someone glancing up.

The window opened into a bedroom. Immediately across from him, its door wide open, was a bathroom with maroon and silver tile. Adjacent to the bathroom was a smaller door that could only be a closet, and nearest to him, hardly two feet away, was a round brass knob surmounting the corner post of a bed. Sunshine reflecting from the polished knob made it gleam with a golden light.

Pulling himself along, he crawled forward another foot so that he was directly under the window. When he raised his head, he could see right inside the bedroom. What he saw made him draw his breath sharply and hold it tightly in his chest. This was something he couldn't have planned.

He had found her, all right. Not only was she in this room, but she was standing in front of her bed completely naked.

4

Monday 8:00 A.M.

Jill Brenner glanced down and saw that her naked body was covered with a light film of sweat. The sunlight pouring through the high window above the brass bed made her skin glisten. She was pleased by the sight of the perspiration, because it meant she was making herself work.

Despite the sunlight, the room was chill, and when she exhaled, white traces of vapor hung in the air. The temperature didn't bother her. For the past five years, winter and summer, she had started her day with twenty minutes of exercise. That was one of the few constants of her life, and during the last year she had been grateful for the routine. Having something definite to do gave her a reason to get out of bed.

She always worked out in the nude, and even in the dead of winter, when frigid air crept through the cracks around the storm windows, it never took her long to generate enough heat to feel warm. Within five minutes, her body would develop a deep sensuous glow that felt almost sexual in its intensity.

She and Jeff had taken advantage of that. It was when she completed her exercises that they had the most energetic and satisfying sex. She was always the first to get up, and he would lie in bed half-asleep watching her nude antics. By the time she finished, he would be out of his pajamas and sitting propped up against the pillows. He would reach out a hand and pull her into bed. His skin always felt cool against her hot and slightly sticky body. Yet he would never let her take a shower first.

She finished the set of twenty-five knee bends and raised her arms above her head to straighten out the kinks in her calf muscles. For a moment she imagined her lean body and small breasts made her look like a figure on top of a trophy, or maybe an automobile hood ornament from the twenties. She missed having someone to admire her. The two years she and Jeff were together had spoiled her. He had openly admired her body, and because she had doubted her attractiveness from the time she was a scrawny and awkward adolescent, his praises meant more to her than they would have to many women.

Not that Jeff was the only person who had ever said nice things about her. Her father was her earliest and strongest fan. She was an only child, and she never doubted her importance to him. Yet except for occasionally telling her, "You look very pretty," he said little about her appearance.

What he cared about was character. "You can't whip somebody who doesn't give up," he would say. Or, "Just do your best, and you'll always win." Even when she was little, she realized he wasn't speaking literally.

Before she turned eight, her father started taking her goose hunting with him. In late fall, they would stand almost knee-deep in the cold water of the marsh, hidden behind stands of saw grass and cattails, and wait for a wedge-shaped flight of geese to come within range. When she was ten, he gave her the single-shot sixteen-gauge shotgun that had belonged to his father and taught her to shoot it.

The shotgun was taller than she was but light enough for her to handle with ease. He showed her how to lead a goose before pulling the trigger and how to nestle the gun's stock in the hollow of her shoulder and brace her feet so she wouldn't be knocked down by the kick.

The only animals she and her father hunted were geese, ducks, and quail. When quail season opened, they would spend a night or two deep in the woods, far from any house. They would hike in with their gear, then sleep under the stars and rise so early the dew was icy cold on her bare feet. After hot coffee and the cold biscuits her mother sent with them, they would spend hours creeping through the woods, trying to get as close as possible to a covey of quail hidden in the undergrowth before flushing them.

By the time she was fourteen, she could make a fire, paddle a pirogue, track a bobcat, and recognize the swampy places cottonmouth moccasins lived. She had also learned to think ahead, move quietly, and act quickly. And she learned not to give up, even when she was tired and discouraged and they were ten miles of hard walking from the car. "I hate a quitter," her father would say. "A quitter might as well lie down and die, because there's always more reasons to quit than to keep going."

Once when she was about fifteen, she asked her father, "Daddy, are you ever sorry you didn't have a boy?" He looked at her as if the idea had never crossed his mind. "A boy would have been all right," he told her. "But I really don't see what difference it would have made." He seemed surprised when she put her arms around him and hugged him tightly.

Thinking about him always made her realize that she would never have gone to Radcliffe if it weren't for him. He would tell her, "Get a good education, my girl, or you'll regret it for the rest of your life." He told her this so often that by the time she was in high school, she would sometimes snap, "I know, Daddy. You've told me a million times." Then she would feel bad about being rude to him. He was telling her not to miss out on what he had missed.

Even though her family wasn't well off, she had enjoyed her childhood. She grew up in a five-room frame house in St. Francisville, a town with a population of three thousand, forty miles from Baton Rouge and one mile from the east bank of the Mississippi River. Her mother taught third and fourth grade, and her father operated Brenner's Grocery, which resembled a general store more than a supermarket.

The town had no bookstore or library, and because her father respected books, the store's stock included a rack of paperbacks and an almost random selection of hardbacks and children's books. That was how she discovered Betsy and Tacy, then Dr. Dolittle, and—most wonderful of all—Nancy Drew. In reading the books, she had to be careful to keep them clean and not spread the pages wide. If she bent the cover, her father might not be able to sell the book.

She could still remember how she always seemed to be waiting for Wednesdays. That was the day the wholesale distributor's truck came from Baton Rouge, bringing bundles of magazines, newspapers, and occasionally books. She persuaded her father to ask the driver to exchange the books she had read for new ones. The driver was reluctant at first, but when he understood the reason, he began to leave extra books just for her to read.

Looking back, she could see that sometime between the ages of twelve and fifteen she had decided to be a writer. It wasn't a career plan really, but just a recognition that one day she wanted to tell stories. Her father had died of heart failure three years after she graduated from college, but at least he had read some of her early magazine pieces. "You're a wonderful writer," he had told her over the phone. She loved him for saying it with a tone of utter conviction.

She lowered herself to the floor and sat on the blue and white rug in front of the bed to catch her breath. She breathed deeply and expelled each breath with a loud whoosh. Jeff had told her that the important thing in breathing was to get fresh air into the lungs so that the oxygen would drive out the carbon dioxide.

Sometimes it worried her that she still thought about Jeff so much. She could recall so vividly what he used to do and say that it seemed no more than a few weeks since she last saw him, and that she would be seeing him again soon. He continued to be more of a real presence in her life than virtually anything but the need to eat and sleep.

Exactly one year ago Jeff had sat alone in his lab late at night and injected himself with a lethal dose of succinylcholine. The drug was a powerful muscle relaxant, and as several of his medical friends told her, he must have died painlessly. He took a dose large enough to inactivate the muscles used in breathing, so when his heart was deprived of oxygen, it simply stopped beating.

When she went to pick up the few personal effects Jeff kept in his office, the people in his lab were quick to mention how easily and professionally he had died. "Medically speaking, he couldn't have picked a better method," one of the research fellows told her. They talked as though by killing himself in such an original way, he had achieved something important. She knew they didn't mean that, but they were too awkward in dealing with people to know how to comfort her.

Jill thanked them, without encouraging conversation, then went about the task of packing. She decided to leave Jeff's books and professional journals in the lab. She had no use for works on molecular biology, biochemistry, and monoclonal antibodies. In the end, all she took away was a squash racquet, gym clothes, and an unframed snapshot of her from the top drawer of Jeff's desk.

In the photograph, she was leaning on the pedestal supporting one of the great bronze rhinoceroses flanking the doors of the Harvard Biology Labs. It had been a summer Saturday, and she was wearing white shorts and a blue tank-top. She was smiling, her hair pulled back off her forehead for coolness. They were strolling around and had dropped in to see if a friend of Jeff's was in his lab. He wasn't there, and they decided to walk to the Square and get a hot fudge sundae at Bailey's. Before they started, Jeff asked her to sit by the bronze rhino so he could get a picture of it. She had felt sweaty and unattractive, and protested. "I just want you there for scale," he told her. "I'm not going to be looking at you." And yet there it was in his drawer.

Of course, the police had already been through everything at the lab, satisfying themselves that Jeff was a suicide. She had found that much harder to believe than they did. The letter he left had both helped and frustrated her. He addressed it to her, then used a safety pin to attach it to the inside of his jacket pocket to keep it from getting lost when his body was moved.

She had known he was given to wide swings in mood, laughing and teasing one day, his brown eyes flashing with slyness, then a few days later becoming morose and withdrawn. Yet he seemed so much more mature than the men she had dated in college. He was somebody she could count on to offer her encouragement and to cheer her up when her own spirits were low. He was so sharp and clever that he could make her laugh without even working at it.

She had been shocked to learn that he had needed very powerful drugs to control his mood swings, because she had never seen him take anything. She had never even seen him swallow aspirin or vitamin C. It was a mystery to her how anyone with such an incapacitating disease could have kept it hidden, yet gone through medical school and then into a postdoctoral fellowship program. Jeff hadn't just scraped by either. He got the grades, the recognition, and the appointments. He was on his way to becoming a superstar in research. It must have been an incredible struggle.

And all so lonely. Why hadn't he at least told her what he was fighting? Sometimes she got so angry at him for what he had done to himself and to her that she was sure she had never cared about him at all. But of course she had. She still did.

When her breathing returned to normal, she stretched out on her back and hooked her toes under the brass railing at the end of the bed. The cold yellow metal felt like a band of fire across the bare skin of her feet. While she was doing her usual thirty sit-ups, the cut shag of the rug tickled the skin between her shoulder blades.

The previous Monday had been the anniversary of Jeff's death. She had tried so hard to avoid remembering it that she couldn't keep from thinking about it. For a month before, she had been aware daily that the date was approaching, and a week before, she made sure she would be very busy when it arrived. She had spent the day doing interviews for a freelance article she was planning. But now it was a week later and she was thinking about Jeff just as much as she had the week before.

She puffed hard as she did the twentieth sit-up, but she didn't stop to catch her breath. As her head came up from the floor and she leaned forward, her body was stretched out before her, and she couldn't keep from being satisfied with what she could see. Tight muscles kept her belly flat between the jutting ridges of her hip-bones, and her firm thighs tapered to the muscular calves of her legs.

Her pubic hair formed a jet black triangle, and a line of tight curls ran upward across her smooth skin to terminate at her perfectly rounded navel. Jeff had loved to run his finger along that line of hair. He said it showed that she was much closer to the animals than most people and that was why she was so sexy when she was in heat.

She got to her feet and stretched her arms out to her sides parallel to the floor. She rotated them in a propeller motion, making such wide circles that her breasts were alternately pushed together then stretched apart. She could feel the muscles of her chest and upper body pull with the strain of her exertions.

She was moving vigorously when she suddenly stopped in the middle of an arm swing and glanced at the window above her bed. The light that came streaming down seemed to have been blocked for an instant. Was somebody spying on her?

She was startled, and she wrapped her arms across her breasts. She stared at the window for a full minute, but when she saw nothing, she decided she was being foolish. The chance of someone spying on her was remote. Oliver Street was in a nice neighborhood and not the sort of place people went around peeping through other people's windows. Certainly not at eight in the morning.

Her apartment wasn't exactly in a basement, because there was still a level below her that really was the basement. But her bedroom was set into the side of a rise of ground that ran the length of the house, and although her window was high in the wall, it was barely above the level of the lawn. It was her private joke that she didn't need any house plants, because she already had grass growing in her bedroom.

After Jeff died, she couldn't afford to keep the apartment they had shared on Broadway, just a block from the Broadway Super-market. Their life together had made her feel more at home in Cambridge than any other place, but she was afraid she was going to have to move to the suburbs. Then the good news came when she was explaining her problem to Kate Springer. Kate had been her college roommate for three years and was now teaching at MIT.

"I didn't know you were even thinking about moving," Kate told her. "I'm doing the same thing. I've got just enough money for a down payment on a house in Brookline, and I'm buying it before the prices go any higher."

For the past three years, Kate had rented a three-room apartment in Professor Horton Smith's house. The day after she told Jill about her plans to buy a house, she introduced her to Mrs. Smith.

Mrs. Smith liked Jill on sight, and the rent was so low by Cambridge standards that Jill made a point of asking whether the figure was for the month. Mrs. Smith laughed and nodded. "We get a lot of tax advantages from renting," she said. "Besides, the ones who can pay high rent are mostly computer and advertising people. We don't want to rent to them. Cambridge is supposed to be for scholars and writers and artists, and they never have any money."

The apartment had been renovated, and its freshly painted walls and polished hardwood floors gave it an atmosphere of cleanliness and freshness Jill treasured. The apartment was at the back of the house and had its own entrance, so she had both quiet and privacy. Since the Smiths lived above her, she didn't feel completely isolated.

She glanced up again. The idea that someone might be watching her made her feel uneasy enough to slip her blue cotton bathrobe around her shoulders and climb up on the bed to look out the window. She never bothered to pull the dotted swiss curtains she had strung on a brass rod above the window, and they were open now. As she stood with her toes digging into the softness of her down pillow and her chin resting on the rough plaster of the window opening, she felt a tingle of fear that ran along her back and made her shiver and involuntarily shrug her shoulders.

She wasn't sure she should be looking out the window, because she wasn't sure she wanted to know if someone was there. What would it be like to see the twisted face and crazed eyes of a stranger staring at you on the other side of the glass?

Yet there was nothing to see, at least nothing threatening. The well-clipped lawn of zoysia grass was beginning to turn green in the warm spring sunshine. The hedge of spirea that separated the Smiths' yard from the one next door wasn't yet in bloom, but the long, arched branches were already covered with delicate spade-shaped leaves. The hedge was less than a dozen feet from her window and dense enough for someone to hide beneath its trailing branches. Yet nothing seemed to be moving in the bushes, and she saw no patches of color or unusual shadows. She refused to give in to her fears and pull the curtains.

She decided that if she had seen anything at all, it might have been a cloud blocking off the sun or a dog or cat wandering past the window. One evening months before, she had almost had heart failure when she glanced up from tying her shoes and saw two glowing eyes looking directly down at her. Even while she was frozen in place, she heard a loud meow and watched a large orange cat paw at the window, asking to be let in.

She climbed down from the bed feeling sure she was just letting her general anxieties get the best of her. One problem with living alone was that you didn't have somebody else around to tell you you were just being silly.

"Cowards die many times before their deaths," her father used to quote to her. He would say it to get her to climb back on a horse after she had fallen off or to walk home in the dark. She had always assumed her father was the source of the wisdom, but discovering he wasn't hadn't changed anything. Even now she associated the words with him and repeated them to herself in the same kinds of situations.

She went into the bathroom, turned on the shower, and adjusted the temperature of the fine spray of water until it was about as hot as she could stand. At first she had missed having a bathtub, but the shower enclosure was one of the nicest features of the apartment. Its fancy tilework gave her the impression of art deco perfection.

She lathered thoroughly with a bar of patchouli soap, rinsed off, then rubbed a discount brand of shampoo into her thick black hair. Her hair was short enough that she could simply towel it dry, so whenever she took a shower, she also washed her hair. That was another of her stabilizing rituals.

She turned off the water and opened the door of the enclosure. She was about to step out when she noticed she had kicked up the edge of the bathmat and exposed a section of the metal frame of the plumbing access panel set into the tile floor. Professor Smith had asked her to be careful not to let water stand on the floor. Otherwise, it would drain into the basement through the cracks around the panel. She tried to keep that in mind, but she was forever kicking the bathmat out of place.

She toweled herself dry, then wrapped up in a thick white bath-sheet before going back into the bedroom. Although she had decided against pulling the curtains over the window, she was still feeling too self-conscious and vulnerable to be comfortable about walking around naked.

Deciding what to wear was ordinarily not a problem for her. She simply pulled on a pair of jeans and a sweatshirt and got down to work. She cared little about what she wore, and since she mostly worked at home, she usually didn't have to worry about what anybody else might think. Today was different. She had to do an interview with the head of the Women's Reproductive Health Center, and she never liked wearing jeans to do interviews. Sometimes people thought you were showing disrespect toward them by not dressing up, and you could end up talking to a person who was a little angry and unresponsive.

The Center was in Cambridge, just off Central Square, and close enough that she could ride her bike. That meant she didn't want to put on a skirt. Looking through the rack of clothes arranged neatly in the small closet adjacent to the bathroom, she chose a pair of loose-fitting gray pants and a white cotton shirt. For a touch of color, she rolled a yellow scarf with silver threads into a narrow band and tied it around her neck. Jeff had given it to her for her twenty-seventh birthday. The weather was too cool for sandals so she slipped on a pair of soft black leather shoes with round waxed laces.

The uneasiness she had felt still lingered, and while she was dressing, she glanced several times at the window above the bed. Yet she saw nothing more than the usual splay of golden light that washed over her bed until around eleven o'clock. Without the sun, the room would become so dark it was almost gloomy. Despite that, she suddenly stepped up on the bedrail and pulled the dotted swiss curtains across the window.

She felt better immediately.

In the kitchen, she juiced two oranges on the glass juicer she had bought at a garage sale the year she graduated from college. She had owned it before she met Jeff. It seemed so fragile, who could have guessed it would outlast him?

She lightly buttered two slices of whole-grain toast and tapped out a tablespoonful of strawberry preserves on the plate beside them. Her mother had taught her to make preserves, and she had put these up herself early the previous summer. "Thinking about how good they're going to be later helps you forget your troubles," her mother would say. That was very much something she needed to do last summer.

She put on the kettle to make the single cup of *café presse* she allowed herself in the mornings, and while the water was heating, she made a list of the things she needed to get done.

First was the interview at the Center. That would take maybe two hours, and later she should write up her impressions while they were still fresh in her mind. On the way home, though, she would have to stop and buy some things for dinner. She and her old roommate Kate still saw a lot of one another, and tonight she was coming to dinner. Kate was easy to please, but Jill wanted to fix her something nice. She would see what looked good at the stores.

Kate wouldn't stay late, and after she left Jill would have to look over the notes she had made on science fiction in general and on

Dune in particular. *Dune* was the focus of Boscon, the national science fiction convention that was scheduled to start on Wednesday. When the editor of *Boston Update* had asked her to cover it, she had agreed immediately. She knew little about science fiction, but she needed the money and she needed to stay on the editor's active list.

She was glad she was going out to do an interview, and she was glad Kate was coming over. Lately she had been feeling very cut off from the world. The main advantage of being a freelance writer was that your time was your own. Paradoxically, that was also its main disadvantage. All that unplanned time could make you anxious, and sometimes she wished she had an ordinary job to go to. It would both give structure to her life and give her a chance to meet more people. However, she knew that once she really settled down to write, she was always glad to be free of the interruptions and schedules of an office. Even with its isolation and loneliness, writing really did suit her best.

The coffee was steaming and aromatic, and its smell filled the room as she poured the brew into the red mug the Smiths had given her for Christmas. Although the liquid was still scalding hot, she couldn't resist the aroma and sipped a little off the top. Her parents had also loved coffee, and some of her most pleasant memories were of her parents sitting around the kitchen table drinking coffee and talking with one another in a good-humored, digressive way.

They would mix in the trivial and the serious so that comments about somebody's hogs breaking out of their pen would be followed by the announcement that somebody else had cancer and could be expected to die before spring. They talked of marriage and betrayal, the size of heaven and the price of cotton, all in the span of a few minutes. She would sit unnoticed in a chair in a corner of the kitchen and let their talk entertain and warm her.

She drank her coffee fast, and she could feel the caffeine take hold and raise her spirits. She cleared the dishes from the table, rinsed them off, and put them in the dishwasher. She dropped a pen and a spiral notebook into her canvas book bag and was ready to go.

As she stepped onto the small flagstone area outside, she pulled the door tightly shut behind her. She heard the spring lock click into place, and she then double-locked the top lock, turning the key sharply to the right to slide the deadbolt into the jamb. Locking the house was the one thing Mrs. Smith had stressed above all others when she had rented Jill the apartment.

Jill headed toward the side door of the garage. She kept her bicycle at the rear of the frame building in the small storage area that also contained the decrepit gas-powered lawn mower, the fertilizer spreader, and other pieces of gardening equipment. The garage also housed the Smiths' car, an aging Volvo they hardly ever drove.

Before she reached the door, she turned and looked back at the house. She glanced up and saw that the rear window of Professor Smith's second-floor study was open a crack to let in some fresh air to combat his pipe smoke. He had probably been at work for even longer than she had been awake. Although he was in his middle sixties, he was a vigorous man and still active as a teacher and a scholar. Jill had come home late some nights to see his study lights burning and to hear the clacking and pinging of his ancient upright typewriter.

She wheeled the bicycle through the small side door and snapped the padlock closed behind her. She tugged on the lock to make sure it had caught. She didn't know what was the matter with her, but she was feeling awfully creepy.

For a moment she toyed with the idea of examining the grass in front of the window that looked into the bedroom of her apartment—then she smiled at her foolishness.

5

Monday 9:00 A.M.

Haack moved down the iron ladder slowly and carefully. The rungs were rusty and wet from the constant seepage of ground water, and the mixture of scale and mold made them treacherously slick. If he slipped and hurt himself, he would never be found. A cry for help would be swallowed up in the brick vault surrounding him, and he would die alone in the moist darkness.

Above him, at the top of the ladder, was the abandoned vat room adjacent to the old morgue of Eastern General Hospital. Except for a narrow pathway, the room was filled by two gigantic galvanized tanks. The morgue began its operation in the 1870s, and in the absence of refrigeration, the vats were filled with a solution of formaldehyde, alcohol, and water to preserve corpses for autopsy or dissection by medical students. When the morgue moved to a new part of the hospital in the 1940s, the vat room had simply been abandoned and forgotten.

Someone straying in by accident wouldn't find much of interest. A casual visitor wasn't likely to notice the flat iron plate with recessed handles in the stained concrete floor. Beneath the plate, a foot below the level of the floor, was the first rung of the rusty ladder he was climbing down so cautiously. He had discovered the room during the time he worked as a security guard.

When he had seen the ad for the job in the *Globe,* he thought he might have trouble getting it. After all, he was ludicrously overqualified. But as soon as he caught sight of the woman in the personnel office doing the interviewing, he knew the job was his. She was under thirty, with neatly trimmed brown hair, and although slightly overweight, she had a pretty face.

After she read through his application, she gave him a puzzled look. "You're a Harvard graduate," she said. "Could I ask how come you want to be a security officer? All it takes is a high school diploma or an equivalency certificate."

.He made his face serious and said, "I want to learn more about life." Then he smiled shyly. "I know that sounds silly, but you know, Harvard keeps you isolated from the real world."

"Are you sure you understand about the job?" she asked. "We're not looking for executive-trainees." She leaned forward and spoke almost in a whisper. "Security jobs can be really boring. I mean, you just stand around and keep an eye on things."

He also leaned forward. "I hadn't planned on telling anybody this," he said in a confidential tone. "Most people would laugh at me, but I want to collect materials for the novel I plan to write. Security guards watch people, and that's what a writer has to learn to do." He paused, wrinkled his forehead, and gave her an earnest look. "Does that make any sense to you?"

She shrugged. "I don't know," she said, smiling. "Is that also why you worked for the tour company? To get experiences?"

"You've got it," he said. "I took trips to Mexico until my stomach refused to go back again." He laughed.

She laughed with him. "I see you have one valuable qualification," she said, turning serious. She glanced at the application form. "You say you have a certificate in locksmithing. Do you have some proof of that?"

"I carry it with me," he said. He took out his wallet and handed her the card certifying that he had satisfactorily completed all the requirements of a correspondence course in locksmithing. The certificate was earned during his sophomore year, when all his college courses seemed boring and pointless.

She glanced at the card, and as she passed it back, her fingers brushed his. "I'm not in a position to offer jobs," she said. "But I would guess that my supervisor is going to be very interested in you."

"I'd appreciate any help you can give me," he said. He looked directly at her, and his voice was sincere. "I would really like to work here."

A week later, he was hired and sent to Eastern General. Within a month, he found the vat room.

He stepped off the last rung of the ladder and turned around. This was when he always had to fight off the panic that began seeping into his mind the way the ground water seeped through the bricks surrounding him. The ladder well was narrow, and without any light from above, the darkness here was total.

The dank air seemed to lack oxygen, and the acrid odor of ancient formalin irritated the membranes of his nose. He could hear his own rapid gasps, and in the stillness they seemed to come from somebody else.

He took a stubby key from his pocket and ran his fingers over the rough planks of the door in front of him. When his fingertips located the smooth face of the lock, he guided in the key, turned it, and pushed against the door with his shoulder.

The swollen wood resisted his effort but finally yielded and swung inward on oiled hinges. The darkness beyond was as complete, but the air was fresher. He closed and locked the door, then groped for the light switch. His fingertips touched the slick, wet surface of the crumbling plaster wall.

He twisted the knob of the old-fashioned porcelain switch, and the lights came on. Immediately, he felt better. He took a deep breath, and as he exhaled, he could feel the residue of panic drain away with the air forced out of his lungs.

The room stretched forty feet to the rear wall, and the ceiling was immensely high. Long ago the walls had been painted a pale green, but now patches of plaster had fallen away, allowing the red brick beneath to show through. Where plaster remained, blisters and scabs had formed as a result of the pervasive dampness. Mineralized water running down the walls had eaten away the paint and left yellowish streaks on the bleached chalky surface.

Once inside the locked room, he felt free to be himself. Like an actor stepping off the stage, he could return to his own reality. Wouldn't Aunt Emily, Mrs. Sanders, and the people he now worked with be amazed to discover what he was really like? They would see how incredibly they had underestimated the strength of his intelligence. His mind was a powerful weapon that could blast their

47

brains to pieces. He was sorry his mother had died before she was able to see his true self. She would be impressed.

For most of his childhood, he hadn't realized how special he was. Before that, he had imagined the difference he sensed involved some inferiority on his part.

"You're so dumb," Allan had said to him. They were eight years old and in the third grade, and Allan had asked him if he knew how women got pregnant.

"I know, but I don't want to talk about it," he said. He thought he knew, but he wasn't sure. He had pieced together his information from vague statements in novels and on television.

Allan wasn't fooled. "You don't want to, because you can't," he said.

"I can, too," he said. Then he blurted out, "Women have holes, and men put their dicks in them."

"Then what?" Daniel pressed him.

"Then they do something like pee," he said.

Allan had laughed. "Wait until I tell everybody that," he said. "They pee! Didn't your mother ever tell you you're a dumb asshole?"

He could still feel his hot embarrassment and recall the struggle to hold back his tears. He knew Allan was just teasing him, yet he still felt sure that Allan must know everything about him and his mother. He never forgot that feeling of shame, and whenever he remembered it now, his face still flushed with humiliation.

Years after he started having his hard dream, when he was fifteen, he finally understood why he wasn't like other people. He was in his second year at prep school when he suddenly realized that Allan was the stupid one and he was the one who was special. This came to him in an instant of revelation while he was reading *Dune*. Before he had completed fifty pages, he realized that he and Paul Atreides were too much alike for the resemblance to be coincidental.

They both were handsome youths of great daring who came from noble houses. Both could endure pain without showing signs of agony, and both had lost their fathers before really knowing them. Paul was a Mentat who could control others by his extraordinary intelligence and the power of his personality. He too could manipulate people by grasping their weaknesses and turning their own motives against them.

Paul was underestimated by everyone, yet he turned out to be the *kwisatz haderach* of Arrakis, the planet Dune. He had no doubt, even then, that he would eventually become a prophet and a ruler.

Dune was just a novel, but Frank Herbert had to be writing out of direct knowledge, because the characters and settings were too vivid not to be real. But how could Herbert know about such things? And why was his own life and character so much like that of Paul Atreides?

His soft dream provided the key to the puzzle. It had started much earlier than the hard dream, when he was no more than six. He is sleeping outside in a clearing surrounded by dense tropical jungle. Above him is a bright silvery sphere that may be the full moon or perhaps a spaceship. More with his mind than his eyes, he senses a dark presence. Maybe it's a person, but whether a man or a woman he can't tell. It's coming toward him, and he feels a terrible fear.

He tries to wake to run away, but he is paralyzed. The dark figure almost reaches him, when suddenly a jaguar silently pads out of the jungle. The tawny animal faces the dark shape, then curls its lip in a blood-chilling snarl that reveals its gleaming white fangs. The figure halts at the sound, then turns and disappears into the jungle. The jaguar lopes past him and follows the figure into the darkness. As soon as the jaguar is out of sight, he falls into an easy and untroubled sleep. The jaguar has been sent to protect him.

When he read in *Dune* about the bene gesserit organization spending centuries arranging for the birth of Paul, he understood that a similar group must have sent people to earth to plan for him. Everything fell into place when he saw a photograph of an ancient stone carving of an astronaut and read an account of how space travelers visited the ancient Mayas in the jungles of Central America. The explorers taught the Mayas science, and the Mayas founded a religion treating the explorers as gods. They became the Feathered Serpent and the Jaguar, but one day the astronauts would return.

Herbert had obviously gotten his information from the Mayas. So it was no accident that Haack was like Paul. He was a descendant of the sky gods and not an ordinary person. The jaguar protected him because it recognized him as a member of an extraterrestrial race. He and the jaguar were both gods. The soft dream was implanted in his mind to tell him he was being saved for greatness.

Haack crossed from the door to the ancient oak autopsy table standing beneath the hanging bulb. He tugged on the leather straps and let them slide through his hand. They felt supple but sturdy, and he could detect a light film of oil on their surface. The heavy brass buckles were free of corrosion but not highly polished. The leather and brass had looked very different before he had decided to restore them.

He slapped his hand on the oak top with satisfaction, then walked to the foot of the table and picked up a black canvas athletic bag.

He put the bag on the table, unzipped it, and took out a rolled bundle. He gave the bundle a shake to make it unroll. It was a jaguar skin, with a deep tawny color and jet black rosettes.

He slipped the skin over his shoulders like a cape and tied the rawhide laces. Broad strips of skin ran down each arm, and sewn onto the ends were hand-forged metal claws filed to the sharpness of razors. He wrapped his hands around the carved wooden handles of the iron claws and slashed at the air.

Once again, he experienced the power and majesty that had come to him when he first put on the skin two years earlier. He had been in the palm-thatched mud hut of a Maya priestess in the Yucatecan village of Xajala. When he clawed the air that time, the man who had guided him to Señora Abanado jumped back in fright, but the old woman simply looked at him and smiled. She seemed to have been waiting for him to come for the skin. He paid her five hundred dollars for it, but if she had known how much he wanted it, she could have charged him three times as much.

He had been back to see Señora Abanado twice. For a fee, she permitted him to watch her perform the ancient rituals of the snake and jaguar gods, and she was happy to supply him whatever he asked for. Her son was just as pleased to transport it across the border.

He untied the rawhide thongs and rolled up the skin. Instead of returning it to the bag, he put it on the lower shelf of the white-enameled instrument stand at the end of the table. He wanted to be able to get the skin quickly when he was ready to use it. At the rear of the shelf was a brown paper bag, and inside it were two pairs of women's underpants.

He stepped out of the circle of light and walked toward the lift. The bare bulb cast his stark shadow on the wall facing him and left everything not directly under it dim and indistinct. The room was the charnel house for the vat room, and bodies no longer needed for autopsy or dissection were lowered from the vat room on the iron slab of the lift.

They were then removed to the street through an opening in the rear wall just large enough for a casket to slide through. He had been disappointed to discover that the steel shutter over the opening had been welded into place.

The iron-framed opening of the lift was to the right of the entry door. He tugged on the doorknob as he passed by, then stopped in front of the knife switch. He pushed down the black handle to test the cable winder, and as soon as he heard the motor activate the winder, he flipped up the switch. Another few seconds and the moving cable would start to make its high-pitched squeal.

Despite the noise, the lift was in good condition. He had oiled the hubs of the pulleys and lubricated the wire ropes to make them slide more smoothly, but otherwise he hadn't found it necessary to make any repairs. Soon he would be using it for its designated purpose, except that the body would be live.

He was satisfied with his inspection, and when he glanced at his watch, he saw he had enough time to update his notes. Keeping an accurate record was a duty he owed to history. He sat at the oak desk he had pushed against the front wall and turned on a goose-neck lamp. He took a black leather-covered manuscript book from the center drawer.

The first page was a scene rendered in colored inks. Tropical trees sprouted from a tangled undergrowth, and birds with yellow, blue, and red markings perched half-hidden in the dense vegetation. At the base of a giant tree, almost impossible to see, was a crouched jaguar. The triangular mask of black fur made its face indistinct, and its pale, glassy eyes reflected no warmth. Hovering over the head of the jaguar, high above the jungle, a pale, silvery sphere seemed to shimmer in the dark blue of the tropical night.

Carefully smoothing the illustration along its crease, he turned to the title page and paused to admire the ornate lettering he had used for *Manual of the Hunt*. He then quickly skipped past the first section. It was called *Kills* and contained data about his four victims, beginning with the girl at Dumbarton Oaks in January of the previous year, going on to the girl in Morningside Park, and ending with Anna Hamilton. The data on the first two were very sparse. Each was a quick pickup, and he hadn't had time to find out much about them.

He had also been terribly frightened the first time, although perhaps that was only to be expected. He had gone to Washington just for the day to see the Maya collection at Dumbarton Oaks. He hadn't planned on killing anyone. Then he met a girl in the museum gift shop and was immediately attracted to her. Her name was Sue. She had long black hair, pale blue eyes, and was almost as tall as he was. She was very attractive. She must have thought he wasn't so bad-looking either, because she was very friendly. He told her he knew nothing about the Maya artifacts on display and asked her to help him choose one of the reproductions as a present for his mother. She said she was an art history major at Georgetown and knew a little about Maya art, so she would be glad to help him.

She was also glad to take a stroll with him along the wooded paths behind the museum. With no real plan, without even thinking much about what he was doing, he suddenly put his hands around her neck and began to strangle her. She fought hard, scratching his face, bruising his legs with kicks, and bloodying his lower lip with her head. She was no match for him, though.

When he was done, he was shaking with fear and elation. He was amazed by what he had done, but also terrified that someone had seen him. He kept his head, though. He dragged the body into a rocky area behind a stand of trees and walked out the visitors' entrance, holding his handkerchief to his nose so that it hung over his lip. He cleaned up in the airport rest room and caught the shuttle back to Boston.

He hadn't imagined it was possible to experience such pleasure. In retrospect, he realized he had even enjoyed the danger and fear. The very next week he took the shuttle to New York. That time he was more cautious. He had realized that he shouldn't approach his prey directly, because someone might see them together. He shadowed, stalked, and lay hidden. He moved in for the kill only when he could do it safely. This time he used a loop of picture wire.

He glanced down at the notebook and flipped rapidly through the descriptions under the heading *Prey Possibilities*. The list had seven names on it. He had carefully compiled it over a period of months of screening the women his current job permitted him to come into contact with. He stopped when he reached the section titled *Hunt in Progress: Jill Brenner*. She was the most attractive of the seven, and there was something intriguing about her. Maybe it was her intelligence.

The first part of the entry consisted of information he had acquired from his own observations and from sources like the Boston telephone directory. Below the raw data was his summary statement:

This attractive female is polite and friendly, although reserved. She seems self-possessed and competent, but she has an appealing air of vulnerability. She is of above-average intelligence and education and so should offer a challenge worth undertaking.

He was proud of the terse, factual style. It was closely modeled on police and autopsy reports he had studied.

Below the description were five numbered items, the first two with marks beside them:

x 1. Locate prey
x 2. Study behavior
  3. Flush
  4. Chase
  5. Kill

On his first two kills, he had let impulse and instinct guide him, but he discovered very quickly that random kills of anonymous women weren't totally satisfying. He needed more personal contact with his victims.

Then he remembered seeing an old film called *The Most Dangerous Game* and realized that hunting was the answer. The woman would also become involved in the action, and she and the hunter would be inescapably bound together by intimate feelings. With its equivalents of flirtation, pursuit, and rituals, the hunt could be like a courtship.

He tested the idea with Marie and Anna. Meeting them, marking them, warning them, and finally taking them had provided him with the kind of feelings he had expected from sex. Everything proved him right about the importance of hunting, but he saw ways of improving his style and making the experience even more intimate. He was learning, developing.

Jill was destined to be the perfect case. Wednesday would be the twentieth day after he took Anna's head and the time coincided both with Boscon and with the day of the Maya calendar dedicated to Cizin, the Death God. He had wanted a special offering.

He uncapped his thick Mont Blanc pen and quickly sketched the floor plan of Jill's apartment, including each potential point of entry. On the facing page, he sketched in the location of the furniture in her bedroom. He worked rapidly, because he still had many practical arrangements to make for the evening. He patted his jacket pocket to make sure he still had the proof he needed.

Although he knew he was rushing matters a little, he couldn't resist turning back a few pages and writing a neat black *x* beside item number three: *Flush Prey*.

6

Monday 8:45 A.M.

The Benjamin Rush Psychiatric Center was on a heavily forested stretch of highway nearer to Waltham than to Cambridge. Firecaster turned into the graveled lot and parked beside a silver BMW. Rush had the reputation of being the country club of psychiatric hospitals, and its patients were mostly wealthy or socially prominent.

He started the familiar climb up the long asphalt drive toward the red-brick Georgian administration building. Scattered around the grounds were the dozen or so cottages housing nonviolent patients. All had white trim and gray slate roofs and looked unchanged since his last visit two years ago.

His eyes sought out cottage B-10 without conscious effort. Alice had lived there for three months, but he couldn't remember what cottage she was in the second time. He had visited her there only once; then she asked him to stay away. He made no protest. By that time she had become a beautiful stranger, a stranger with delicate features and dark-honey hair.

He would always remember the five good years they had together. During that time he was working his way up in the department, fascinated by every day he spent on the street. The people, the problems, even the constant undercurrent of threat and danger, thrilled him. He knew from the first day that becoming a cop was the right move for him.

His pleasure was increased by the satisfaction of knowing that Alice's career hadn't been damaged by leaving Washington. She was doing even better than when he had met her. Her reputation as a printmaker was sufficiently established for her to be represented by galleries in New York, Chicago, Dallas, and Los Angeles, as well as Boston. Several museums and a number of large corporations had bought her work to display.

"It's a good thing you asked me to call you for a date," she would say to him. "Otherwise I would still be piddling away my time in D.C." Then she would add, "Now that I know how shy and reserved you are, I can't imagine what made you bold enough to slip me your number."

"Simple," he would say. "I couldn't live without you."

Then Alice had changed both their lives completely when she threw a heavy china bowl through the plate-glass window of a restaurant where she was having lunch with a friend. She had seen a hideously distorted face staring at her from inside the glass.

"It was the one I call Ostra," she told him. "He's been saying awful things to me about sex and telling me he was going to take over my life." She sighed and slumped down on the bed. "I've been feeling so dull, so heavy, that I'm not sure I care whether he does or not."

The diagnosis was schizophrenia. When Alice was discharged from Rush, she came back home to live in the large Victorian house he had inherited from his grandmother. He hoped things would return to normal, and in some ways they did. She went back to work in her second-floor studio, and he spent most evenings reading or doing paperwork in the study next door. He would hear her humming or singing snatches of old top-forty songs as she worked on a sketch or dug her carving tools into the hard wood of a print block. It seemed as if they could enjoy the same separate but companionable experiences they had shared before.

But they could not. It was as though body snatchers had been at work and substituted a pod creature for the real Alice. She was a different person. Once her cobalt blue eyes flashed with interest in everything around her, but now they had turned blank and cold. She worked on prints, but she never made any progress. Her feelings toward him changed, and she could no longer stand for him to touch her. After two weeks, she started sleeping in her studio.

He missed the person she used to be and found it impossible to stay at home while she ignored him. He became one of the people he had always felt sorry for, those who used their job as a substitute for a personal life. Then after her second stay at Rush, she returned to California to live with her parents. Three months later she asked him for a divorce, and he agreed to it. He saw no alternative. Alice was beyond his reach.

He thought he had hit bottom, but during the divorce process, his father died in his sleep of a cerebral hemorrhage. When Firecaster attended the services at Memorial Chapel, he heard his father praised as a teacher and scholar. But what he remembered was the gentle, somewhat distracted man who had worked at home as much as possible so he could spend more time with his son. He had lost the dad who never seemed to mind when he was interrupted by a kid who wanted him to look at a crayon drawing or help find the right kind of screwdriver.

Two important people in his life had disappeared. He had known that one day he would have to lose his father, but he had never imagined he would lose Alice. Even now as he passed cottage B-10, he could feel the muscles tugging at the corner of his eye, and the administration building seemed surrounded by a soft gray haze that blurred its lines and colors. "Alice, Alice, Alice," he whispered as he walked up the broad limestone steps.

Ted Castle was director of the Psychiatric Profile Research Institute. He was forty-five, with a sharp face and a complete inability to sit still. "The only difference between Ted Castle and a manic patient is that patients aren't allowed to wear ties," is the way Alice's psychiatrist once described him to Firecaster. Firecaster liked him, perhaps partly because he sensed Castle liked him.

Castle shook hands and motioned Firecaster to a chair. He dropped into the opposite one, then immediately got up. He walked behind his desk, picked up the red-covered folder of reports and photographs Firecaster had sent him, then sat down again. He put the file on the corner of the desk where he could reach it.

"I spend most of my professional life thinking about human beings at their worst," Castle said. He tapped the file and shook his head vigorously. "I'll have to admit, though, your job is nastier than mine. These pictures are just awful."

"Now you see why we've got to catch this maniac without wasting time," Firecaster said.

Castle shrugged and let out his breath in a long whoosh. "So you want me to try to say something useful about this guy?" he asked. He glanced at Firecaster in an almost challenging way.

"I've got a special task force primed and ready to act, but we're stymied, because we have essentially no information. Even a few guesses might help us move off square one."

"I'm not going to guess anything," Castle said. He spoke softly, as though talking to himself.

"Sorry, I put it badly," Firecaster said quickly. "What I mean is, tell me what you think it's reasonable to believe about this guy." He took a tan leather notebook from his jacket pocket and gave Castle an expectant look.

"All right," Castle said. He shifted in his chair and tapped his fingers on the upholstered arm. His whole body seemed to be in constant motion. "Let's take it for granted that our perpetrator is a serial killer; that means he's not going to fit everybody's idea of a raving lunatic. He's not going to be babbling or drooling or saying his cat told him to kill people. In public, he's going to act like you or me." Castle smiled slightly. "Maybe more like you," he said.

"And I certainly prove that looks can be deceiving," Firecaster said, returning the smile. Then he became serious again. "Are you saying this isn't somebody who has hallucinations or flashbacks?"

"It's not likely," Castle said. "To all appearances, he has an intact functioning personality. He may be physically attractive, and chances are good that he's friendly and even quite charming. He's not a schizophrenic or a schizoid personality. I'm quite sure about that."

Firecaster took a deep breath and let out a sigh. "Ted, you've now told me nineteen things this guy isn't," he said. "So what is he?"

Castle unclenched his hands and spread them out in puzzlement. "He's somebody with a serious personality disorder that we don't really understand yet," he said. "He's what older diagnostic systems used to call a psychopathic or sociopathic personality."

"A psychopath," Firecaster said, nodding his head.

"That's as good a term as any. Whatever you call him, he's a sexual sadist. Beneath his charm, he is vicious, violent, and absolutely merciless. He keeps a significant part of his personality hidden, like a snake in a box. When he feels safe, he lets out the snake."

"Now this is beginning to sound useful," Firecaster said. He leaned forward in his chair. "It might be even more useful if you could say what makes him feel safe."

"Control," Castle said. "He's got to have everything under control to fight off depression and a sense of worthlessness."

"Physical control?"

"Physical control, psychological manipulation, whatever," Castle said, waving his hand in a broad gesture. "He's probably good at getting his way, because we also know from studies that he's likely to be quite intelligent." He gave Firecaster an appraising look, then added, "Maybe even smarter than you or me."

"That I'm willing to believe," Firecaster said. "He's already made me feel like an idiot, and I know he doesn't make stupid mistakes."

"Don't expect him to," Castle said in a tone of warning. "He's not somebody who wants to get caught or who is so emotionally wrecked he doesn't think about the cops. He's a perfectionistic personality, and he'll be meticulous in his planning and execution."

"That gives me an idea," Firecaster said. "If he's so smart and likes control so much, could he be somebody close to the investigation?" He paused, then said, "I mean, somebody like a cop?"

"Could be," Castle said. "At the least, he's likely to have an interest in the police and how they operate."

Firecaster jotted down some notes, then glanced at Castle. He was out of his chair and pacing in front of the picture window. He tugged absently at the bottom of his red and gold striped tie.

"Would it help for me to just speculate about his childhood?" Castle asked. He turned around to face Firecaster. "I'm not talking about guesses, but a reconstruction based on statistical data and the few theories we have."

"It could help a lot," Firecaster said. He shifted in his chair and stretched out his legs. Castle's constant motion was beginning to make him jumpy.

Castle nodded, then turned to stare out the window. "He's somebody who was abandoned or abused during the first six or eight years of his life. The abandonment might not have been literal or the abuse physical. Maybe he lived with his family, had enough to eat, and nobody laid a hand on him."

"Psychological abuse," Firecaster suggested.

"Emotional," Castle said, nodding. "It's enough that somebody important was indifferent to him, never expressed any love toward him, never treated him as a worthwhile person."

Castle paused for so long Firecaster began to wonder if that was all he was going to say. When he finally started to talk again, he spoke in a regular, cadenced tone, as though reciting a memorized passage.

"He's a young man filled with incredible anger against whoever rejected him," Castle said. "Probably his mother, because mothers get left with children. The father abandons the mother and the child, and perhaps in unconscious retaliation, the mother emotionally abandons the child. The perpetrator is enraged by this, but he learns to hide his anger so he can win her love and keep her from abandoning him completely."

"I'm following you," Firecaster said. He sat straight in his chair again as the pieces Castle was offering began to fall into place.

"The anger gets mixed up with sex," Castle went on. "The two fuse, and the only real sexual satisfaction he's likely to get comes from vicious acts of destruction." Castle leaned on the window ledge and crossed his arms over his chest. "This kind of killing is more like rape than most murder. It's driven by rage, by a cold merciless fury."

Firecaster felt slightly giddy as he absorbed all the information. It was as if his mind were literally racing. He could sit still no longer and got up and leaned against the edge of Castle's desk.

"How about the mutilations?" Firecaster asked. "They look like they were made by claws. Do you think that's significant?"

"Very likely," Castle said. "The perpetrator surrenders to the murderous rage he ordinarily forces himself to keep under tight control. He gives himself permission to act like an animal, and for that time, he becomes an animal. He wants to let himself be totally unreasoning and driven by impulses."

Firecaster swiveled around to face Castle. "But why do you think he calls himself the Jaguar instead of the Tiger or whatever?" he asked.

Castle shook his head and shrugged his shoulders. "To know that we would have to tap into his own private symbol system and fantasy structure."

"You seem very sure those exist," Firecaster said.

Castle sat down at his desk, but his fingers couldn't stay still. He pulled out paperclips from the plastic box in front of him and began to string them together. Hardly glancing at Firecaster, he paid very close attention to sliding the open end of each clip onto the closed loop of another.

"He's got a fantasy structure all right," Castle said. "It's very elaborate and detailed, and you can be sure that, unlike his real life during childhood, in his fantasies he plays the role of the power figure. Everything revolves about him, and he is always in control."

"You think he acts out those fantasies?" Firecaster asked. Castle was concentrating on the paperclips and seemed far away in his own thoughts. "Do you?" Firecaster asked in a louder voice.

Castle nodded without looking up. "The fantasies both prompt his impulses and reinforce them," he said. "They probably started when he was a kid, and he's added to them over the years. He was almost certainly acting out part of the fantasy when he killed his first person."

"You mean Thomas?" Firecaster asked.

Castle looked up from his task and fixed Firecaster with a steady gaze. "Not necessarily," he said softly.

Firecaster felt the shock of a sudden realization. "You're right," he said. He stood up, then sat down on the edge of his chair. "She may be just the first we know about."

He silently cursed himself for ignoring what he considered an essential rule of police work. He called it the brown-shoe rule. As he would say to new detectives, "You can't tell me how many people you've seen today were wearing brown shoes, because you weren't looking for brown shoes. Remember, you can only discover what you're looking for." He had learned the rule from studying the history of science, then found it also held for criminal investigation.

He had let himself become so wrapped up in the two cases he knew about that he hadn't considered the possibility of their being connected with others. Even one other case with some hard physical evidence might give him a lot more to go on than he had now.

"Anyway," Castle continued, "that killing has been added to the fantasy structure, giving it a sort of reality. So now the fantasies and the actions begin to feed on each other. Imagining himself doing something makes him want to do it, and having done it provides more material for the fantasy."

"Then he's caught up in his own feedback loop," Firecaster said.

"Exactly," said Castle. "As the cycle turns, a kind of reality is generated. What he had previously only imagined now comes to be a part of real life." Castle looked up from the paperclips. "Having our fantasies become real is what all of us think we want."

Firecaster stood up and crossed his arms over his chest. He stood looking thoughtfully at Castle. "I was convinced before I came here that this is somebody who is going to kill again," Firecaster said. "Does that square with your analysis?"

"Absolutely," Castle said. "Once a sexual sadist kills one person and finds out how much pleasure it gives him, there's no stopping him."

"Do you think he's likely to try to fool us by making the next murder quite different?"

"No, no, no," Castle said, shaking his head vigorously. "No fundamental changes. But expect him to start getting more elaborate. He may decide to do things that make scenes in real life match up more closely with scenes in his fantasies. Because, remember, he wants to make those fantasies real."

"This is so frustrating," Firecaster said. He jammed his hands in his pants pockets. "It sounds like if we knew this guy's fantasies, we'd have a roadmap to his house."

"Not quite," Castle said. "This isn't going to be somebody easy to catch."

"Yeah, but I'm going to do it anyway," he said flatly. He took out his notebook and glanced at a page. "If this guy hates women so much, do you think we're looking for an unmarried or unattached man?"

Castle threw down the paperclip chain and got up from his chair. He walked to one of the tall bookshelves and began scanning the books level with his gaze. He seemed to be looking for a book to give him the answer.

"Not necessarily," Castle said. He turned and spoke to Firecaster directly. "He can keep himself sealed off from a wife or girlfriend so completely she would never suspect him of anything worse than being selfish and ignoring her needs. And of course a number of men fit that description."

"From what I've seen in this job, women almost invariably know when their husbands or boyfriends are concealing something from them," Firecaster said. "They may not know what they're hiding, but they know they're hiding something."

Castle nodded. "Most of us give ourselves away by being too casual or by overreacting. People sense there's something we feel guilty about."

"So?" Firecaster was puzzled. Castle seemed to be contradicting what he just said.

"No remorse," Castle said, as though providing an obvious explanation. "He doesn't act guilty, because he doesn't feel guilty." He pulled his head down and his shoulders up in a movement that might have been some kind of exercise. "His victim is just a toy."

"That's exactly it," Firecaster said, not bothering to hide his excitement. "That's what I felt when I looked at Hamilton's body. That's what pissed me off at him so much. He sees his victim as a

60

puppet, as a doll he can do anything to. He doesn't think of her as having feelings."

"That's because he views her only as an instrument to achieve his own ends," Castle said.

"Then I don't think I'm following you," Firecaster said, letting his puzzlement show. "I don't see how he can manipulate people if he doesn't identify with them."

"He may have a shrewd intellectual understanding of what motivates people," Castle said. "But he doesn't have any real empathy. He isn't able to identify with his victim any more than you can identify with a football you're about to kick."

"That all makes good sense to me," Firecaster said. "But what about the most bizarre feature of these killings? Do you have any ideas about the missing heads?"

"Nothing helpful," Castle said. "Serial killers often take trophies from their victims. Usually these are body parts—a finger, an ear, a tongue—but sometimes just a piece of flesh."

Castle walked to his desk and placed the palms of his hands flat against the smooth brown surface. "It's not clear why they do it. Maybe the object has some symbolic meaning to them or maybe it proves to them that they've done what they fantasized about."

"If he takes the heads because they have some private significance, that may be worth exploring."

"Maybe," Castle agreed. "But the connection may be so private we can never guess it. Or it might be an obvious one. His mother might be a hairdresser or sell wigs or something of the sort."

"Is that meant to be a joke?" Firecaster asked.

"Absolutely not," Castle said. "That's just the sort of association that might trigger his actions."

"Then it's something to keep in mind," said Firecaster. "It may be more helpful than you think."

The beeper on Castle's belt went off, emitting a series of high-pitched tones. Castle picked up the telephone and punched four numbers. He identified himself, listened a moment, then said, "Tell Blake he doesn't have to take the medication. Say I'll be there soon and we'll talk about it." He hung up.

"I've kept you too long," Firecaster said. "But just a couple of quick questions."

Castle dismissed the apology with a wave and leaned back in his chair.

"Is our perpetrator likely to have been in trouble with the law?" Firecaster asked. "We're going to look at males charged with sex crimes. What are the chances he'll be on the list?"

"Almost zero," Castle said. "If he's been arrested, it was for a crime unrelated to sex. Maybe burglary, because a lot of these guys get turned on when they break into a house."

Castle stood up, then sat on the edge of his desk, letting his feet swing free so that he could tap his heels against the closed drawers. "If you want to check records," he said, "you'd be better off checking people charged with cruelty to animals or stealing panties."

Firecaster felt a tingle of surprise. The inventories of items found at the crime scenes were not in the materials sent to Castle. "Why do you say stealing panties?" he asked.

"Sexual sadists get an erotic thrill from underwear. Some steal it, some dress in it, and some do both. It's a common fetish for that particular diagnostic category."

Firecaster slipped his small leather notebook back into his inside jacket pocket. He looked at Castle, who was tapping his heels and glancing around the room.

"You've given me a good picture, Ted," Firecaster said. "I've got a lot better idea of who I'm up against, and knowing your opponent is half the game. I'll eventually get him, unless he decides to quit or to go off to Canada."

"He's not going to do either," Castle said. "He's just hitting his stride. Because he's been successful, he's going to be drawn more and more into his own fantasy. He's going to start acting it out in more and more detail."

"Maybe the warning call to Hamilton shows that," Firecaster said. His smile was grim. "Eventually, he's going to start getting too cute. He'll take risks that will give him away, and that's when I nail him."

"I hope you do it soon," Castle said. He stood up and held out his hand to Firecaster. "I'll get you a written version of the high points of this," he said.

Castle held the door for Firecaster, then followed him into the hall. As they walked toward the elevator, Castle asked, "Do you ever hear anything from Alice?"

"No," Firecaster said. "I never do."

Castle used his key, and the elevator door slid open just in time to save Firecaster from the awkwardness of continuing the conversation.

7

Monday 11:15 A.M.

It was past eleven by the time Jill completed her interview and pushed open the bright blue and yellow door of the Women's Center. The chill of the morning was gone, and Central Square was crowded with shoppers enjoying the sunshine.

She hadn't expected the interview to last so long, but Dr. Neff, the director, was a dynamic woman who talked eagerly about her organization. Jill felt buoyed up by their conversation. It made her remember when hard days didn't get her down, because she had guided her life by her dreams. Surely she hadn't changed so much, though. Maybe she could even get back to the novel she had stopped working on when Jeff died.

It was her second attempt at a novel, and she had started it with his support. She had been serious about fiction, and after she graduated from college, she worked part-time at a business library to give herself time to write. In a year of hard work she completed a novel, which she then spent another nine months persuading publishers to read. Those who did liked her writing but not the book.

She was so discouraged she didn't want to begin another novel. Instead she quit her job and started doing freelance articles. For almost two years she did lots of local stories that sank without a trace. Then the *New York Times Magazine* bought "Fair Harvard?," about the treatment of women at Harvard. That established her reputation, and editors started calling to ask if she was interested in doing something for them.

She met Jeff while doing a piece on a new genetic test for susceptibility to heart disease. He wasn't directly involved in the research, but he volunteered to explain the technical details to her. The explanations continued over dinner, and as soon as he found out about her first novel, he encouraged her to start a second one. "If you're a writer, you've got to write," he told her. "Writing novels is art, and publishing them is business. The two don't always go together." While they were living together, she finally began the second novel, but after he died, she hadn't felt like going on with it. Now the idea suddenly seemed very appealing.

She stopped walking, not in a mood for shopping and reluctant to return to the dullness of her apartment. She caught sight of a white rabbit in a blue jacket munching a carrot on the sign of The Lettuce Patch Restaurant and decided to splurge on having lunch out.

The restaurant was crowded. The booths along the walls were filled, and only a few small tables in the center were vacant. She walked to the self-service counter at the rear and asked for a chicken salad sandwich and a bottle of seltzer with lime. She gave her first name so she could be called.

She found a table near the front and dropped her blue canvas book bag on the opposite chair. The hanging plants and white and green wallpaper gave the room a springlike air. With the sunlight streaming through the window and the gentle buzz of conversation around her, she could imagine she was having lunch in a garden.

"Jill!" the woman at the counter called out.

After paying, she picked up the plastic tray and turned to go to her table. Then she saw Richard Klore standing in front of her. He was smiling, but his pinched face and blond moustache gave him a rabbity look. He was wearing a gray tweed jacket, a silver-striped tie, and black shoes polished to a high gloss. For a moment she wasn't sure who he was. Then she had to make herself look surprised to keep him from noticing that she wasn't particularly glad to see him.

"I came in at just the right time," Richard said. He smiled again, showing small sharp teeth. "What brings you to Central Square?"

Richard's lab had been down the hall from Jeff's, and their offices were in the same suite. "He's arrogant and greedy," Jeff told her once. "I don't hold it against him, because he's bright. But except when he's talking science and medicine, he's about as interesting as a boiled potato."

About a month after she and Jeff became a couple, she met Jeff at his office one evening and he introduced her to Richard. The next day Richard called to ask her out. "I can't," she told him. "Jeff and I are very involved."

"I don't mind," he said. "I'm willing to see you whenever you get the time."

"That's flattering," she said. She was polite but careful not to say anything encouraging. "Right now, though, I'm not interested in anyone else."

"Let me know when you get free again," Richard said.

After that conversation, she had seen Richard a number of times, but only when she was with Jeff. Richard soon became involved with Sarah Cray, a doctoral student in genetics who worked in his lab.

64

Sarah was bright and charming but intellectually insecure. A few times, when it would have been awkward to do otherwise, Jill and Jeff had gone out to dinner with them, but Richard was so condescending toward Sarah that the evenings were painful and embarrassing.

Ironically, she didn't have to tell Richard when she became free again. He was the one who found Jeff's body. Because their offices were in the same suite, when Richard saw Jeff's door was open, he walked in to say hello. That was how he happened to be the physician who checked the vital signs and made the official judgment that Jeff was dead.

When she came to the lab that night, Richard had made an effort to be consoling. The attempt seemed more calculated than sincere, but she told herself she was being unfair. Still, when Richard called her two weeks later and asked her out, she refused. Not only was he still involved with Sarah, but something about him was too predatory to allow her to feel comfortable. When she moved to her apartment, she hadn't sent him her new address. Now here he was again, making an obvious effort to be casual and pleasant.

"I did an interview at the Women's Center," she said to answer his question.

"I've been keeping an eye out for you at the Coop and the Broadway Super," he said. He showed his small teeth in another smile. "I didn't expect you to show up on my doorstep."

"Your doorstep?" Jill asked. "Do you live around here?"

"I moonlight at the Center clinic."

"I didn't know that," Jill said. She was immediately aware of how fatuous that sounded. She knew nothing at all about what Richard was doing nowadays.

"I'll get something to eat and join you," Richard said.

"Please do," she said. She couldn't say anything else, without being deliberately rude. "I'm up front." She nodded her head toward the table.

By the time she cleared off the other chair, Richard had returned. "Granola yogurt, skim milk, and an orange—all very healthy," he said, putting his tray on the table.

Jeff would have made that sound ironic, but Richard's tone was smug. As soon as the thought occurred to her, she told herself not to compare the two any further. It was pointless.

"I thought about calling you a couple of times," Richard said, "but I've been so busy I never got around to it." He leaned across the table, but she felt crowded and shifted back in her chair until the distance was comfortable. "I guess you've been putting together a new life with lots of new people in it."

"There's nobody new," she said. She turned her face away from him, then looked back. "I do my work, and maybe a couple of times a week I have dinner or go to a movie with a friend." She shrugged. "Otherwise, I keep pretty much to myself."

She hoped she had avoided giving Richard the impression she was needy and lonely. She particularly didn't want him to think she was offering him any encouragement.

"You shouldn't be by yourself so much," Richard said. He sounded genuinely concerned. "You need to keep active, see people, and go out and have fun."

She sipped some seltzer directly from the bottle and nodded at him. "I've got plenty to keep me busy," she said. Then to shift the conversation away from her personal life, she quickly asked, "How is Sarah? You haven't said anything about her."

"She took an offer from New Haven Hospital," he said. His tone was conversational, but anger showed in the tone of his voice. "I told her my leaving Cambridge was out of the question and it was either the job or me. So three months ago, she took a walk."

"I'm sorry," Jill said. She felt hypocritical, because she was actually glad Sarah had found the courage to leave. Yet it would be pointlessly cruel to tell Richard that.

"Everything is just fine," Richard said. He waved his hand in a dismissive way. "To tell you the truth, I was getting bored with her. If she hadn't left, I eventually would have tossed her out. Now I'm living alone and liking it."

"Speaking of living alone, I had a strange experience today." Jill was determined to change the subject again. "I had the feeling while I was doing my exercises that there was somebody spying on me through my bedroom window."

"But you didn't see anybody?" Richard sounded interested.

"I didn't see anybody," she admitted. "And there probably wasn't anybody to see." She forced a short laugh.

Richard leaned forward and rested his forearms on the table. He gave her a tight, professional smile. "Probably just an anxiety reaction," he told her. "Is there anything going on to cause you any stress?"

She realized he had forgotten that the anniversary of Jeff's death had just passed. Of course, there was no particular reason he should remember. "I suppose you could say things haven't been exactly normal for me for over a year," she said.

Richard still didn't make the connection. He drank some milk and looked at her, obviously waiting for her to go on. She suddenly decided she didn't want to go on. Despite what she told Richard, she was now beginning to feel virtually certain someone had been watching her.

"I might actually have seen someone," she said. She looked directly at Richard, and this time she was no longer smiling.

"It's possible," he admitted. His tone suggested the possibility was remote. Then he seemed to lose interest in the question. He glanced at his watch. "I've got to get out of here," he said. "Before I go, I want to make plans for us to get together."

She remained silent. She was annoyed at his presumption that he could make plans for them both without first asking her if she wanted to get together with him.

Richard stood up and pushed in the chair. "In fact, have dinner with me this evening," he said.

"But we just had lunch." Jill stood up. "We'll do something again before long, I'm sure."

"Why not tonight?" Richard pressed her.

"Because my friend Kate Springer is coming to dinner." She tried to keep the annoyance out of her voice.

"Then how about if I drop around for a drink later?" Without giving her a chance to reply, he asked, "Are you still living on Broadway?"

She found his persistence annoying, but if she put him off now, he would simply call her later. At least with Kate around she wouldn't have to deal with whatever romantic advances he might have in mind.

"I moved several months ago," she said. She picked up her blue canvas bag. Then she made up her mind. "We're having dinner rather late. So how about coming around eleven?"

"Let me get your address then," Richard said. He smiled and looked pleased with himself.

8

Monday 3:00 P.M.

So far as Firecaster could tell, the space hadn't been converted into anything. It was just a dusty loft where somebody happened to live.

The large, open room had tall, uncurtained windows on the east and west walls. The toilet was enclosed by a partition without a top, and next to the toilet, a white porcelain sink was bolted to the rough plaster. At the rear, another room had been carved out by unpainted plywood nailed to raw two-by-four frames. The hardwood floors were rough and splintered, and at places splotches of oil and neatly drilled holes marked where machinery had once been bolted down.

In the corner of the room farthest from the windows, a king-sized mattress with dirty, rumpled sheets lay on the floor. Beside the mattress were a blue vinyl airline bag and two cardboard boxes filled with clothes. One of the boxes was brightly printed with smiling yellow grapefruit below bright green letters that spelled out *Florida Tre-eat*. A small red TV set perched on top of a large, gray-painted wooden spool that once had held telephone wire.

Alfred Dabney had agreed to talk to them without a lawyer present, but for the last five minutes, he and Renuzi had discussed nothing but the Bruins. Firecaster had sat silently, giving Renuzi a chance to establish some rapport with Dabney and get him accustomed to answering questions.

"What do you do for a living, Mr. Dabney?" Renuzi asked, shifting the direction of the conversation. His tone was polite and respectful.

Firecaster estimated that the man sitting in the heavy wooden armchair weighed at least three hundred pounds. His face was a long oval that seemed inflated much beyond its normal size. The enormous amount of fat made his features soft and indistinct and gave his face a surprisingly delicate appearance. Each breath was a moist, labored wheeze. He was thirty-nine years old, but rolls of fat had kept his skin free of wrinkles.

Velma McArdle, who had called to give them his name, told Renuzi he was known as Big Al. "He says he knows something about that girl that was killed down by the river," she said. "I don't know what it is, because he wouldn't tell me."

Big Al's chair was the only one in the room that looked sturdy enough to hold him. Firecaster sat front-to-back in a metal-framed dinette chair, and Renuzi perched on the upholstered top of a wicker stool.

"I'm a stone mason," Big Al said, answering Renuzi's question. His voice was surprisingly thin and high, lacking in resonance.

"Got a lot of work?" Renuzi asked.

"Yeah, I guess," Big Al said. "Depends on what you mean by a lot. I got a job starts next week up to Wheaton College. It's a ten-million-dollar job with lots of stonework, mostly walls."

"How did you get that job?" Renuzi asked.

"I know a man that always calls me if he's got anything," Big Al said. "He's a contractor. Henry Shea's his name. Works for Otley Engineering over in Newton. You can check it out."

"When's the last time you had a job?" Renuzi asked. His voice was casual, and he didn't seem to be paying much attention to the answers.

Big Al shook his head. "Depends on what you mean by a job," he said. "I did a couple of piddling things last month for private individuals, but I hadn't had no real job since last November." He looked at Renuzi seriously. "You know, there's not much stonework going on during the winter. Concrete and mortar freeze and don't set right. You've got to tear everything out and start over. Waste of money."

Big Al apparently intended to go on talking, but Firecaster cut in. "How well did you know Anna Louise Hamilton?" he asked sharply.

The big man turned his face toward Firecaster. He seemed undisturbed by the question. His eyes looked small, peering past the mounds of fat that framed them, and they searched Firecaster's face, as though trying to discover the reason for the question.

"I never did know her," he said at last. "I never set eyes on her."

"We think you did," Firecaster said. He made his voice crack like a whip. "We think you're lying to us."

"You'd better go ahead and tell him," Renuzi said gently. "The Lieutenant can be a hard man, if you don't go along."

"You can't tell us you never heard of her," Firecaster challenged him.

Big Al shook his head slowly, and the fat on his cheek swung in a gentle rhythm. "I didn't say I never heard of her," he said. "I told you I didn't know her."

"We've got a witness who says you did," Firecaster snapped at him.

"You've got somebody feeding you a line of bullshit then," Big Al said. He hesitated a moment, then said, "And I bet you dollars to doughnuts I know who it is." He turned to look at Renuzi. "It's Velma, ain't it? She's the one who told you." He seemed more curious than angry.

Renuzi kept his face noncommittal. "Just tell the Lieutenant all you know," he said. "He's not trying to get anything on you. He just wants to help you, if you're in some kind of trouble."

"Tell us what Velma you're talking about," Firecaster ordered the man.

"Velma McArdle," Big Al said. "I've known her about two years, maybe closer to three. She works for Otley. She's about as old as I am, but she's got a real good job in the timekeeper's office. She's a nice lady and awful pretty." Then he added as an afterthought, "She's not married, though."

"Why do you think she might have told us you were a friend of Anna Louise Hamilton?" Firecaster interrupted him.

Big Al sat quietly for a moment. Then he said, "I guess she must have thought I knowed more about the killing than I do."

"Isn't that because you told her more than anybody but the killer would know?" Firecaster insisted. "We've got evidence that puts you at the scene. We've got a witness and we've got evidence." He paused to give Big Al a chance to think, then said harshly, "We've got enough to arrest you on suspicion of murder."

"Go ahead and tell us about it, Al," Renuzi said softly. "Don't worry about how you say it, because you can't shock me and the Lieutenant. We've been around the block a few times." He gave Big Al an encouraging nod.

"I don't have nothing to tell you," Big Al said. He sounded exasperated. He raised his thick arms off his lap, then let them fall back. His upper arms were so large that only his wrists rested on his legs. "Velma just misunderstood something I said to her."

"What did you tell her?" Renuzi asked. "Just tell us what you told her, and I'm sure that'll clear everything up." He sounded encouraging.

The big man took a deep breath, then let out a long sigh. "I was walking down toward the river when the cops found that girl's body. Anna Hamilton, I mean. I stood around with a bunch of other people and watched what was going on." He shook his head. "I didn't see much, really. Just a bunch of blood on the ground, and I heard somebody say her head was missing."

"How did you know her name?" Firecaster asked.

"I didn't know it then," Big Al said. "I read about the killing in the *Globe* and saw it on TV. That's how I know her name."

"What did you tell Velma McArdle?" Renuzi prompted.

"Oh, Lord," Big Al said. He shook his head and looked away. "It's too embarrassing. I don't even want to have to think about it, much less talk about it."

"I told you we've heard everything," Renuzi said.

Big Al looked at Renuzi, then took a deep breath and started. "Well, I'm real fat," he said. He forced a laugh. "As if you hadn't noticed. Anyway, it's a little bit hard to get women to go out with me, unless I can impress them. You know, so they'll get past their first impression and get to know me." He avoided Firecaster's eyes and looked at Renuzi.

"I know what you're saying," Renuzi told him.

"When I went out to fill out the papers for the Wheaton job last

Friday, I saw Velma in the office," Big Al said. "I was shooting her this line about how I knowed more about the Hamilton killing than the TV did." He shook his head and his jowls wobbled. "All I meant was I heard that the head was missing, and they didn't put that on the TV."

He glanced left at Firecaster, then turned back to Renuzi. "I told her, if she'd go out to a hockey game with me, well, I'd tell her all about it."

"We've got your picture," Firecaster said.

"Picture, where?" Big Al asked, turning to face him.

"Where Anna Louise was murdered," Firecaster said.

"I already told you I was there," Big Al said. His voice took on a slight whine.

"What were you doing there?" Firecaster asked. "Did you just come around to see if you'd left anything behind?"

"You'd better say what you were doing there," Renuzi said.

"Nothing," Big Al said. He voice was beginning to take on a sharp desperation. "I wasn't doing nothing there. I was just walking back from a store when I saw a big crowd down in the park, and I just went down to see what was going on."

"I thought you told us earlier you were walking through the park," Firecaster said.

"I did say that," Big Al admitted. "I went to see what was happening, just the way any normal person would do."

"What store were you coming from?" Firecaster asked.

Big Al hesitated, then said, "Tom's Trains on Garden Street."

"What sort of place is that, Al?" Renuzi asked. In contrast to Firecaster, he spoke in an easy conversational way.

"It's a place that sells trains," Big Al said. He shrugged. "I don't know what else to say about it."

"Toy trains?" Renuzi asked.

"Yeah," Big Al said. "Only they're called models. You know, like model railroads." He sounded slightly embarrassed.

"What were you doing there?" Firecaster asked.

"I was buying some stuff," Big Al said. "It's kind of a hobby with me, you know? I don't get much work during the winter, and I don't have all that many friends. So I just try to stay out of trouble by putting together my own railroad."

"How about showing it to us," Renuzi suggested.

"You think I don't have one?" Big Al asked. "It's right there at the back." He gestured toward the opposite end of the room.

"We'd like to see it," Firecaster said. "You can show us what you bought at Tom's Trains."

The big man pulled himself into a standing position by rocking

71

forward and pushing down on the arms of the chair. He took a deep breath and started toward the back. His whole body seemed to swing to one side then the other as he walked. Yet he moved surprisingly fast.

The opening in the partition had no door. They let him walk through first, then followed a few steps behind him. Big Al turned on an additional overhead light.

Most of the floor space in the partitioned area was taken up by sheets of green-painted plywood resting on sawhorses that formed the base of an elaborate train system. Big Al leaned over and flipped a row of toggle switches.

Firecaster had never seen anything to compare with the elaborately created scene. He bent over to be able to make out the details.

In mountain valleys, tiny towns with white clapboard houses, paved roads, and supermarkets were divided into sections by a small railroad track. The track itself was lined with automatic coal loaders and brightly illuminated stations. A freight train stood motionless in front of one of the stations. The train's refrigerator cars, hoppers, flatbeds, and container cars stretched out for over a foot along the track.

Big Al switched on a transformer and moved a lever. At once a sleek passenger train with silver cars and a boxy tandem diesel at the front began to move across a sandy desert landscape. Along the track, signal lights glowed green.

"You constructed all this yourself?" Firecaster asked. He had dropped his sharp questioning tone.

"Yes, sir," Big Al said. "I've been working on this setup for about three years now. It's a lot of trouble, but it's a great pleasure to me. Sometimes I just come in here and set down. Maybe I won't do nothing but study the layout or try to think up some changes. When I leave, though, I always feel better than I did when I come in."

"What's the scale?" Renuzi asked.

"HO," Big Al said. He picked up a cardboard box with a cellophane window in the front. "This here is what I bought at Tom's," he said, showing the box to Renuzi. "Trees. These are fir trees, but you can get maples, sycamores, whatever kind you want. I'm thinking about putting in a big forest right outside of town." He pointed at a place beyond the white clapboard houses.

Firecaster felt moved by Big Al's enthusiasm. He now found it impossible not to think of him as an overgrown child, the sort of friendless, unattractive boy forced to develop a hobby to protect himself from despair.

* * *

"So what do you think?" Renuzi asked when they were on the street again.

"I think Big Al did a terrific job of solving his problems," Firecaster said. "Too bad Crazy Cat didn't do as well."

9

Monday 1:30 P.M.

Kate Springer's attitude toward food took the pressure off having her to dinner. She liked everything she ate, and Jill knew that to please Kate all she had to do was please herself.

She usually bought everything she needed at the Broadway Super, but since Mrs. Smith talked about how wonderful the produce was at the stand on Brattle Street, Jill decided to go there. The fruits and vegetables did look wonderful. She quickly selected heads of romaine and Bibb lettuce, found both tarragon and basil, then turned her attention to fruit.

Nestled in the artificial grass behind the papayas, she saw exactly what she wanted—New Zealand raspberries. The dusky purple of the berries reminded her of the soft hues of an impressionist painting. The raspberries were ruinously expensive, and for a moment she started to put back one of the half-pint boxes. Then she realized how silly that was. If she was going to make a special dinner, a couple of dollars extra hardly mattered.

She walked a few doors down and went into Sage's. The couple of dollars extra were about to become several times that, because Sage's sold only the best of everything. She bought feta and Parmesan, a plastic-wrapped tray of fresh pasta, unsalted butter, heavy cream, and half a dozen crunchy rolls.

When she reached home, she put away her bicycle and set down the groceries on the flagstones while she got out her keys. She opened the lock with the deadbolt, then the keyhole lock. She picked up her bags and carried them to the kitchen. She put the cheese and raspberries in the refrigerator and, after thinking about it, decided that was the place for the pasta also. She filled the sink with water and dropped in both heads of lettuce.

She went to the bedroom to change into jeans and a sweatshirt. She untied her scarf and pulled open the middle drawer of the dresser to put it away. She reached inside to lay it on the stack in the drawer, then jerked back her hand as though she had touched a snake.

She felt the short hair on the back of her neck bristle, and her shoulders squeezed together into an involuntary shudder. Something was wrong about the drawer. The scarves were still folded into rectangles and stacked in a single soft pile, but they weren't right. She never stacked them so the corners were perfectly square, but now the scarves were completely twisted out of alignment. It was as though somebody's thumb had riffled through the stack.

Somebody's thumb, she thought, and the phrase seemed to stick in her mind. The idea that someone she didn't know had gone through her clothes struck her with a sudden force. She didn't feel so much afraid as violated, her most private possessions fingered and tampered with.

The window! Somebody must have come through the window. She hadn't been imagining things. She untied her shoes, kicked them off, and climbed on the bed. The latch was still fastened and the pins in the sides of the frame were still in place. No one could have come in that way. But just because someone looked through a window didn't mean he would break in that way. She had other windows.

She hurried through the entrance hall, past the door to the kitchen, and into the next room. The kitchen had no windows, and both windows in her living-dining room were still fastened. Neither showed any signs of tampering.

While she was pulling a curtain back into place, she glanced out toward the garage and saw Professor Smith pulling weeds from around the spirea bushes. He was wearing gray suit pants that were old and baggy, and his green plaid flannel shirt was faded from years of washing. Kneeling on the walk by the garage, he looked more like somebody's yardman than a Harvard professor. It flashed through her mind that perhaps he had gone through her things, but she immediately rejected the idea as ridiculous.

Then she thought about her jewelry. She walked swiftly back to the bedroom and pulled open the top drawer of the chest that stood against the wall next to her bed. She reached beneath the underwear and moved her hand around until she found a rectangular brass box. She thought it had been moved, and she was sure she would find it empty.

She flipped open the lid and saw with relief that the gold necklace with the ruby pendant her father had given her for her eighteenth birthday was safe. It was the only valuable piece she owned. Yet everything else was in the box also—the opal earrings Jeff gave her their first Christmas together, the jet necklace she bought for herself in Baton Rouge just before leaving for college, and several other pairs of earrings set with various semiprecious stones.

She opened the bottom drawer. It was filled with shorts, bathing suits, and shirts she hardly ever wore. She couldn't swear to it, but she thought someone had been through that drawer as well. She reached under the clothes and came up with a photograph album covered in cracked blue vinyl. Several yellow drugstore envelopes of photographs and negatives were stuffed inside.

She checked the first envelope and saw that it held the pictures she and Jeff made during their week at Falmouth. The weathered gray house they rented was in the background of the photograph on the top of the stack. Jeff was in the foreground. He was wearing a skimpy white bathing suit that made his long legs look even longer, and he stood facing the camera with his hands on his hips and his feet spread apart. He was smiling, and the wind from the sea had blown his dark hair into a fantastic twisted shape. She quickly put the photographs back into the envelope and returned the album and the packages to the bottom of the drawer.

She slammed the drawer closed and decided she simply wasn't going to look anyplace else. Even though things didn't seem quite right, nothing appeared to be missing. Maybe her imagination was being overactive because she was startled by whatever it was that crossed her window that morning. She would talk to Professor Smith and see what he thought about it.

Professor Smith was still on his knees tugging out clumps of coarse grass, but he stood up and brushed his hands when he saw Jill walking toward him. He pulled out a dark blue handkerchief and rubbed it across the top of his bald head.

"If you want to start thinking it's summer, just do a little manual labor," he said. He smiled and looked down at her.

She made an effort to return the smile in a natural way, but he recognized immediately that something was wrong. His large gray eyes narrowed, and he cocked his head slightly to the side. "Are you feeling ill?" he asked. "If you are, I'll call Ellen to come out here and she'll tell you exactly what you have to do about it."

Her smile was more natural this time. Professor Smith had a way about him that was comfortable and reassuring. Just seeing him standing there in his baggy gray pants and faded flannel shirt made her feel much better.

"I'm not sick, but I am a little upset," she said. "Have you sent anybody to clean or do any repairs in my place?"

Professor Smith didn't answer at once. He seemed to be giving the question thorough consideration, running through his file of memories. Then he shook his head. "No one has done any work in your part of the house since the fall," he said. "That's when we had the radiators bled and the furnace cleaned."

"Did somebody come to the door or anything like that?"

"I've been in my study most of the day, and I don't believe there's been anybody here." He carefully folded his handkerchief and put it in his hip pocket. He then looked at her closely, his head bent so that he could peer into her face. "What's this all about, Jill?" he asked. "I've never seen you so worried."

"I think somebody was in my apartment while I was out this morning." She felt a great relief in just telling someone.

Professor Smith whistled softly. "That is upsetting," he said. "Are you missing anything?"

"So far as I can tell, nothing is gone," she said.

"That's good at least," he said. "I'm sure you didn't fail to lock the door."

"I double-locked it, and it was still locked when I got home." She couldn't help feeling defensive, but she hoped she didn't sound that way. She had done nothing to bring this on herself.

"Any signs of a break-in?"

"I can't see anything," Jill said. "And the windows are all locked."

Professor Smith rubbed his chin and looked puzzled. "This is awfully strange," he said. "Just what makes you think somebody was in your place?"

Jill tried to explain about the scarves and her feeling that someone had been through her drawers. "I can't be certain, of course," she said when she had finished. "There's nothing I can hold in my hand or point to for other people to see."

She waited expectantly, as though Professor Smith were going to render a judgment. He only nodded and looked at her with mild gray eyes. "Have you given your key to any friends?" he asked.

"I haven't even had any duplicates made," she said.

"I don't know then," he said. "Do you want me to call the police?"

"I haven't thought about it," she said. "What's your opinion?"

"Useless," he said. "No theft, no signs of a break-in." He shook his large head slowly. "They would take your name, fill out a report form, and that would be the end of that."

"I'm sure you're right," Jill said. "They would think I was just another nut." She shrugged. "I guess the best thing to do is to forget it."

"I suspect that's sensible," Professor Smith said. He hesitated, then spoke in a deliberate way, as though to be sure of choosing the right words. "You've had a fright, but I don't think there's anything you need to be afraid of. Still, I'm going to have the locks changed on that door."

"I hate for you to go to that expense," Jill said. "There really doesn't seem to be any good reason for my feelings."

"That's all right," Professor Smith said. "The locks need changing anyway. I didn't change them when Kate left, and I don't know how many keys she may have passed around."

"Are you going to do it today?"

"Too late today," Professor Smith said. "I'll call Tom Sims right now and ask him to come over first thing in the morning."

"Thanks very much," Jill said. "I know I'll sleep a lot better after tonight."

10

Monday 11:00 P.M.

Kate settled herself on the blue velvet Victorian love seat and stretched out her legs. Jill came in from the kitchen with the tray of demitasse cups and brandy and placed it on the low table in front of the love seat. Kate shifted her feet so she could get past.

Kate was tall and lanky with the sort of blond good looks that led people to think she might be a model. She was actually a computer scientist in MIT's artificial intelligence program. She had finished her doctorate and received a faculty appointment only the year before.

"Dinner was absolutely wonderful," Kate said. "I don't know why you don't open a restaurant and charge a hundred dollars a meal. You could be like Alice what's-her-name in Berkeley and make a fortune."

"I don't open a restaurant because I don't want to have to work for a living," Jill said. "That's why I took up writing, remember? It pays about the same as panhandling, but you don't have to spend as much time being nice to people."

She poured an inch or so of the pale brandy into each glass, then handed one to Kate. She slipped out of her shoes and sat at the opposite end of the love seat with her feet curled under her.

"You do all right for yourself," Kate said. "Did you go to the science fiction convention? What do they call it?"

"Boscon—for Boston Convention," Jill said. "It doesn't start until Wednesday. I was going to stay up late tonight and write down some interview questions, but now that the charming Richard Klore is dropping by, I'll have to postpone that until tomorrow."

Kate gave her a sympathetic look. "I'm sorry I can't stay to protect you from death by arrogance," she said. Kate had met Richard only once and had detested him within five minutes. "But if I'm not in bed by midnight, then the next day, the computers are smarter than I am."

Jill laughed. When the two of them were alone, they joked around and teased one other as though they were still undergraduates having a good time before the reality of finals caught up with them. Even when times were hard, Kate always made her laugh and raised her spirits. To keep from destroying the feeling of fun, Jill hadn't mentioned her uneasiness that morning or her fear that someone had been in the apartment. Kate would make a joke of it, but that really wouldn't make Jill feel reassured. Better just to keep quiet.

"I wish I had a fireplace," Jill said. "I would like to be sitting here staring into the fire, watching the flames leaping around and just dreaming."

"I used to wish that too when I lived here," Kate said. "Now I've got a fireplace in the living room and another upstairs in the bedroom. The catch is, I don't have anybody to sit in front of it with."

"You could if you wanted to," Jill said. "I never really understood why you broke up with Charlie Ranger."

"I sacrifice everything for my work," Kate said. She held a hand to her forehead in a melodramatic gesture, then glanced at Jill and shrugged. "This sounds awful, but I just got bored with him. It wasn't merely that he told me more about junk bonds than I wanted to know, although that counted. The real problem was, I thought he had two sides to his tape, but one side turned out to be blank and he played the other too many times to make me want to go on listening."

"He was good-looking."

"And rich," Kate said quickly. "Don't forget rich. Now I'm going to have to meet mortgage payments with a salary based on the modern notion that everybody has the benefit of two incomes. That's capitalism's revenge on women."

"You'll find somebody else before long," Jill said. She knew Kate well enough to respond to her real worry. After breaking up with someone, Kate felt she would never find anyone to take his place. "You always have," Jill reminded her.

"That was before I developed standards," Kate said. "But enough about me and my fascinating love life. Let me get your ideas about one of the burning topics of our day."

Jill played it straight. "Cleaning up the environment? Nuclear destruction? Racism? Saving endangered species?"

"Nope," Kate said, shaking her head at each suggestion. "I'm talking of nothing less than—furnishing my living room." She paused. "I don't know whether it should look like a set from *Metropolis* or a Ralph Lauren cottage."

"That does give us a little scope to work with," Jill said.

Jill poured out more brandy, and for the next twenty minutes they talked comfortably about the furniture styles, chintz and dark wood, and the high price of everything.

Kate let the last drop of her brandy slide down the snifter onto her lips, then got up from the love seat. "I really need to go," she said. "I thought I was going to be around to ease your misery for a few minutes, but maybe you're not going to need help anyway. It doesn't look like Richard is going to show up."

As though the name were a cue in a play, there was a series of sharp raps on the door. Jill got up, looked at Kate, and opened her eyes and mouth as though giving a silent scream. She went to the door.

"I know I'm late," Richard said. "You didn't tell me your apartment was at the rear of the house."

"Oh, I thought I did," Jill said, knowing she had.

"I've been up and down the street trying to find the place."

"I'm sorry about the trouble, but you're here now," Jill said. "Come on in and have some brandy."

Kate walked from the living room into the entrance hall. "Hi, Richard," she said. "I'm Kate Springer. We met a couple of years ago when Jill and I were having ice cream at Steve's and you came in with your girlfriend."

"Right," Klore said. He shrugged out of his coat and handed it to Jill.

"Could you get my coat while you're at it," Kate said. Then she turned to Klore. "I wish I could stay," she said, "but it's getting late."

Jill helped Kate on with her coat and opened the door for her. "Thanks for coming," she said. "Give me a call."

"I will," Kate said. "You'll have to come over and help me make some measurements. It was a wonderful dinner." She squeezed Jill's arm, then turned to face Klore. "Don't keep her up too long," she said. She closed the door firmly after her.

"Come and sit down," Jill said. "Is brandy okay? I've got scotch and some white wine."

"I like brandy," Klore said. He picked up the bottle from the coffee table and looked at the label. Without saying anything, he set the bottle down again and sat on the love seat where Kate had been sitting.

Jill poured the liquor into Klore's snifter, then added a small amount to her own. Klore swirled the brandy around, then took a sip.

"This is quite good," he said. "No offense, but I wouldn't have expected it." He glanced at her.

"Were you expecting a nice peach cordial?" Jill asked. She found it hard to avoid sarcasm when she talked to Richard.

"Don't get angry," he said. "It's just that you never struck me as somebody who would know the difference between aged brandy and raspberry Ripple."

"I really don't know much more than that," Jill said. She was determined not to let Klore get to her. She had agreed to let him come over for a drink. Now he was her guest and she had to treat him that way.

"I could teach you a lot," he said. "Wine is one of my hobbies, but I also know quite a bit about brandies and single-malt scotches."

"How did you get interested in wine?" Jill asked.

The question was all Klore needed to prompt him into a lengthy account of wines and vineyards and the astonishment of those in his wine club at how swiftly he had acquired his expertise. Eventually she stopped paying attention to what he was saying and concentrated on remembering the fun she had with Kate.

Then suddenly she heard Klore say, "You know, I've been thinking about you ever since we met at lunch."

"I'm flattered," she said. "You shouldn't get in the habit of that, though." She sat up straight and leaned into the corner of the love seat.

"Why not?" He turned to face her. "I think I'm even more attracted to you now than I used to be." He set his glass on the table, then moved toward her and put his hand on her arm.

His action caught her by surprise, and she tried to shrug off his hand. He tightened his grip and began pulling her against him. Then as he leaned forward to try to kiss her, she jerked away from him and stood up.

"Let's get something clear," she said. She rubbed her arm where his fingers had dug into the flesh. "I invited you here for a drink, and that's all. If you had some other plans, I'm sorry."

Richard's face was stiff with anger and his smile was forced. "That's okay," he said. "I plan to make your plans the same as mine."

She was about to make a sharp reply when the door buzzer sounded with a dull rasping that seemed very loud in the small apartment. The noise startled them, and they stared at each other in a quizzical way.

"I'm not expecting anyone," Jill said.

She wasn't sorry for the interruption, but she couldn't imagine who it might be. She glanced at her watch and saw that it was a minute or so past midnight. It was too late for the Smiths, too late for anybody to be dropping by casually. Maybe Kate had forgotten something.

She hurried to the door, then another idea made her hesitate. Could it be that everything wasn't over, that there was someone out there in the dark waiting for her? No, that was too absurd. She turned on the outside light and pulled open the door.

No one was there. She peered into the night beyond the white dazzle of the porch light, but it made the darkness impenetrable. She listened, trying to catch even the faintest sound, but she could hear nothing. She decided she would at least move outside the circle of light and take a look around. She couldn't just close the door and pretend nothing had happened.

She had already taken the first step outside when she noticed the box. It was so near the door that it was only when she looked straight down that she saw it, and she dodged to the side and almost fell to avoid planting her foot squarely on it. It was a long white florist's box tied with black ribbon. Without giving the matter a second thought, she picked it up and tucked it under her arm. She stepped back inside and closed the door. It was much colder out than it had been, and she shuddered from the chill of the air.

Richard was standing at the entrance to the living room watching her. "I didn't know you could get florists to make deliveries this late," he said. "I guess I'm not your only admirer. Maybe I should've taken the subtle approach and sent flowers." He sounded angry.

"I don't think these came from a florist," she said. She held the box out for Richard to see and pointed to a noose of black ribbon that dangled from the top of the box. "Look at this."

He took the box from her, held it high and rotated it to catch the light. He peered carefully at the noose, then glanced toward her as he lowered the box. "A hangman's knot," he said. "It's got thirteen twists at the top, if I counted right."

"I don't understand," she said.

"The thirteen turns mean it's a hangman's knot," he repeated. He gave her a patronizing smile. "It's the kind they use to hang criminals on the gallows."

She felt herself turn cold, even colder than she had felt from the night air. She stared at the small black noose hanging from the white box, then shook her head violently, as though that would make the sight go away.

Richard said, "When I was a kid, we believed it was against the law even to tie a hangman's knot. We thought that if you tied one, that meant you were going to kill somebody." He shrugged. "For all I know, maybe it is against the law." He suddenly noticed the rigid expression on her face. "I didn't mean to scare you," he said. "You look upset."

"I am upset," she said. She took a step back and half turned away from Richard and the white box. "I am very upset."

He took her by the arm in a surprisingly gentle way. "If you think you're going to faint, you should sit down and lower your head."

"I'm not going to faint," she said. She noticed a tremble in her voice, even though she had meant to sound annoyed. "I don't want to open that box. I want to get rid of it, so please take it out by the garage and dump it into the garbage can."

Richard shook the box, and it made a muffled clunking sound. He looked at her and shrugged. "It's got to be flowers," he said. "I can't imagine there's anything dangerous in it."

She said nothing, and Richard walked past her into the kitchen. In a moment she had made up her mind and followed him. She stood beside him by the sink.

"You're right," she said. "We should at least see what's inside, and maybe there's a card that will tell us who it's from."

"It can't hurt to open it," Richard said.

"Probably not," she agreed. "But I'm going to be the one who does it. After all, it was left on my doorstep."

Richard looked at her with surprise. She expected him to object and assert his authority over her on some grounds or other, but he made no protest. He put down the box on the countertop and stepped back to give her room. She took a pair of kitchen shears out of a drawer and cut the black ribbon. She used the tip of the scissors to push the ribbon away from the box. She had no wish to touch the box more than necessary.

"Wait a minute," Richard said. He spoke sharply, and she paused and looked at him. "This is spooky," he said. "I thought somebody was just sending you flowers, but I'm not so sure that's all there is to it."

She put down the kitchen shears beside the box and stood back from the countertop. "What are you thinking of?" she asked. "A bomb?" As she spoke the word, the possibility seemed less absurd than she first thought.

"We can't be sure it's not," Richard said. "Maybe somebody got you confused with someone else."

"It's possible," she admitted.

She stood at the counter hesitantly, looking down at the white box. Then she made up her mind, and without saying anything to Richard, in a single decisive gesture, she jerked the lid off the box and threw it to the floor. Maybe the box concealed something just as dangerous as a bomb, something they hadn't even thought of. Her muscles stiffened in sudden fear.

The box was filled with flowers. Beneath the green tissue paper wrapping, at least a dozen flowers with white trumpet-shaped blossoms were crowded together in the narrow box. Her fingers trembled as she pulled back the edges of the thin green paper. Richard had taken a step backward when she pulled off the lid, but he had said nothing. Now he moved back by her side and leaned over to examine the dead-white blossoms.

"Lilies," she said, picking up a single stem. "They're what my father used to call graveyard flowers, because you see so many of them at funerals. I guess that fits right in with your hangman's knot."

She dropped the lily back into the box and tucked her hands under her arms to still the trembling of her fingers. Nothing has happened, she told herself. They are just ordinary flowers in an ordinary box, and there is no reason to get upset.

Yet she couldn't stop the trembling, and it now seemed to pervade her whole body, a small but uncontrollable tremor that made her arms and shoulders quiver as though she were freezing to death. Something was happening, even if she couldn't figure out what it was. She was scared, and she didn't even know what she was scared of. A shapeless dread surrounded her, a fear so unfocused it wouldn't even permit her to marshal her efforts and face it directly.

Richard pulled back the green tissue paper at the bottom of the box and pulled out an envelope. It was white, letter-sized, and made of obviously cheap paper. "Look what I found," he said. "Do you want to leave it here?"

"No, open it," she said.

The flap was not sealed but tucked inside. Richard pulled out the flap, peered into the envelope, and extracted a color photograph. He held it by the corner while he examined it carefully. He held it close to his face, then he smiled and passed the photograph to Jill. "This seems to be a picture of you," he said.

She glanced at the picture and almost dropped it in disbelief. It was a nude shot Jeff had taken of her the first summer they were together. They were spending a week at the Vineyard in a borrowed house, and each day they lived out their erotic fantasies. She was coming out of the water, naked as Venus, and walking across the beach directly toward the camera. Her wet hair, quite long at the time, was twisted together and hung like a dark rope over her breast. The small bands of white skin ordinarily covered by her bikini sharply contrasted with the deep tan coloring the rest of her body. She was smiling, but she was also blinking, trying to get the salt water out of her eyes.

Jeff had suddenly pulled the camera out of the beach bag and snapped a shot. "I want to record you for your own posterity," he told her. "Forty years from now, you may not believe you once looked so good." She hadn't protested. She was flattered, but more than that she wanted to memorialize that moment, that time. It was the only nude photograph ever taken of her, and now someone was using it to play some kind of perverse game with her.

"There's something on the back," Richard said. "It looks like some kind of insignia."

She turned the photograph over. A skull and crossbones was crudely stamped in red ink in the center of the white expanse. The eye sockets of the skull seemed abnormally large, and the large bones crossed below the lower jaw appeared too symmetrical to be real. Although the fine details were blurred, there was no doubt about what it was.

"What is it?" Richard asked.

"A death's head," she said.

"What do you mean?" Klore asked.

Jill didn't answer. "I want you to drive me to the police station," she said. "Immediately."

PART THREE

April 26
Tuesday

11

Tuesday 12:20 A.M.

He twisted the steering wheel sharply and maneuvered the white Mazda RX-7 into the exact center of two parking spaces. He slammed the door, producing a hollow echo in the underground garage, dropped the key into his pocket, then headed toward the stairs leading to the lobby.

Without breaking stride, he suddenly leaped up and slapped his hand against the concrete ceiling. Success and anticipation were working in him like drugs, and he was feeling powerful and dangerous. Instead of standing silently in the darkness, he could have taken her when she opened the door. The guy with her would have caused no trouble. But the Jaguar didn't do things just because he was able to. Shaping the world required control and patience.

Make the prey aware of your presence, the plan said, and he had executed the step in a sophisticated way. His methods were more subtle than he had ever used before, but then Jill was going to be a perfect case. She was going to be his homage to the sky gods, his demonstration that earth had its own kwisatz haderach.

He pushed open the heavy fire door and stepped into the Great Hall. The concierge glanced up from the paperwork on the standing desk. He was a round, heavy man in his sixties who wore the required uniform of a blue suit, blue shirt, and maroon tie.

"Good evening, Mr. Haack," the concierge said. "Still a bit nippy out, isn't it?" The man's smile was professionally friendly and in no way personal.

"It's chilly, but spring really is here," Haack said. His smile and tone matched the friendliness of the concierge. He preferred that kind of relationship, pleasant, yet structured and formalized.

He had lived at Cambridge Court for a year and a half. Before that he was in a disgusting one-room apartment on Prospect Street at Central Square. Even when his Uncle Dick died and left him more money than he had ever dreamed of, he didn't move. He hadn't wanted to give his mother another reason to disapprove of him.

In her distant, controlled fashion, she had made it obvious that she was furious about his inheritance. "A person who can't get a decent job isn't someone who knows how to handle money," she had told him when they met with the executor of Uncle Dick's estate. "I never realized Richard Holton was such a fool, and I'm glad my sister died before she had to find out. The money properly should have come to me. Dick got most of it from Emily, and it was family money."

"But it's still in the family," he told his mother.

"Only technically speaking," she said. She gave him a look of acid disdain, then fell silent.

He knew Uncle Dick left him the money because he felt sorry for him. He could remember one Thanksgiving at his uncle and aunt's house on Long Island when they had all gone for a walk after an early dinner. He was about seven and was running ahead along the road picking up stones to throw at the pinecones hanging off the trees.

"Stop that," his mother told him sharply. Then when he threw one last stone, she said, "You are stupid and worthless." Her voice was cold and hard.

"Helen, that's no way to talk to a child," Uncle Dick said. "You might as well slap him in the face." He sounded angry.

"I do not need your advice, Richard," his mother replied. "Now let's have no more words on this subject."

"Helen is right," Aunt Emily said. "It's none of your business."

He was glad Uncle Dick didn't say anything more to antagonize his mother. When she was angry, she wouldn't speak to him at all, not even to criticize him. Once she had said nothing to him for almost a week. She had pretended he didn't exist and left it to Mrs. Sanders to carry out her orders. "You're a lucky boy," Mrs. Sanders would tell him. "Some parents whip their children or worse, but your mother never lays a hand on you."

Uncle Dick sent him nice presents, but the family hardly ever got together. His mother was too busy with her research, too busy helping people get well. When they had family affairs, his mother prepared him in advance to play his role properly. "No one cares what a naive, uneducated boy thinks," she told him. "No one wants to be bored by a child. So after dinner, just excuse yourself and find something to do."

After college, he saw his mother at Thanksgiving and Easter, the two holidays she considered to be family obligations. Christmas she had always ignored as no more than a commercialized pagan custom. Usually she called him two weeks before each holiday to let him know when she wanted him to arrive, but otherwise she made no effort to communicate with him. He had learned through bitter experience that she didn't welcome his calls. They lived lives that rarely intersected.

Ironically, the meeting with Uncle Dick's executor in October of the previous year was the last time he saw her. Six months afterward, with no warning, she died of a heart attack. By the time he was notified, she had been cremated and her ashes scattered at sea. The housekeeper called him two weeks later.

"She wanted no services," Mrs. Sanders said. "She left me instructions about that. She wanted me to get in touch with her lawyers but notify nobody else. At first I thought she meant that applied to you, but then I decided she probably just forgot about you. Anyway, I decided to call you. A boy should know when his mother dies."

He expected he would feel grief for his mother, the way people on TV and in movies did. Instead, he had felt nothing but relief and a growing elation. He realized that his mother's death had released the power he had been hoarding inside himself.

His mother died in April, he learned of it in May, and by the end of that month, he had bought his apartment in Cambridge Court. He didn't give up the Prospect Street place though. He continued to pay the rent on it in cash and to use the name he had rented it under, the same name he used at his job.

As soon as he moved into his new apartment, he realized he resembled Paul Atreides after the death of his father. He was becoming the person he was destined to be. His mother's death had made it possible. Sometimes, though, he couldn't believe she was really dead. He knew she was, but he felt as if she weren't.

When he had gone to Dumbarton Oaks in September and met Sue, the girl in the giftshop, she made him remember his stolen photograph of his mother, the one taken before he was born. Sue hadn't really resembled his mother, but she had given him a hint of the same vitality he saw in the snapshot. She seemed to possess the same inner secrets that allowed his mother to exercise such power over him.

If only he could understand that power, if only he could strip away the layers and penetrate the mystery hidden deep inside her, maybe he could gain the power for himself. Then he would be the one in control.

He had felt what it meant to have that control when he strangled Sue. His mother's power now belonged to him. A week later he had exercised it again in Riverside Park, choosing a woman whose name he didn't even know, a woman to whom he spoke not a word. That second time, he realized he could never think of stopping. He needed the feelings that violence, struggle, and death itself evoked in him. He needed them in order to be alive.

But if he wanted to go on feeling alive, he would have to be careful. He had been stupid to act from impulse. Planning was also part of the pleasure. Marie and Anna had helped him learn, and Jill would be perfect. She was perfect in other respects as well. He had seen that when she first walked into Bookkeepers and came back to where he was working. He had sensed in her the same power he detected in the stolen snapshot of his mother, the same power he wanted both to possess and destroy. It also shone out of the photograph of Jill he had found in her bottom drawer.

He walked past the concierge toward the Tazza d'Oro coffee bar at the rear of the building. Usually he would stroll through the lobby at a leisurely pace, appreciating its travertine marble floors and vaulted ceiling with frescoes of Isis and Osiris. Cambridge Court was surely the equal of the palace of the Atreides. Now, though, he moved with a sense of urgency. He had a lot to do to carry out his original plan.

He turned left into a short corridor, then stepped into a cubicle with a glass-paneled door. The closet-sized room was carpeted and contained a small desk. He sat in a chair and pulled the telephone toward him. Humming to himself, he dialed from memory.

"Eastern General Hospital, Operations Desk, Mrs. Partree. May I help you?" She delivered her message in a pleasant singsong voice.

"This is Field Superintendent Malley of the Allen Protection Agency. I'm doing a spot check on field personnel, and I want to ask you to look at your sign-in sheet to verify that Security Officer Jim Thompson is on duty this evening." He paused, then added, "That's Thompson with a p, by the way."

"Just a minute please," she almost sang to him. She left the line open, and he could hear the rustle of paper and the scraping of clipboards being shifted around on a hard surface. Finally, she said, "I show Thompson signed in at twenty-four hundred."

"People like you sure make my life easier," he said. "Since this is a random integrity check, I'd appreciate it if you wouldn't mention this call."

"I understand," she said. "Now I've got another call."

He held down the switch hook, released it, then tapped out another number. Knowing Thompson was still working for Allen simplified matters.

"State Police, Motor Vehicles." Once more the voice was female, but this time it was flat and official.

"This is Officer Thompson, badge 2551 with the Allen Agency at Eastern General Hospital," he said in the same matter-of-fact tone.

"We've got a vehicle blocking our emergency area, and I need a registration."

He paused to give her time to punch in the badge number and confirm its legitimacy. The real Thompson would probably be making several of these calls during the night.

"Go ahead," she said.

"Honda Civic, blue sedan, Massachusetts license George, Fox, X-ray 1149."

"Hold," came the command.

He took a short pencil and a slip of paper from the holder at the top of the desk, and by that time she was back on the line. "Make-license match," she said. "Engine number PB80067394689. Registered to Richard Carleton Klore." She spelled the last name. "Address, 2951 Harvard Street, Cambridge. Occupation, physician and research fellow, Eastern Medical School. Business address, 1266-Annex Eastern General Hospital."

"You might know, it was one of our own doctors," he said. "Thank you, and have a nice night." There was no response, and he hung up.

He pushed the chair back from the desk and looked at the information he had written on the slip of paper. When he was a freshman someone had told him, "If you stand in Harvard Square for a week, you'll see everybody you know in Cambridge by Wednesday and everybody in Boston by Saturday." Cambridge was a small town. He and Klore lived on the same street, and both were connected with Eastern General Hospital—he knew exactly where Klore's office was.

And of course they both knew Jill Brenner. But during the week he had watched her house, he had never seen her with Klore or with anybody else. So what was she up to now? She was wrong if she thought hanging out with Klore was going to be of any help to her. She would have to realize that Klore was just another of the sheep, as helpless to protect her as she was to protect herself.

He still had one more phone call to make. He tapped out Jill's number. The image in her photograph was still in his mind: the long slim legs, the dark patch of pubic hair accentuated by the pale skin surrounding it, the taut, well-shaped breasts. Her eyes were almost closed, but she was clearly laughing. Arrogant bitch. But he would change her. They would become more united than even the most passionate lovers could imagine.

He allowed the phone to ring eight times, more than enough for a small apartment. She might not be answering the phone, but it was more likely she had gone to the police. She would be there for a minimum of an hour and a half, and round-trip travel time would add another half hour. Even if she left immediately after getting the flowers, she wouldn't be back before 2:15 at the earliest. He had more time than he needed. He hung up the telephone and began humming again.

Even the basement of his building was more pleasant than his old apartment on Prospect Street. The floor was covered with gray industrial rubber sheeting, and the walls were plastered and painted a bright white. Fluorescent fixtures hung from chains and provided green-yellow light round the clock.

Very little was in the basement. The building's air-conditioning and other service equipment was in a subbasement one level down, and since each condominium had its own laundry hookups, the basement contained no washers, dryers, or clotheslines. A wine cellar with an insulated steel door took up the central part of the space, and the rest of the area was divided into storage rooms, one for each condominium.

He worked the built-in combination lock of the door of his room by dialing in the numbers. Except for a workbench and a metal tool cabinet, the large room was relatively bare. The air was stuffy, and he could easily detect the sharp odor of ammonia mixed with a peculiar musky smell.

The odor came from the two glass aquariums that sat next to one another on a large folding table pushed against the wall. Each aquarium was covered with a wire screen of heavy hardware cloth. On top of the wire of each was a single brick to make sure that the screen stayed in place.

Inside the aquarium nearer the door, a thick-bodied lizard with a stubbed tail and black and yellow scales crouched with its nose pressed against the glass. Although the lizard's eyes were open, it seemed permanently frozen in its posture.

In the other aquarium, a snake was half-hidden under a layer of wood shavings that covered the bottom to a depth of three or four inches. The snake was close to two feet long, but because it was partially coiled, it seemed shorter. Its body was marked by rings of yellow and red separated by narrower bands of black, and its highly polished scales gleamed in the brightness of the overhead light.

He walked past the cages and picked up a soft-sided plastic gym bag and a blue cloth laundry bag from the workbench. He put down the gym bag on the table behind the cages, removed the brick from the snake cage, and took off the wire cover.

The snake's head was resting on the top of its coiled body, its round eyes shining as brightly as its scales. He reached into the cage, and in one deft, swift motion, he grasped the snake behind its head and, using his other hand, lifted the mass of coils from the aquarium. He dropped the snake into the cloth bag and pulled the drawstring tight.

The snake had not resisted being picked up and, in fact, had hardly moved at all. The cool temperature of the storage room had rendered it sluggish. He dropped the cloth bag inside the plastic one and fastened the long zipper along the top.

The god Itzamna was now ready to play his role in the plan. He would wrap his scaly body around Jill's smooth skin and pierce her soft flesh with his needle-sharp fangs. Screaming with terror, begging Itzamna to free her, she would be dragged below into the dark place of the gods, into the place of the twisted roots, where he and Itzamna would be one, united in her.

12

Tuesday 12:30 A.M.

Jill had never been inside a police station before, and she was surprised to find it looked like any other municipal office. The room had the same vinyl floor, colored plastic furniture, and long tubes of glaring fluorescent lights. She might have come to get a dog license or pay a traffic ticket.

Richard hung back while she approached the uniformed woman at the information counter. "How do I report a crime?" she asked.

The woman barely glanced at Jill. "Take a seat and wait for the complaints officer," she said. She spoke the sentence as if it were one long word.

She and Richard sat in molded gray plastic chairs pushed against a dirty white wall. The complaints desk was behind a narrow line marked in yellow tape on the green tile floor, and an elderly woman with thin, scraggly hair dyed the shade of copper occupied the visitor's chair.

Jill watched the woman fumble in her purse for her glasses, put them on carefully, then bend over to peer at something the officer was pointing to with the tip of his yellow pencil. The woman's beige coat was dragging on the floor, and its hem was dirty with grime and splattered mud. Everything she did seemed to take tremendous effort, and Jill wondered what had happened to make the woman come to a police station in what must seem the middle of the night to her.

Perhaps nothing had happened. Perhaps she was just lonely. The police probably thought talking to her was a waste of their time. Jill hoped they wouldn't think that about her problem.

The officer was almost the opposite of the woman. He was young, black, and dressed in a sharply creased uniform. Despite the hour, he was also very alert. As soon as she and Richard sat down, he glanced over and gave them a quick nod.

Richard seemed anxious. He kept crossing and uncrossing his legs and turning his head from side to side to see what was happening in the room. He hadn't objected when she asked him to come inside with her, but now he appeared to regret his decision.

His restlessness and silence were getting on her nerves. Finally, without turning to face her, he said, "You should do the talking here." He then glanced at her to gauge her reaction. "I mean, it's your apartment that was broken into and all," he said.

"It may surprise you, but I'm aware of that," she said. Ordinarily, she would have tempered her sarcasm with a smile and made a joke of it, but now she didn't feel like bothering to protect Richard's feelings.

"You don't have to worry," she told him. "I'll handle everything and sign a statement or whatever I have to do." She looked at his bland, smooth face and felt herself becoming angry. "You may have forgotten I'm here because I'm worried about my safety," she said coldly.

"If I could do anything more to help, I would," Klore said. "Don't take this the wrong way, but you're obviously in no danger now. I just meant I didn't see any point to my getting involved in something I don't know anything about and don't really have time for." He gave her a look that invited her sympathy.

"Is the time really what's bothering you?" Jill asked. "Are you sure you're not just a little frightened?"

"Frightened of what?" Klore looked at her and shrugged. "Somebody stole a picture and sent it back to you with a bunch of flowers. Maybe that's supposed to scare you, but I don't have any reason to be scared."

"Don't you?" she asked. "If you're around me, you might be there at the wrong time."

"Jill, Jill," Richard said, sounding exasperated. He shook his head. "You're making too much out of this. You're just upset by what is probably a practical joke."

She didn't bother to answer him. She didn't know what to say, really. She wanted to think he was right and that she was making too much of the whole situation. But she couldn't convince herself of that. Although she worked hard to look calm and behave normally, the fear was deeper and more pervasive than anything she had felt before.

The elderly woman finished her business and walked away from the desk. Jill rose and took a few steps toward the yellow line. She didn't look to see whether Richard was coming with her. When the officer glanced up, she crossed over to the desk and took the chair the woman had vacated.

She shifted slightly so she could see Richard. He was sitting where she had left him, his head turned away from her. She knew then he had abandoned her. She felt a flash of anger, but caught herself. She didn't need him.

"What seems to be the problem?" the officer asked. He spoke in a brisk but friendly way.

"My apartment has been broken into," Jill said. She had decided the police would take her more seriously if she focused on the break-in. But now as she spoke the words she could hear her voice crack with strain. Tears came to her eyes, and she had to clear her throat. "Sorry," she said.

"Don't let it bother you," the officer said in a gentle voice. "There's nothing like a little paperwork to take your mind off your troubles." He opened a drawer of his desk and handed her a form with numbered lines. "We'll need a list of everything that was taken."

She used a finger to wipe the tears from the corners of her eyes. She then glanced at the paper and shook her head. "Nothing valuable was taken," she said. "Quite frankly, it's not the break-in itself I'm most concerned about. I'm really worried about myself." Her voice sounded thin and constricted.

"It's very frightening to have your apartment entered," the officer said. He sounded genuinely sympathetic.

Jill sighed and said, "I'm not being very clear." She paused a moment, then blurted out, "I think I've been threatened."

"What do you mean?" The officer sounded more suspicious now.

"Around midnight a box of white lilies was left at my door," she said. She began to tell her story rapidly. "A hangman's knot was tied in the black ribbon around the box, and inside there was a picture of me stolen from my apartment earlier in the day. The back of the picture had a skull and crossbones stamped on it." She went on to talk about feeling watched and about sensing that someone had broken into her apartment. "I couldn't be sure then," she said. "But now that I have the picture, I know I wasn't just imagining things."

While she was talking, the officer's doubt seemed to disappear, and he nodded encouragingly. Yet his face showed no surprise. She had expected him to ask her a great many questions as soon as she finished. Instead, he said, "Excuse me a second," then consulted what looked like a photocopied list of names.

"You've got a very unusual story," he said. "I'm going to ask you to tell it again to Detective Karen Chase. Her office is on the third floor, just to the left as you step out of the elevator." He gave her a friendly smile and said, "I think she'll be able to help you. She's really terrific."

Jill felt better after telling her story. Although nothing had changed, she felt confident she would be able to handle whatever came up. Now she would have the police to help her.

She went over to Richard and stood directly in front of him. Looking down at him, she said, "I have to go up to the third floor. You can come with me if you want to, but I don't want you to feel you have to."

Richard made a show of looking at his watch. He studied it a moment, as though lost in a difficult calculation. At last he said, "It's getting pretty late, and I have to meet somebody for rounds at seven tomorrow morning."

"Feel free to go home," she said. "I'm sure you've had a long day, and you're probably very tired."

Richard either failed to notice the irony or decided to pay no attention to it. "I am exhausted," he said. "I don't want to ruin tomorrow by stretching out today too long." He tilted his head to look up at her. "But how will you get home?" he said. "Don't you think I'd better stay?"

His offer was so patently insincere she thought he must be parodying himself. Then she realized he believed he was showing genuine concern. "That's not necessary at all," she said, adopting the same earnest tone. "I'll insist that the police give me an escort."

"That's a great idea," Richard said. "That makes me feel I'm not just abandoning you." He stood up. "I'm sorry we didn't get to have our drink. Maybe as soon as this mess is cleared up, we can try again."

"Maybe," Jill said. "I'd better go now. Somebody's waiting to see me." She abruptly turned and walked toward the door to the stairs.

"Just a minute," Klore called to her.

She stopped and turned to face him.

"Promise me you'll give me a call tomorrow and tell me how things worked out," he said. His look was sincere, and she wondered if she had misjudged him.

"I'll call you," she promised.

13

Tuesday 1:00 A.M.

The Smiths' house slowly emerged into view as Haack jogged toward it. The porch light produced a dazzling glare that shone through the fretwork trim and spilled onto the sidewalk. The light turned the house into a carnival castle promising him a night of enchantment and illusion.

Haack went past the house, but as soon as he was out of the pool of light, he crossed the few feet between the sidewalk and the spirea bushes. He worked his way down the line of bushes toward the back of the house until he reached the place he had hidden earlier. The spireas were not yet in bloom, and he could smell only the faint indefinite odor of damp vegetation as a slight breeze stirred the branches. The bulb above Jill's door was burning, and while it was not nearly so bright as the ones in front, it made it impossible to enter that way.

Walking rapidly, he left the protection of the bushes and crossed in front of the garage to the drive. The rubber soles of his shoes were silent on the smooth asphalt, and without slowing his pace, he moved along the drive to the corner of the house, then turned and started down the basement stairs. He moved slowly, sliding the toes of his shoes across each step to avoid the litter of dried leaves.

When he reached the bottom, he stood with his back pressed against the cold stone wall beside the door. The muscles across his stomach were stretched tight, and his hearing was so acute that even distant noises seemed loud. Mass Ave was two blocks away, but he could detect the whine of an accelerating engine and the hesitation of an automatic transmission as it shifted to a higher gear.

He unzipped his athletic bag and took out his black pigskin gloves. He forced his hands into them, flexing his fingers to stretch the thin leather. He then tried the knob of the basement door. It was locked, but it had four panes of glass at the top, and getting past it would present no problem.

Removing a four-inch roll of cellophane tape from his bag, he quickly cut off short pieces and pressed them onto the lower right pane. He took care to leave free a narrow curved path from the right side of the panel to the left. Bearing down hard on the shaft of a glass cutter, he traced out the path with the cutter's diamond blade. Using the knuckles of his clenched hand, he gave the glass a sharp tap. The semilunar segment came free, but the tape kept it from falling onto the concrete floor. He reached inside with his left hand and opened both locks.

The basement was warm, but as he moved away from the door, the darkness became total. He switched on his penlight, and a narrow finger of brightness darted out from the hooded halogen bulb. He turned the beam upward and moved it around until he located the water pipes running to Jill's bathroom. He traced them across the ceiling and found what he had been looking for—the plumbing access panel.

An aluminum stepladder hung on the wall in front of him, and he eased it off its hooks and positioned it directly below the panel. The opening was too narrow to squeeze through without his clothes snagging or binding, but he would just be able to wriggle through in his bare skin.

He slipped the dark velour top over his head and dropped it on the floor between the legs of the ladder. The silence was so complete that the falling shirt made a discernible plop. He pulled off his running shoes, then stepped out of the velour pants and put them on top of the shirt. The small drafts that stirred the air of the basement felt chill against his bare skin, but in his aroused condition, the minor discomfort was almost pleasurable.

He removed the drawstring bag with the snake from the blue carrier, folded down the stepladder's bucket shelf, and held the bag in place while he climbed to the top of the ladder. He had not been able to avoid jostling the bag, but there was no sign of activity from the creature inside. The cold had slowed its bodily processes almost to a standstill.

Holding the penlight in one hand, he pushed against the cover of the access hole with his other hand. He felt his level of excitement increase when the cover moved upward without any great effort. It carried the bathmat with it, but that was no problem. He let one edge of the cover rest on the bathroom floor, then slid the cover to one side. He worked fast but made virtually no noise.

No light came from the bathroom, and the loudest sound was his own rapid breathing. He reached through the opening and placed the cloth bag gently on the tiled floor. He then took two steps up the ladder, held his hands above his head as though he were about to dive, and squeezed his shoulders past the pipes. One of the pipes was so cold it seemed to burn his skin as his thigh pressed against it.

Once in the dark of the bathroom, he felt his excitement rise even higher. He had violated a rule, and someone might discover him at any moment. But for now, he was hidden and secret, powerful and irresistible. The sweet scent of Jill's soap and the sense of her presence evoked jumbled feelings of lust and fear that frightened him with their intensity. He felt powerless to control what was happening to him.

He calmed himself by concentrating on the warm dampness of the air against his naked skin. It felt intimate, personal, as though he were in direct contact with Jill. As he thought about what he was going to do to her, he touched himself lightly with the tips of his fingers. As his erection grew, he began to stroke himself in a rapid, machinelike way, chanting under his breath, "You'll be sorry, you'll be sorry, you'll be sorry. . . ."

He used the penlight to locate the toilet paper holder and pulled off a long segment of paper. He wiped himself clean, then checked the floor for spots. Seeing none, he wadded up the paper and left it at the edge of the access hole to take with him on the way out.

He stood in the bathroom doorway for a moment, then stepped into the bedroom. Light coming from the porch and shining through the windows produced a pearl gray darkness that was nothing like the blackness of the basement and bathroom. Yet the light was not strong enough to reveal more than the outlines of things, and he clicked on the penlight.

The bed was neatly made, with a patchwork spread tucked carefully under the pillows. He started to pull back the spread when he noticed an electric cord hanging down beside the table lamp. He followed the cord with the narrow beam of the penlight until it ended in the control box of an electric blanket. The weather was chill, and someone accustomed to using an electric blanket would probably still be turning it on. He couldn't have planned anything better.

Without pulling the bedspread loose, he picked up one of the pillows and moved it to expose the blue and white striped sheet beneath. He then untied the knot in the drawstring of the cloth bag and gently dumped its contents onto the bed, right where the pillow had been.

The snake was so motionless with the cold it seemed dead. It had looped back on itself and balled into a sinuous knot in an effort to preserve its heat. Tumbling it out of the bag and onto the bed disturbed its security, and it uncoiled slightly, moved its blunt head in a sharp arc, and flicked out its tongue. Threatened by its exposure to new surroundings, it tightened its coils and pulled its head back so that it was almost hidden by the tangled loops. The snake's bright bands of yellow, black, and red looked startlingly out of place against the sheet.

He replaced the pillow with the snake directly underneath it. He then straightened the bedspread so the bed looked wholly undisturbed. He smiled and said softly, "Itzamna will be pleased to welcome you to your bed."

14

Tuesday 1:15 A.M.

Detective Karen Chase was tall and solid, with a long face and short, dark blond hair. She spoke in a husky voice made huskier by cigarettes. She also had a warm smile and a good-humored laugh, and Jill found no difficulty in telling her what had happened from the time she felt someone was watching her to the time she opened the box of lilies.

"My God," Chase said. "I see why you decided you needed some help." She shook her head. "That's one of the weirdest stories I've ever heard, and if anything even remotely like that happened to me, I'd be trying to *move* into the police station."

"I was afraid no one would take me seriously," Jill admitted.

"We don't have to see actual blood before we take people seriously," Chase said. "In fact, I want to tell my boss your story. Can you wait right here a couple of minutes?"

"Of course," Jill said.

"Great," Chase said, as though Jill were doing her a big favor. "There's coffee on the table by the elevator, if you want any." She gave Jill a quick smile, then hurried down the hall.

Firecaster was in his office looking through Renuzi's point summary of the backgrounds of Marie Thomas and Anna Louise Hamilton. Renuzi had listed the friends of each victim, each school they had attended, addresses they had lived, places they had worked, and every club or other organization they had belonged to. Firecaster read through item after item, but nothing matched.

They were making no progress on either case. Standard investigating procedures weren't producing any results. Unless something changed, they could go along the same way for a few more weeks, but eventually they would even run out of long shots to try.

He considered whether it would be useful to widen the scope of the investigation and increase the number of categories for point comparisons. Maybe they could check out the people in Hamilton's various dance groups, and see if any of them knew Thomas also. They might not have to go in that direction, though. Renuzi had people interviewing joggers along the Charles, and that might turn up something. Also, Murphy might find something helpful. It was too early for despair.

He had been awake since five-thirty and was beginning to find it hard to concentrate. Still, he didn't want to go home until he was exhausted enough to fall asleep without having time to think. He didn't want the forlorn and bloody images of Thomas and Hamilton floating through his consciousness like pale ghosts. He was glad when Chase walked in.

"I've got something that just may be a Crazy Cat lead," Chase said. She looked casual as she leaned against the partition forming the front wall of his office, but her voice was tight with excitement.

"Tell me everything you know," Firecaster said without hesitation. His tiredness and boredom evaporated, and he leaned forward in his swivel chair.

When Chase finished her summary, Firecaster didn't say anything. Instead, he leaned back and stared up at a crack in the ceiling plaster. He wanted to think without being rushed. He wanted to see if any new pieces would fit together with the ones they already had. He had been staring at the crack since Thomas was killed, watching it grow larger. Now smaller branches were starting to sprout from the main crack. Disorder was increasing.

"Interesting," he said softly. He sat up straight and looked at Chase. "What about phone calls?"

"Nope." Chase shook her head vigorously. "And no mention of a jaguar. Do you want to talk to her anyway?" She now sounded more hopeful than excited.

"Definitely," Firecaster said firmly. "She's the best thing we've come up with, so bring her in here. But she's your find, so you do the talking." He closed the file folder and pushed it away. He knew he shouldn't get his hopes up, but despite himself, he felt the muscles of his stomach tighten with anticipation.

When Chase introduced her to Eric Firecaster, Jill could hardly keep from staring at him. He shook hands and offered her the chair in front of his desk. He was lean and tall, and his light brown hair was cut short and pushed back from his forehead. Yet she was most fascinated by his dark blue eyes. They were set deep in his face above high cheekbones, and the skin at the corners was creased into a network of permanent lines.

"Am I going to have to tell you my whole story again?" Jill asked. She could hear the petulance in her tone.

Firecaster laughed and shook his head. "We only make suspects tell their story over and over," he said. "Detective Chase gave me an outline of what happened, and I thought if she and I worked together, we might be able to figure out how to deal with your problem."

"I'm sorry," Jill said. She was starting out the wrong way without meaning to. "I'm just getting tired."

"Do you know of anyone who might have a grudge against you?" Karen Chase asked. She sat down and turned her chair so it faced Jill. "A neighbor or friend you've had an argument with?"

"I can't think of any arguments," Jill said.

"Maybe somebody at work?" Chase suggested.

"I don't go to work," Jill said. Then she quickly added, "What I mean is, I don't go to an office with people. I'm a writer, and I work at home." She shrugged. "It just isn't possible that somebody I know has a grudge against me."

"Then how about something you've written?" Chase asked. "Have you gotten any threatening letters or phone calls?"

"No one's ever threatened me before," Jill said, shaking her head. "The last piece I published was on ice cream in the wintertime. Not very controversial." She stopped and thought a moment, then again shook her head. "Even the articles I've done on social issues are about institutions or policies, not people."

"Think about flowers," Chase said. "Do you have any associations?"

"No personal ones," Jill said. "They're all conventional or symbolic." She paused, then said, "Lilies with funerals, to be specific."

"Or flowers with lovers," Chase said. "Anybody you've been out with ever send you flowers?"

"I haven't been out with anyone in a long time," Jill said. The statement seemed to hang in the air, and she felt the need to explain it. "The friend I was living with killed himself last year. I haven't felt much like starting any new relationships." She didn't dare give in to her feelings and lose control. She worked to keep her tone detached, as though discussing someone else's life. She didn't look at Firecaster.

"What about Richard Klore?" Chase asked.

"Tonight was the first time I've seen him in several months," Jill said. She gave a humorless laugh. "I think you can also say it was our last evening together."

"You're not going to give him a chance to help a damsel in distress?" Chase asked. "Isn't that what every man craves?"

"I think Richard has already had more chances to help than he wanted," Jill said. "As I told you, I was already having Kate Springer to dinner, so when I ran into Richard, I gave in to a little pressure from him and invited him over for a drink afterward. I thought that would allow me to be polite to him without getting involved."

"We'll want to talk to Kate to see if she saw anything when she left your house," Chase said. "But you're saying you have no romantic interest in Richard Klore that might make somebody jealous."

"I have no romantic interest in Richard Klore," Jill said emphatically.

Firecaster said, "Let me break in here." Jill turned to face him. He was leaning across the desk, resting on his forearms but looking very tense. "Do you know Marie Thomas or Anna Louise Hamilton?" he asked.

His voice was serious, and she made herself think carefully about the question. "I've never heard of either of them," she said finally. "Is there some reason I should have?"

"Not necessarily," Firecaster said. "I'm just taking some random shots." He shrugged, and she thought he looked disappointed. "Let me try another one, though. Do you know anybody who refers to himself as the Jaguar?"

"The Jaguar?" she repeated. "You mean the animal, I assume, not the car?"

"I had forgotten that was the name of a car," Firecaster said. He smiled and seemed genuinely amused at failing to make the obvious connection. The smile changed his face, releasing its lines of tension and making his eyes seem brighter.

Jill found herself smiling in response. Then she gave Firecaster a quizzical look. "Do these questions have anything to do with me? Is there somebody called the Jaguar who breaks into people's apartments?" She glanced at Chase. Her expression was pleasant, but she said nothing. Jill turned toward Firecaster again.

He was leaning back in his swivel chair with his knee braced against the edge of the desk. The smile was gone, and despite his casual posture, he didn't look particularly relaxed.

"We're looking for a perpetrator who calls himself the Jaguar," Firecaster said. He spoke in a level academic voice, as though outlining basic facts in an objective way. Yet behind the dry tone she could sense powerful feelings of some kind. "He's a dangerous guy, and he may give warnings before he does anything. So far as we know, though, he doesn't break into houses."

Jill nodded to show she was taking in the information. "You don't think it was the Jaguar in this case?" she asked. *This case!* She seemed to be denying her own involvement.

"I know you said nobody could have a grudge against you," Firecaster said. She saw he was avoiding answering her question. "But in a day or two, you might remember somebody who made a pass at you at a party or somebody who knows you but isn't a part of your conscious thoughts."

"I'll think about it," she promised. "I don't expect to come up with anybody's name, though. Whoever did this is not somebody I know."

"You may be right," Firecaster acknowledged. His tone changed, becoming less didactic and more gentle. "I don't want to minimize your fears," he said. "But the incident has the appearance of nothing more than a malicious prank."

"Because of the flowers and the photograph?" Jill asked. She felt herself blushing. Under the circumstances, it was foolish to feel embarrassed about the nude snapshot, but she couldn't help it. Maybe if Firecaster weren't so attractive, she wouldn't be reacting in such a way.

"Partly," said Firecaster. He appeared not to notice her flushed face. "Plus the fact that it's obviously not a burglary attempt."

"It couldn't be somebody who was going to rob me and got scared off, then decided to take out his frustration on me?"

"Unlikely," Chase said. She crossed behind Jill and positioned herself in the doorway. "Burglary is an occupation like any other. Thieves break into places to make a living, not to look around. Yet you say nothing of value was taken and there were no signs of entry."

Chase smiled and raised a finger. "That suggests somebody with access to your apartment," she said. "Maybe somebody with a key, somebody you've forgotten you gave a key to." She shook her head. "Also, a professional thief wouldn't waste time playing games with you."

"You do think I'm telling the truth?" Jill asked. She turned toward Firecaster. "I know all this sounds unlikely."

"We don't have any reason to doubt you," Firecaster said. He sounded reassuring.

"I said a professional thief wouldn't play games," Chase said.

"Someone is, though, and people who play games with you are usually people you know."

"You may think no one you know is capable of doing something so strange and frightening," Firecaster said. "Yet people can surprise you. Some have a peculiar thread woven into their personalities, and sometimes their craziness comes out in ways you would least expect."

"I know that's true," Jill said. "Probably there's a story for me there, but I don't think I want to pursue it right now."

"I've got some writing for you to do," Chase said. "Come on back to my office and fill out a complaint form." She laughed and took a step into the hallway.

Jill felt disappointed at having to leave. She was beginning to see why people came to the police with their paranoid worries. Probably that was why the old woman at the complaints desk had come. By making you the center of attention, the police made you feel secure and important. Then she caught herself. Her worries weren't paranoid. Something *had* happened to her.

Looking directly at Firecaster, she asked, "Do you think I'm in any danger?"

"If you want my judgment, I would say that you aren't," he said. He hesitated to judge her reaction, then continued. "The perpetrator had the chance to harm you, if he wanted to."

"So I should just go home and go to bed?"

"That's right." Firecaster nodded in agreement. "I'll turn your name over to the dispatch office and have the patrol officers keep an eye on your apartment for the next couple of weeks."

"That will make me feel better," Jill said. She stood up. "This may sound naive, but I've got to ask anyway," she said. "How about fingerprints? Some could be in my apartment or on the box the flowers came in."

"It's possible," Firecaster agreed. "I'll let you in on a trade secret, though. Despite what you see in movies and mystery novels, it's uncommon to find definite and usable fingerprints at the scene of a crime. So for an ordinary breaking and entering, we don't even look."

"What if I brought in the box, would you check it?"

"All right," Firecaster said. "But just having somebody's fingerprints doesn't get you very far. Unless they're on file someplace, the most you've got is evidence to confirm, but not to identify."

"I can see that," Jill said.

Firecaster got up and walked to her side of the desk. "Do you have a way home?" he asked.

"I could take a cab," she said, her tone tentative.

"That's not necessary," Firecaster said. "I was about ready to leave before you arrived, and I can drive you myself. By the time you've signed the complaint form, I'll be ready." He then added as though it were an afterthought, "I could also pick up the box of flowers."

"That would be great," Jill said.

Chase walked briskly down the narrow corridor to her office, but Jill followed more slowly. She was pleased Firecaster wanted to take her home. She liked the way he looked and talked. She liked his dark blue eyes, and his smile, the smile that often seemed so pained. She was attracted to him, and she sensed the feeling was mutual. She was no longer angry at Richard Klore for abandoning her.

15

Tuesday 2:15 A.M.

Firecaster pulled into the driveway of the Smiths' house and drove to the back.

"Just in front of the garage will be fine," Jill told him.

He stopped the car and switched off the ignition. The muscles of his face had relaxed, and he no longer felt the steady tug at the corner of his left eye. Yet he was extremely tired and had to fumble with the switch before he could turn off the headlights. Despite his fatigue, he felt an edge of excitement and heightened awareness.

He hadn't felt that way in such a long time he found the reaction almost frightening. Something was happening to him he had no control over, and he didn't like becoming so vulnerable. He particularly didn't want to make a fool of himself by letting Jill see how much she affected him.

"Are you sure you wouldn't rather spend the night at a hotel or with friends?" he asked.

"I'll be okay here," she said. "The Smiths are right upstairs, if I get into trouble."

"You aren't scared?" Firecaster asked.

He glanced at her and saw her face in profile against the dark background of the car window. The outline was as finely drawn and delicate as a carving on a cameo, and at that moment, he thought he had never seen anyone more beautiful. He found resisting the impulse to reach across and touch her almost physically painful, but he didn't dare do it. He barely knew her, and only officially at that. Even though he generally trusted his responses, things were happening too fast this time.

"I'm not very scared now," she said. "I was earlier, but after talking to you and Detective Chase, I'm much less worried."

"Don't get so confident you become careless," Firecaster quickly said. "I don't want to tell you everything is fine, because it may not be."

"I understand," Jill said.

"Why don't I go in with you to get the flowers," he suggested. "That way I can take a look around."

"Would you mind?" Jill asked. She sounded relieved. "I do dread going inside by myself. My imagination must be in overdrive, because I have an image of somebody pouncing on me just after I close the door."

She was making an effort to keep her tone light, but he suspected she was on the verge of tears.

"I don't mind at all," Firecaster said.

"I never thought of going home as returning to the scene of a crime," Jill said. She spoke ironically, but he could still hear tension in her voice.

"That's what you're doing," Firecaster said. He hesitated a moment, then plunged on, not allowing himself to consider what he was going to say. "Don't take this wrong, but I live in a big house with lots of spare room, and you're welcome to stay with me tonight." Then wanting to match her tone, he quickly added, "No strings attached, because I'm too tired to attach any anyway."

Jill reached across and put her hand on top of his. She left it there a moment, pressed his fingers gently, then took her hand away. The gesture was simple, but she made it intimate. In just a touch, she conveyed not only warmth and tenderness, but an erotic interest that caught him by surprise.

"You're very nice," she said. "It's not necessary, though, and probably not even a good idea."

"I understand," Firecaster said. He wanted to sound matter-of-fact, but instead his voice sounded strained.

"Maybe not," Jill said gently. "I'm not sure we're talking about the same thing." She looked toward him. "What I mean is, when something happens to scare you, then you're supposed to make yourself do whatever it is you're afraid of doing. That way you don't turn into a permanent coward."

"I wasn't thinking about that," Firecaster admitted. "I don't believe you're in any real danger or I wouldn't let you stay alone. I was only thinking about your feeling nervous."

"That's what I've got to face up to, instead of running away," she said.

"Sounds reasonable," Firecaster said. "Is that a lesson you learned at your mother's knee?"

"Actually, I learned it from my daddy," Jill said. "When I was a kid, I turned over a pirogue in a swamp pond, and after he fished me out, he made me go right back and paddle across the pond."

"What's a pirogue?" Firecaster asked.

"It's a boat like a canoe," she said. She thought for a moment. "I guess you could call it a dugout, because it's made from a hollowed-out log."

"Were you very scared?" Firecaster asked.

"I was when I fell out," she said. "I just knew the gator that lived in that pond was going to get me. I could almost feel the jaws latching onto my leg, biting right down to the bone. When my daddy pulled me out, I didn't want to do anything but go home."

"But your father wouldn't let you?"

"He certainly wouldn't," she said. Firecaster could hear the pride in her voice. "I begged and pleaded, but he wouldn't budge. As soon as I got my breath back, he picked me up and sat me in the pirogue and told me he'd meet me on the other side."

She laughed at the memory. "I did it," she said. "I was sure I was going to turn over again, and I thought every ripple in the water was the alligator coming after me. But I got across."

"Do you know you begin to sound very Southern when you talk about that?" Firecaster asked. "It's not just an accent, but the whole way you talk. Where did you grow up, Mississippi?"

"Watch your language," Jill said. "People from Louisiana can't imagine it's even possible anyone could think they're from Mississippi."

"Sorry," Firecaster said. "Your childhood must have been a lot more exotic than mine. I spent most of my time playing pinball in the winter and trying to get somebody to take me to the Cape to go sailing in the summer."

"Now, that's exotic," she said. "I never even heard of the Cape until I came up here to college." She suddenly leaned toward him, and he put his arm around her. He pulled her close, then as she turned her face upward, he kissed her.

For a few minutes, they simply sat together, holding each other. He nuzzled her hair with his nose and kissed the smooth skin of her forehead. The fragrance of her soap and shampoo filled his nostrils with an almost forgotten feminine sweetness. Under the arc of his arm, she seemed surprisingly small and fragile, and he pulled her closer against him.

"I want to hear more about your childhood," he said softly.

"I want to hear more about yours," Jill said.

"We've got a lot to talk about," he said.

Jill leaned away from him and sat up straight. "We're going to have to do it some other time," she said. "Now that I'm not scared anymore, I think I'm on the verge of total collapse."

"I'm sure you are," Firecaster said. "I wasn't thinking, because I guess I could sit here with you all night. I'm sorry."

"Don't be," Jill said. "We'll get together again." She touched his hand gently, then opened the door of the car.

While Jill waited just inside the front door, he walked through each room of the apartment. He looked into each closet, peered under the bed, and checked to see that all the windows were fastened. He opened the glass door of the shower enclosure, then slid it back into place. He noticed the bathmat was askew, and using the toe of his shoe, he moved it so it covered the metal seam in the tile floor.

"All secure," he said. "Let's get the flowers bagged up, and I'll be gone." He shook out the folded plastic garbage bag he had brought with him. "I want you to slide the box in yourself so we don't get another set of prints on it."

She did as he asked, then watched while he filled out the chain-of-evidence tag and attached it to the bag with a piece of yellow tape.

"We'll have to get your friend Richard Klore's fingerprints so we can eliminate them," he said. "Of course, we'll also need yours."

"Don't call him my friend," Jill said. "I guess you'll have to have this too." She held up the plain white envelope that had been in the box. "I put the picture back inside. The picture of me, I mean."

"I've got a small bag for that," Firecaster said. Jill dropped the envelope into a clear plastic bag with *Evidence* stamped on it in red letters. He zipped the bag shut. "I'll make sure as few people as possible have access to the photograph," he assured her.

"It's not the strangers who bother me," she said. He noticed she was blushing. She looked away from him and said, "Jeff took it." Then she raised her eyes to meet his. "We were very much in love."

"Please don't feel embarrassed," he said. "You don't need to be."

He folded the bag and slid it into his pocket. "My invitation to spend the night still holds," he said.

Jill smiled and shook her head. "I'm going to lock my door and put the chain on and get a wonderful night's sleep."

He took a business card from his wallet and handed it to her. "My home number is here," he said.

He picked up the bag with the florist's box, and Jill opened the door for him. He paused in the doorway, and the wind from outside felt cold as it blew past them. She took a step toward him, then leaned against him, her head on his chest.

"Call me," he said softly. "For any reason or for no reason."

"I will," she said, almost whispering.

For a moment, their eyes were caught together. Then, as though by previous agreement, they kissed one another gently.

16

Tuesday 2:30 A.M.

Jill clicked on both locks and fastened the chain into its slide. She stood for a moment, staring at the back of the door and listening to the whining noise of Firecaster's Saab as he backed down the driveway. She smiled from the pleasure of having someone to think about and knowing he was thinking about her.

She hadn't had such a feeling for a long time, and realizing that made her remember Jeff. It was easier to think about him now. Although she still felt the pull of affection, he seemed more remote, less a presence than he had been only that morning.

She glanced at the card Eric had given her, then placed it on the table by the telephone. Although she was exhausted, she didn't think she could just climb into bed and fall asleep. Too much had happened. She needed to unwind.

She went into the living room and poured herself a generous amount of brandy. As she swirled the glass, the pale brown liquid felt cool against her fingers. She took a sip and felt the heat of the alcohol spread all the way down her throat. She walked the perimeter of the living room, studying the prints on the wall and reading the titles of the books in the bookcases. She stopped at her desk, then sat in the uncushioned chair behind it.

She had long ago given up attempting to keep her desk neat. Bills were piled on the right front edges, and next to them were brochures and junk mail. She pulled a Bean's catalogue out of the pile and a blue postcard fluttered to the floor. She bent down and picked it up. *Bookgram from Bookkeepers* was printed across the top. She puzzled over the card, then she remembered. Below *The book you requested is now available,* someone had written *Dune* in blue ballpoint pen.

The same day she asked for the book at Bookkeepers she bought a copy at the Coop. She had known she would be able to get one somewhere around Harvard Square. That's why she hadn't wanted to order it, but the man working there insisted on filling out the card for her. She had mentioned doing a story on Boscon and talked with him about *Dune,* so she felt she had to let him. That he was quite good-looking also probably had something to do with it.

She threw the blue card into the wicker wastebasket under the desk, then finished her brandy in a large swallow. She took a hot soapy shower, and by the time she had brushed her teeth and put on her long red-plaid flannel nightgown, she was sure she would be able to sleep.

Tomorrow she would talk with Eric, and they would get together. Was he married? The thought startled her. He hadn't been wearing a wedding ring, but that didn't mean anything. He said he lived by himself, but that didn't mean much either. Maybe he had a wife who refused to divorce him. Maybe he had five kids. Christ, maybe he was a bisexual or a homosexual who had never been able to accept the fact. Maybe he even had AIDS. She told herself to stop thinking such absurd thoughts; she would know more about him soon enough.

She sat on the edge of the bed and moved the dial on her electric blanket to its lowest setting. The bedroom was chilly, and she wanted the blanket to take the edge off the cold of the sheets. She pulled the covers back slightly, slipped her feet under them, and settled gratefully into bed. The touch of the sheets was almost painful, but as the blanket heated up, she could feel herself becoming enveloped in a cocoon of warmth. She surrendered to the heat and to the softness of the bed and passed into sleep with no awareness of a transition.

How long she slept before something began to disturb her she couldn't say, because she didn't wake at once. She came back into consciousness very slowly. She was like someone pulling herself out of a deep hole with muddy, slippery sides. Exhaustion was getting the better of her, yet it seemed terribly important that she come awake. It seemed essential that she pay attention to what was happening.

At first she was aware of a distinct movement by her right shoulder. She felt it through the bed. It was not something touching her, but something moving in the bed.

Then something *was* touching her. Something brushed against her arm, then pressed against her hip and thigh. She could feel the weight and movement against her skin through the soft flannel of her nightgown.

She brought her right arm down to her side slowly, sliding her hand across the smoothness of the sheet. As soon as she touched it with her fingertips, she knew what it was. Its body was cold and surprisingly rough-textured. She could feel the muscles under the dry skin move and curve the body toward her.

She literally jumped out of bed, and in a single motion, she whipped the covers off so they fell in a heap on the floor. She jerked the chain on the table lamp, then jumped back from the bed as though it were about to explode.

The snake was uncoiled and stretched almost straight in the middle of the mattress. The reptile looked incredibly large to her. It was at least two feet long but seemed much larger. The yellow, red, and black rings circling its body looked surreal against the pale blue and white vertical stripes of the sheets. The effect struck her as horrible.

The warmth of the electric blanket had restored the snake to full activity, and as soon as it was exposed to air and light, it sensed a threat. It raised its head a few inches from the bottom sheet and flicked out its tongue to test the atmosphere. The tongue was velvety black, and it darted from the rounded snout, then back again in rapid succession. The scales along the sides of the narrow slit of the mouth had a metallic glint. The snake opened its mouth, revealing an interior like pink-tinged silk, but the jutting fangs were as sharp and menacing as hypodermic needles.

The snake's head then moved in a slow, short arc. Its round, lidless eyes seemed to fix on Jill for the first time. She stared back into their black glassiness, until the snake suddenly pulled itself into a tight coil on the bed. Its head quivered as the blunt nose pointed in her direction. The tongue continued to flick in and out, checking the surrounding air.

The snake struck, without warning, hurling itself toward her for what seemed half the length of its body. She could hear the harsh hiss coming from its mouth, a noise that absurdly reminded her of air escaping from a toy balloon. The needlelike teeth caught the light from the table lamp and glistened with saliva.

Jill was stunned by the suddenness of the attack, but her body needed no commands. It reacted without reasoning, and she hurled herself backward, almost falling on the polished hardwood floor.

Her breath caught in her chest, and for a moment she was too paralyzed even to gasp. She was frozen with horror and fear and the nearness of death. Then her body's need for air overcame the paralysis and she began breathing in ragged, rapid gasps.

The snake pulled back from the edge of the bed and once again looped itself into a coil on the sheet. It held its head high above the constricted mass of its body. Its blunt snout swayed back and forth in an unvarying arc, the glittering dead-black eyes always fixed on her.

She moved away from the snake, backing across the room until she was standing pressed against the wall. Only then did she feel secure enough to think.

Free from immediate threat, the snake uncoiled itself and began attempting to slither toward the end of the bed. Its brightly banded body contorted with the motion, but it seemed to make little progress. The smoothness of the sheets apparently made its advance difficult.

She realized then that if the snake made it onto the floor, she could easily become trapped. She wouldn't be able to get out her bedroom door without having to pass directly by it.

She saw what she must do.

She snatched her pillow from the floor, where it had fallen in her leap out of bed. Holding the pillow in her left hand, suspending it by a corner, she dangled it in front of the snake. She then swung the pillow back and forth with a gentle motion.

The snake reared up half a foot from the surface of the bed and struck at the pillow without coiling. Jill jerked back the pillow. Then while the snake was off balance, her hand shot forward and grabbed its tail. As she grabbed, she jerked backward and swung the snake in a wide arc with such force that its body was as straight as a twirled rope.

She could feel the dry, rough skin and the ripple of muscles as the snake tried to break loose. She held tight, her jaw clenched and her breath coming in rapid gasps. Her arm kept moving through its arc, then with a dull cracking sound, the snake's head hit the polished hardwood floor several feet away from the bed.

She immediately turned loose from the tail. Then she stepped back, her muscles tensed and her face distorted. The snake drew its body together into a writhing contraction of its own muscles. Its mouth snapped shut again and again in a frenzy of useless biting. Then all at once the snake went totally limp. It lay unmoving, its head stretched out, its body twisted into a loose knot.

Jill took a deep breath. Then she took another. She was almost panting. Her hands were shaking so much she seemed to have lost control of them. They might have been someone else's. She paused for only a moment to look at the snake. It wasn't dead. It was only stunned, but she wanted to be sure that at least it wasn't moving.

Her first thought was to slam the bedroom door and call Firecaster or Mr. Smith. But she immediately realized that by the time she could tell anybody what was happening, the creature would wake up and crawl into a hiding place. The next person going into her bedroom would have the dangerous task of searching for an alert and aggressive snake. It would be better for everyone if she could get rid of the problem herself. Without hesitating longer, she turned and ran from the room and into the kitchen.

She couldn't get the large bottom drawer of the cabinet open. She yanked it so it started out at an angle and jammed in its tracks. She pulled as hard as she was able, but the drawer refused to move. She could hear the wood creak as she tugged on the drawer handle. Sweat made her hands slippery, and the drawer handle slipped from her grasp.

She pounded the front of the drawer with her fists, tears of frustration running down her cheeks. Her pounding shoved one side of the drawer back along its track, and she saw then what she was doing wrong. Using her knee, she banged the drawer shut. Then she pulled it straight toward her, and the drawer slid out easily.

She found what she was looking for on top of the knives. She snatched it up, barely avoiding the sharp blade of a boning knife, then ran back to the bedroom. She forced herself to approach the snake again.

It was still alive. Not only was it alive, it was beginning to move. It was throwing its coils into loops, looking for a grip on the polished hardwood floor.

As the snake saw her, its motions became more agitated. It reared up and struck at her, then pulled back and struck again. Jill dodged in and out, closer and then back away. She had the pattern now. She moved toward the snake.

It struck. Then while it was pulling its head back toward its coiling body, she struck back. She brought her heavy cleaver down right behind the snake's oval head.

Blood spurted out, a fine red spray, then the snake's body writhed and flopped with a dry, scratchy sound against the wooden floor. The head continued to flop and twist, the black tongue flickering out and the eyes catching the reflected light and shining like wet black glass beads. The satiny pink mouth opened and closed and once bit its own disconnected body.

Jill let go of the cleaver, and for a moment it remained upright, stuck in the wood of the floor. Then the weight of the handle was too much for the blade to support, and the cleaver fell over with a thud. The writhing body of the dying snake moved the cleaver from where it had fallen. The blade made small scraping noises as it rubbed the floor.

Jill stood against the front wall of the bedroom, a good ten feet away. She rubbed her right hand against the softness of her flannel nightgown, trying to erase the tactile memory of the dry, cold body of the snake in her clutched hand.

Her head was bent forward and her eyes were fixed on the scene in front of her. It was horrible to watch the snake die, but she didn't feel sorry for it. More than anything, she simply wanted to assure herself that the snake was genuinely dead.

At last the snake's body stopped writhing. She waited for several minutes, just to be sure. Then she turned and walked out the bedroom door.

She saw the small, white rectangle of Firecaster's business card by the telephone on the hall table. Calling him now seemed pointless. She had done what had to be done.

She spilled the brandy while she was pouring it, but she hardly noticed. It didn't seem important.

17

Tuesday 8:45 A.M.

Someone was pounding on her door hard enough to shake the frame and make the safety chain rattle. Jill sat up on the couch. She was startled by the noise but so disoriented by sleep she didn't know where she was. The green-plaid stadium blanket had slipped to the floor, and she felt stiff and cold.

She answered the door automatically, and it was only when she had unhooked the chain and was pulling the door toward her that she realized how stupid she was being. She should at least ask who was there.

Bright sunlight flooded through the open door and blinded her. She held her flattened hand above her brow to ward it off, but even then she had to squint her eyes before she could see anything. The man standing in front of her was middle-aged and weathered. A red cap with earflaps was pulled down low on his forehead, and the twisted black cords of the flaps hung down past his cheeks like thin Indian braids.

"Sorry for beating on your door," he said. His pale blue eyes lighted on her face, then darted away. "I rung the bell, but I didn't want to walk in and maybe embarrass somebody." He laughed nervously, still not looking at her.

"I'm awake now," Jill said. She realized he was looking away because she was wearing only her nightgown.

"I'm Sims," the man said. "Professor Smith asked me to replace the lock here." He tapped the doorknob with a finger.

"He told me," Jill said. She couldn't get her thoughts together. She knew that for some reason she shouldn't let him change the lock. Then in a rush of detail, she recalled everything. Particularly the snake. She shuddered and tucked her hands under her arms.

"It won't take me long," Sims said. He gave no sign of noticing her fit of trembling.

"Not today," she said, making a deliberate effort to speak clearly. "I had a break-in last night, and I want the police to see everything the way it was."

Sims nodded, but showed no surprise. "All right, but I'd put me a new lock on here PDQ." He tapped the doorknob with the flat of his finger. "The only kind of people this piece of tin will keep out are the honest ones."

"I'll tell Professor Smith to call you," Jill said.

"I'll give him a call myself," Sims said. "People are always wanting me to come right now," he grumbled. "When they need something, they need it last week."

"Thank you for coming," Jill said automatically. As she closed the door, Sims adjusted his hat in what might have been a polite tip.

She leaned against the closed door for a moment. Her legs still shook a little, but now that she was fully awake, she felt more in control of herself. Even so, the idea of going into her bedroom was still too horrible to consider. She rubbed her hands together, trying to get rid of the prickling, cold feeling of the snake.

116

She crossed the few feet to the telephone table and dialed Firecaster's home number. When he answered, she told him quickly what had happened. "The emergency is over," she said. "But I think you ought to come over."

"Give me fifteen minutes," Firecaster said. "Please don't clean up anything until I've had a chance to survey the scene."

"I've seen the movies," she said. She thought how nice it was to talk to him. He brought out her inclination to joke around, and with that, she could feel her confidence returning. "Is it okay if I make some coffee?" she asked.

"It's okay," Firecaster said. "Just don't throw away the grounds." He paused, then in a serious tone he asked, "Jill, are you really okay?"

"I really am," she said. "I'll be even better when I see you." She was thinking that, but she surprised herself by saying it.

She hung up the phone, loaded the coffee maker, and turned it on. She felt warmer, and the aroma of the coffee made things seem more normal. While the coffee was dripping, she decided she could face going into her bedroom. It was either that or spend God knows how long wearing the same red-plaid flannel nightgown and going barefoot.

She crossed from the bedroom door to the closet without looking toward the opposite side of the room. She held up her hand at the left side of her face to shield her eyes. Keeping her head turned, she searched through the closet and found a pair of jeans and a sweatshirt. She put them on without underwear. Her underwear was in the dresser, and it was too close to the part of the room she was avoiding.

She needed to use the toilet badly, and the urge to duck into the bathroom was irresistible. As she pulled open the door, her heart was pounding and her mouth was dry. She flipped the light switch and glanced around quickly. The silver tiles shone softly as though illuminated by an inner light, and she could see nothing unusual.

By the time she had washed her face, brushed her teeth, and combed the tangles out of her hair, she was in a good mood. She felt better than she did most mornings. She was proud of herself. She wouldn't have believed she could be so tough.

Then for a moment her good feeling disappeared; she felt nothing but a dark coldness that gripped her from the inside. She couldn't believe she had done anything to anyone that would justify or even explain what was happening to her.

18

Tuesday 9:30 A.M.

Firecaster knocked on the door and called out, "Jill, it's Eric." She hurried to open the door, then as soon as he came inside, she threw her arms around him. He held her tightly and neither of them spoke for a while. Then Firecaster said, "I'd better go to work."

"The bedroom," Jill said. "On the right side of the bed."

She poured herself another cup of coffee and sat down in the living room. She was still sipping the coffee when Firecaster returned a few minutes later. As he sat down, he gave her a puzzled look and shook his head. She didn't understand why until he started talking. Then she realized she had impressed him.

"I saw the snake," he said. "I can't believe you actually cut off its head."

"That was easy," she said. "Stunning it was the hard part. I had to pick it up by the tail and wham it against the floor." She glanced at Firecaster, and he shook his head again. "I'm deathly afraid of snakes, but what can you do if you wake up and find one in bed with you?"

"Run," Firecaster said. "How come you didn't just run?"

"By the time I realized it was a snake, it was crawling down the sheet, and all I could think of was that if it got on the floor, I'd be trapped. I had to do something."

"You sure did it," Firecaster said. He seemed to relax a little, as though just realizing the danger was over. "I thought maybe you'd majored in herpetology or snake charming."

"No such luck," she said. "But you can't grow up in Louisiana and not hear lots of snake stories." She hesitated, then said slowly, "I think I just remembered where I got the idea of slamming that one on the floor."

"From your father?"

"My grandmother," Jill said. "I remember my grandmother going to gather eggs and just as she stepped inside the hen house, a snake dropped around her neck like a necklace. She grabbed it by the tail and popped its head against the wall."

"Another unexpected advantage to growing up in the country," Firecaster said. "You did good, as they say in my business."

She started to say something, then hesitated. Firecaster's face had acquired an almost blank expression. He stood up and crossed his arms over his chest; then his whole body swayed slightly backward and forward. He seemed agitated and distracted at the same time.

"What's going on here, Eric?" she asked after a moment. "Do you still think somebody I know is doing this?"

The question brought him back to awareness. He stopped swaying and looked down at her. "I don't know," he said in a flat voice. "Last night I thought I did, but now I don't."

"Do you think it's the Jaguar?"

He shot her a sharp glance. After hesitating a moment, he said, "I'm beginning to think it's possible."

"But you're not sure?"

He paused for a long time. "I need to think about it," he said. "It could still be someone with a grudge against you, or even someone you don't know who might see you as a target." He paused again. "Has there been anyone around doing surveys, trying to sell you things, calling up to offer memberships in clubs, anything like that?"

"No," said Jill, shaking her head.

Firecaster reached for the phone. "Well, right now I'm going to get the crime scene unit over here. Maybe we can get more to work with."

Jill stood up. "Unless you need me, I should go upstairs and let the Smiths know what's happened."

"Go ahead," Firecaster said. "Tell them we'll want to talk to them later this morning."

Professor Smith was at the university, but Jill told her story to Mrs. Smith. She was horrified by what had happened in her own house. "You are so brave," she told Jill. Her eyes grew wide as she imagined the situation. "It makes me shudder to think that while you were fighting the snake, Horty and I were sound asleep."

"You didn't hear anything, then?" Jill asked.

"We were both in bed by eleven, and nothing woke us up," Mrs. Smith said. She shook her head. "You should have called us. We would have come right down."

"I did think about it," Jill said. "But by then the emergency was over."

Mrs. Smith's face suddenly drew tight with worry. She leaned toward Jill. "I find this is all very frightening," she said. "How could someone get into your apartment without breaking a window or forcing the door?"

"That's what the police are trying to find out," Jill said. "They're also going to want to talk to you and Professor Smith later today."

"Good," Mrs. Smith said firmly. "I'll ask them what they plan to do to protect us tonight." Then the worry came back into her voice. "Do you think we should hire our own security guard for a few days?" Her fingers tugged at the edges of her blue apron, smoothing it over her dress.

"I don't think that's necessary," Jill said. "I'm sure the police will be on watch." Then feeling herself blushing, she added, "The lieutenant in charge is a friend of mine. I'll talk to him and make sure you have protection."

"That would be very helpful," Mrs. Smith said. "But what about you? Are you going to stay in your apartment?"

"Not tonight," Jill said. "I think I'll have to spend a couple of days with a friend."

"Goodness, I don't blame you at all," Mrs. Smith said. "I feel so nervous about this I may ask Horty to take me to visit some people we know in New Hampshire."

Mrs. Smith glanced up and gave Jill a look of sudden concern. "I think it's a good idea for you to go away for a few days," she said. "You must still be careful. Promise you won't take any silly risks."

Jill smiled, touched by the older woman's obvious concern. "I'll do my best," she said.

She said good-bye to Mrs. Smith and left by the back stairs. On the asphalt apron in front of the garage, she saw a white van parked beside Firecaster's Saab. The van had *Crime Scene Investigation* lettered in blue along its side. A tall man with red hair and a lightly freckled face was coming out her door, and he stepped to one side to let her pass. He nodded to her, and she thought he looked very tired.

Firecaster was hanging up the phone, and she could hear people in her bedroom conversing in the casual joking tones used by those accustomed to working together. They might have been a group of carpenters discussing how to tackle a job. When Firecaster turned to look at her, he smiled but said nothing. She suspected he was uncertain about how he should treat her in the circumstances.

"Have you found anything?" she asked.

"A little," he said. "Ed Murphy's people are doing the bedroom and bathroom now, then they'll do the basement. They're going to take the snake to somebody for identification."

"It looks like a coral snake," Jill said.

"That's what we think, but we need to be sure so we can try to trace it," he said.

"How did somebody get in?" Jill asked abruptly. She rubbed her hands against the thigh of her jeans, and tried not to let her mind go back to the scene in her bedroom.

"The basement door was the entry point," Firecaster said. "The perpetrator cut the glass to get inside, then crawled into your bathroom through the plumbing access hole."

"I never even thought about that," Jill said.

"No reason you should," he said. "At least you're one-hundred-percent safe now, and we are going to see to it that you stay that way."

"Your place instead of mine?" Jill asked.

"If it's okay with you," Firecaster said. "You don't want to be around here for a while anyway. You wouldn't want to see how Ed Murphy and his crew are going to mess up your apartment."

"Are you doing all this just because of me?" Jill asked. "I mean, just because of us?" When Firecaster said nothing, she answered her own question. "You're not, are you? You now think what's happening to me is tied to the other cases, to the Jaguar cases."

Firecaster fixed her with a level gaze, and his eyes seemed the deep blue-black of glacial ice. She was sure she never wanted him to look at her in anger or disapproval.

"I'm still not sure," he said, "but even though we have no direct evidence, I'm beginning to think it's likely." He paused. "The possibility is enough to justify a thorough investigation. It's also enough to make me want to hide you away for a while."

"That sounds good," she said. "I told Mrs. Smith somebody would talk to her later, and she wanted to be sure they would have some protection."

"They will," Firecaster said. "We're going to keep a close eye on this place for the next few days. Now, are you ready to get out of here? If you are, I can take you myself. If we wait, I'm sure to get called away."

"Can I take some clothes?" Jill asked. "I need at least a few things." She made it sound like a protest.

"We know that," Firecaster said. "Just check out everything with Ed. I'm sure he'll let you take whatever you want, but he's got to put it on a list and you've got to give him a set of your prints first."

Jill shook her head. "Being a victim doesn't stop when the crime ends," she said.

19

Tuesday 9:50 A.M.

A dozen or so people were hanging around the door of Bookkeepers Bookstore when John Haack arrived for work.

Bookkeepers did business fourteen hours a day, opening at ten in the morning and closing at midnight. Yet the hours were never long enough for some, and he was accustomed to pushing his way through the crowd always gathered around the entrance. Usually he wasn't too careful with his shoving, and he didn't mind if he accidentally stepped on a foot very hard. He always smiled sweetly and even apologized if he felt like it.

Today he didn't have to resort to games for satisfaction. The flawless working of his plan testified to his intellectual powers, and its execution proved his courage. He was a worthy scion of the House of the Jaguar. The source of potential trouble wasn't one he could have foreseen, but dealing with it was going to provide an interesting afternoon. His mind was working at double its usual speed, and in his stomach he could feel the churning of excitement.

He rapped on the frame of the door, and Sharon Gino, the assistant manager, turned the lock and held the door open for him. The group waiting outside looked up expectantly, but Sharon quickly snapped the door closed.

"Why anybody should be so anxious to get into a bookstore is a mystery to me," Sharon said.

Sharon was in her early fifties, divorced, with three adult children who had all moved to California. She was easy-going, cheerful, and always ready to help. Haack liked her, because unlike the other employees, she had no intellectual pretensions. She pointed out to everyone who worked with her that she never read books and so far as she was concerned she could be selling hardware or pickles.

"I wouldn't be here if I didn't have to work," Haack told her. "But I bet you would." His voice had a teasing lilt.

"You're probably right," Sharon said, then laughed. "It's because I don't have anything else to do. A handsome young man like you could be out having fun."

She liked to laugh, and that encouraged him to tease her, which she also liked. He suspected she thought her interest in him was motherly, but it really had more to do with sex. Sex was always the key. He saw it everywhere.

He didn't mind Sharon's interest. She gave him the chance to create the character he wanted those at the store to accept. Besides, he liked using his special powers to make others think he didn't have any.

He stepped up to the counter separating the office from the rest of the store and took a time card from the gray metal rack hanging inside. Leaning over a little farther, he picked up a ballpoint pen from the desk. John Horace Haack then wrote *John Charles Webb* on the red line opposite the time notation.

He had used the name for more than a year and a half. He started right after his Uncle Dick made him rich and he had realized that this was the sky gods' way of telling him to start preparing for his role as kwisatz haderach. Getting a social security card, driver's license, and even a passport had been absurdly easy. Then when his mother died, he knew he was being sent the message he had been waiting for. He was free to be himself, his complete self. Like a butterfly slowly emerging from its cocoon, he was coming to be the person he was meant to be.

"I'll take your card, John," Doris Wyden said. She was in her early twenties, with bleached blond hair cut short and a round, almost cherubic face. "I've got to enter it in the ledger anyway." She was seated at a desk behind the counter and had to stretch to reach the top of the partition.

"How long do you want to work today?" Doris asked. She was responsible for both scheduling and time-keeping. "We could use you until two for sure, then maybe until six, if you want."

"Two is fine," Haack answered. "I don't want to turn into a Rimmer." They exchanged smiles. Peter Rimmer was the manager, a sallow, pudgy man who left the store to spend long periods of time with his girlfriend. He would be gone for hours, then come back and try to create the impression he had been working in the store all the time. He claimed twice as many hours as anyone else.

"I'll give you until two, if that's what you want," Doris said.

Doris was always particularly nice to him. She smiled a lot, caught his eye, and engaged him in chit-chat whenever she could. He had wanted a friend in the office, so he had started by flirting with her after a couple of weeks on the job. But he knew that if he wanted to keep her hooked, he would have to let her make the first move. After a month she realized he wasn't going to ask her out, so she gave in and asked him. He had stammered a little and made a show of being uncertain, then agreed with obvious reluctance.

Doris lived on the far side of Somerville, but she insisted on meeting him at Harvard Square to save him the trip. They took a bus to Porter Square and had dinner in the comforting bustle of Cambridge Seafood. He ordered soft-shell crabs, and since she had never eaten them before, he convinced her to taste one. She took the tiniest bite, made a face, and said, "How can you eat this? It tastes like stale corn chips."

"I thought New Englanders ate everything that comes out of the sea," he teased her.

"Only the ones that taste good," she said. He laughed as though she had said something very funny. That made her laugh, and he knew then he had made her feel witty and attractive.

They walked back to Harvard Square, holding hands and enjoying the warmth of the evening. Doris suggested they go for a drink at the Golden Quiver on Arrow Street. "I think the name is so clever," she told him. "At first you don't think anything about it, then you see the joke."

He laughed and pretended she was very clever to see the name as a pun. "That's what I get from you," he said, squeezing her hand. "A golden quiver right down my back."

He couldn't afford to lose control of himself, so by ordering tonic water twice, he managed to drink less than one gin and tonic, while giving the impression of drinking three. Doris actually drank three.

The noise from the videos and the shouted conversations was loud, and after they finished the first drink, he bent across the narrow table to speak. "I could feel a force attracting us from the first day I saw you," he told her. He spoke in a low voice that made her lean so close to him their foreheads were almost touching.

"I expected you to ask me out," she said. Her face showed her puzzlement. "Then when I asked you, I thought at first you were going to say no. What was the problem?"

He made his face expressionless, then turned away. He faced her again and leaned even closer. "I'd rather not tell you now," he said almost too softly to hear. "Let's just enjoy this evening." He kissed her gently on the lips, then sat back and smiled.

While they danced, she held tight to his hand and pushed her body against his. It was past one when they left the Golden Quiver, and during the cab ride, she leaned against him and turned up her face to be kissed. He could taste the sweet, flowery flavor of gin in her mouth. "Stay over," she whispered to him.

He stayed until early morning light fringed the edges of the window shades. He had been a careful and thoughtful lover, and he made sure Doris was satisfied. He fought off the nagging boredom that would push him to increase the power of his lovemaking into violence by recalling details from his experience with Sue at Dumbarton Oaks. He was a little rough with Doris, but not so rough as to make her complain. His immediate satisfaction came from the subtle way he exercised control over her. His real satisfaction would come later.

The next day was Sunday, and in the afternoon he called Doris and asked her to go out for coffee. When they met, she was shy about looking directly at him, but her smile showed she was thinking about the secret they shared. He let her take his hand, even though he didn't respond to the pressure of her fingers.

"I have a lot to blame myself for," he told her solemnly. He stared at the coffee brewing in the glass and chrome pot on the table in front of them.

Doris looked puzzled for a moment, then reached across and took his hand. "You don't," she said. "Nothing happened that I didn't want to happen."

"It's not that," he said. He smiled at her. "I haven't been totally honest with you." He looked into her eyes. "I'm already involved in a relationship with someone in New York."

She pulled her hand back, her eyes filled with shock. "What about us?" she asked.

"That's just it," he said. "I don't want to break up the other relationship. I'm really in love." He frowned and shook his head. "I should have stayed away from you," he said. "Now I feel horrible."

When she said nothing, he went on talking. "If you want to hear something strange, her name is also Doris," he said. "She's studying sculpture at the Art Students League, so she can't move here. I go down to see her every couple of weeks. Long-distance love affairs are hard to keep up." He sighed. "Maybe that's why I let myself get involved with you."

"What do you want to do?" Doris asked. She couldn't keep the hurt from her voice.

"I don't think we should go out anymore," he said gently. "We should just stay friends and treasure our memories."

"If that's what you want," she said. Then her voice cracked as she said, "But will you let me know if something happens?"

Doris never asked him out again, but she hadn't given up on him either. He was sure she expected his New York romance to fail, then she would be there waiting to catch him before he hit bottom. Her hope gave him a handle on her.

The New York relationship was the story he used with everyone who asked him about his social life. The story let him be friendly without having people think he was gay and without having to fight off pathetic creatures like Doris. He had seen enough of people and their girlfriends in college. He couldn't stand the way they tried to fill up your life, crowding in until they smothered you.

They thought they understood you, never realizing how impossible that was. "I'm sure I could make you happy," Doris had said. Ridiculous. If there were places he couldn't go himself, it was stupid for them to think he could open himself up and let them look inside.

"Talk to you later," he said to Doris. He liked to keep her hoping a little. Since she kept the time cards, she could let someone work at hours different from those noted on the card. Twice he had applied the charm, and she had obligingly made the changes he asked her to.

Haack straightened out the science fiction shelves, made a mental note of titles needing restocking, and went to the stockroom to locate them. He stacked the books alphabetically in a cardboard box, returned to the front, and began filling in the empty places in the rows.

He heard the snap of a lock that indicated that Sharon had opened the front door and let in the knot of waiting customers. He looked up the long aisle between the shelves toward the front to try to locate Rimmer. He saw him standing by the door watching customers come in, and as the last one walked through the door, Rimmer walked out.

Haack walked quickly to the office counter. Doris was hard at work with a calculator, but as soon as she noticed him, she looked up. She seemed slightly surprised to see him again so soon, but her look of puzzlement was replaced by a warm smile.

"Change your mind about your hours?" she asked.

"You're psychic," Haack said. "I need to take my car to be inspected this morning, so I can get my license plates." He took his wallet out of his back pocket and pulled out a folded piece of pink paper. Since the paper was blank, he showed it to her without unfolding it. "I just realized it a few minutes ago or I wouldn't have agreed to work today."

"I doubt if we can get anybody to take your place now," Doris said. She looked worried, concerned for him. "Nobody is going to want to rush in, even if I could find somebody."

"I know," Haack said. "I'm really sorry even to have to bring it up." He sounded contrite and slightly embarrassed. Then changing to a flirtatious tone, he said, "Do you suppose you could just cover for me a little? I mean, I'll certainly put in the time, but I just can't do it now."

Doris looked quite unhappy. "How about Rimmer?" she asked.

126

"He'll be gone for two or three hours, maybe more, then when he comes back, tell him I took my lunch break and was planning on going to the wholesalers to pick up some special orders. Tell him I'm doing it on my own time—I will too." Haack talked fast, making the story sound plausible.

"He may not even ask about you," Doris said. She was obviously convincing herself to do what he wanted, and he knew he had her. Then, as though suddenly remembering, she asked, "How about Sharon?"

"You can tell her the truth," he said. "Let's not tell her I'm going to make up the time later, though. I mean, Rimmer is the one who has to review the time cards, so Sharon doesn't have to know anything about how we work this."

Doris still hesitated. Her head was turned down toward the desk. Her face was hidden, and he could see only the blond swirl at the crown. He reached across the barrier and took one of her hands in his. He squeezed it gently and in a soft voice said, "I won't forget this. When I get all this taken care of, maybe we can go out and grab a drink." Doris looked up and smiled. She nodded without saying anything. Then she lowered her eyes to the desk top again.

He spent enough time checking the shelves of the women's literature section to make sure no one was watching him closely. Just to play it safe, he waited until Sharon was busy with a customer, then went into the storeroom. Without pausing to read the titles, he chose one hardcover book and two paperbacks to take with him. They would be his proof that he had picked up the special orders.

He left by the service entrance.

20

Tuesday 11:00 A.M.

The apartment on Prospect Street was a third-floor walk-up in a crumbling red-brick building. As he breathed in the sour odor of its decay, he realized how glad he was he no longer lived there.

Yet for practical reasons he was glad he had kept the apartment. John Webb lived there, but it was also where John Webb and John

Haack intersected, merged, then separated again. Someone tracing Webb would never find Haack.

The air inside his apartment carried a heavy musty scent that initially seemed sweet but quickly became cloying. He had made an attempt to control the smell by scattering around several packages of mothballs, and the harsh odor of naphthalene was mixed with the sweetish scent.

He always got used to the odor after breathing it for a while, but at the beginning, it was hard not to gag. He unlatched one of the two front windows and pushed it up as far as the paint-clogged track would permit it to go. He was careful to pull the dusty brown curtains back into place.

The apartment consisted of one room with a daybed and desk and a kitchen alcove shut off from the main room by a pair of folding doors. The doors were too warped to close completely, and he put a hand on the edge of each one and shoved them back. Even in daylight, the dirty hole that was the kitchen was dark, and he swept the air in front of him until he encountered the hanging cord of the ceiling fixture. The cord felt greasy as he gave it a sharp tug.

The suddenness of the light caught the roaches by surprise. A dozen, two dozen, too many to count, began to scurry for the cover of darkness in the cracks of the floor and around the walls and cabinets. The hard chitin of their feet made rapid scrabbling sounds on the worn dirty linoleum. He made no effort to kill them but paused to give them the chance to get out of his way.

The rusty set of white-painted steel cabinets had been installed at least forty years earlier. Blackened rings of grease and dirt surrounded the handles of the cabinets, and the porcelain of the sink was worn away around the drain, allowing an orange circle of rust to form on the cast iron. The drainboard had been covered with the same pattern of linoleum used on the floor—a basket of red and blue flowers repeated endlessly on a muddy yellow background.

On the drainboard was a large rectangular object draped with a pale green sheet. At the top, he had allowed the sheet to dip low to form a natural pocket he could fill with mothballs. He now scooped up the mothballs and dropped them into an empty saucepan. Working carefully, he unwrapped the sheet and let it fall to the floor. He then kicked it out of his way.

The object exposed was another glass-sided aquarium tank with a wire screen over the top. The tank was somewhat larger than the two in his basement, and the wire covering was the fine mesh of a window screen. At first sight, the tank seemed to be filled only with uncoiled rolls of white cotton batting. He peered into the tank, and when he could see nothing happening beneath the cotton, he rapped sharply on the glass.

As though he had thrown a switch, the inside of the tank burst into motion. What seemed to be thousands of small carpet beetles with black bodies and iridescent green heads began swarming over and through the cotton batting. The beetles were now in utter turmoil. Most were simultaneously running and climbing on the cotton in purposeless ways. While some fell back and then started over, others pushed upward until they could crawl across the underside of the screen. He tapped the screen several times to knock the beetles off, then removed it. Using long-handled kitchen tongs, he peeled back the cotton wrapping.

In the middle of the tank was the head of Anna Louise Hamilton. Not that anyone would have been able to recognize her. Very little flesh remained—some patches of skin attached to the top and sides, a few shriveled fragments hanging from the forehead, and a few more kept in place by the muscles attached to the hinges of the jaws. Certainly not enough soft tissue was left to form any distinctive human features.

The beetles had very little work left to do. The suture lines of the skull were mostly visible now, and the skull itself could be seen to be a dull yellow-white color. The cartilage of the nose was eaten away, and nothing but the thin bone of the septum remained to mark a division in the gaping hole in the middle of the face. The eye sockets were dark hollows, and the seething multitude of beetles used them as a route from inside the skull to its surface. He used the tongs to wrap the layers of cotton around the head once more. It was just as well they were so close to finishing, because he wanted to have plenty of beetles available for the next trophy.

He put the screen over the top of the tank, then draped it again in the green sheet. The beetles would do nothing unless they were kept in the dark. In the light, they would run around in senseless, disorganized ways. He dumped the saucepot of mothballs on top of the sheet.

He took hold of the handle of the cabinet above the tank. He felt his heart jump in anticipation, and a mixture of horror and pleasure spread through his body like a warm liquid. "I think you'll like this, Mother," he whispered, his voice small and childlike. He pulled open the metal door, and staring out at him was the clean and very white skull of Marie Thomas.

He was proud of the way it had turned out. After the carpet beetles worked on the head for two weeks, he then boiled it in a large stockpot for two days, making sure all traces of flesh and fat were removed. Afterward, he soaked the skull for a day in a solution of hydrogen peroxide. The natural yellowish color bleached away and the bone turned a clean white. To preserve the look, he coated the skull with paste floor wax and polished it to a high gloss. He then used nylon cord to articulate the jaws. The job had taken hours, but when he was done, the jaws moved up and down in a natural way.

In preparing the skulls, he had followed the directions in Alfred Taylor's *Textbook of Taxidermy*. He had wanted to employ the same methods the Maya used, but he had been unable to learn anything about them. Eventually, though, he would honor Maya ways and pay homage to the sky gods by building a Wall of Skulls like the one at Chichén Itzá. Except his wouldn't be carved limestone. His would be a wall of real skulls.

Above the skull, on the middle shelf of the cabinet, stood two glass laboratory jars. With their thick, heavy lids, they looked like the jars holding packages of peanuts in old-fashioned candy stores. Except these jars were filled with brains floating in formalin, one in each container.

The brain that had been Marie Thomas's had been clumsily removed, and thick strands of grayish white matter floated out from its base like peculiar anatomical structures. Both hemispheres showed signs of damage—strange blunt dents like those in a package of cream cheese. To avoid sawing open the skull, he had tried to take the brain out through the occipital foramen without enlarging the opening adequately.

He had done much better in removing Anna Louise Hamilton's brain. Now it sat preserved in its glass vessel, looking as though it might still be capable of thinking and feeling. His technique was improving.

He wanted to become so technically proficient that he could rebuild the collection of Lucite-encased specimens his mother had displayed on the shelves of her study. He missed those brains. They should have been his, of course. She shouldn't have given them to the medical school. She shouldn't have given them the money either. "We view the gift as an enduring monument to her long service to this department," the head of Neurosurgery had written to him. "Long after those who knew her as a skilled surgeon have departed, her legacy will continue to benefit those suffering and in need."

Suffering and in need. That's what he had been, and she had done nothing to help; really, she had done her best to keep him that way. And then she didn't even leave him the brain specimens, much less the money. By cutting him out of her will, she was telling him one last time what she had told him all his life. "You're my accident. We have to live with the consequences of our accidents, but we don't have to like them."

She would always say it with a slight, cold smile, as though inviting him to enjoy the joke. This one was nothing like the warm, pleasant smile in the photograph of her he had stolen. The picture had been taken only a year before he was born, and he was sure it proved she was right about him. He had ruined her life. But how?

Whatever he had done, it must have been awful. For as long as he could remember, his mother had hinted, but never told him directly, that he was responsible for spoiling her happiness. One morning when he was about to turn thirteen, he awoke feeling sick. He had a dull, aching pain beneath his genitals.

Scared and miserable, he turned to her for help, but she had sympathy only for herself. "Now you can be glad that nothing happening to you will ever be as bad as you happening to me," was all she said. He hadn't asked her to explain, because she would only say something just as cruel, then laugh at his incomprehension. Within a few days, the pain between his legs went away. Then his hard dream had started.

He had never told his mother about it. Sometimes he felt that she was inflicting it on him, that she had found some way to control his mind. Maybe that was why he had experienced such immense relief when Mrs. Sanders told him she was dead and cremated, her ashes scattered in the ocean. But the dream hadn't gone away, and before the year was over, he began to wonder if she *was* dead. After all, he had never seen her body or even her ashes.

He wanted to be sure. He wanted her brain floating in one of the thick glass jars. He wanted her dead. He wanted to kill her.

Thinking about her made him angry. He slammed the doors of the cabinet, rattling the thin metal panels. He pulled the light cord, then jerked the folding doors toward him. As the warped edges jammed together, the wood creaked and popped.

He sat at the desk and opened the bottom drawer. He took out a copy of the Boston yellow pages a year out of date. Its cover was dirty and torn, and a heavy red rubber band ran across the middle to keep the pages from flopping open. He removed the rubber band and opened the directory. The first quarter inch of pages opened together. They had been glued to one another to serve as a lid for the hollowed-out space cut into the center of the directory.

Nestled inside was his Astro HT-5000. It was hardly larger than an electronic beeper, and its general shape and appearance made it almost indistinguishable from one. However, the two contact probes sticking out at the top weren't like anything found on a beeper.

He picked up the Astro and slipped the plastic cover off the end opposite the probes. He took a rechargeable nine-volt battery from his pocket and attached its terminals to the clips inside the battery compartment. The battery had been charging for days and was at full capacity.

The single battery could produce a current of sixty microamps and forty-five thousand volts at a pulse rate of twenty per second. As little as one-second contact with the probes would disrupt the normal pattern of electrical activity and cause an instant and massive spasm of the involuntary muscles. Like a hammer blow, the electricity would knock anyone to the ground. When used on the head or neck, it would render a person immediately unconscious. The Astro worked silently and instantly, and because it caused no damage to the nervous system or heart, it never left telltale signs. It was an elegant instrument and the perfect tool for his purposes.

He held the stun gun in front of his eyes, tilting it slightly away from him. He then used his thumb to slide the switch into the "on" position. An electric arc leaped between the two probes with a sharp crackling sound. The arc was pencil-line thin but as bright as lightning, and after the crackling he could smell for an instant the metallic odor of ozone.

A change of clothes and the proper ID and he would be ready.

21

Tuesday 11:45 A.M.

The house was a massive red-brick Victorian with a broad covered porch that ran across the front and curved around the east side. Firecaster punched in the code to deactivate the alarm system, then opened the door and stepped aside to let Jill enter.

He was surprised by how self-conscious he felt about taking Jill to his house. His few unsatisfying romantic efforts during the last couple of years had always been conducted on neutral ground or someone else's territory, and Jill was the first woman he had invited home since Alice left. He wanted Jill there so he could be sure she was safe, but he also wanted her there for himself.

The experience of feeling warmth and concern for someone was once a constant feature of his life, a piece of the background that he took for granted. Now, though, the experience seemed so fresh and surprising he could barely believe he had ever felt anything like it. The same was so with the sexual attraction that pulled him toward Jill. Something had happened to him, something he couldn't quite believe.

Jill stood in the hall and glanced into the living room with its ornate furniture. On the opposite side, she could see into the dining room, with its double fireplace, long mahogany table, and marble-topped sideboard. Directly in front of her, a delicately curving grand staircase made a gentle left-hand turn as it spiraled up to the second floor. The polished banister gleamed. "It's all so beautiful," she said.

"It belonged to my grandparents—my mother's parents," Firecaster said. "When they died, my mother wanted to keep it in the family. Since my parents didn't want to live here, they gave the house to me."

"So you used to come here when you were a kid," Jill said. She turned her head to the side slightly and looked at him as though trying to picture him as a child.

"All the time," he said. "My grandfather even had a fishpond dug in the backyard so I would have a safe place to skate in the winter. He was afraid if I went to a real pond, I might fall through the ice and drown or freeze to death." Firecaster laughed. "The fishpond was about two feet deep and almost never had any fish in it."

"But you did skate on it?" Jill asked.

"I was a good skater," he said. "And I always had an audience. Grandpa would stand in the kitchen and watch to make sure nothing happened." He hesitated, remembering. "I'd skate for maybe an hour, then when I came inside, Grandma would make cocoa, and the three of us would sit in front of the kitchen fireplace drinking cocoa and eating oatmeal cookies."

He suddenly felt self-conscious talking so much about himself. It was the first time he had talked about his grandparents for years, maybe even since he and Alice had moved into the house almost eight years ago.

"They must really have loved you," Jill said.

"They did," he said, nodding. Then he gave her an apologetic smile. "I'm not sure what made me start telling you all that. I'm not usually so sentimental."

"I hope it had something to do with me," she said. "So much has happened, I think I'm feeling the need to be sentimental too."

She took his hands and pulled him toward her until they were standing toe to toe. She released her grasp, then wrapped her arms around his waist and pressed against him. Their first kiss was gentle, but the following ones were lingering and aggressive.

"Do we have time for this?" Firecaster asked quietly. They stood in the hall holding each other, their foreheads touching. Her head was turned up, and her lips brushed his with soft kisses.

"We don't have time for anything else," she said. She looked at him with frank openness, then lowered her eyes again. "I saw that last night. I was thinking about us, and I realized I don't even know if you're married." She spoke with a whispery softness, as though someone might overhear them.

"I'm not," Firecaster said. "I used to be married, though." He hesitated. "I was married to somebody I loved very much."

"Did she die?" Jill asked.

"Only in a sense," he said. "Something triggered a schizophrenic episode. She got better for a while, but she became a different person."

"You left her?" Jill asked.

"I never would have," Firecaster said. His voice was firm. "But she wanted to get away from everyone, including me. Maybe even particularly me. She didn't give me any choice in the matter."

"Like me," Jill said. "I loved Jeff more than I thought you could love somebody, but I didn't have any choice either."

"I know," Firecaster said. "That occurred to me when you told me about him last night."

She pulled away from him suddenly, and for a frightening moment, he thought he had said something to make her angry. "Let's not talk about the past anymore," she said. "At least not right now. For the first time in a year, I feel more interested in somebody real than in a memory."

"I understand," Firecaster said. "I've also been in love with what used to be." He shrugged. "Now it seems absurd."

They held one another tightly, then broke apart again, both smiling as if everything were amusing.

For Firecaster the feeling didn't last. For a moment, he had found it possible to forget about mutilated corpses and his fear for Jill. Now, though, the tightness on the left side of his face was beginning to return.

"I'm starting to feel a little antsy," Firecaster said. A scowl replaced his smile. "I ought to get back to your apartment and keep the investigation moving down the track." He massaged his left cheek and rubbed the back of his head.

"Won't it go along without you for a while?"

"It will," he admitted. "But I feel frustrated not to be out trying." He pulled his shoulders back, then slapped a fist against an opened hand with a sharp crack. "I've got to see if anything we have will tell us whether it's the Jaguar who's after you."

"You haven't made up your mind?" Jill asked.

"I still don't know," he said. "This afternoon I'm going to call my group together, and we'll see what we can figure out. We'll talk about Thomas and Hamilton, as well as you."

"You didn't answer my question," Jill said. "You said you didn't know, but I asked if you had made up your mind."

"I'll give you the same answer," Firecaster said. "I haven't had enough chance to think things through." He hesitated. "But I'm going to assume you're in danger from the Jaguar, because that's the only reasonable hypothesis."

"The *only* reasonable hypothesis?" Jill asked.

"Right." Firecaster nodded. "First, let's use Occam's razor and not assume we're dealing with two crazy people, if we can account for the same events with one."

"But that means you think what happened to me is like what happened to the other two women," Jill said.

"That's what I haven't thought through yet," Firecaster admitted. "But that's my feeling at the moment." Without pausing, he said, "There's a second consideration that makes the assumption reasonable, but it doesn't have to do with evidence."

Jill looked puzzled.

"It has to do with the value of what's at risk," Firecaster said. "Since your life is at stake, it's reasonable for us to assume a worst-case possibility, and that means assuming a psychopath is out to kill you." Firecaster paused, then said softly, "You did fine with the snake, but you might not be able to handle the next episode."

"You're sure there's going to be another?" Jill asked. Her tone asked him to deny it.

"Assuming my hypothesis is right, I'm virtually certain," Firecaster said. He looked into her eyes with the hard stare he used in interrogations. "Aren't you?"

"Yes," she said. "But I was hoping you'd tell me I was wrong." She sighed and nodded her head. "Whether he's the Jaguar or not, I think he's somebody who makes plans and then carries them through."

"Or tries to," Firecaster said. "I'm sure he thinks he's smart, very smart. But he doesn't know how smart we are."

"Are we?" Jill asked.

"We both went to Harvard, didn't we?" Firecaster said with obvious irony.

"I think I'll repeat the question," Jill said.

"We can beat him," Firecaster said. His voice had become grim. "Crimes aren't committed by disembodied spirits. Everybody leaves a trail, because that's just the nature of the world. You've got to talk to people and let them see you. You've got to work at some kind of job, and you're almost sure to leave some kind of physical evidence at the crime scene."

"Even when you know enough to take precautions?"

"Even then," Firecaster said. "The perpetrator violates the normal order of things when he breaks into a house or rapes or murders someone. The world shows the marks, and every perpetrator will tell you about himself, if you just listen carefully."

"And that's where expertise comes in," Jill suggested.

"That and a lot of tedious and boring work," Firecaster said. "A task force like mine can take a lot of inherently insignificant strands and trace them out. Most will lead nowhere, but if you're lucky, you can weave some of the strands together. Then, all at once, you've got a net you can use to snare the bastard."

"I'm a lot more interested in police work today than I was yesterday," Jill said.

Firecaster laughed. "Even so, that's enough lecturing for now. Come on and let me show you the den and kitchen, then you can choose your room." He turned to pick up the small canvas suitcase she had brought with her.

"Hold it a minute," Jill said. "If you think I'm going to stay in a room by myself, you are wrong. I want a roommate." Seeing Firecaster's quizzical look, she said, "I know we haven't even had our first date, but I think we're already past that point."

"I didn't want you to think I was pressuring you."

"So you wanted me to pressure you," Jill said.

"I hadn't thought of it that way," Firecaster said. "But maybe so." He smiled, then picked up the suitcase.

"Wait," Jill said. "There's one thing I've got to do. I've got to call Richard Klore."

Firecaster's face froze.

"Don't worry," Jill said. "I told you that last night wasn't a date. Believe me, I'll be happy never to see him again."

"So why do you have to call him?" Firecaster tried to make the question sound neutral, but he could hear the edge of complaint in his voice.

"I promised I would let him know what happened," Jill said. "If he can't reach me at my apartment, he might start to worry, and he's not somebody I want worrying about me . . ."

"All right," Firecaster said. "The kitchen phone is closest." She had said exactly the right thing.

"Here's a line of poetry for you to think about while you're waiting—'And we shall new pleasures prove. . . .' "

"That's only part of a line."

"It's my whole line," Jill said. "Take it or leave it."

The call to Richard Klore lasted less than two minutes.

22

Tuesday 12:00 P.M.

He decided to enter Eastern General Hospital by the back way, through the emergency room, just as he did when he had worked there.

He avoided the patients' entrance and pulled open the unmarked fire door that led directly into the treatment area. That way he didn't have to go through the waiting room. An Allen Agency officer would be on duty there, because that was where trouble broke out. Dopers high on angel dust were as wild as wolves, and almost as bad were the drunks who threw up on the floor and started fights if somebody told them to use the toilet.

Yet he had enjoyed dealing with the slime that came to the ER. He felt he was doing good by keeping them in order and protecting others. He particularly remembered the big redheaded man with a knife slash across his cheek. The blade had cut loose a half-moon flap of flesh that hung down from his cheekbone and exposed his teeth. Somebody had pushed him through the ER door and taken off.

The man was bleeding like a slaughtered hog, but he was also strung out on angel dust. He was hallucinating that he was a dog doctors wanted to experiment on. "I'm not going to let you cut me," he said over and over in a blurred voice. "I'm a very valuable husky." He made snarling noises and backed against the wall. When three staff members tried to get him into a treatment room, he knocked two of them to the floor and gave a nurse a very serious bite on the arm.

Haack was too clever to confront him directly. He offered him some water in a soup bowl, and when the man reached for it, Haack clicked one handcuff around his wrist, snapped the other around a water pipe, then knocked his feet from under him. Haack held on to both feet and let the redhead swing in the air by one wrist. A tech then stepped in and knocked him out with an injection. Everyone in the ER—doctors, nurses, techs, and even patients—had applauded.

Something like that was always happening. Not for the first time, it occurred to him that he probably should have become a cop. Maybe he still could. He wasn't too old, and they would be impressed with his background.

The curtains were pulled in two of the six treatment rooms, and the only person in sight was a nurse wearing a print smock over blue pants. She glanced at him, and he saw her eyes move down to check for a photo ID. When she saw it, she lost interest in him. Ralph Majors was the name on the laminated card, and the job title was Radiology Technician. The card was one of three he had stolen from lockers in the staff changing room.

The nursing station was unattended, and he leaned across the counter and picked up the red-bound paging directory. He looked up Klore's beeper number and office extension. He put the directory back, then pushed past the steel-clad door into the carpeted hall.

The elevator was opposite the door, and to the right of it was a bank of telephones. Without hesitating, he picked up the house phone and dialed the extension for Klore's office. After half a dozen rings, a woman sounding much out of breath answered.

"Is Dr. Klore available?" he asked.

"He's in his lab," she said. "Are you a patient?"

"This is Ralph Majors in Radiology," he said. "We just finished MR imaging on a lady, and a new tech misplaced her data sheet. We don't know who she is, but we know Dr. Klore was asked to do a consult. We need to get the results to her attending ASAP. If you know who she might be, I can check it out."

"Mrs. Halprin is the only patient Dr. Klore has consulted on in the last two weeks," she said. "I don't see how it could be her, though. She admitted with severe pneumonia and had a chest X ray, but she was discharged yesterday. It doesn't sound like our patient."

She stopped suddenly, then grew cautious. "You're going to have to check with Dr. Klore though, and his lab doesn't have a phone. I really can't tell you anything."

"I understand," he said, letting her know he was joining the conspiracy that she had given him no information. "I'll be sure and talk to him."

He hung up the receiver then immediately picked it up again and dialed the number for the paging operator. "Please page 35-35-40 and have Dr. Klore call extension 5631," he said, reading the number off the phone he was using. "This is a code two page." Code one was used only for a major disaster, so unless Klore had turned off his beeper, he would call back quickly.

He leaned against the wall and surveyed his surroundings for a moment. He had to make sure the two things he needed for his plan were available. Three small conference rooms used for talking with families of patients were on the same side of the hall, and he quickly checked them all, opening the doors and glancing inside. All were empty.

Solid walnut doors, acoustical tile, and heavily padded carpets made the rooms virtually soundproof. Attached to each door was an aluminum holder with a reversible sign. He changed the signs on all three doors from "Staff Only" to "Conference: Do Not Disturb."

He picked up the phone on the second ring. He said, "ER, Dr. Wilson speaking."

"This is Dr. Klore," Richard Klore said. "You paged me."

He was surprised to hear how whiny Klore's voice sounded. Jill should have done better. She was too good-looking and intelligent for him. But it didn't matter about Klore, really. As soon as he could get close enough to her for her to experience the awesome power of his mind and personality, she would blend herself with him, and her thoughts of inferiors would blow away like smoke in the wind.

"Thanks for calling, Dr. Klore," he said. "We've got a lady named Mrs. Halprin here who just came in with respiratory acidosis, and the relative tells us you're her doctor."

"I just did a consult," Klore said. "Call Dr. Carter."

Haack ignored the interruption. "We've got her on a Ventimask with forty percent O_2 concentration. We think she's going to be okay for the moment, but the relative is worried about brain damage."

"Probably not," Klore said. "I know the lady, and I'd guess part of the problem is a panic reaction."

"Maybe so," Haack said. "Anyway, the relative insists on seeing you before he'll consent to more treatment. We're worried we're going to get alkalosis with her and he's going to keep us from doing anything."

"I don't remember any relative," Klore said.

"I think he's a brother," Haack said. "I do know he's a lawyer. He was quick to tell me that." He paused to let Klore digest the information. Then he said, "I got the impression he wouldn't mind suing all of us."

"He wouldn't have a case against me," Klore said.

"With lawsuits you lose even when you win," Haack said. "You could make us all happy if you'd just talk to this guy."

"It's not my job to make anybody happy," Klore said.

"That was just a way of speaking," Haack said.

There was a pause while Klore obviously thought the matter over. "All right, I'll come," he said, not bothering to hide his exasperation. "But tell him no more than ten minutes. I don't have time to waste on Mrs. Halprin."

"I'll tell him," Haack said. "I'll put him in a conference room, and I'll be there to introduce you." He smiled at his success. People like Klore were so arrogant they never expected to encounter a superior intelligence. "I really appreciate it," he added in a sincere voice.

Klore hung up without saying anything.

He estimated he had about ten minutes before Klore arrived. That was plenty of time, because the second thing he needed was also easily available. Parked against the wall next to the ER were two special laundry carts. The top level of each was covered with stacks of towels, sheets, and pillowcases, and the lower level was hidden on all sides by green surgical drapes. The laundry was merely a prop; the carts were gurneys specially rigged to keep patients from guessing that their true function was to remove corpses to the morgue. No one wanted to confront death directly, particularly in a hospital.

A group of residents came out of the elevator. Laughing and talking, they headed down the hall toward the cafeteria. He waited until they passed, then pushed the gurney toward the conference room. He held open the door with one hand and shoved it inside with the other. He then removed the Ralph Majors badge and pinned on one that identified him as Richard Wilson, M.D., Emergency Medicine. He closed the conference room door quietly behind him.

He had gotten a good look at Klore coming out of Jill's apartment, and he had no trouble recognizing him as he stepped out of the elevator. Klore stopped in the middle of the hall and looked around him. He face was tight with annoyance.

Haack walked toward him and held out his hand, ready to shake Klore's. "Dr. Klore?" he asked. He smiled in a twitchy, hesitant way.

Klore barely glanced at him and ignored his outstretched hand. "Take me to this guy and let's get this over with," he said.

"He's here in the first conference room," Haack said. Klore stopped and waited for Haack to open the door. Haack pulled the door partly open, then stepped behind Klore, forcing him to enter the room first.

Klore stood with his back to the door and glanced around. "There's nobody here," he said in an angry voice.

Klore was in the process of turning around when the electrodes of the Astro-5000 made contact with the skin just above his shirt collar. As the forty-five thousand volts entered his nervous system, it forced his involuntary muscles into massive clonic seizure.

He fell to the floor without uttering a sound.

23

Tuesday 12:30 P.M.

Haack knew he had to work quickly.

Klore was stunned, but he wasn't dead. When his head cleared he would start wondering what had happened. That might lead to a noisy and totally unnecessary confrontation.

He turned the lock on the conference room door, then took out a bite-restrainer from a deep cargo pocket of his corduroys. The device consisted of a strong elastic band attached to a block of soft gray rubber. In surgery it kept anesthetized patients from clamping their jaws shut and blocking off the endotracheal tube keeping them breathing.

He had helped himself to many such items from the hospital. When his shift was over, he would prowl the hospital's corridors until the early hours of the morning, using his master key to open any door that seemed interesting. He had assembled an impressive collection of scalpels, bone saws, retractors, clamps, a staple gun, and probes of various shapes and sizes.

He spent most of his time in the autopsy suites, though. They were always empty at that time of morning, and he was free to examine the corpses stored away in the refrigerated stainless steel drawers. If he were lucky, he would find a partially dissected cadaver. Then he would become fascinated by the complexities of the body's inner structure and gaze for long periods at the exposed organs and tissues as if contemplating a piece of fine sculpture.

He never dared to steal a head or any other part of a body from the morgue, because he was afraid of triggering an investigation. He did the next best thing, though, and put together an album of autopsy photos he took from the filing cabinets. An attendant had come to work early one morning and seen him closing a file. The man said nothing, but Haack was almost sure that was one of the reasons the Allen Agency fired him. It may have been that incident that made them suspect he stole the fitted-leather pouch of autopsy equipment.

He took a thin, white washcloth from the stack on the cart, folded the cloth into a rectangle, then jammed it into Klore's mouth. He inserted the rubber block on top of the washcloth. He then fed the free end of the elastic band into the slide fastener and pulled the device tight. He held the tips of his fingers in front of Klore's nostrils to make sure his patient's airway was not obstructed. He didn't want Klore to die of suffocation.

From the opposite pocket, he took out thin, white rubber surgical gloves and a roll of three-quarter-inch filament tape. He pulled Klore to a sitting position and slipped off the white coat covering his clothes. He unbuttoned the blue-striped shirt, slipped it off, then pulled off Klore's shoes, pants, and underwear. He avoided looking at Klore's naked body, with its slack muscles and pale pimply skin. It made him feel vaguely embarrassed.

Klore was starting to move a little. His shoulders twitched together and his head rolled to the opposite side. Haack backed off, then touched the probes to Klore's neck once more. Klore's body convulsed. His arms and legs drew together toward his trunk like the contorted legs of a dying insect. Then immediately all his limbs straightened out in rigid lines and a shudder racked his torso. He lay still on his back with his eyes closed. The bite-restrainer had not changed its position.

Haack slipped the Astro back into his pocket and pulled on the surgical gloves. Kneeling down, he picked up Klore's unresponsive arms and braced them together on top of the abdomen. He then unrolled a foot of filament tape and wrapped it around one of Klore's wrists. He picked up Klore's other arm and held its wrist against the taped one. He straightened the arm so that the palms of both hands were flat against each other. He wrapped the wrists together, taking turn after turn with the roll of tape. Without cutting the tape,

142

he began wrapping the hands. He wrapped the thumbs together, then the fingers, then the entire hand. He cut off the tape with a razor-sharp survival knife, which he then returned to a scabbard on his belt.

He pulled up the green surgical drape covering the lower part of the gurney. With little effort, he picked up Klore by the shoulders and slid his body onto the cold steel platform. He used filament tape to fasten each of Klore's ankles to the welded metal rods supporting the upper platform.

He bent Klore's bound hands above his head and taped them to the rod on the left side of the gurney. To make sure Klore wouldn't thresh about and make noise, he placed rolled-up towels under his head. His neck was bent forward so far he wouldn't be able to move it in any direction. He used the remainder of the tape to attach Klore's trunk and hips to the gurney's steel platform.

He wrapped up the clothes in the white lab coat, put the bundle between Klore's legs, and lowered the drape that hid the bottom of the gurney. He then unlocked the door, and after a glance to confirm that no one was in sight, he maneuvered the gurney out of the narrow confines of the conference room.

He paused a moment to step inside the ER and drop the bundle into the decontaminate/burn hamper. The materials would be saturated with antimicrobial agents and then incinerated. It was unlikely anyone would notice the clothes, much less connect them with Klore. He considered getting rid of the surgical gloves he was wearing but decided against it. With AIDS around, some workers wore gloves all the time while on duty.

He was headed away from the public sections of the hospital, and into the work areas. Laundry, food service, and maintenance were toward the back, as were testing labs and storage areas. The research facilities were there too, hidden away to keep the public from being shocked. No one would want to stroll by the neurophysiology labs and see the cages of monkeys with electrodes implanted in their skulls or go by the dog labs and watch surgical residents trying to learn their skills.

Past a set of swinging doors painted a cheerful blue and yellow, he entered a section of the hallway marking the boundary between the public and private sectors. The carpeting was a stained and dingy green, and the cream-colored walls were marked and scarred by carelessly handled carts.

He stopped in front of the oversized elevator and pushed the "down" button. The elevator was used to move large equipment, radioactive substances, biologically hazardous materials, and anything else that either didn't fit or shouldn't be transported in the front elevators. Since that included violent patients and dead bodies, he was at the proper place.

While waiting for the elevator, he glanced down the hall and saw a policeman coming toward him. It wasn't an Allen Agency officer, but a Cambridge cop. His first thought was to pretend he didn't see him, to look down or away or anywhere else. Then almost immediately, he had the opposite impulse. He felt a need to stare at the cop, to watch his every move.

He reminded himself of his training, the rules he had imposed on himself. He looked at the policeman, caught his eye, smiled and nodded, then looked away again. He began to fiddle with the laundry on top of the cart, straightening the edges of the stacks, changing their order, shifting pieces from the bottom to the top.

The elevator doors rattled open as the policeman arrived. Haack quickly shoved one end of the cart into the elevator. The doors started closing as he was stepping inside, then the policeman's hand snaked out and shoved the rubber bumper. The doors jerked open again.

"Thanks a lot," Haack said. He pulled the gurney toward the back of the elevator. The policeman pushed on the other end, and the large rubber tires bumped over the gap between the elevator and the metal sill.

Haack smiled again in a show of appreciation. He stepped to the front of the elevator, but instead of pushing the number of the floor he wanted, he touched the "close" button. The door rattled in its track and pushed against the policeman's hand, but the officer held the bumper firmly in place.

To Haack's surprise, the policeman stepped inside. He removed his hand from the rubber bumper, and the door slid closed with a solid clunking sound. Haack had to move backward to give the cop some room. The cop was now the one close to the buttons.

"Where would you like to go?" he asked. He was a large, burly man with a red face and a broad stomach that stretched his shirt tight. His wide shoulders and thick hands made it obvious that being overweight didn't make him less formidable.

"Six, please," Haack said, giving him the wrong floor.

The officer glanced at Haack's cart. Then Haack saw him peering at the ID badge hanging from his pocket. Haack realized he had neglected to change his ID to the Housekeeping badge. It was a fault, an error, a stupidity. It could have been avoided. He felt his stomach muscles tighten, but he forced himself to keep a slight smile in place.

"I didn't know doctors had to deliver laundry nowadays," the policeman said.

"Only at Eastern General," Haack said. He kept his tone bantering. "They're trying to find a new way to keep up profits. I also have to cook breakfast on Sunday." He shook his head and said in mock seriousness, "Being a doctor's not what it used to be."

The officer laughed. "You make it sound like my job," he said. He took a careful look at the piles of linen on top of the gurney. "Seriously, Doctor, what are you doing pushing a laundry cart?"

"This really isn't a laundry cart," Haack said. He responded to the change in tone by sounding serious himself. "It's just supposed to look like one."

"No kidding," the policeman said. He looked at the gurney again. "What is it then?"

"We call it the Uptown Express," Haack said. "The psychiatric unit is on the sixteenth floor, and we use this cart when we have to move people in restraints up there. We restrain them and hide them under the laundry so other patients don't become frightened. I guess a policeman knows how people can act when they see you tie somebody up and take him away."

"I sure do," the policeman said. "Sometimes they just go crazy and start beating on you." He glanced at the cart. "Have you got somebody under there now?" He stepped back and reached for the sheet.

Before he could raise it, the elevator door opened, and Haack gave a hefty shove to the gurney. It rolled into the hall, and a nurse with a clipboard stepped quickly to one side to avoid being hit. "I soon will have," Haack said. He half turned to face the policeman.

"Be careful, then," the policeman called out. "Those psychos can kill you."

24

Tuesday 1:00 P.M.

The sixth floor was for cardiac cases, but he had chosen it because of the passageway linking it to the old Rycroft Pavilion.

He crossed into Rycroft and loaded the cart onto the freight elevator. When he reached the basement, the doors slid open on a wide area with gray rubber flooring. Fluorescent tubes glowed with a greenish white light, and the tires of the gurney made a clicking noise as they rolled across the raised pattern of the floor.

The room marked *Metal Supplies* was at the end of the hall behind the second of two doors. The lock on the door was not part of the hospital's master system. The only key was kept in the Security Office and was used only by a group including an administrator, a bacteriologist, and a security officer. He hadn't dared remove the key, but duplicating it from a wax impression was no problem.

The heavy metal door was windowless and sealed with rubber gaskets. He pushed the gurney inside. The door clicked shut, and the gaskets made a soft sighing sound as they were compressed by the weight. Attached to a steel frame on the back of the door was a half-inch-thick metal bar painted red. He rotated the bar counterclockwise until its end came to rest snugly in brackets welded to the heavy frame.

Several metal-working machines were bolted to the gray-painted concrete floor. A power hacksaw with a two-foot-long blade stood next to a grinding wheel eighteen inches in diameter. Newer machines were in another shop, but he was sure the old machines worked. He had been a member of a team that opened the doors for a repair crew and stood by while they used the giant grinder to cut down a swage too large for the newer machines.

He shoved the gurney to one side to reach the red button on a control box. Air pumps kicked into action and began the noisy labor of reducing the atmospheric pressure in the room. The pumps were basic to the room's new function. A three-phase arc furnace stood under a fume hood in the center of the room. The furnace could convert sixty-cycle current to 960 and vaporize biological agents placed in its crucible, ones like the cholera bacillus and the AIDS virus. The negative atmosphere was to keep them from escaping. He set the pressure gauge at 14.5 psi, only a pound under normal pressure but enough to make the pumps work. He wasn't worried about anything escaping. He wanted the noise.

The suction pumps produced a dull, repetitive thumping sound that was accompanied by the rattling whine of an exhaust fan. From somewhere, he could hear the strong steady whoosh of air as it was forced out of the room and through long sheet-metal ducts to vents on the roof.

Haack flipped back the green drape on the gurney. Klore was awake and alert. His face was pale, and his dark eyes stared out, wide and unblinking. He rapidly shifted his gaze, trying to discover where he was. The folded towels used to hold his head in place limited his angle of vision.

A few thin trickles of blood had run down his arms from his wrists. He had struggled against the filament tape enough to make it dig into his flesh and break the skin. The tape was twisted into a narrow cord, but not a single strand of the fiber had broken.

Haack knelt down by the gurney and released the catch on the bite-restrainer. He pulled the block of gray rubber out of Klore's mouth, then extracted the washcloth. Klore began taking harsh, gasping breaths, his thin chest heaving with the exertion. Haack stood back, looking down at the figure of Klore, trussed and helpless. He made his smile friendly and warm. In another kind of situation, an onlooker might have said the look was an understanding one.

"I hope you're all right," Haack said. His eyes narrowed in a show of concern. "I had to tie you quite tightly, but the beauty of that tape is it doesn't cut off circulation the way rope or wire does."

He studied Klore's face for a moment, and when Klore didn't say anything, he continued his monologue. "I suppose being gagged is the worst part, because it must seem you're about to choke to death. Your body wants to fight against the gag, but if you do, then the feeling of suffocation becomes worse. Your mind has to bring your body under control, make it do what is best for itself."

Haack's voice became calm and reflective. He might have been analyzing a formal problem in mathematics. "You started gasping immediately when I untied you," he said. "Yet I doubt you were really suffering from oxygen deprivation. I suspect the gasping was just psychological. You needed to assure yourself that you could breathe freely." He nodded as though agreeing with himself. "Strange, isn't it, how much of what we do is dictated by our fears, rather than the facts?"

"You're the one who called me, aren't you?" Klore said. His voice was a raspy croaking noise from deep in his throat. "There wasn't a patient, and you're not really a doctor."

"You're wrong," Haack said. His smile seemed benign and reassuring. "You're someone who is acted on, and that makes you the patient. I'm going to do the acting, so you can regard me as the doctor."

"I don't know you," Klore said, sounding puzzled. "Did I ever treat you for anything? Did I do something to make you angry?" His voice was less raspy, but fear made it higher, thinner.

Haack pulled the survival knife out of its scabbard. As soon as Klore caught sight of the bare blade, he tugged against the tape attaching his bound hands to the gurney. Haack reached out with the knife, and with one flick cut the tape around the support rod.

Klore brought his hands toward his chest, then shifted his shoulders on the steel platform.

"You'll find that a lot more comfortable," Haack said. He stepped back and leaned against the long pipe-support bed of the power grinder. "Now I'll answer your questions. No, you've never treated me for anything, and no, you never did anything to make me angry."

"What do you want from me?" Klore asked. "Is it drugs?" His voice rose in volume, but even then the sound was lost in the continuing thud-thud, thud-thud of the reciprocating pump evacuating the air. The pump's pattern and rhythm seemed to mimic the frantic beat of a laboring heart.

Haack smiled and shook his head. "Maybe you're just scared, but aren't you being a little stupid about this? We do have a friend in common, you know."

Klore looked painfully and desperately puzzled for a moment, then all at once his face showed understanding. "Jill," he said. "You must be the one who's been after Jill." His face immediately changed to reveal his fear.

"That's right," Haack said. "You probably know her better than I do, but soon she and I will be closer than you and she could ever be." His tone was soft and wistful, as though he were talking about a lost love.

"I don't know her very well," Klore said. "I used to know her boyfriend, that's all." He shook his head, his eyes wide and staring. "I wasn't even planning on seeing her anymore."

"I'm glad we agree," Haack said. He nodded slowly.

"About what?" Klore asked.

"That you won't be seeing her anymore."

"Is that all?" Klore asked. His voice was hesitant, poised between doubt and relief. "I promise you I will never see her again, if that's what you want." In a rush he added, "And I'll forget I ever saw you too."

Haack straightened up and turned his back to Klore. He began loosening the automatic feed rack attached to the grinder's carriage. He slid the rack in the machined grooves, moving it forward with the adjusting wheel. He turned around again. "You are more intelligent than that, Dr. Klore," he said. "We're here because I need to keep you from interfering with my plans for knowing Jill Brenner. Now that we've met, it's necessary for me to carry out my original plan."

Klore struggled to a half-sitting position on the gurney. He leaned to one side, supporting himself on an elbow. "You're mistaken," Klore said. "It's not necessary. You haven't done anything to me, and you haven't really done anything to Jill. There's time to keep things from getting out of control."

"Nothing is out of control," Haack said.

"I mean, it's not too late to back off from doing something you'll regret," Klore said. "You seem very intelligent. If you think things through, you'll see I'm right."

"Right about what?" He made the question very innocent.

"That you don't have to kill me," Klore said. His voice had lost all trace of hoarseness and was now loud and passionate. "I promise I will stay away from Jill Brenner. I won't tell her about meeting you. I won't talk to her at all."

Klore stopped to see what effects his words were having. Haack's interested but bemused look encouraged him. Klore said, "I'll forget about meeting you myself. I can do that, if you give me the chance. Nobody will ever know."

"That's literally false," Haack said. "Two of us would know. What you mean is, nobody other than us would know."

"That's right," Klore quickly agreed.

Haack started tinkering with the grinder again. He seemed to be considering Klore's proposal. He pushed the red button on the machine's control panel, and the grinding wheel slowly began to rotate. He pushed the black button, then turned to face Klore once more. "Did you ever study decision theory in medical school?" he asked.

Klore nodded. "I learned some of the basic principles." He spoke quickly, his tone betraying an eagerness to please.

"Would you order a kidney biopsy for somebody who comes in complaining about a sore back?"

"Probably not," Klore said.

"Why not?"

"Because it would be risky for the patient, and it wouldn't tell me much about the patient's problem."

Haack smiled and looked pleased. "You are sharp," he said. "Maybe that's what Jill likes about you." Very briskly he said, "A poor cost-benefit ratio. You risk a lot—the patient's life—for little or no gain. Do you follow me?"

"Oh, God," Klore said.

Haack laughed. "That's right," he said. "I have nothing to gain and everything to lose in a case where two people know about my interest in Jill and about our meeting."

Haack stopped talking and cocked his head to the side to look down at Klore. "You can't deny the logic of that, can you?" he demanded.

25

Tuesday 1:30 P.M.

Klore's face turned ashen, and he began coughing and choking as though he might throw up. He turned his face away from Haack and let his head loll to one side.

"I hope you don't think I'm angry or hate you," Haack said. "We're both intelligent and well educated, probably have the same background and tastes. I bet you like Mozart and Ridley Scott movies, don't you?"

"Yeah, I do," Klore said. He sounded eager to claim a shared identity.

Haack nodded, an almost somber look on his face. "I guess two men who pick out the same woman probably are a lot like each other in some deep way," he said. "Although I've only just met you, I feel we're friends. You probably think that's strange."

"I don't," Klore said. The coughing fit was over, and he lifted his head again to look at Haack. "I can feel what you're talking about too," he said. "I wish you would call me Richard, because that's what my friends call me."

"All right, Richard," Haack said. He smiled at Klore. "I'm glad we feel the same way. That's a comfort to me. I don't want you to hate me for doing what has to be done."

"You don't *have* to do it, I told you," Klore said. His voice had become a whine again, the voice of a child pleading with a parent.

"Oh, come on, Richard," Haack said. "I just demonstrated to you there's only one rational outcome for you and me." Sounding almost sad, he added, "I know you can't afford to see things the way I do."

"Wait a minute," Klore said. His voice was high and rushed with excitement. "I just thought of something important. I know something I think you want to know."

"I'm sure you do," Haack said. "I'm sure you know more about many things than I do."

"That's not what I mean," Klore said. He couldn't keep his desperation hidden. "I mean I have some information you need, some information about Jill."

150

"What?" Haack snapped out. His voice was suddenly hard, and the bantering tone was gone.

"It wouldn't be rational for me to tell you while you're still planning to kill me and I'm tied up," Klore said.

"You are absolutely right," Haack said. His good humor seemed to return. "But let's do things in stages to protect both our interests. I'll cut the tape holding your feet so you can stand up, but I'll leave your hands bound."

Without waiting for Klore's response, he pulled out his knife once more and sawed through the layers of tape that secured Klore's ankles to the supports of the gurney. Klore swung his legs over the edge of the metal platform and planted his feet on the floor. He leaned his elbows on his thighs, his back bent at a sharp angle, but he made no effort to stand up.

"That's stage one," Haack said. "Now tell me what sort of information you have about Jill, and I'll decide whether we move to stage two."

"I know she's moved out of her apartment," Klore said. "She did it this morning."

"Interesting, but not surprising," Haack said. "I suppose you know where she's gone."

"I know the street and I know whose place it is," Klore said. He was staring at the gray concrete floor. "I wrote down the telephone number, and I could give it to you."

"It wouldn't make you feel bad to do that?" Haack asked.

"But we're friends," Klore said. "I'll help you, and you can help me."

"You mean I can let you live," Haack said.

"That's all I want," Klore said. "I'll tell you what I know, and then I'll forget about everything. This will be our secret, and this time I would have something to lose too."

"Maybe so," Haack said.

"I really would," Klore said earnestly. "If somebody hurt Jill Brenner and I set her up for it, I would be legally guilty of a crime." Sounding desperate, he added, "I would be a co-conspirator, for God's sake."

Haack made a show of mulling over the matter. He stood silently, a slight smile turning up the corners of his mouth. Then at last he said, "Okay, Richard, we can move to the next phase. You can stand up now."

Klore got to his feet, but he seemed too unsteady to stand alone. He leaned against the top of the gurney, his elbow on the laundry and his bound hands held in front of him as though he were praying. The pale skin on the backs of his thighs showed deep red lines made by the edge of the gurney. His scrawny body trembled all over.

"Will you untie my hands now?" he asked.

"I'm sorry, Richard, but I can't do that," Haack said. "People who are desperate act in desperate ways, and you might overpower me."

"I need a guarantee before I tell you anything," Klore said. "I need to know how you're going to let me get out of this."

"Why should I give you guarantees?" Haack asked. "What's to keep me from simply demanding that you tell me what you know?"

"I won't do it," Klore said. "I know you were going to kill me, so it won't do you any good to threaten me."

"Good point," Haack said.

"So I need a guarantee," Klore said. He kept his face averted, as though denying making a direct demand.

"How about this . . ." Haack began. Before he could go on, Klore was running for the door. His bare feet made wet slapping noises on the concrete floor, and his gasping for breath sounded almost as loud as the mechanical wheezing of the air pumps.

Klore hit the steel door with his whole body, as though he could force himself through it. Then his taped fingers were fumbling with the red metal bar. Using his hands together, he pushed upward, swung the bar free, and let it drop. He fit the tips of his fingers around the doorknob. But the steel bar continued to swing through its long arc, and before he could turn the knob, it smashed into his hand. Klore gave an involuntary cry of pain as the heavy steel crushed his fingers.

Klore jerked his bound hands away, then reached for the door-knob again. His right hand was rendered useless by the blow, but he succeeded in lodging the metal knob between his index and middle fingers and was trying to use the thumb of his other hand to provide the needed power. But he was too late. The jolt from the stun gun threw him to the floor.

Haack smiled to himself. He was amused by Klore's attempt to escape. Klore had done exactly what he had expected him to do—tried to distract him with conversation, then run for it. People were so predictable. They thought they were so smart they could trick their way out of every situation. Yet they had never been up against a true cerebe, someone who could think their thoughts just by using reason.

Haack reached down and picked up both of Klore's feet. He then walked backward in rapid shuffling steps, pulling Klore's inert body across the floor. Klore's head rolled from side to side with the motion, but the surface of the concrete was smoothly finished and the body slid easily.

He moved the body parallel to the long pipe-support carriage of the grinder. He then dropped Klore's feet, and raised the body by grabbing it under the arms. He rested it for a moment against the metal frame of the carriage. Then in a single heave, he raised the body to the level of the carriage and dropped it onto the support rack. Klore's head was pointing toward the flat surface of the grinding wheel.

He took out a new roll of filament tape and quickly wrapped ten turns around Klore's neck to secure it to the support rack. He cut the tape with the survival knife, then taped both Klore's ankles to the rack.

When Klore regained consciousness and tried to look around him, he couldn't turn his head. Bands of tape wrapped around his forehead attached his head to the carriage of the grinder. He attempted to jerk free by whipping his head from side to side, but the tape permitted no lateral movement. He then attempted to throw his head forward, but the tape around his neck and head made it impossible.

Klore could move only his eyes. They were now wide and staring with fear, dominating all other features of his ashen face. They darted back and forth within the narrow limits of their scope, conducting a frantic search for any shred of hope.

Klore was absolutely silent. He didn't try to talk to Haack or cry out for help. He seemed stunned and frozen, like a blinded rabbit transfixed by the headlights of a speeding car. In the absence of a human voice, the constant thumping of the reciprocal pump and the whooshing noise of the exhaust fans seemed to grow even louder.

"It was only natural for you to try to get away," Haack said. He stepped forward so Klore could see him. "I don't hold it against you, and I'm not angry." Klore's eyes focused on Haack, but he maintained his silence. "I'm going to let you give me the information you wanted me to have," Haack said.

"And then you'll just go away and leave me here?" Klore asked. His speech was halting, and his voice was flat.

Haack shrugged. "I don't see why not," he said.

"But I don't know where we are," Klore said. "Maybe nobody would ever find me." His voice was now stronger and livelier.

"I'll make sure somebody finds you," Haack said.

"I'll trust you," Klore said. He licked his lips, then hesitated a moment. Then all in a rush, he said, "She's staying in the house of a police lieutenant. His name is Eric Firecaster, and he lives on Victor near Davis Square. I don't know the number."

"I'm disappointed in you, Richard," Haack said. "Like most people, you've overvalued the worth of your information. I could have found out the same thing with a telephone call to Professor Smith. Is that all you've got to offer?"

"I'll help you get her," Klore said. The desperation was strong in his voice. "We can do it together—you and I. I'll set her up for you, and then you can do whatever you want to do."

Haack laughed. "I suppose I should be insulted at the suggestion that I need your help. I'm not, though, because your offer just shows I was right to suspect that we're really very much like each other."

"Are you going to keep your part of the deal?" Klore asked.

"If you mean, am I going to go away and leave you tied up, that's a promise I always intended to keep." Haack stepped out of Klore's range of vision. "But before I go, I've got to make sure everything is set up the way I want it."

He adjusted the level of the carriage so the grinding wheel cleared it by a small fraction of an inch. He turned the small wheel that moved the pointer along the graduated line inscribed at the edge of the carriage. He stopped the pointer at a position near the middle of Klore's larynx.

He moved to the front of the grinder and punched the red button on the control panel. The two-foot wheel began to spin at a relatively slow rate, but as it turned, it picked up speed. According to the stamped plate on the housing, the wheel turned at a rate of six thousand feet per minute.

Soon it was nearing that speed. The rough, granular surface, covered with diamond grit, began to sparkle as it caught the overhead light. Then the wheel became a gray blur, a flat featureless disk. The noise changed with the speed. The soft whirring sound at the beginning grew louder and louder and then changed into a high-pitched whine. The sharp whining served as a background drone to the dull and slower thud-thud, thud-thud of the air pump.

Haack waited until the wheel was turning at its highest speed. He then slid down the lever that activated the grinder's automatic feed mechanism.

Klore was already screaming when the wheel sheared away the hair from the crown of his head and then cut into the skin and bone of his skull.

Rivulets of bright red blood mixed with white fragments of bone and gray-white brain tissue were running together. They were forming a puddle on the yellow-painted safety area around the machine as Haack opened the door to leave.

26

Tuesday 4:45 P.M.

Firecaster stopped in the outer office and poured a Styrofoam cup full of coffee. He took a sip off the top and grimaced; it tasted oily and bitter.

With his stack of files tucked under one arm, he took the stairs down to the conference room for the task force meeting. He was going to need more coffee before this meeting was over, but at least now they had something real to talk about. That was part of what put him in a good mood.

Jill was the other. He had left her lounging in bed, beautifully naked, except for a pale blue sheet draped around her shoulders. The phrase "like a dream come true" had been running through his head ever since. It didn't even seem hackneyed.

The conference room was dominated by an oval mahogany table polished to a gloss and armchairs upholstered in green leather. The walls were paneled in walnut, except that in the manner of municipal government decoration, the paneling was vinyl-clad wallboard. What really made the room appealing was that it lacked the odor of stale smoke and disinfectant that lingered in the interrogation rooms.

Don Renuzi, Karen Chase, and Ed Murphy were chatting when he came in. Renuzi and Chase sat together, with Murphy across from them. Chase laughed at something Murphy said. File folders were stacked in front of everyone but Renuzi.

Firecaster put his own folders on the table and took the chair at the end. The cheerful banter began to subside, then everything became quiet. Like students in a class, they all turned toward him.

"I want to tell you a little about my conversation with Ted Castle at Rush," he began. "Don and I decided a psychiatric profile might help us."

"It's better than calling in a psychic," Renuzi said.

Firecaster opened the folding blackboard behind him. He picked up a piece of yellow chalk and wrote *fantasy* and *power* at the top. "Castle says that as the Jaguar continues to get away with his murders, the more likely it is he will be pulled into the world of

155

his own." He tapped a knuckle on the blackboard. "His fantasies will become more elaborate, and he'll try to make reality fit them." Firecaster paused, then said, "That's my major reason for believing it's the Jaguar who is after Jill."

Since Jill first asked the question, he had thought the matter through carefully. His conclusion was based on the logical principle of "inference to the best explanation." Given what he knew about all three cases and given Castle's analysis, the best explanation was that the Jaguar was the perpetrator. Even in the absence of any hard evidence joining Jill to the other two cases, he knew he was right.

"You mean he's escalated his warning from a phone call to a full-scale production number," Chase said.

"I think so," Firecaster said. "He's staging a play. He's cast Jill as the female lead, and she's probably acting just the way he wants her to."

"So he knew the snake wasn't poisonous?" Renuzi asked.

"Right. He set things up so they would play out according to his plan."

"He couldn't figure Jill would kill his pet," Chase said.

"It wouldn't matter, though," Renuzi said. "If he just wanted to scare her to soften her up for later, it wouldn't make any difference if the snake bit her or she bit it."

"That's disgusting!" Chase said forcefully. She looked at Firecaster. "Do you think he expected Jill to go to the police?"

"Probably," Firecaster said. "I don't imagine that worried him." He tapped the other word on the blackboard. "Castle suggested the Jaguar probably thinks of himself as so powerful he doesn't have to worry about the police. He believes he's smarter, quicker, more daring, more knowledgeable—whatever it takes, he thinks he's got it."

"He's been right so far," Chase said. "But we're going to nail his ass this time."

"Absolutely," Renuzi said.

Firecaster brushed the chalk off his hands and sat down. "We've got a lot to talk about, but let's hold off for a minute," he said. "I want to deal with the Brenner case first, then connect it with the other two. Ed needs to get back to the lab, so let's hear from him first." Firecaster glanced down the table at Ed Murphy. "What have you come up with, Ed?"

Murphy sat up in his chair in an obvious effort to look alert and groped for the file folder in front of him. It was red, the highest priority file in the Forensics unit. He opened the file and looked over the first page. Eventually he said, "I'm afraid we don't have much that will help."

"Don't be sure," Renuzi said. "I once nailed a guy because I found out he had overdue library books."

Murphy smiled faintly. "The front door lock was picked. We found a few unoxidized dents and scratches on the wards. That suggests the perpetrator started out trying a skeleton key, then switched to picking the lock."

"Did he know what he was doing?" Chase asked.

"Absolutely," Murphy said. "Your average burglar barely knows how to use a key. This is somebody with training."

Firecaster turned to face Renuzi. "Don, have somebody check B-and-E arrests for the last two years." Then remembering what Castle said about burglary suspects, he added, "Look for lock skills, but also check for perps who made off with underwear or did anything perverse at the scene."

"Like what?" Renuzi asked.

"Masturbation, trying on women's clothes, writing on the wall, slashing pictures—anything like that."

"Will do," Renuzi said.

Murphy looked at Firecaster to make sure he was finished. "No attempt was made to pick the basement lock. He just used tape and a glass cutter." Murphy shook his head. "Since we found no prints or fibers, that suggests he was wearing nonfabric gloves, probably leather."

"How on earth do you know that?" Chase asked.

"The impressions on the tape's adhesive surface show a grain pattern, but plastic or rubber gloves leave spikes when they pull up the adhesive. Since the gloves aren't fabric, they're probably leather."

"I see," Chase said, sounding slightly chagrined.

Renuzi leaned forward. "Let me interrupt you," he said to Murphy. "Eric, do you think this business of cutting glass suggests somebody else went through the front door? Are we talking about two people?"

Firecaster shook his head. "My guess is he knew he would be hidden in the stairwell. Even if you're good at picking locks, it's much faster to cut the glass, turn the knob, and walk in."

"Makes sense," Renuzi said. "But now we've got him standing in broad daylight picking a lock in front of God and his sister. Does that make any sense?"

"He's the plumber Professor Smith thought he saw, for Christ sake," Chase said.

"It doesn't take a rocket scientist to figure that," Renuzi said. "But that doesn't answer my question."

"Yes, it does," Chase insisted. "It's broad daylight, he's dressed as a workman and carrying a toolbox. It wouldn't matter if half the people in Cambridge saw him working on the door."

"You're right," Renuzi said, reversing his position. "The plumber could also fit the description we got from one of the joggers we questioned in Hamilton."

"Remind me," Chase said.

"Caucasian, six feet or better, blond or light brown hair, well-built but not beefy." Renuzi spoke as if reading from a page only he could see.

"Don, have we got some people checking the neighborhood to see if anybody else saw the plumber?" Firecaster asked.

"We're doing it right now," he said. "I've also got some people calling every plumber listed in the directory to see if they made any service calls in the area yesterday."

Murphy noisily turned sheets of paper in the red folder. He was clearly impatient with the interruptions. "We've got to get this Richard Klore's prints," he said. "We need them for elimination in the apartment and on the flower box. We aren't hopeful about prints, but we're doing our best. We're going to use ninhydrin in the bathroom and the bedroom, places we're sure the perpetrator spent the most time."

"Did you do a sperm wash?" Firecaster asked.

Murphy shook his head. "Short of washing down the whole apartment, it would be hard to know what to test."

"Did you do a UV test?" Firecaster asked.

"We didn't think it was appropriate," Murphy said, shaking his head. "Since it wasn't a sex crime, we didn't expect to find seminal fluid."

"We should look anyway," Firecaster said. "If this guy gets a sexual thrill out of breaking in, we might find something."

"I get the point," Murphy said. He took a pen from his pocket, clicked the top, and made a note in the red file.

"The snake," Renuzi prompted.

Murphy smiled and nodded his head. "You already know it's nonpoisonous. I took it to Dr. Gordon at the MCZ. He hauled out trays of skins, and jars, and bones, and I don't know what-all for over an hour." Murphy looked down at his notes. "Here's the bottom line. The snake is not even related to the coral snake, although its markings are similar. If you really want to know, it's a *Lampropelitis triangulum annulata*—at least the way the Jesuits taught me to pronounce Latin. It's also called a Mexican ringed milk snake. It lives in parts of Texas and Mexico and nowhere else."

"Did this Dr. Gordon say where you might get one?" Chase asked. "I don't imagine you can buy them at K-Mart."

"He said a few places around the country specialize in importing exotic reptiles to sell to zoos and research labs."

"So could the Jaguar have just ordered 'One snake, hold the poison'?" Chase asked. Everyone but Murphy laughed.

"Dr. Gordon said not," Murphy said. "He doesn't think they sell to private individuals."

"Let's check the importers," Renuzi said. "Write out the scientific name so I can give it to my people."

"We should ask the importers whether they've had any inquiries at all," Firecaster said. "He might have tried to make a buy, even if they wouldn't sell."

"Maybe we ought to check the zoos too," Chase suggested. "See if they're missing any of their fangy friends." Then she said, "I volunteer to take that one, Don." Renuzi nodded and Chase wrote something in a chunky notebook.

"We've got the Nissan wagon," Murphy said. "No prints. It was stolen yesterday morning out by Fresh Pond. It was on the list this morning, but it wasn't found until Don let the traffic people know we were interested."

"Those guys just like to give tickets," Renuzi grumbled. "I hope my car never gets stolen."

"Let me guess where they found it," Chase said. "Back in Fresh Pond."

"Wrong," Murphy said. "It was parked on Memorial Drive about two blocks from the Boylston Bridge."

"Same difference," Chase insisted.

"What do you mean, same difference?" Renuzi asked. "It takes ten or fifteen minutes to get to Fresh Pond."

"We're not talking the other side of the moon, are we?" Chase responded. "The Jaguar doesn't stray far from his territory. Fresh Pond is as far away as he goes, and he probably went there because he wanted to steal a car a long way from home."

"Got it," Renuzi said. He moved to the edge of the chair. "He sticks close to the center of Cambridge, because he lives here."

"He could be across the street right now," Chase said, nodding in agreement. "Maybe he was even standing behind me in the checkout line at the Broadway Super last night." She crossed her arms over her chest and rapidly twisted from side to side as though shaking off a chill. "God, what an awful idea."

Murphy paused, then looked at Firecaster and nodded slightly. "That's all I have for you right now," he said. "We're examining the flowers and box, but we haven't found anything yet. We've vacuumed at Brenner's, and we'll do a fiber check with the other two. Now if you don't need me, I'd like to finish up a couple of things so I can do the UV screening and maybe a sperm wash this afternoon."

Murphy eased the door closed, leaving a dead silence behind him. Renuzi shattered it. "I hate to think that this creep is smarter than me. You know what I mean?"

"He's no smarter," Firecaster said. "We just aren't used to dealing with somebody like him. He's intelligent, but trying to think the way he does would be like trying to imagine what the world looks like to an alien from another planet."

"So how do we catch him?" Renuzi asked.

"By doing what we're doing," Firecaster said.

"I agree," said Chase. "But what do we do next?"

Firecaster glanced down at his notes. "When we had only Thomas and Hamilton to deal with, we got nowhere trying to figure out how the Jaguar picks his victims," he said. "Nothing matched or made sense. Now we've got Brenner. Let's throw her into the mix and see if we can come up with anything new."

Chase and Renuzi exchanged glances, then looked back at Firecaster. "He picks by sex and age," Chase said. "That's all we can say on our information. The only point-matches we got with Thomas and Hamilton are the same here."

"One more—they're all from Cambridge," Renuzi said. "That's what Brenner adds."

"But Brenner doesn't help," Chase said. "He still seems to choose victims at random."

"I don't believe it," Firecaster said. "This is a control freak." He rapped his knuckles softly on the bare wood of the table. "If we find the string that connects the three cases, we can make a noose for the Jaguar."

"Let me play with the Cambridge angle then," Renuzi said. "The Jaguar stands on the corner at Harvard Square and watches women pass by. He sees somebody he likes, follows her around, then when he's ready, he kills her."

"Possible," Chase said. "Or he works in a bank. He sees a woman he wants, gets her name and address off her checkbook, then he knows where to find her."

"That's better," Renuzi said. "Or maybe a clothing store, a hair salon, or anyplace else somebody might write a check."

"That's what we'll go with," Firecaster said. "We'll start with seeing if the three women shopped at the same grocery store, used the same bank, and so on."

"I know how to do that fast," Chase said. "We've got the computer program they developed in Seattle to look for patterns in the

Green River case, and I've got a guy who knows how to use it. He's been bugging me to let him."

"Using a computer is a good idea," Firecaster said. "When can you start?"

"Tod says he can have the program up and running in three hours," Chase said. "Then we can start inputting the data."

Renuzi turned to face Chase. "Correct me if I'm wrong," he said with heavy irony. "I know about computers like I know about knitting, but I believe you have to have the data before you put it in. Right?"

"Right," Chase said. "But we've already got the crime-scene inventories and the interview reports."

"They don't even scratch the surface," Renuzi said. "The interviews aren't going to give you the names of everybody who knew the victim, but you're going to have to know that if you're really looking for links."

"We can get that," Chase said.

"We can if we reinterview everybody in all three cases," Renuzi said.

"Nobody said it would be easy," Chase said.

"And the crime-scene inventories are pretty thin stuff," Renuzi went on. "They aren't going to tell you where the victims bought their pantyhose."

"You're right, Don," Firecaster said. "We're going to have to reinvestigate each case in a lot more detail. Do you have any better ideas?"

Renuzi shook his head. "I just wanted to say that the computer's not going to work any magic. We could be at this for a long time to come."

"Maybe we'll get lucky fast," Chase said. "You can never tell."

"Don, send a couple of people to reinterview Thomas's boyfriend and a couple more to talk to Janet Quick again," Firecaster said.

"Lists of friends, family and church members, co-workers, club memberships, hobby organizations—that sort of thing?" Renuzi asked. "See if anybody shows up in all three cases?"

"Or even two," Firecaster said. "Maybe we can establish a connection with number three later. That's not all, though. Let's get some people going through the credit card slips, canceled checks, and receipts in all three cases."

"How many people?" Renuzi asked.

"Whatever you need," Firecaster said. "Two each ought to be enough."

"Plenty," Renuzi agreed. "Then what do you want? If we find

two of them bought a dress at the Gap, do we go there and show pictures and ask questions?''

"Right," Firecaster said. "But we also want to develop inventories of the things they bought or did recently. The computer may be able to spot a pattern or score a hit that we missed."

"Standard police work," Chase said.

"Exactly," Firecaster said. "We want to get the computer to do what we could do if we had an incredible amount of time."

"It's a good idea, I'll admit," Renuzi said.

"Last matter," Firecaster said. "I'm taking responsibility for Jill Brenner, because I want to make damned sure nothing happens to her. As I'm sure you know, I have a personal interest in her." He examined their faces, trying to read their responses. If anything, the expressions were sympathetic. "Even though the Jaguar hasn't hurt her yet, we all agree that as sure as the stars shine over the deep blue sea, he's going to try again."

Firecaster looked from one person to the other. Tapping the tip of his finger on the table for emphasis, he said, "I want us to keep close enough to her to read the label in her shirt." The other two nodded in understanding.

"One more thing we shouldn't forget," Renuzi said. "The twentieth day is tomorrow."

27

Tuesday 9:00 P.M.

The dark blue Buick belonged to an elderly woman who lived on his floor at Cambridge Court. She drove the car only during the summer months and would never know it had been out of the garage. He had duplicated the keys when she had asked him to leave them with the concierge for her niece to pick up. Haack had always thought of the car as a backup. No one ever noticed a blue Buick.

He had parked three houses up from Firecaster's and on the opposite side of the street. This gave him a perfect diagonal view. He had been at his post for an hour and was now sure Jill was in the house alone. The garage at the rear was empty, and lights were on in only one room. He had watched enough houses to know that one person usually stays in a single room, while two people move around.

He got out of the car, crossed the street, and walked toward the house. The houses were all large and widely separated. The trees along the curb formed an arching canopy of bare branches, and from time to time, an easterly breeze made them rattle and scrape. The noise kept the sound of his steps from carrying through the crisp air. Heavy clouds blocked even the light of the stars, and he pulled his gray scarf tight. He glanced at the house and let his eyes follow the sweep of the porch as it curved around to the side and disappeared into the darkness.

A startlingly bright bulb shone above the front door beneath the covered porch. Within the circle of light, he spotted the code box of the alarm system. He hadn't expected a police lieutenant to have a security system, but then he hadn't expected a policeman to live in a mansion either. An outside box meant an old-fashioned two-wire alarm, and it would present no problem.

Not that he intended to break in. He saw nothing to make him alter his initial plan. One day people could read *The Book of the Jaguar* and find out how he had done everything, but they would never be able to duplicate it. Compared to the race beyond the stars, humans were pathetic creatures.

He was dressed properly for the neighborhood. He had bought the clothes at Sears to wear on the New York shuttle. They made him look like a sales rep who wasn't quite top-drawer. The suit was dark gray, and with it he wore a white shirt and a blue tie with a pattern of small red anchors. His shoes were black oxfords with soles still slick from lack of wear. His black topcoat was not tweed, but its herringbone pattern was supposed to look like it.

He completed his slow tour up and down the block, climbed into the Buick, and settled down for what could be a long wait. It would be disastrous for Lieutenant Firecaster to interrupt the operation; he needed to return and then leave again for at least an hour. Making sure Firecaster left was within his power, but first the lieutenant had to come home.

He counted lighted windows and cars passing down the street. Tomorrow would be Cimi, the day named for the God of Death and the beginning of a new lunar month. It was almost time for Jill to visit the place of the tangled roots. He would offer her to the jaguar god and to the gods of the sky and the underworld. Marie hadn't known he was behind her; Anna had known but not suspected any danger. He had prevented both from screaming, but he would let Jill scream. He wanted her to know him.

He first saw the flash of headlights in the rearview mirror, then his eyes followed the ruby red taillights as the car slowed and turned into the driveway. The lights disappeared behind the raised porch, and in a few minutes, a tall man wearing a sports jacket and scarf came around the corner and walked up the front steps. He punched in a code and opened the front door.

Haack smiled in the darkness and felt a surge of pleasure course through his body like an electric current. The only piece over which he had no control had fallen into place. From now on, the game was his for the running. No one was clever enough to stop him.

He looked at the glowing green numerals on his digital watch and waited exactly five minutes. He then drove to the corner, turned left, and pulled into an all-night Mobil station. Two cars were stopped at the self-serve pumps, and the drivers stood by them, squeezing the handles and watching the red numbers count up the money and the gallons. He parked the Buick by the white-painted curb near the air hose.

He walked to the bank of vending machines adjacent to the cashier's booth, dropped two coins into a machine, and punched in the code for a package of peppermint chewing gum. He unwound the red strip opener and dropped it into the trash barrel. He unwrapped the paper from five pieces of gum, put them into his mouth, and started chewing them. He worked his jaws to reduce the rubbery wad to manageable size.

The pay phone stood on a steel pedestal behind the cashier's booth. The woman inside was counting packages of cigarettes and making notations on a form. He was sure she was paying no attention to anything else, but even if she wanted to see who used the phone, she wouldn't be able to. That was a reason for choosing the Mobil station. He dropped in his money and punched the number. After this call, he would go back to the house to make sure the lieutenant was gone. Then he would come back and make the second call.

"Hospital Security," a woman answered. Her voice was sharp and clear. He moved the wad of chewing gum to the front of his mouth. Speaking in a voice that he made thick and slurred, he delivered his message.

"Please repeat that and give me your name," the woman said.

Instead of answering her, he uttered a guttural growl. Then he gave a vicious snarl that might have been made by an animal.

They were the same noises he had made while sacrificing Marie and Anna.

28

Tuesday 9:30 P.M.

They took their coffee into the den and sat together on the over-stuffed sofa. Jill drew her feet under her and leaned against the cushions. Firecaster sat with one leg crossed over the other, his foot swinging back and forth in a rapid arc.

They both seemed preoccupied and drank the coffee in a nervous silence. Finally, Jill put down her cup and said, "Tell me about the other cases. I can't remember their names."

Firecaster turned to look at her. "Thomas and Hamilton," he said. "Are you sure you want to know?"

"Wouldn't you?"

"I would. But that doesn't mean you should."

"I do," she said.

She listened attentively while he talked and nodded her head in encouragement, just as she did when she was interviewing. His account was succinct but detailed, and she interrupted him only a few times to ask questions.

"Now you know almost as much as I do," Firecaster said.

"Thanks for telling me," Jill said in a grim voice. "At least I have an idea of what I'm up against." She gave a tight smile. "I now know I'm not being pursued by a phantom."

"The Jaguar is real," Firecaster said. "All too real."

"What you said about him giving warnings triggered an association for me," Jill said. "When I was a kid I used to go hunting with my daddy." She felt a sudden need to avoid a misunderstanding. "We'd hunt quail or ducks, never deer or even rabbits."

"I wouldn't have guessed you'd hunt anything."

"I couldn't do it anymore, but I used to have my own shotgun," she said. She smiled at the recollection, then said proudly, "I was a pretty good shot, too."

"I'm sure you were," Firecaster said with conviction.

"But what I started to say was that I remember how we used to move very quietly through the woods, then when we were ready, we'd make a lot of noise and flush the birds." She waved her hands in front of her. "They'd fly up in absolute panic, and that's when we'd shoot."

"That's your association with the Jaguar's warnings?" Firecaster seemed puzzled.

"There's more," Jill said. "One of the reasons I gave up hunting was that I read a short story in high school that made a big impression on me. Have you heard of 'The Most Dangerous Game'?"

"It sounds vaguely familiar," Firecaster said. He shook his head. "I don't remember it though."

"It's about a rich Russian named General Zaroff who lives in a castle on an island. He uses lights to lure ships onto the reef, and when the survivors come to his castle, he feeds them, gives them dry clothes, and sends them out into the jungle armed with a knife. Then he hunts them down and kills them for sport."

"So humans are the most dangerous game," Firecaster said.

"Exactly," Jill said. "I think the Jaguar is hunting people the way General Zaroff did."

"Possibly," Firecaster said. "It's got to be something like that, but he probably doesn't think of it in those terms."

"The Jaguar is crazy, isn't he?" Jill said abruptly. "Not just because he kills people, but the way he does it for no reason. Just for the thrill, I guess. And even General Zaroff didn't mutilate his victims."

"But that fits with your idea that the Jaguar is hunting game— big game," Firecaster said. "Taking trophies, Ted Castle called it."

Memories from the night before suddenly came back to her, and her shoulders shuddered as though she were chilled. She wrapped her arms across her chest to keep from shaking. "I'm glad I'm not by myself in my apartment," she said.

"I'm glad you're right where you are," Firecaster said. He picked up her left foot and ran his fingers across the arch of her toes. "This way I get to keep more than an eye on you."

She smiled, but she was distracted. "I gave up hunting, because I didn't like getting pleasure from death," she said. "That's the big impression the story made on me."

"I don't understand," Firecaster said.

"I never realized death and pleasure could be connected until I read the story," Jill said. "I didn't want to be like General Zaroff. He mixes up love and death and talks about hunting and killing as if they were foreplay and sex." She shook her head. "It's all quite bizarre. I'm glad there are guys like you to hunt the hunters."

She smiled at Firecaster, then fell silent. She was abstracted from the moment, lost in thoughts that had just come to her. Finally, she turned to look at Firecaster. "Why do you do it? You could do so many other things."

Firecaster didn't respond immediately. When he did, he spoke carefully, as though he knew the answer but wasn't sure how to put it into words.

"I can intellectualize my job and tell you I do it because I enjoy solving problems," he said. "I like taking little unrelated fragments and putting them together in my mind to form a sort of topographical map. Then if I can find the right road on the map, it will eventually lead me to the killer."

"Almost like some kind of science," Jill said.

"That's exactly it," Firecaster said. "I try to invent a hypothesis to explain all the facts surrounding the murder, and that involves identifying the murderer."

"But if you're really intellectualizing now, it's not just the pleasure of solving puzzles that makes you do your job."

"That's right," Firecaster admitted. "It's exciting to feel you're matching wits with a killer who thinks he can outfox you." He paused. "Still, if I were satisfied with solving abstract problems, I wouldn't have become a homicide detective. But I like to see my ideas translated into reality, and catching a killer is about as real as you can get."

Firecaster smiled faintly, then his face tightened again. "Any cop can tell you that when you confront a killer and try to take him, you enjoy the thrill," he said. "You may have nightmares later, but in a peculiar way, you like the danger. No matter how careful you are, your life is on the line, and that makes you see everything with a special clarity and interest that's exhilarating."

"That sounds exactly like what people say about hunting dangerous animals," Jill said.

"Exactly like it," Firecaster agreed. "That's why General Zaroff, the Jaguar, and I are partly brothers under the skin." He held up an index finger. "But there's one thing that sharply divides me from them."

"What you do is legal," Jill said.

"Our aims are different," Firecaster said, ignoring her suggestion. "I don't set out to kill anybody, but I do have to balance the moral books. Every day I get my nose rubbed against the hard fact that a victim's life was wrongly destroyed." His voice took on a sharp edge. "By the time I'm on a case, a person—a human being—is gone forever. Family and friends remember that, and even though I'm a stranger, I can't forget it. My job won't let me."

"So you become the victim's champion."

Firecaster nodded slowly. "I do what victims can't do for themselves," he said. "I can't restore their lives, but I can give them back their dignity as human beings by making their killers feel the teeth of the law."

Firecaster turned toward her, and she thought she could read pain and sadness in the rigid lines of his face. "That makes me different from General Zaroff and the Jaguar," he said. "Still, like them, I can never escape thinking about death. I just don't happen to enjoy it."

"How horrible," Jill said. She felt a sudden rush of sympathy. She moved closer, put her arms around him, and held him tightly. She kissed him gently and felt him relax a little.

"Enough," Firecaster said emphatically. He leaned back on the couch. "Can't we think of something cheerful to talk about?"

The telephone in the kitchen rang. Firecaster seemed not to notice the first ring, then he was out the door before Jill could answer his question. She could hear no words of the conversation, just a few low murmurs. When he returned, she thought he was sick. His eyes were half-closed and his skin was pale. Yet his face wore the same hard-set look she had noticed when he questioned her.

"That was Don Renuzi," he said. His voice caught, and he cleared his throat. "I'm afraid I've got bad news about Richard Klore." He paused, and she nodded for him to go on. "Klore was killed sometime today at Eastern General. It looks like the Jaguar did it."

"I was right," she said in a dull voice. She felt no surprise and no sadness; only a general numbness.

"What do you mean?"

"I told Richard I was dangerous to be around. That's what he believed, but he couldn't admit it. He laughed at me for telling him." She touched her cheek lightly with her fingertips. "And now the Jaguar has killed him instead of me."

"Not *instead of*," Firecaster said. "I suspect he killed Klore to get him out of the way and to prove he can kill you whenever he wants to. He's notifying us that he's not intimidated."

"Poor Richard," she said.

"I've got to go to the scene," Firecaster said. His voice was steady, but he looked unwell.

"I don't suppose I could come?"

"You wouldn't want to be there," Firecaster said earnestly. "It's not like in the movies. Something horrible seems to linger at the scene of a violent murder." He paused to find the words. "Fear and rage still hang in the air like a rotten odor, and you can almost imagine you smell them." He waved his hand in a wide gesture. "It's frightening."

He spoke slowly and reflectively, and she thought he was addressing himself as well as her. He was telling her once more that he wasn't just a spectator who could protect himself by turning away. He had to draw close to the victim, close to death. He had to look at the wounds and smell death's smells.

Jill moved toward him, and they clung together tightly. "Don't think about that. Just remember that we're alive," she said. "Death is still far away." She tried to sound confident and reassuring, for her own sake as well as his.

"Not for Klore, though," Firecaster said. He touched her hair and cheek with his fingertips, then stepped away. "Before I leave, I've got to make sure you'll be all right." He walked toward the wall phone and picked up the receiver. "I'm going to have an officer come and stay with you while I'm gone. Would you prefer a man or a woman?"

"Neither," Jill said. "If I were in my apartment, I'd want somebody, but I'm perfectly safe here." She saw Firecaster's skeptical look and kept talking. "I want to go to bed early, and I don't want somebody around bothering me. You're letting your feelings for me make you too cautious."

Firecaster sighed and hung up the receiver. "I have no reason to think you wouldn't be safe by yourself," he said. "But I'd feel a lot better if you'd let me send somebody."

"There's no need," Jill insisted. "Nobody who could possibly cause me trouble knows where I am. Just show me how to operate the burglar alarm, and that's enough."

"Do you promise to call me if anything unusual happens?" Firecaster asked.

"Of course I will," she said. "I don't want another night like last night."

29

Tuesday 11:00 P.M.

Firecaster found the smell of blood in the room almost overwhelming. It was a sickly sweet odor that hung thick in the air and caught in his throat so that he had to swallow to avoid gagging. He found himself clearing his throat again and again.

The air pumps were off, and the forensic crew was waiting outside the double doors. Renuzi was standing just inside the room. Firecaster could hear people talking in the distance, but the room itself was silent.

He glanced around at the equipment bolted to the concrete floor. He recognized a screw-cutting lathe, but the purpose of some of the machines escaped him. Finally, reluctantly, he walked forward and stood at the back end of the power grinder. He moved carefully to avoid stepping into the broad path of blood that led from the front of the grinder, across the gray floor, and out the door.

Nothing had been disturbed, Renuzi assured him. Except for turning off the air pumps, everything was as it had been found. Klore's naked body was still attached by bands of filament tape to the metal rack of the grinder's carriage. The tape at the wrists and ankles was rolled and twisted to the narrow diameter of a wire, and the skin and flesh at those places were worn into deep raw wounds. Klore had struggled.

The grinder had turned off automatically when it reached the setting on the carriage. Klore's head was gone, and the stump of his neck was jammed against the flat abrasive face of the grinding wheel. The body and the surrounding area were covered by a slick reddish brown layer of blood mixed with pulverized bone and tissue. Fragments of brain, bone, flesh, and teeth had been thrown to the sides in a regular pattern by the spinning of the wheel.

Firecaster looked up and saw that even the ceiling was splattered with the debris. The same was true of the rubber-tired gurney with its stacks of towels and sheets that stood ten feet away from the grinder. Virtually everything in sight was stained with the color of coagulated, partly dried blood.

Firecaster turned away from the machine. Then with no warning, a wave of unreality washed over him. It was as if a black fog had come between him and his surroundings, leaving him in a darkened world of vague shapes and shadowy forms. The vision in both eyes was blurred, and his ears were ringing. Sounds that reached him seemed distant and distorted.

He stood still for a moment. He was aware Renuzi was waiting for him, but he didn't look in his direction. Nothing was wrong with his thinking processes. He knew exactly where he was and why he was there, but his body was telling him he should leave. *It's just an anxiety attack,* he told himself. *It will go away.*

He slowly made his way over to Renuzi, exercising elaborate care to avoid as much blood as he could. Blood was everywhere. Death was everywhere. This was the worst episode he could remember in almost two years.

"No telling how long it would have been before the body was discovered," Renuzi said. "Maybe a week or two. If anybody had gone through the double doors, they could have seen the blood running under this one." Renuzi indicated the door with a nod of his head.

Firecaster glanced at the metal door and noted the heavy red steel bar that allowed it to be fastened from the inside. He forced himself to think. The bar would make it difficult for anyone to break into the room, but it would also make it hard for anyone to get out of the room. The Jaguar must have felt confident he wouldn't be disturbed or he would never have put himself in a room with only one way out.

Renuzi continued his account. "Mary Parnell is the name of the security officer who took the call," he said. "They don't have a taping system here, but she's sure she remembers everything. After she answered, he said, 'A murdered doctor is in A-42, and the Jaguar is everywhere.' "

"Did she try getting him to talk?"

"She asked him to repeat the information and to give his name."

"He didn't play?"

"She says he growled and snarled like an animal, then he just hung up." Renuzi shrugged. "That was it."

"What time was the call?" Firecaster asked. He was making an effort to appear normal; he wondered if Renuzi noticed anything.

"Roughly nine-twenty," Renuzi said.

"So did this officer, Parnell, rush right down here?"

"She was the only one on duty in the office, so she had to call her supervisor," Renuzi said. "His name is John Clarence, but he didn't go right down there either."

"How come? I know they see a lot of dead bodies in hospitals, but they don't get murdered doctors every day."

"He was following standing orders," Renuzi said. "This is where they destroy dangerous biological waste." He glanced behind him suspiciously. "You have to go through a special procedure to come in here."

"Did that slow up reporting the crime?"

"Not as much as you might expect," Renuzi said. "Everybody hurried, and we got the call at nine-thirty-four."

"Who has control of the key?"

"Security," Renuzi said. "Chase is up in the office talking to Parnell and Clarence. She's also going to get the duty officer from the last shift to come in, because that's when the homicide must have occurred."

171

"Why do you suppose he decided to call us on this?" Firecaster asked. "The other ones he let us find for ourselves."

Renuzi shook his head in puzzlement. "He probably wanted to jerk us around, and he realized if he didn't tell us where to look, it might be a couple of weeks before we found out what he'd been up to."

Firecaster stood silent for a moment, making himself think. Lacking any safe place to rest his gaze, he looked down at his feet. He noticed that the polished black edges of Renuzi's soles were stained with reddish brown splotches. He was also aware that Renuzi was looking at him very closely, but Renuzi knew when to keep quiet.

Firecaster shifted uneasily from one foot to the other. There was something he couldn't quite grasp, something just beyond the range of his awareness. Something connected with the call and with Klore.

Nothing was coming to him.

"Let's let Murphy take over and go someplace else to talk," Firecaster said. "I've seen all I want to."

30

Tuesday 11:20 P.M.

She tried not to think about Klore. In a way, she was responsible for his death, but thinking about it only reminded her that the same person was trying to kill her. She had to be careful not to let such thoughts take control of her, not to let her imagination cripple her. If she tried, she could resist the danger. She knew that from experience.

When she had started going hunting with her father, she was frightened of the woods. She would lie awake in her sleeping bag and hear the whispering noises of the night, then wait anxiously for something to happen. When nothing did, she would still remain vigilant, making herself exhausted and miserable with dread.

Finally, she would say, "Daddy, I can't sleep. I'm scared." Her father would reach across and take her hand, but he never told her there was nothing to be afraid of. "You've got to use your head," he would say. "If you just go by your feelings, you'll be scared of the wrong things."

He would explain that she was hearing birds rustling their feathers as they settled in the trees or a possum crunching through dry leaves on his way to drink from a slough. "When your head tells you everything is okay, make yourself think about something nice." She could still hear the reassurance in her father's soft drawling voice.

When she was eight, she would think about the giant Sears store in Baton Rouge and pretend she was buying all the clothes she wanted for Ruth, the doll her Aunt Mae had given her. Now she made herself remember how good it felt to have Eric hold her and how much she liked touching him. She was lucky, very lucky.

She switched on the alarm system the way Eric had shown her and returned to his den. For twenty minutes she did nothing but scan the books in the bookshelves. Her mind was restless and distractible, and nothing was appealing. She finally turned away from the shelves and picked up her own paperback copy of *Dune*. She was still planning to go to Boscon tomorrow, and although she had completed the novel, she had put off reading the appendices.

She stretched out on the overstuffed sofa with an embroidered pillow under her head. She thought she would have trouble concentrating, but she was soon immersed in Herbert's account of the religion of Dune. She felt herself relax and give in to the pervasive fatigue that had built up during the last two days. Her eyes closed, and she began drifting gently into sleep.

The shrill ringing of the telephone startled her awake. She got up, knocking her book to the floor, but for a moment she stood unmoving. Her mind was fuzzy with sleep, and she couldn't recall where the telephone was. Then she remembered and hurried across the hall into the kitchen. She snatched up the receiver, but it almost slipped from her grasp and she had to fumble to recover it. The accordion wire coiled around her wrist like a thin, white snake.

"Miss Brenner," a man's voice said. "I'm Detective Robert Nashua, and I'm calling for Lieutenant Firecaster. Is everything all right there?" The voice had the official and slightly bored sound of a man doing his duty, but the tone was friendly.

"Everything is fine." Her voice was thick with sleep.

"I didn't wake you?" he asked. He sounded even friendlier now, and the question was slightly teasing.

"I was just reading." She made an effort to sound more awake than she felt.

"I'm glad you hadn't gone to bed, because the Lieutenant asked me to drive you to Eastern General Hospital."

"Does it have to do with identifying Richard Klore's body?" She felt genuinely puzzled.

"I don't know, Miss Brenner. He just told me to go get you and bring you down." He started talking faster, not giving her a chance to interrupt or even to think. "The Lieutenant is worried about you opening the door for the wrong person," he said. "He told me to work out a code with you."

"What kind of code?" Jill asked.

"I'll ring the doorbell two longs and a short," he said. "You shouldn't open the door for anybody until you hear that. Then you should come out on the porch, and I'll escort you to the car. I'll be driving an unmarked blue Buick."

While he was talking, she heard a car engine start up. Traffic noises were in the background. He must be at a pay phone on the street somewhere. But what was he doing outside, if he had just been talking to Eric at the hospital?

"Could I talk to Lieutenant Firecaster?" she asked.

"Sorry, but I'm not where I can reach him." He hesitated just a moment, then said, "I'm out getting my car. I had to call from a street phone, because our guys were tying up all the hospital lines, and the Lieutenant told me to hop to it."

She came awake with a shock. Detective Nashua sounded so sincere, and everything he said sounded plausible. Yet he also seemed too ready to answer questions she hadn't asked. Besides, Eric surely would have called her himself. A shiver ran up the back of her neck, and she realized what she had to do.

"Lieutenant Firecaster's assistant, Sergeant White, drove me last time," she said. "Do you know why he's not coming?"

She felt her heart beat faster while she waited for his response. "Lady, you don't seem to understand." He spoke like someone who has tried to be reasonable and is now losing patience. "Everybody's busy with this investigation. Sergeant White just can't get loose now."

As she listened to his answer, she began to feel unsteady on her feet. Her breath caught in her chest, and her hand on the telephone turned sweaty and cold. She didn't doubt that she was talking to the man who was planning to kill her. She wanted to slam down the telephone and run away from it. She felt as though he could reach through the phone line and touch her. She didn't think about his hurting her. Just touching was enough.

Then she became angry. A rage born of fear and frustration sprang up from somewhere deep inside, and it was all she could do to keep from screaming curses into the telephone. How dare this worthless piece of shit think he could get away with tricking her! It was almost worse than breaking into her apartment, threatening her life, and making her run away, although they made her furious too. She felt insulted by his arrogance, by his assumed superiority.

But she had enough experience from hunting to know that anger could make you do stupid things. You had to keep your head. She clenched her jaw, and her hand tightened on the telephone as she fought to control herself. The effort paid off, and she suddenly acquired a cold clarity of mind that evaporated her anger. Now that she was thinking like a hunter herself, she grasped a possibility that pleased her—*she would trap the Jaguar*.

Instead of being his victim, she could turn him into her prey. But she would have to control herself to keep from scaring him off.

"I'm sorry to ask so many questions," she said apologetically. "I just want to make sure I do the right thing."

"Perfectly all right," he said. "I'm used to dealing with people in trouble." The impatience was gone, and he sounded friendly and reassuring once more.

"Let's see if I've got it right," she said. "You'll ring the bell in a code and I'll come out."

"I'll ring two longs and a short," he said. "You'll step out on the porch then. Tell you what, you just think about those rings and don't worry about anything else."

"Maybe that will keep me from getting so jittery."

"See you in a few minutes," he said. He could have been an old friend eager to meet her after a long absence.

As soon as she hung up, she took a deep breath and let herself shake. "Oh, my God, what have I done?" she said out loud. She rubbed her hands over her face and pushed her hair back from her forehead.

She picked up the receiver again and dialed 911, but before the first ring, she hung up. If the police came, they would almost certainly scare the Jaguar away. The opportunity to trap him would be lost. The only reasonable thing was to let Eric know the Jaguar was about to show up on his doorstep.

She dialed the switchboard number of Eastern General Hospital. She had called Jeff dozens of times, so it didn't surprise her that she remembered the number. But she was glad she did, because she needed all the time she could get.

A female operator answered on the sixth ring, and Jill asked for Security. The line clicked and popped, then she found herself listening to the repetitious buzz of a busy signal.

"The line is busy," the operator said.

"This is an emergency," Jill said. "Can you break in?"

"I'm not supposed to do that," the woman said. "The police have taken charge of the Security phones."

"But this is a police matter," Jill said, her voice rising from frustration and anger. "I've got to talk to Lieutenant Firecaster."

"I cannot override," the operator insisted. Jill was about to protest more, but then the operator said, "I think a line is free now." Jill let out a sigh of relief as she heard the phone at the other end begin to ring.

"Snack Bar," a rough male voice said.

"I was trying to get Security," Jill said.

"Then you've got the wrong number, don't you?"

"Can you switch me back?" she asked.

"I don't know nothing about that," the man said. "You can call back." He slammed the phone down so hard it hurt her ear.

She rapidly punched in the hospital number once more.

"We've been having trouble with the lines," another operator told her when she explained what had happened.

"Could you try again?" Jill asked. Her voice was almost pleading.

"The line is busy now," the operator said. "Why don't you call back in a few minutes."

"I really don't have much choice, do I." She didn't slam the receiver down, but she didn't replace it gently either.

She was starting to feel worried about the time she had wasted. How much time before the Jaguar showed up? She had no way of knowing. It might be half an hour or ten minutes. Her hands began to shake as she realized that if he came before she could get Eric, she would be unprepared to defend herself.

Besides, even if the Jaguar didn't break in and attempt to kill her, he would leave, and then they would then be no closer to catching him. If she was going to be a hunter, she had to think like one.

Jill made two decisions. She would wait exactly five minutes before trying again to get through to Eric. Meanwhile, she would look for something she could use as a weapon. Just reaching these decisions gave her a greater feeling of confidence.

She turned away from the telephone and glanced around the kitchen. The most likely weapon was a knife. She started pulling open cabinet drawers. She found cocktail napkins, placemats, measuring spoons, poultry shears, pot holders, skewers, lobster picks—everything but knives. She slammed each drawer shut and went on to the next. Time was running out.

Every kitchen had knives. But where were they? She had opened all the drawers on one side of the room when she noticed a shallow cabinet of dark wood above the stovetop.

She pulled open the door and saw the cabinet was filled with knives of every kind: chef's knives, boning knives with stiletto-thin blades, slicing knives, curved butcher knives, and various sorts of utility and paring knives. She selected a large chef's knife and slammed the door of the cabinet. The knife was over a foot long, with a chromed steel blade, and a jet black handle. It was a marvel of craft, a formidable weapon.

Her hand curved around the shaped wood in a tight grip. A slight projection at the back of the handle kept the knife from slipping out of her grasp. She made a few passes in front of her, swinging it as if it were a sword. The blade made brief whooshes as it sliced through the air.

With a weapon in her hand, she felt a surge of power. For all that, however, she knew she would have difficulty stabbing the Jaguar with the knife. When she thought of ramming the shiny steel blade into the body of a living person, it made her feel sick. It was so contrary to her feelings and her sense of herself she doubted she would be able to do it.

She felt a comfort in having the knife, but as she looked at it, she realized a gun would be better. She could use a gun to threaten, and the Jaguar would pay attention. With a gun she'd have distance. But if she was going to find one, she was going to have to act fast. The clock was running out, and she couldn't waste time searching the whole house.

Where would Eric be likely to keep a gun? She put the knife down on the countertop and stood still for a moment. She would have to forget about time slipping away and just make herself think.

The den! That was where he said he spent time when he was at home. It served as a transition point between working and resting, so it was the place he would keep anything connected with his work.

She hurriedly crossed the hall into the den and glanced around quickly. The library table at the end of the room across the window caught her attention. If Eric sat there doing his paperwork, it would also be a good place to store things.

The table had two large, shallow drawers. She slid out the first, but she saw at once that it contained nothing more interesting than blank paper and a plastic tray filled with paperclips and rubber-bands. An unopened roll of picture-hanging wire in a plastic bubble-pack jammed against the table as she attempted to close the drawer. Telling herself to hurry, she left it open and jerked out the other.

At first glance, the second drawer seemed equally disappointing. It was filled with letters, memos, and receipts thrown together in no particular order, but two objects caught her attention. On the right was a pocket-sized camera, and shoved to the back was a slender aluminum cylinder with a nozzle-shaped black plastic cap.

A white label with red letters identified the cylinder as containing Chemical Mace. Below the large red letters, a dense block of text listed the components of the substance and cautions concerning its use. She picked up the metal tube without wasting time reading the text.

She slid the cylinder into the front pocket of her jeans and hurriedly returned to the kitchen. She had gone over her five-minute limit, and she could feel the tension in the muscles of her shoulders and neck. She was beginning to listen for the doorbell and half expected it at any moment.

She would make one last effort to call Eric. If she couldn't get through on the first try, she would have to call the police.

Holding the receiver in her left hand, she punched in the Eastern General Hospital number. But something was wrong. She couldn't hear the tones as she touched the numbers with her finger. She put the receiver to her ear. No dial tone, no sound at all.

The line was dead.

She dropped the telephone and ran to the alarm box in the far corner of the kitchen. She pushed the button to send a signal to the police to set off an alarm bell.

Nothing happened.

Only then did she notice that the red ready-light on the box was no longer glowing.

31

Tuesday 11:30 P.M.

The employees' lounge was a large room with furniture too dilapidated to be used elsewhere in the hospital. Candy and soda machines were arranged along the back wall, and plastic-topped tables formed a semicircle in front of them.

While Renuzi was talking to Murphy, Firecaster walked to an unoccupied sofa pushed into one corner. In the opposite corner, three men and a woman sat at the row of telephones Renuzi had arranged to have assigned to them. Starting with Klore's mother in Newark and then with members of the hospital staff, everybody associated with him would be getting a phone call.

They would be asked about their relationship with Klore and what they knew about his relationships with others. The callers would be looking for evidence to connect Klore with somebody who also knew Jill, and each person would be asked for additional names. Eventually the net might snare the Jaguar.

Renuzi had the effort organized and running before Firecaster even arrived at the hospital. Although the work was tedious and time-consuming, it was standard police procedure. The possibility of uncovering significant information was slim, but the data would allow them to build up a picture of Klore's ordinary life so that anything unusual would stand out.

Firecaster was glad to see the operation proceeding so smoothly, and he was grateful to Renuzi for taking responsibility. It freed him from having to worry about organizational details of the investigation. Of course, the additional freedom only increased the pressure on him to come up with some ideas. He rubbed the left side of his face vigorously, as though he could massage away the tension.

"Ed says he can't start yet," Renuzi said, coming over to the couch. "Klore has to be declared, and we're still waiting for the M.E.'s office."

"I think it's safe to say a man without a head is dead," Firecaster said. "But I don't see any reason to hurry, because I suspect we're not going to learn much that isn't already clear."

Renuzi sat at the opposite end of the couch. "That depends on who is doing the looking," he said. "What were you saying earlier about obvious conclusions?"

"It's obvious that the room where Klore was killed is one only somebody familiar with the hospital would know about," Firecaster said. "I think we can take it for granted that the Jaguar either is or was on the staff of Eastern General, and that opens some possibilities for investigation."

"You bet," Renuzi said. "Let me tell you something else, because it's another piece of the same color that helps make the picture." He took a deep breath and tugged down his vest. "I got the name of Klore's secretary from Security, and while we were waiting for you, I called her. She said someone identifying himself as Ralph Majors from Radiology called the office around twelve-thirty. She wrote down his name, the way she does everybody who calls. He said he needed to talk to Klore about a patient, but he didn't know the patient's name. At first she thought he must mean a Mrs. Halprin, but then she remembered Mrs. Halprin had been discharged."

Renuzi took another deep breath, then continued to speak rapidly. "That made her suspicious, and she wouldn't tell him anything. She did say that Dr. Klore was in his lab and this Ralph Majors would have to talk to him."

"Is there a Ralph Majors?" Firecaster asked.

"Not here," Renuzi said. "At least not now. I had the personnel director run the name through their computers, and she told me Ralph Majors quit his job over a year ago. He moved to San Francisco and works at the University of California Medical Center."

"Let's confirm it," Firecaster said. "But I'm sure we both know what the story is likely to be."

"Ralph Majors is still in California, and the Jaguar somehow got his hands on Majors's ID tag," Renuzi said. "He pinned it to his lapel, then walked around the hospital like the Pope in Vatican City."

"Exactly," Firecaster said. "Is that what you meant about another piece of the same color?"

"That's it," Renuzi said. "Not only does he have an ID tag, but judging from the way he talked to Klore's secretary, he knows how things are done around here. He knows the right words, and he knows the music that goes with them."

"He's got insider knowledge," Firecaster agreed. "He knew how to get Klore out of his lab and down here, for one thing. By the way, have you checked Klore's lab yet?"

"I sent Donna Korvall to take a look," Renuzi said. "There's no sign of a struggle, but we also got a little more than that. The guy in the lab across the hall from Klore's was still working, and he said he saw Klore leaving around twelve-thirty or one o'clock. He also didn't see him come back."

"It's hard to believe Klore would make arrangements to meet somebody down here. I doubt he could even find this place."

"I think that's where the laundry cart played a role," Renuzi said. "I don't know if you looked at it, but it's got tape wrapped around the support poles. I imagine the Jag got Klore to meet him someplace, knocked him out, tied him to the cart, and wheeled him down here."

"Find out where the cart came from," Firecaster said. "Probably that's where Klore met up with the Jaguar."

"Right," Renuzi said. "We'll also look for a witness who saw somebody they didn't recognize pushing the cart."

"Good," Firecaster answered absently. His mind had returned to the Jaguar's telephone call. Something about it wasn't right. Why would he tip them off about Klore's body? How could it do him any good?

"Here's what to do first," Firecaster said, pulling himself out of his reverie. "Get the hospital personnel office to pull the records of every white male between twenty-five and fifty who is currently on the staff or who has been within the last three years."

"You've got it," Renuzi said.

"Next, call Ted Castle and tell him I would appreciate it if he came over here and took a look at the work of the Jaguar. Then get him to go over the personnel records with you, and see if he picks up on anything." He sensed that he was making the right decisions. Yet at a deeper level something about the phone call was still distracting him and keeping him from concentrating completely on the problems at hand.

"You've got it," Renuzi said again. He turned toward the open door, then hesitated. "This is a nasty one, isn't it?"

"The worst yet."

"I guess it must hit you pretty close to home," Renuzi said gently. "In a way, Jill is our best bet, isn't she? I mean, we do know he's going to be looking for her."

Suddenly Firecaster's heart seemed to catch, then stop. He saw in an instant that Jill was in more danger than ever. *Jill had called Klore.*

Klore was the only one who knew she was staying at his house, and Klore could have tried to save his own miserable life by telling the Jaguar where to find Jill. That's why he had broken his pattern and called to tell them where to find Klore's body. He wanted to get Firecaster out of the house so Jill would be there alone.

"I've got to go," Firecaster said sharply.

Then he was on his feet and pushing past the people standing in front of the lounge door. He rushed through the door and began running down the hall. He felt too sick with fear to be angry at his own stupidity.

As he ran through the blurred light of the hall, something seemed to grab at his feet, slowing him down despite his effort. He felt as if he were running down an endless tunnel half-filled with dark, bloodstained water.

32

Tuesday 11:45 P.M.

She felt sick. For a moment she thought she was going to throw up. Her stomach was knotted, and the muscles across her chest were so tight she could breathe only in short gasps. She never imagined she would have to face the Jaguar alone.

Running or hiding made no sense. He had to be near the house, because he had cut the phone line. If she ran, he would kill her in the street, and if she hid, he would break in and find her. Besides, how long could she cower in a dark closet, knowing a killer was searching for her?

Then it occurred to her—*she could still set a trap for the Jaguar.* Even if she couldn't capture him, she could make sure he got caught. She had told herself to think like a hunter, and that's what she should be doing. The prey was more cunning than she had realized, but now that she was more in control of herself, she realized she had a little time. He would want her to believe he had driven from Eastern General Hospital. Otherwise, she might get suspicious.

Even while she was thinking about having some extra time, a plan was beginning to take shape. She went back to the den and got out the package of picture wire from the library table. She ripped off the cardboard and pulled the roll out of its plastic bubble. She jerked open the other drawer and took out the camera. The frame-counter showed eight exposures still remained. That would be more than she needed. She examined the flash attachment, and to be sure she knew how it worked, she flashed it once. The sharp whiteness of the light made her blink.

She returned to the kitchen and put the camera on the countertop next to the porch door. The fact that the porch curved around to the front of the house was the basis of her plan. The door itself was a slab of solid oak, and she couldn't see out.

She examined the wire. It was double-stranded and strong enough for her purpose. She turned off the lights in the kitchen. No need to backlight herself in the doorway. Wherever the Jaguar was hiding, he wouldn't be in a position to view the whole house, and most likely he was watching the front.

She turned the deadbolt, then clicked back the spring lock. She set the latch so that if the door slammed shut, she wouldn't be locked out. She then pulled the door open slowly and felt a slight change in temperature. The air caught between the oak door and the aluminum storm door was colder than the air in the kitchen. She opened the storm door as wide as it would go. The outside air was even colder, and her sweatshirt and jeans felt inadequate. She held the door open and moved the metal slide on the door-closer until it reached the cotter pin at the end. She tugged against the door, but it didn't move.

She stepped silently onto the porch and immediately backed up against the wall. She stood for a moment to allow her eyes to grow accustomed to the dark. She listened, straining her ears for even small sounds. She could hear the faint noise of traffic and the rattling of the trees in front. The yew bushes growing beside the porch made their own small scratching sounds.

She worked her way toward the front of the house. She walked with her back flattened against the wall to avoid presenting a silhouette. The floor of the porch creaked slightly. It was a faint noise, but to her ears, each creak sounded like a small explosion.

She reached the point where the porch turned the corner and the back of the house was sharply separated from the front. There was nothing to tie the wire to at the apex of the curve, but a few feet behind it, in the direction of the kitchen, a faucet jutted out from the wall two feet above the porch floor.

The ornamental bib was in the shape of a small animal. She knelt down, staying closely pressed against the house, and tied the end of the wire around the valve stem. She then wrapped half a dozen turns around the bib. She jerked on the wire to make sure it wouldn't come loose.

Paying out the wire from the spool, she crept across the porch to one of the columns. The decorative trim at the top was hardly above eye level, and it was an easy matter to pass the wire between two pieces of fretwork. She pulled the wire attached to the faucet until it was tight, then wrapped the wire twice around the trim.

The wire now cut a taut, straight line between the faucet and the trim. It slanted from a height of five feet to two feet and was invisible in the darkness. She pushed against it with the flat of her hand and was satisfied it was securely anchored.

She left the storm door propped open, but quietly closed the inner door and threw the deadbolt into place. She took a deep breath, then expelled it with a great sigh of relief. She turned on the lights again. She patted her pocket to reassure herself that the can of Mace was still there. Next she put the chef's knife on the counter by the door and arranged the handle so it stuck out. She then placed a small stepping stool beside the door. The stool was heavy enough to use as a door prop but light enough to be shoved aside without difficulty.

She checked the camera again and moved the film forward to be sure the first shot would be on an unexposed frame. She slipped her left hand through the dangling black strap so the camera would stay attached to her, even if she dropped it.

She again turned off the kitchen lights, leaving on the small bulb above the stove. She sat down on the stool and avoided looking in that direction. She wanted her eyes to become adjusted to the dark. The next move was the Jaguar's. All she had to do was wait.

33

Tuesday 11:55 P.M.

She settled herself on the stool, pushed her knees together, and crossed her arms. She took a deep breath, exhaled slowly, and told herself to relax. Her ragged breathing became smoother.

Then the doorbell rang. Only it didn't really ring. Instead, chimes struck one another and tinkled out a three-note sequence. The chimes resonated for a moment in a soft, gradually diminishing hum before lapsing into silence. They tinkled once more, then again. The signal was supposed to be two long rings of the doorbell then a short one, but pushing the button only made the chimes strike. Short and long rings were impossible. That would give her time. He would assume she was confused.

She opened the kitchen door and clicked the spring lock so it would latch automatically when the door slammed shut. She placed the stool in the doorway to keep that from happening accidentally. Once on the porch, she quickly flattened herself against the brick wall.

While waiting for her eyes to adapt to the deeper darkness, she took the can of Mace out of her pocket. She held the canister near the top so her index finger could reach the valve. She moved down the porch rapidly, almost at a run. She stayed on her toes and didn't worry about creating a silhouette. She knew where the Jaguar was and he couldn't see her.

She felt an increasing excitement and warned herself to move carefully and do nothing to give herself away. She slowed as she approached the column with the wire. For her to run into it and trip would turn her plan into a deadly farce. She ducked her head and crossed under where the wire was highest.

She crept to the wall and flattened her back against it so she could peer around the corner. Through her sweatshirt, she could feel the cold bricks pressing against her skin. She no longer felt chilled, though. She leaned forward and turned her head toward the front door. The fixture above it spilled out a pool of light illuminating everything within the circle with an intense white brightness. She could see him perfectly.

Her first impression was that she had made a terrible mistake. A killer might be attractive, but would he have such a stylish haircut? Would he wear his overcoat with such flair? This wasn't somebody who had crawled out of the gutter. Even the way he held his body showed he was used to being in charge of things.

He was standing directly in front of the door, his arms crossed over his chest. He was smiling faintly and kept his eyes on the door. He didn't seem tense or hurried. He could have been a man whose lover has invited him to come by for a late-night drink and who is patiently waiting for her to answer the door.

He seemed so familiar it was even possible she had met him somewhere. He wasn't somebody she had ever spent time with, but she could have been introduced to him. She might have talked to him for a few minutes in a class or at a party or while waiting in line.

His appearance had made her hesitate, but as he reached forward to push the doorbell again, she acted. She stepped around the corner, stood with her feet slightly spread, and raised the camera. She looked through the viewfinder to get the subject in sight but made no effort to correct the focus. It would have to do. She triggered the shutter with her eyes closed.

As the flash exploded in the darkness surrounding her, the Jaguar turned toward her. She had the camera raised in front of her, but she gave up all thought of taking another picture. For a moment she stood transfixed by the change that had come over him. His face was distorted with rage, his lips pulled back in an angry snarl that exposed his teeth. His eyes were opened wide and seemed to protrude from his face.

The flash must have blinded him, but nevertheless, he was rushing in her direction. His response was as automatic as a machine's, and with a hollow feeling, she sensed it was too late to run. He had crossed at least half the distance separating them, and by the time she turned, he would be on top of her. She had to try to stand her ground.

She released the camera and let it swing by the wrist strap, then spread her feet farther apart and held the can of Mace in front of her. She pointed the nozzle directly toward him. He came rushing at her against the bright light, his form huge and dark, like a truck bearing down on her. It was all she could do not to look away, but she stood as if welded to the spot.

When he was within ten feet, she pressed the button on the Mace can. A jet of chemical shot out in a hissing stream, but it lacked the power to reach his face. The stream curved downward and struck him on the left leg. An irregular pattern of white appeared on his dark trousers, and the air was fouled with biting fumes.

He looked surprised, as though he couldn't believe she was fighting back. He checked his headlong rush toward her for a fraction of a second. But since she had missed his head, the Mace had no apparent effect on him. If anything, he became angrier and more menacing. His mouth was opened wide, and he was breathing heavily, almost panting.

Her eyes smarted from the acrid chemicals that filled the air, but she held out the can to spray another stream. Once more she held down the plastic button, pushing so hard the ridges on its surface bit into her finger. The can emitted a soft hiss, but nothing came out the nozzle.

Her body reacted without any orders. She threw the can right into the face of the Jaguar. Although he raised an arm to protect himself, it was too late. The cylinder smashed into his cheek directly beneath his eye. She was running before she knew what she was doing. The rubber soles of her shoes gripped the slick surface of the porch and gave her the traction needed to keep up her sprint. She pumped her legs, almost falling forward in her hurry. Her shoes made dull thudding sounds as they slapped against the smooth planking.

Immediately behind her, she could hear the echoing repetition of a dry, rasping noise as the slick leather of the Jaguar's shoes scrabbled on the floor. For a terrifying instant, she confused the dry noises of the shoes with the leathery rustling sound of the snake. She could feel twin points of pain in the calf of her right leg.

Then she felt herself flying forward as the Jaguar shoved with his fingertips against her back, causing her to lose balance. She hit the floor with her hands and experienced burning pain as the skin of her palms scraped against the wood. She scrambled forward on her hands and knees, crawling like a dog. She thought she was out of range, but then his hands were around her right ankle, grasping it above the top of her running shoe.

She twisted her body around and dropped flat onto the floor. Her ankle turned in his hands, and he was thrown off balance. She kicked with her right foot, and as she did so, she bent forward and swung the camera on its strap through a short arc. The camera connected with his head, making a surprisingly loud thud, but the camera strap broke off her wrist and the camera itself went skittering across the floor.

When the camera struck him, he made no sound but he jerked his head backward. She then pulled her right leg toward her with all her strength. His grip didn't break, but his fingers slipped so they were on her shoe instead of her ankle. She twisted her foot loose, leaving the shoe in his hand. Then she was up and running again.

The skin on her palms burned, and her chest was hurting. She was breathing in ragged gasps. But he was still behind her, and she could hear his breathing above her own. The sound drove her on, as though it were a force pressing against her.

Then the wire was directly in front of her. She couldn't see it, but she recognized the column. She veered left toward the edge of the porch. She didn't dare turn and look, but the dry slapping sounds now seemed to come from her right.

The night was black, but the bushes at the edge of the porch seemed reassuringly familiar. She wondered for a moment whether something so peculiar could be happening to her, then a wave of hopelessness washed over her. Time was suspended, and she felt frozen in place.

Then she heard a guttural expression of rage and frustration behind her. A chill went through her, then a surge of energy. She threw herself forward and ducked under the wire. Almost immediately, she heard a dull twanging followed by a tumbling crash. She turned her head and saw the Jaguar lying facedown on the porch floor.

An extraordinary sense of relief flooded through her. She stopped running and stood staring at the fallen figure, as fascinated by the horror it represented as she had been by the writhing body of the stunned snake. In the shadowy light, she could just make out that his hands were thrown forward and his head was flat against the floor. She took a step closer, wanting to make sure he was unconscious. She could hear the breath rasp in his throat. She bent over to get a better look.

His hand shot out to grab her. She jumped backward, and the

hand flailed the empty air. Before she turned completely around, he was up and coming toward her once more.

An almost suffocating desperation drove her forward. The kitchen door stood wide open no more than fifteen feet in front of her; in no more than six steps she could be safe. She counted each step up to five, then she threw herself across the threshold. She knocked the stool to one side, and while it was still clattering on the floor, she grabbed the edge of the heavy door and shoved it toward the opening.

The door was within inches of clearing the inside of the frame when the heel of the Jaguar's hand hit it from the outside. She threw herself against the door, and immediately felt a countervailing pressure from the other side.

Without her right shoe, it was hard to get a grip on the slick surface of the kitchen floor. She placed both hands flat against the door and pushed with her left foot. If everything depended on a shoving contest, she would lose.

The Jaguar's hand reached inside the door, and his fingers curled around the edge. That made it impossible for her to close the door and activate the spring lock.

"You can't get away," he said. His voice sounded strained with effort. "You belong to me now."

She jammed the side of her left foot against the door, letting the rubber sole of her shoe act as a doorstop on the varnished floor. Stretching out as far as she could reach, she snatched the chef's knife off the countertop.

A sudden shove on the door forced her to throw all her weight against it. He knew he could wear her down. He was pushing steadily, letting up the pressure, then pushing again. Soon he would give a single hard shove, and she would lose her balance. The shoe wouldn't help anymore.

He eased the pressure once again, and she turned the knife in her hand so she was grasping it by the handle. She raised the heavy blade over her shoulder, ready to bring the sharp edge down on the Jaguar's fingers. But she realized she couldn't do it; she couldn't cut off somebody's fingers.

She felt the pressure on the door increase again, and she quickly changed her grip on the knife and held it underhanded. Then without hesitating, she jabbed the point of the knife at the row of fingers curled around the door. She felt the point stick into flesh, and it was horrible. She saw blood spurt from the damaged fingers, then the hand jerked back.

She dropped the knife and shoved against the door with all the weight and power she could summon. The door slammed into the frame with a bang, and the spring lock clicked into place. She immediately snapped on the deadbolt.

Something then hit the door, rattling and shaking it. Another blow fell. He was kicking the door, she decided, seeing if he could break the locks loose. The door was old but solid, and there was no sound of splintering. She hoped a neighbor would hear him, and call the police.

The pounding on the door ceased abruptly. She put an ear against the panel, but she could hear nothing. It occurred to her she should be able to look onto the porch from the windows in the dining room. She picked up the knife and pushed past the swinging door.

The room was dark, and she wasn't sure where the furniture was. She dropped to her knees and crawled along the floor, feeling her way with her fingers. She found the edge of the rug, then crossed the cold hardwood floor until she felt the drapery. She stood up and inched sideways to the window nearest the kitchen. She teased back the edge of the curtain.

The dining room was so dark the porch seemed almost lighted. He was still there, hardly six feet from where she was standing. She shuddered, her hand tightening around the hilt of the knife.

He was on his knees and moving his hands around, his actions mimicking her own trip through the dark. Except he seemed to be searching for something. The camera! Of course that's what he was looking for. He wouldn't want to leave a photograph of himself behind. He suddenly stood up and jammed something into his coat pocket. He walked along the porch toward the front of the house. *What was he doing?*

She stood up and guided herself into the living room by touching the wall. She wanted to be able to look out the living room windows and keep a watch on him.

Shuffling her feet on the carpet and groping for the next piece of furniture, she made her way slowly through the dark living room. When she was a yard away from the pale rectangle of the large front window, it exploded in a loud crash of splintering glass. She reeled back and threw a hand in front of her face to ward off fragments, but the drapes kept the glass from flying out. Shards fell harmlessly to the floor with a crystalline tinkle that sounded inappropriately cheerful.

She froze in position, holding the knife in front of her with its blade pointing toward the window. She waited for the Jaguar to push aside the curtains and rush toward her.

She was ready to fight or to run, and she was not scared anymore.

He wouldn't expect her to be waiting for him, and this time she would steel herself. She couldn't expect to stay alive unless she did her best to kill him.

She waited, still as a painted panel, the knife raised and her hand steady. But no one came through the window. Holding the knife in front of her like a sword, she made her way toward the right side of the broken window. She felt along the floor with the toe of her shoe to keep from cutting her right foot on the shards of glass.

She pulled back the edge of the drape and looked out. She saw jagged glass in the frame, but she also saw something that surprised her. Inside the window was an ornamental iron grating, hidden from the outside by the frosted glass of the panes.

Beyond the grating, she could see nothing but the gray darkness of the porch. *But where will he try next?* she wondered. Maybe a basement window, maybe a door she didn't know about. She could only wait and listen.

She then heard faintly the high shrill note of a police siren. She turned her ear toward the window and in another moment was sure the siren was coming nearer. Rapid footsteps crossed the porch, then she heard a car start out front and the whine of an accelerating engine.

She let the corner of the drape fall back into place and began to feel her way toward a light switch. The siren was much louder, and as she turned on the lights, the squeal of brakes reached her.

Then she heard the front door open and Eric's voice calling her name.

34

Wednesday 2:30 A.M.

Jill was leaning against the counter slowly stirring a saucepan on the stove when Firecaster came into the kitchen through the back entrance. The sound of the door startled her, and her heart began to pound in her chest. She reminded herself that she was safe now and took a deep breath. She held it until her pulse slowed.

Firecaster sat down at the butcher block table without saying a word. She started to say something about how he'd frightened her, but he looked so worn out she kept quiet.

Despite the chill night air, Firecaster's forehead glistened with a thin film of sweat. Deep lines ran from the wings of his nose to the corners of his mouth, and his hair was as tousled as if he had just climbed out of bed. His shoulders slumped forward, but his eyes were still alert. In the brightness of the kitchen's hanging globe, they shone with the hard light of dark blue glass.

The forensics crew working on the porch had just packed up their equipment and left. Jill had heard Firecaster asking Murphy's assistant when he could expect the results, then saying good-night to them. Now, after the lights, noise, and commotion of having the police searching the backyard, scouring the porch for evidence, and boarding up the broken window, the kitchen seemed strangely quiet. The loudest noise was the scraping of her spoon against the pan.

"What are you making?" Firecaster asked. His voice was thick with fatigue. "It smells good."

"Cocoa," she said. "I needed something to calm me down, and I remembered your talking about how your grandmother used to make cocoa. So I opened a few cabinets, and there was the can. You want some?"

"Only if you've got enough."

"I've got enough for you," she said.

Jill took two white mugs from the cabinet beside the sink and poured each full of hot chocolate. Steam rose from the dark frothy surface of the cocoa. She put one mug in front of Firecaster, then sat with hers across from him at the table.

It was the first time they had been alone since she had hurriedly given him an account of what had happened. He had immediately taken charge of the search and insisted she stay out of the way. She was happy to agree; it was a great luxury just to feel secure and protected. She spent over an hour by herself in the den. At first she had paced the room like a caged animal, unable to relax at all, but eventually she calmed down some. Now she felt settled enough to be curious about what had been happening, but Firecaster looked so tired she resolved not to ask him any questions. She could wait until tomorrow.

"He's vanished like a ghost in the daylight," Firecaster said. He sat silently for a moment, then took a sip of the cocoa. It seemed to revive him a little. "I ordered a four-square-block search centering on the house and put out an area-wide bulletin on the car, but

191

nothing's turned up yet." He shrugged. "Of course, once he got out of the neighborhood and hit Mass Ave, he could have been ten miles away before we made our first move."

He looked up from his cup and gave her a rueful smile. "What's ironic is that it's entirely possible I drove right past him when I was coming and he was going."

"You couldn't have known what kind of car to look for until I gave you the description," Jill pointed out.

"I did pass a dark blue car that might have been a Buick," Firecaster said. "And it had just one man in it, too."

"It could have been him," Jill agreed.

"It's possible he lives so close that he ducked home before we could get the search going," Firecaster said. A current of anger seemed to pass through him. The muscles of his face tightened, widening his eyes and drawing his mouth into a narrow line. "That's what makes everything about the Jaguar so damned frustrating. I know he's right under our noses, yet we can't touch him." As he talked he jabbed the table with the tip of a finger, as though by his action he could pin down the Jaguar.

"Have you called off the search?" Jill asked.

"I canceled the extra people," Firecaster said. He took a deep breath and let it out as a long sigh. "If you don't make a collar in the first half hour of a search, your chances become very remote. And I kept things going full steam for close to two hours." He shook his head. "It's in the hands of the regular patrols now. They've got your description and orders to stop and question anybody driving a dark blue Buick."

"I wish I could tell you more to help," Jill said.

"You've given us so much that if we can't catch this guy, we ought to be sued for malpractice," Firecaster said. "We know what kind of car he was driving, and we've got a blood sample from the knife. We've got his physical description, and we'll probably find his hair on the clothes you were wearing." He paused. "We've also still got you."

"I'm not complaining," she said. "Too bad you don't have his picture, though." She gave Firecaster a pained smile.

"I can't imagine what possessed you even to think of trying that," he said. He shook his head in disapproval, but she thought she could detect pride in his voice.

"I don't know what went wrong," she said. "Things always work out for Nancy Drew."

"She's had a lot more experience," Firecaster said. He smiled at her, but he still looked tired. He took a sip of cocoa. "Now that you've had a couple of hours to think things over, do you think the Jaguar is somebody you know?"

"I've actually been trying *not* to think about him," Jill said. "My nerves are pretty shot after two days of this."

"I know that's true," Firecaster said. He gave her a sympathetic look. "I don't like asking you." He hesitated. "Do you understand that I have to?"

Jill nodded. "I'm sure I never met him," she said. "I told you I thought I might have seen him before." She hesitated. "I'm not even sure about that, though. What I meant was that he seemed like someone I *might* know."

Firecaster looked puzzled. "I don't understand," he said. "You mean he's somebody you can imagine knowing?"

"That's it," Jill said. "He looked well taken care of, and he had a certain flair that's hard to describe."

"You think he might be a professional? A doctor, lawyer, professor, somebody like that?"

"Could be. Maybe a scientist or an executive. Something that makes you accustomed to having people look up to you."

"Think he could be a cop?"

"Maybe," Jill said. "He certainly did a good imitation."

"A better imitation than mine," Firecaster said. He lowered his eyes. "My stupidity almost got you killed."

"You can't blame yourself," Jill said. She reached across the table and placed her hand on his. "I'm the one who insisted on being left here alone."

"That doesn't alter the fact that I had a failure of imagination," Firecaster said. "I knew about Klore, but I didn't see how he could pose any threat. That's the failure."

"You were distracted," Jill said. "We were both distracted." She gave his hand a reassuring squeeze.

Firecaster glanced up at her and shook his head slowly. "We've got to be exceedingly careful," he said. "You were on the Jaguar's schedule for today, because it's been twenty days since he killed Hamilton. You messed up his plans, but you can be sure he's not going to give up. If anything he's even more dangerous now, because he's a wounded animal."

"Because I hit him in the face and stabbed his hand?" she said. "They weren't serious wounds, you know."

"Not in themselves," Firecaster agreed. "But they were significant ones."

Jill nodded to show she understood. "You mean I wounded his pride."

"Right," Firecaster said. "You humiliated him, so now he wants to hunt you down to get his revenge."

A feeling of dread took possession of her, and she suddenly became cold all over.

Firecaster got out of his chair and moved quickly around the table. He knelt down by her chair and put his arms around her. He held her tightly for a moment, kissed her, then pulled her close against him once more.

"Don't worry," he said, his voice husky. "Now that I've found you, I'm never going to lose you."

"I know, I know," was all she could say. She sounded tight and choked. Then, to her surprise, warm tears began to trickle down her cheeks.

PART FOUR

April 27
Wednesday

35

Wednesday 11:00 A.M.

Jill was sitting in his office on the same metal chair she sat on the night they met. Only now she sprawled out in a careless way, her body turned sideways and her feet stuck out in front of her. He thought she was attractive then, but now he realized she was beautiful.

"I've got to keep working," she said. "I can't put my life on hold because of some maniac."

"I understand," Firecaster said. "But I would feel happier if I could keep you in my hip pocket until we know you're absolutely safe."

"But that won't be until you catch the Jaguar," she said.

"We've got a lot better chance of doing that than we did twenty-four hours ago."

"But you still don't know when it will be," Jill said. "It might be tomorrow, and it might be two months from now. We're back to square one—I can't put my life on hold."

"How much risk do you think going to the convention involves?" Firecaster asked.

She raised one shoulder slightly. "Almost none, I imagine. It's a huge public affair. Over two thousand people are supposed to be there, and I can't imagine the Jaguar attacking me in the middle of a crowd."

"It's true that he doesn't seem to work that way," Firecaster said. "Where is the convention?"

"The Cambridge Plaza."

"At least it's a public place," Firecaster said. "I don't guess it's any more risky than anyplace else."

"Except for your hip pocket." She smiled.

"Or my vest pocket," he said. "How about if I have somebody drop you off and pick you up?"

"That's okay," Jill said. "But what I don't want is somebody tagging along and watching me." She paused and looked at Fire-

197

caster to see if he was going to object. He said nothing, and she went on. "Having a bodyguard would make me self-conscious and cramp what little journalistic style I've got."

"What if I insisted on protection?" Firecaster asked.

"I would say I'm not under arrest," Jill said. She sat up straighter in the chair, and her voice sounded strained. "I would say you don't own me, and I'm free to do whatever I want without interference." She looked at him without blinking.

Firecaster nodded. Then after a long pause he said, "Stay with the crowd and don't get isolated."

"I will," she promised. She slouched back in her chair and smiled shyly, as though she had surprised herself by her own vehemence.

"Just one other precaution," he said. He opened a desk drawer and took out a small black plastic box. He lifted the hinged lid and removed a silver octagonal pin with a raised green enamel circle set in the center. He handed it to her.

"It's very heavy," she said. She weighed it on the tips of her fingers. "It's also rather clunky." She turned the pin over and examined the single post with its threaded fastener.

"It costs over eight hundred dollars," Firecaster said. "I had to leave a departmental charge form for that amount with Special Services."

"That doesn't make it pretty."

"It might make it useful, though," Firecaster said. "It's a transmitter with a button-sized lithium battery and a silicon chip. If you lift the green circle, it starts broadcasting at a fixed frequency." He held up a device the size of a small transistor radio. "This is the receiver. I'm clipping it on my belt. Where are you going to attach the pin?"

Jill shrugged. "I've never been wired up before. How about on my shirt?" She glanced down and touched a spot above her left breast.

Firecaster came from behind the desk, surveyed her for a moment, then shook his head. "Not so good," he said. "It would be too easy for it to get torn off in a struggle. How about the waistband of your pants? Corduroy's tough, and the waistband is extra thick."

"Whatever you say," Jill said. "Except you're going to have to help put the fastener through." She handed him the pin, then stood up and moved close to him. She turned her body so he could easily reach her hip.

"Above the belt okay?" Firecaster asked. He inserted the point of the thick post through the black corduroy, then twisted on the fastener.

"When am I supposed to push the button?"

"You don't push it, you pull it," Firecaster said. "And you do

198

that whenever you feel you might need help. Don't let the possibility of a false alarm make you hesitate."

"Can you really get the signal this far away?"

"Special Services said it would carry for five miles, even with buildings in the way," Firecaster said. "The hotel is less than three from here. That seems like a safe margin of error."

"It looks perfect there." She twisted her head to look down at the pin. "I don't know how I ever lived without it."

The irony of her remark struck them both at the same time. She looked at him, and he could see she was more frightened than she admitted. She said nothing, but she suddenly moved closer and embraced him.

"Don't forget what I said last night about the Jaguar being more dangerous than ever," he told her. He rubbed his cheek against the top of her head. Her hair smelled of the same sweet herbal odor he had noticed the night he had driven her home.

"I won't," she said earnestly. "And don't you worry about losing me." She kissed him tenderly, then slipped out of his embrace. She turned toward the door and pulled it open. "Who's going to deliver me?" she asked. "I need to leave or I'll be late for the press lunch."

"Karen Chase has somebody lined up," he said. Jill placed her hand in his, and for a moment they stood not moving, just looking into one another's eyes. "Be careful," he said. His voice was almost a whisper. .

"I promise," Jill said. She gave his hand a final squeeze that left his fingers tingling. Then she was gone.

He longed to call her back and ask her not to go, even order her not to go. At the same time, he felt guilty because he hadn't been completely honest with her. He had let her believe he was going along with her refusal of police protection. Yet when Jill reached the convention she would be watched. Detective Helen Kim had orders to stick to her and intervene at any sign of trouble. Four other people were there to keep an eye on the entrances and assist Helen if need be.

He put his head in his hands and looked down at the scarred surface of his desk. He wasn't at all sure he had handled the situation well. The only possibilities open to him had been unacceptable. If he had refused to let Jill go to the convention alone, it would have caused serious conflict between them. He had already seen how much she valued her independence, and he didn't doubt it was enough to make her leave him. Yet by allowing her to go at all, he was letting her take a terrible risk.

Until they had the Jaguar, she was going to be as vulnerable as a tethered lamb staked out to attract a tiger.

36

Wednesday 11:45 A.M.

The conference room was hot and reeked of stale cigar smoke. Karen Chase added to the foul atmosphere by lighting a cigarette as soon as she took her place at the mahogany table. Don Renuzi gave her a look of disapproval and fanned the smoke away from his face.

Firecaster had asked Ted Castle to join them, and he was sitting with Ed Murphy on the opposite side of the table. They were bent over a page filled with columns of abbreviations and numbers.

"Ed has priority again," Firecaster said. "He has to be in court in an hour." He stood at the head of the table, resting his hands on the back of the green leather chair. The aspirin he had swallowed half an hour earlier still hadn't stopped the dull pain in his head.

Murphy took the paper from Castle and looked down at it. "We did the sperm wash the Lieutenant asked for," he said. "We recovered a residue of seminal fluid from the edge of the plumbing access panel. We rehydrated it, but we found no sperm cells." He glanced up from his notes. "That's unusual and is compatible with either some medical condition in which sperm isn't produced or a vasectomy." He nodded toward Ted Castle. "Dr. Castle agrees that a vasectomy is more likely."

"Aspermia is relatively uncommon," Ted Castle said.

"You couldn't find out the blood type?" Renuzi asked Murphy.

"Not without cells," Murphy said. "We do have the blood sample from the knife. I took it to Genident last night, and they sent the results over this morning. This is what we call a genetic fingerprint." He held up a sheet of photographic paper with fuzzy black bars against a white background. "The pattern of these bands is unique to an individual."

"Is there a central file of genetic prints?" Chase asked.

"Not yet," Murphy said. "There's just talk."

"Then what good is the damned thing," Renuzi said. "We need a blood type to help the investigation."

"Sorry," Murphy said. "I misled you. The technique also identifies the blood group." He glanced at the typed page. "It's O-positive."

"Why didn't you say so," Renuzi said. "Eastern General's per-

200

sonnel files include the blood type of everybody who ever worked there."

Firecaster cut him off. "If nobody has any questions, let's let Ed go, and then we can get down to those kinds of details." He looked around, then nodded to Murphy, who gathered up his red files and left. "Okay, Don, back to screening the hospital records. What have you and Dr. Castle come up with?"

"Nothing," Renuzi said. "What's so frustrating is that I feel sure the perp worked there or still does, but I don't know if we can pick out his file."

Ted Castle tapped his finger on the stack of green and white paper in front of him. "The printout doesn't give us enough personal information about these people to establish psychiatric probabilities," he said. "I was just glancing through, and I see dozens of people with O-positive blood."

He looked down at a page. "Here's somebody who's twenty-seven, worked in maintenance, and has one felony conviction." He looked up at Firecaster. "On the basis of this much information, he's a good bet."

"We'll get the computer to list people like that, then run them down," Renuzi said. He puffed out his cheeks and made a whooshing noise. "I was hoping it could be quicker."

"May I look at the file?" Firecaster asked. Castle put the pages in order and handed him the folder. Firecaster took it and sat down.

The others were quiet while he flipped through the printout. Chase lit another cigarette, and Renuzi scowled at her.

Firecaster skimmed the pages, reading nothing with any particular care. He saw the names of people identified as physicians, nurses, secretaries, dieticians, clerks, and respiratory therapists. Then all at once he realized something was not there. A whole category was missing from the entries, and it might be just the one they were looking for.

"Ted," Firecaster said. "Didn't you tell me it was likely the perpetrator might be associated with the police in some way?"

"The data we have show there's a high statistical correlation," Castle said. "One theory is that the police represent power and authority, just what such people lack. They are attracted to the police to try to fill that void." He leaned forward on his elbows, then sat back in his chair. "The statistics aren't just for police professionals. It's equally likely the perpetrator might be a special deputy, corrections officer, or even a citizen ride-along."

"Or maybe a security guard," Firecaster said. That was the missing category. "Maybe at a hospital."

Castle's eyes opened wide and his lips parted. "Exactly!" he exclaimed. "I think you've got it." His voice was loud and excited. "May I see the file again?" He stood and reached along the table. Still standing, he began turning through the file. The accordion-fold pages unfurled and piled on top of one another. "We completely missed it," he said.

"Don't forget about the slow learners," Chase said.

"Nobody in hospital security, past or present, is on this list," Castle said. He dropped to his chair and perched on the edge. "We've got doctors, office staff, laundry workers—everybody you can imagine—but we don't have a single name from security."

"And I know why," Renuzi said. He spoke quietly. "The hospital doesn't have its own security department. They contract with the Allen Agency, so we need their personnel files too."

"Can you get them?" Castle asked.

"I don't anticipate a problem," Renuzi said. "Should they take priority over the hospital files?"

"Absolutely," Castle said, speaking forcefully. "If the perpetrator worked for the hospital, the probability is high he worked in security."

"Current or past files, though?" Renuzi asked.

"Past," Castle said immediately. "Chances are he got fired. Either he came into conflict with a supervisor or he was found doing something dishonest or peculiar."

"How could you possibly know that?" Renuzi asked. He seemed more amazed than skeptical.

"I can't," Castle said. "I'm telling you data-based probabilities again."

"That's what we needed to narrow the search," Renuzi said. He slapped both hands on the table. "We can start going through names this afternoon. I know people at Allen."

Renuzi started to stand but sat back down when Chase spoke up. "I've got something that might be important," she said. "But you know the way things go. You think you've got something nailed down, then it turns out to be your own foot." She gave a hoarse laugh.

She tapped a cigarette on the ashtray in front of her. "We got the Seattle program running last night and fed it the inventories in all three cases." She lit the cigarette and continued talking. "We got several hits. Hamilton and Brenner have accounts at Coolidge Bank, and Thomas and Hamilton have a Sears credit card."

"That's not interesting," Renuzi said. "Three young women in the same city are bound to have a few things in common."

"Give me a break," Chase said. "However, we did turn up one

match that's out of the ordinary." She drew smoke deeply into her lungs, then exhaled it.

"Come on," Renuzi said. "We've got work to do."

"Chill it," Chase said. "I didn't interrupt you." She removed two blue postcards from a plastic evidence bag and dropped them in front of Renuzi.

"What are you showing me?" he asked. "Don't make me guess. I'm not in the mood for it." He read the address on one of the cards, then turned it over and looked at the back.

"The cards are from Bookkeepers Bookstore," Chase said. "One was sent to Marie Thomas and the other to Jill Brenner." She took another drag on the cigarette. "Both are notices that a book they wanted can be picked up. *The Space Merchants* for Thomas and *Dune* for Brenner." Chase paused. "I believe both are science fiction novels."

Firecaster felt his heart speed up and his chest tighten. Jill and Marie Thomas asked for science fiction books at the same store, both books were unavailable, and both people were sent cards. The connections seemed too close to be coincidental.

"How about Hamilton?" Firecaster asked. "Is there anything to tie her to Bookkeepers?"

"Possibly," Chase said. "Janet Quick said Anna Louise read a lot, and her apartment was filled with science fiction books. She must have gone to Bookkeepers some time, just because it's so big and so close." She rubbed out her cigarette in the ashtray. "One other thing. I'm no expert, but I think the handwriting on both cards is the same."

Firecaster took the cards from Renuzi, and while comparing them, he began to see in a shadowy way their role in the crimes. His headache had shrunk to a three-inch disk of numbness in his left temple. If it would just go away, he could concentrate better.

"Listen to this," Firecaster said. Then for what seemed an eternity, nothing came to him and he sat motionless. Finally the words started to flow. "Suppose the Jaguar works at Bookkeepers. A woman comes in, and he likes something about her. He gets her name and address by convincing her to let him fill out a blue card. If she refuses, he drops the matter, because he doesn't want to look suspicious."

"But what if they have the book she wants?" Renuzi objected. "She wouldn't have any reason to let him fill out a card."

"Maybe if she asks him for the book, instead of looking for it herself, he lies to her," Chase suggested. "He says they don't have it, but he'll be glad to order it." She shrugged. "Or he just forgets about women who don't want him to order a book, even if he finds them appealing."

"I don't think he would give up so easily," Firecaster said. "I can think of two other possibilities." He got up from his chair and wrote the number one on the chalkboard. "Suppose he starts talking to a woman about science fiction and tells her about a book she would like. Unfortunately, he says, we don't have it in stock. Would she mind requesting it? It wouldn't obligate her to buy it, and the store should have it anyway."

"He would have to know enough about science fiction to talk a good line," Renuzi said.

"People who read science fiction at all usually know a lot about it," Chase said. "I remember that from high school."

"Why would he mail the cards, unless the woman had really wanted him to order a book?" Renuzi asked.

"Because it would be suspicious if he didn't," Chase said. "The customer might start to wonder or maybe his boss might."

"Here's a second possibility," Firecaster said. He wrote the number two on the board, then turned around to face his audience. "Convincing women to let him fill out a blue card is just one of the ways he uses to get their addresses. Maybe he tells some he's putting together a mailing list of science fiction fans or that the store is considering giving away books in a promotion. Whatever he says, he can probably charm most women into giving him their address. He's good-looking and intelligent."

"He could use several techniques," Renuzi said. He spoke softly, as though talking to himself. "Maybe he just happened to use the same one with Thomas and Brenner."

Firecaster brushed the yellow chalk dust from his hands and sat down again. His eyes focused on the fake paneling at the end of the room, but he noticed nothing about it. He was thinking hard. He felt as if he were in a trance and some other intelligence was supplying him with thoughts. He was only a conduit to reach others.

"Maybe he builds up a file of women," Firecaster said. "Then he decides who he wants to follow up on. He picks one and watches her for a while." He stared at the paneling as if at a movie screen, then nodded his head as he settled a point.

"Maybe he considers two or three. Eventually he narrows the field to one. He goes after her, but he's cautious at first."

He fell silent a moment and felt a great reluctance to go on. "He spends weeks, maybe even months, planning exactly what he wants to do. Then he kills the woman he's picked. He cuts off her head, he mutilates her body—he does everything he has imagined. Maybe that's Thomas."

The words stopped coming automatically, and he rubbed the aching spot on the side of his head. He remained silent until, finally, the words began to flow again. "Everything goes just as he's planned, and he sees he's in no danger of getting caught. Also, he got more pleasure from the killing than he imagined possible. Not only does he want to do it again, he's got to do it. It's become his way of life, the way he denies the possibility of his own destruction. Maybe then he kills Hamilton."

He spread his hands flat on the surface of the table, leaned forward, and bowed his head. He gazed at the varnished mahogany as though peering into a mirror. "He's discovered a system he can use to control the world. Now he's free to turn everything into an elaborate and deadly game."

Firecaster shook his head. "That's when he chooses Jill and forces her into the role he's designed for her." Then in a voice softer than before, a voice wholly his own, he added, "And it isn't over yet."

37

Wednesday 1:00 P.M.

Haack arrived at the Cambridge Plaza Hotel in a dark blue stretch limousine. The driver pulled the car under the porte cochère, stepped out, and waved away a doorman in a rumpled brown coat. The doorman had braced his shoulders and attempted to look smart when he caught sight of the limousine, but the chauffeur's manner made clear he considered only himself worthy of opening the car door.

The car had soft leather upholstery, a well-stocked bar, digital stereo, a videotape player, and most important, windows tinted with a layer of burnished gold. Haack found it immensely satisfying to gaze out at people without their knowing he was watching them. They were animals in a zoo.

The chauffeur opened the door in a single sweeping gesture, then stood with one hand on the handle and the other held stiffly at his side. Attached to the front of his cap was a silver medallion of a springing lion, its mouth opened in a ferocious snarl—the emblem of Lion Limousines.

"Come for me at six o'clock, Clarence," Haack said. "I'll wish to go to dinner, then return afterward." He spoke in a formal fashion but didn't consider himself acting.

"Very well, sir," Clarence said. His tone was respectful, and if he felt self-conscious about playing a role, he kept it hidden.

Haack had arranged for the car three months earlier. As soon as he saw the necessity of attending the convention, he recognized he would need to travel in a limousine. His image and dignity would be compromised if he were forced to maneuver his own car through the traffic, then drive around in search of a parking lot not already filled.

The chauffeur waited attentively as Haack stepped onto the broad red carpet spread from the curb to the great bronze doors of the hotel's main entrance. Haack stood unmoving for a moment, his head erect, eyes fixed ahead of him. He was determined to soak up the experience to recall later and savor it in detail.

His arrival was attracting the attention he imagined it would. No one, not even famous science fiction writers, arrived at a convention in a chauffeured limousine. He glanced at the crowd. Fifty or sixty people, perhaps more, were milling around outside the entrance, and they all turned to look at him.

People in the crowd were jostling one another with much talking and laughing. When they caught sight of him, they seemed to freeze for a moment. Their actions stopped dead and the noise died away for an instant. Then very swiftly it swelled to an even greater volume. *They were talking about him.* Those about to enter the hotel stopped at the door and turned to look. A few people were pointing him out to those who had been too confused or distracted to know what the crowd was responding to.

He noticed with satisfaction that a number of those in the crowd were dressed in costumes representing science fiction characters. A Luke Skywalker in an orange flight suit and a Princess Leia with her hair rolled into flat coils were holding hands. On the opposite side of the red carpet was a man in an old-fashioned double-breasted suit wearing a wig of green tentacles. Haack guessed he was supposed to be one of the mutant telepaths from *Slan*. Four or five cyberpunks with pink and green hair and ripped black vinyl clothes were scattered here and there. Haack realized that what made him unusual was the appropriateness of the clothes he was wearing. Any fool could see they were not a mere costume but an expression of the nature of the wearer.

He took the first few steps up the carpet, and as he did the crowd

206

fell back, moving quickly out of his way. Then, as though the scene had been orchestrated, the people lined up on either side of the crimson path. It was as if they had been waiting for him and had made plans to provide him with a triumphal entry.

He was wearing a black stillsuit made by the Los Angeles costume company that had produced costumes for the movie of *Dune*. The suit was a replica of the ones Dr. Kynes had brought to Paul and his father to prepare them for their first trip into the desert of Arrakis. That was the suit Paul was wearing later when he put his hand on the rock shrine containing his father's skull, quoted from Bomoko's Legacy, and was recognized by the Fremen as one for whom all limitations are removed—the kwisatz haderach.

The suit fit him closely from neck to feet, like a scuba diver's wetsuit. It was made of ripstop nylon with an inner layer of soft insulating fiber. A black sash was wrapped around his waist. Attached to the suit on his left side was a black leather holster containing his stun gun.

Attached to the opposite side was a black high-impact plastic scabbard holding his crysknife. The knife was supposed to be made from the tooth of a sandworm, but his was actually the Tek survival knife he always kept with him. Its handle was black steel, and its wedge-shaped stainless blade was sharp as glass.

In honor of the occasion, he had draped across his back a crimson cape that hung from his shoulders to his knees. Surrounding his eyes was a mask of black silk. He hadn't planned it as part of his uniform, but he hadn't expected Jill Brenner to be able to identify him. The mask had the advantage of hiding the bruise below his eye on his left cheek. Two fingers on his left hand were bandaged with flesh-colored tape.

He was sure that since Jill was supposed to write about Boscon for *Boston Update,* she would be there. She wouldn't change her plans out of fear, and he liked that about her. Anyone could swat flies like Marie and Anna, but a true contest demanded a worthy adversary. *The Book of the Jaguar* could not astound its readers if there were no obstacles to overcome.

While the crowd watched in silence, he walked directly toward the great bronze doors. He held his head high, pulled his shoulders back, and looked neither to the left nor right. He stole surreptitious glances at the crowd out of the corner of his eye.

A woman standing somewhere near him said, "Wow, he's handsome." Her voice was at a conversational level, yet it carried across the still air like a shout.

Another woman said, "It's Paul, Paul Atreides!"

"Muuad-'Dib!" a man shouted. "The kwisatz haderach."

"Muuad-'Dib! Muad-'Dib!" a few people began chanting.

The chant was immediately taken up by the entire crowd. "Muad-'Dib, Muad-'Dib, Muad-'Dib . . ." was repeated again and again. Those lining the carpeted pathway raised their hands in salute. When Haack reached the bronze doors, the doorman in the rumpled coat pulled one open, then stood back to allow him to enter.

Haack turned to face the crowd. He smiled, then held up his right arm, his palm turned toward them. "I accept your water as tribute," he said in a booming voice. Without waiting for a response, he turned abruptly and walked through the doorway. As he did, he heard from behind an outbreak of applause.

Then the heavy bronze door closed behind him, and he quickly lost himself in the crowded hotel corridors.

38

Wednesday 1:15 P.M.

Firecaster and Karen Chase walked side by side down the main aisle of Bookkeepers. Firecaster said nothing but pointed toward the red plastic sign hanging in front of the office area. Karen Chase nodded.

Behind the counter, a young woman was seated at a desk. Firecaster noted automatically that she was in her early twenties, had a round face and short, blond hair. She was quite attractive.

"Are you the manager?" Chase asked.

"He's out right now," the woman said, looking up.

"Please check my identification." Chase held out a leather folder with her shield pinned to one side and her photo-ID opposite it. "We're police officers on official business. I'm Detective Chase and this is Lieutenant Firecaster."

"I'm Doris Wyden," the woman said. She looked startled, then stood up and awkwardly shook hands with each of them. "I don't know when Mr. Rimmer will be back. He's the manager."

"Maybe you can help us," Chase said. Her manner became warmer. "Who sends out cards to notify customers that books they wanted have arrived?"

"I do that." Doris Wyden seemed surprised by the question.

"Oh, good," Chase said. "We want to show you something." She took a manila envelope out of her blue canvas bag, unfastened the clasp, and extracted two glossy black and white photographs.

"Are the cards in these pictures like the ones you send customers?" Chase asked.

She examined each of the photographs carefully. "Ours are blue, but they look the same," she said.

"Do you remember sending either of these?"

"Not really." Doris Wyden shook her head and smiled. "The sales people give me dozens of them to mail. I hardly glance at them."

"How about the handwriting? Do you recognize it?"

Doris Wyden held a photograph in each hand and glanced from one to the other to compare them. "It's John Webb's," she said.

Firecaster felt his heart thump, as though it had skipped a beat. His face remained immobile, and he silently congratulated Chase for keeping her own excitement hidden.

"You're sure?" Chase spoke mildly, obviously trying not to spook Doris Wyden.

"I'm sure," she said firmly.

Firecaster felt himself relax. He was certain they had the right person. He knew it.

Doris Wyden then seemed to decide she had said too much. Spots of color stood out on her pale cheeks. She started to say something, then hesitated. Eventually she said, "I wish you would tell me what this is about. I'm not comfortable answering all these questions without knowing the reason."

"All I can tell you is that it's police business and we really need your help so we can help someone else," Chase said. She spoke casually and smiled. Then before Doris could realize her question hadn't been answered, Chase asked, "Does John Webb happen to be working today?"

"He's not scheduled," Doris Wyden said. "Most days he puts in a few hours, but he's off today."

"We'd like to talk to him," Chase said. Then she added, as though it had suddenly occurred to her, "Could we have his address and telephone number?"

Doris Wyden hesitated a moment, then said, "I'll get it for you." She sat at her desk and flipped through a roll-file. She wrote out the information on a sheet of paper and handed it to Chase.

"What does he look like?" Chase asked. "We don't want to pass him going out and not recognize him." She laughed.

"He's about six feet, well-built, blue eyes, sort of blond hair," Doris Wyden said. "He's twenty-nine, but he looks younger. He's very attractive."

"In case we miss him at home, do you know if he's supposed to work tomorrow?" Chase asked.

"From ten to six," Doris said. To explain the promptness of her answer she added, "I do the scheduling."

"You're being so helpful," Chase said warmly. She inclined her head to the right to get a glimpse of Firecaster. He nodded and moved forward so that he was standing beside her.

"Ms. Wyden, if you do the scheduling, does that mean you keep track of the times people work?" Firecaster asked.

"That's right," Doris said curtly.

"What sort of system do you use?" he asked.

"I hand a time card to everybody when they come to work or go on break," she said. She spoke slowly, as though reluctant to part with the information. "They fill it out and give it back to me."

"Do you still have the cards for the last couple of months?"

"I don't, because at the end of the week, I transfer the times to the ledger. Then I throw away the cards."

"If anybody wants to know about last month, then you can check the ledger?" Firecaster asked.

"That's right," Doris said. A change had come over her with the question. She almost whispered her answer, and she lowered her eyes. Before she had just been curious, but now she looked frightened. Something was upsetting her that hadn't before.

"I want you to check a date for me," Firecaster said. "Thursday, April seventh."

"Does this have something to do with John?" Doris suddenly asked. "I don't want to do anything that might get him in trouble."

"Are you pretty good friends?" Chase asked.

"In a way, I guess," Doris said. "We went out once, and I sort of had a crush on him." She shook her head. "But he's so loyal to his girlfriend in New York he didn't want to start anything with me."

Chase nodded at Doris while she was talking. "He sounds like a nice guy," she said. "Maybe I can stretch the rules and tell you a little bit more." She glanced at Firecaster as though seeking his permission. He nodded to show Chase he was willing to go along with her strategy.

"I think you'll feel better talking to us if you know we're trying to trace the movements of the women who received the cards," Chase said. "We're interested in what happened to the women, and we don't have anything against John Webb. But since he filled out the cards, we naturally think he might be able to tell us when he last saw the women."

"So that's why you need to know about the times?"

"That would certainly help," Chase said. She smiled at Doris. "The first is Thursday, April seventh."

"It'll take a minute," Doris said. Her doubts seemed to have vanished, and she pulled out a thick ledger with a green cover from the row of books hidden by the overhang of the countertop. She turned the pages quickly, then said, "It's right here."

"Did John Webb work that day?" Firecaster asked.

She was silent for a moment, then said, "My records show he worked from four in the afternoon until eight o'clock." Her voice was almost inaudible.

"No breaks for dinner or anything?" Firecaster asked. Something else was obviously bothering Doris Wyden, but he wanted to get the information they needed before she decided not to cooperate.

Doris shook her head. "I've got him down for being here the whole four hours."

Firecaster felt his certainty drain away. Webb couldn't be the Jaguar. The time wouldn't work. Before four o'clock was too early for Hamilton to be killed, and after eight was too late.

However, the Charles River wasn't very far away. Somebody in good shape could run the distance in less than ten minutes. If the store had been crowded with customers, Webb might have been able to slip away, kill Hamilton, then get back before he was missed. If anybody wondered where he was, he could say he had run down to Mass Ave to grab a sandwich.

"Did Webb work on Friday, March eighteenth?" Firecaster asked.

Doris took longer to find the entry. She answered the question without looking up. "I've written down that he worked from six until midnight," she said.

Thomas's body had been found shortly after eleven, and even if Webb drove, he couldn't have made the round trip from Bookkeepers to the motel and committed a murder in anything less than an hour. It wasn't possible.

Then something clicked, and he understood why Doris Wyden was starting her answers with expressions like "my records show" and "I've written down." They were phrases lawyers told their clients to use to avoid outright lying. There was something about the ledger entries she wasn't telling them.

Firecaster said nothing for a moment. He kept his eyes on Doris Wyden as she closed the ledger and put it back under the counter. "Is there anything else I can help you with?" she asked. Her voice now sounded unnaturally bright, and she avoided looking at either of them.

"You can tell us the whole truth about those entries," Firecaster said. "I don't want to arrest you for concealing evidence and obstructing justice, but I will if I have to." His voice wasn't loud, but he made his tone sharp and official.

Doris Wyden looked shocked. "I haven't done anything illegal," she objected.

"We can let a court decide that," Firecaster said. Then he added more softly, "But with a little cooperation, things will never have to go that far."

Doris Wyden's pretty face took on a scared and defeated expression. "I've never done anything really wrong in my life," she said. "I shouldn't have done what he asked me to, but it seemed harmless enough." Her voice was whispery, and she avoided looking at them.

"Done what?" Firecaster asked her.

"Made the wrong ledger entries," she said. "John told me it was because he didn't want Mr. Rimmer to know he wasn't working when he said he was," she said. "He always made up the hours, too. But the days you asked about are ones he wasn't here at the times the ledger says."

"How are you so sure about that?" Firecaster asked.

"I put a little mark on the pages," she said. She pointed to a tiny circle of black ink just below the green-stamped page number in the ledger. "It was so I would know. I didn't like making a change and not having any record of it at all."

"And Mr. Rimmer doesn't know," Firecaster said.

"He could fire me if he found out," Doris Wyden said. She looked up at Firecaster with eyes wide with worry.

"If he ever has to know, we'll talk to him," Firecaster said. "I'm sure we can convince him not to fire you."

"I hope you're right," Doris Wyden said. Then as though in repayment, she said, "I also changed John's time card yesterday. He wasn't really here from ten to two."

Firecaster exchanged glances with Chase. "We're going to want to talk to you again," he said.

"Tell no one about this conversation," Chase told her. "If you do, you can be charged with obstructing justice."

"I won't say anything to anyone," Doris Wyden promised.

Only Chase heard her. Firecaster was already hurrying toward the front door.

39

Wednesday 1:15 P.M.

Jill Brenner allowed herself to be swept along by the crowd pouring out of the banquet room where the Boscon media luncheon had taken place.

She glanced over her shoulder to be sure Susan Hooper was keeping up with her. Susan had sat next to her at lunch. She was a tall, thin high-school junior, with lanky brown hair and round metal-rimmed glasses that gave her a serious look. She was bright and talkative, and Jill found it easy to make conversation with her.

At the beginning of the luncheon, before she began talking to Susan, Jill had a hard time. The official welcoming talks were predictably boring, and while the convention organizers droned through their speeches, her mind kept drifting back to the night before.

Although she was sitting in a banquet hall full of people, she still saw the Jaguar lying unconscious on the porch floor. She recalled how she made herself approach him and how her heart almost stopped when, with no warning, he suddenly came awake and clutched her foot. She remembered the shock, then the numbing fear, as she struggled to break loose.

Her body remembered just how it felt to be running and to feel the Jaguar right behind her. Her skin flushed hot, then cold, and her breathing became rapid and shallow. He had looked so ordinary at the front door, but when she had taken the photograph, his face had become distorted and cruel. She could still see his blank blue eyes staring at her. She shuddered at the recollection.

Once the speeches were over and she and Susan had started talking, she felt much better. Coming to Boscon had been the right decision, and she was right to insist that Eric not stop her. Otherwise, she would have had nothing to think about except what had happened to her. It would be like watching the endless cycling of a film loop showing a gruesome accident.

Jill also felt she couldn't have had better luck than finding Susan Hooper as a guide. Susan knew a great deal about science fiction and its fans. She had answered Jill's questions patiently and made suggestions about what she should read, and now she was taking her to see someone she thought Jill would like to interview. "He's a well-known figure in fandom," Susan said. "His name is Steve Davis, and he teaches courses in science fiction."

Jill had been surprised by the people at the press lunch. Except for the camera crews and a few people like the neatly dressed man from the Associated Press, those who attended seemed to be science fiction fans like Susan, rather than professional reporters.

That was one of the things Susan had explained to her. "Nearly everybody here is a fanzine publisher," Susan said. When she saw Jill's blank look, she said, "That's short for fan magazine. They aren't ordinary magazines you can buy at a newsstand. They're publications written by fans, for fans."

"Are you a publisher?" Jill was beginning to sense she was dealing with a subculture more complex than she had first imagined.

"I took over *Annals of Arrakis*," Susan said. "The guy who started it went to Princeton and didn't have enough time to keep it going. Everything we publish is connected to *Dune*. Tod did it all with a mimeo machine, but I've switched to a Macintosh with a laser printer. We've got a terrific look." She hesitated then said somewhat shyly, "We've been nominated for a fanzine award for Best Graphics."

"Great," Jill said. "When will you know if you've won?"

"At the awards ceremony tomorrow night. That's when they announce all the prizes."

"I saw a list of the prizes in the press packet," Jill said. "I was surprised there were so many."

"It's like a family gathering," Susan said. "The prizes compensate for having people think you're weird." Jill saw that Susan's idea of fans as outsiders would be a good peg to hang interviews on.

"Some of the contests are pretty interesting," Susan said. "Did you see that right before the Galactic Ball tomorrow there's a Best Costume contest? That's always fun."

"I noticed it," Jill said. "I won't be able to tell who the people are supposed to be, though."

"I've already seen the guy who's just got to win," Susan said. "He's Paul Atreides right down to the ground, blond hair, stillsuit, and all." She shook her head in wonder. "You should try to find him, just so you can see what the kwisatz haderach looks like. He's too good to be believed."

"I'll keep an eye out," Jill had promised.

A camera crew from Channel 6 stood outside the broad center door and filmed those coming out from the luncheon. The outside corridor was a good forty feet wide, but it was jammed with people hoping to catch a glimpse of the convention's guest of honor.

"Go straight across the hall," Jill heard Susan say from behind her. "That's the Press Room, and I'm sure he'll be there."

The room was a cavernous expanse. A table just inside the door was piled high with press packets in white envelopes. Farther away from the door, a bartender stood behind a long table with buckets of ice, glasses, and bottles of liquor.

The rest of the room had been organized into interview areas. Groups of two or three chairs arranged around a small table were scattered about the room. Jill thought the place looked like a cocktail lounge.

"That's Steve Davis," Susan said. She pointed to a bearded man in a long brown cassock talking to a woman at the drinks table. "You find a place to sit, and I'll bring him over." When Jill looked doubtful, Susan said, "Don't worry about being pushy. Steve loves to be interviewed."

Jill claimed one of the tables far enough away from the door to be quiet, and in a few minutes Susan was back with Steve Davis walking beside her. After she had introduced them, she said, "I'm going to leave you two to talk. I need to find Tod and ask him about our mailing list." She then turned to Jill. "If you want any more introductions or want to get in touch, just pin a note to the message board in the lobby."

Jill thanked Susan for her help, and after she left, she took a closer look at Steve Davis. He was tall, with a lean athletic build and dark brown eyes. She guessed he was around thirty, maybe a little older, but it was hard to tell. His neatly trimmed beard and straight short hair had been powdered white, and his face and hands were covered with makeup that made him seem heavily tanned.

"Thanks for letting me talk to you," Jill told him. "I'm afraid you're dealing with a real science fiction novice."

"Don't worry about it," Davis said. "I teach at Concord Community College, so you can't ask me anything I haven't heard before."

"I'm sure I should recognize what character you are, but I actually don't," Jill admitted.

"Then you haven't seen the *Star Wars* movies," Davis said. He smiled at her, showing even white teeth. "If you had, you'd know I'm Obi-Wan Kenobi. Darth Vader and I are the last of the Jedi knights, except he went over to the Dark Side."

Davis stood up and raised his arms out to the sides. Jill could see that under the coarse brown cassock he wore a white robe cinched at the waist with a heavy leather belt. He then patted a black cylindrical object that hung from the belt. "My lightsaber," he said. "It's like a laser, except it draws its power from the Force." Seeing Jill's blank look he went on. "The Force is an energy field that surrounds us, and a Jedi knight learns how to tap into it to gain power."

Davis laughed, then dropped into the chair beside the small table. "That's who I am," he said. He looked across at her and asked, "Would you like a drink?"

"None for me," Jill said. "But you go ahead."

"A Jedi doesn't drink alcohol," Davis said.

"Do you see yourself as a Jedi knight?" Jill asked. "I mean, is this more than a game for you?"

"In a sense," Davis said. "I like the movies tremendously, because they have an important message. They tell us to try to be at harmony with ourselves and the universe. A Jedi is someone who has succeeded, so I say I'm a Jedi to remind myself of how I should try to live."

"Then you really do think of yourself as a Jedi."

"But only in the way a Christian might think of himself as Jesus or a Jew might think of himself as Abraham," Davis said. He laughed as if something suddenly struck him as amusing. "I don't confuse the real world with the world of *Star Wars*, if that's what you had in mind."

"What about other fans?" Jill asked. "Do you think some blur the distinction between the worlds of science fiction and ordinary life?"

"I guess it's possible," Davis said. "But even unhappy kids who turn to science fiction to escape the bad things in their lives probably don't cross the line between fantasy and reality."

He held out his hands with the palms up. "Let's face it, we all have our daydreams, and I don't think science fiction fans are any more likely to get lost in theirs than anybody else."

"Wait just a second," Jill said. She took a spiral pad out of her purse and jotted down a few notes. She glanced up at Davis. "You said you looked to science fiction for ideals. Do you think supplying ideals is its primary purpose?"

Davis shook his head. "It's supposed to entertain, first of all. But like all fiction, it's got to have a moral point of view, and I think science fiction maintains values like tolerance, respect for those who are different, and the importance of scientific knowledge. Anyway, that's what those who consider themselves a part of fandom believe."

"Both you and Susan refer to *fandom*," Jill said. "Why don't you just say *fans*? What does *fandom* mean?"

"You've touched a nerve with that question," Davis said, shaking his head. "Have you seen people here wearing buttons with FIA-WOL or FIJAGH on them?"

Jill shook her head, unsure of what he was saying.

"You'll see some, if you look," Davis said. "The words are acronyms. One stands for 'Fandom is a way of life,' and the other for 'Fandom is just a goddamned hobby.' That's the split."

Davis glanced at Jill to see if she had followed his explanation. She nodded to keep him talking.

"Those who consider themselves *real* fans build their lives around science fiction the way some people do around religion," he said. "All their friends are fans. They read all the science fiction they can get their hands on, then write the authors to tell them what they think. They watch old *Outer Limits* reruns and all the science fiction movies, even the atrocious ones. They publish fanzines or at least write for them, and of course they go to conventions like this one."

"And the other group doesn't do all that?"

Davis smiled. "Actually, most of them probably do the same things, but they don't spend as much time at it. Also they don't try to get their sense of identity from science fiction. Most of the FIJAGH people are older and have jobs they like and families, so they aren't searching for something to belong to."

"Would you say the way-of-life group is made up mostly of adolescents?" Jill asked.

"Mostly, but not exclusively," Davis said. "Some are just people who find their ordinary lives unsatisfying."

"Are Trekkies in that group?"

"They could be," Davis said. "But it's also true of fans interested in specific writers like Cordwainer Smith or books like *Dune*."

Steve Davis was knowledgeable and articulate, and as the conversation continued, Jill found she enjoyed talking to him. After three quarters of an hour, she had learned more about the history of science fiction, its authors, fans, and current trends, than she could have by investing a day in a library. Now, thanks to the combined efforts of Susan and Davis, she had enough background to feel comfortable writing about the convention.

Jill shook hands with Steve Davis and thanked him for his help, then asked, "By the way, are you a FIAWOL or a FIJAGH?"

"That's what students always want to know," he said. "I tell them I don't see anything to gain from splitting the world of science fiction into two parts. From my perspective, it has so many pieces it looks like a mosaic."

"Fair enough," Jill said. "Would you mind if I quoted you?"

"I'd love it if you did," Davis said.

40

Wednesday 1:50 P.M.

Jill made her way out of the press room and back into the entrance area. It was still crowded with people moving from one talk to another or searching out friends from past conventions. The congestion was worsened by a crew from Granada TV. A cameraman was at the head of the stairs, shooting down at those who were trying to make their way upstairs against the downward flow. A woman with a microphone stood directly in front of the stairs, forcing the crowd to break and swirl around her as though she were a rock in a river.

Jill usually hated being caught in a crowd, but she found herself not minding so much this time. She didn't feel trapped or suffocated or frustrated by not being able to get somewhere else. The time she had spent talking to Susan and Steve Davis had given her a favorable impression of science fiction fans in general. The people surrounding her were young, and they were having a good time just being together.

Thinking about Susan made Jill decide to go to the lobby to leave a note for her. If Susan were willing, she wanted to attend Awards Night with her. Susan would be able to identify the celebrities, as well as provide her with a commentary on what was happening.

Too many people were trying to use the central stairway, and Jill angled her way toward the more sparsely populated area near the elevators. She knew from the briefing at lunch that twenty-five hundred people had paid their registration fee, and when spouses, children, and free-riders were added, the total would be over three thousand. The convention was spread out on four floors of the hotel.

She waited for the elevator with five or six people who were chatting together. Two elevators stopped, but each was already filled to capacity. The people were packed so tightly, there clearly was not enough room for even one more person.

"This is hopeless," a woman said. "We might as well walk."

"But look at the stairs," a man told her. They all glanced toward the jammed central stairway.

"We can go down the fire stairs," the woman said. Others ex-

218

pressed agreement, and the group filed through the door several feet down the wall from the elevator.

Jill started to follow them, then hesitated. She wanted to stay with a crowd and not become isolated. But probably all the elevators were going to be filled, and if she went down the stairs with the people who just left, she wouldn't really be alone.

She pulled open the metal fire door and stepped onto the landing. She could hear laughing and talking coming from the group that already seemed to be one floor below her. She glanced behind her as the pneumatic closer slammed the door shut with a solid clunk.

The light in the stairwell was dim, but she had no trouble seeing the unpainted concrete steps, their edges protected from crumbling by a strip of scored metal plate. The air was cool and unmoving, like the air inside a cave. Then below her a door opened and slammed shut with a solid clunk. The noise of talking and laughter had stopped. Presumably the people she was following had been going down only one or two floors. Now it was much quieter, and her footsteps echoed on the stairs, each step making a dull slapping sound.

She had walked down a floor and a half when she heard a door open above her, maybe on the floor she had just left. She thought nothing about it at first, then she paused and listened to the footsteps. They were barely audible, but they were there. It was as though someone were trying to keep from being noticed. Even while she listened, the footsteps stopped.

Was somebody following her? She could sense the edge of panic beneath the level of consciousness, and she suddenly felt sure someone was after her. Then like a wind coming from nowhere, a rush of fear drove all thought from her mind, and she felt herself automatically beginning to run down the stairs.

She moved faster and faster. Almost at once, she felt she couldn't get enough breath into her chest, and she repeatedly sucked at the air. The echoes of her feet slapping the steps overlapped one another and made a rapid, cracking noise like a burst of gunfire.

She could hear the steps above her grow faster. All doubt disappeared. Someone *was* following her. Someone was after her. She made an effort not to let herself think of the night before: of the darkness, the desperate struggle to flee, the terror of having her foot caught. She tried to turn off her mind.

She reached a landing, started to go through the door, then changed her mind. The steps sounded too close, and she thought that if she paused to open the door, she would be caught.

She immediately realized she wasn't thinking clearly. She could have been in the safety of the public area beyond the door. Without slackening her pace, she turned her head to look behind her. She saw the dark, looming form of a shadow. The pale yellow light made the shadow dense but indistinct, and it moved against the painted plaster wall of the stairwell as though it were alive.

She made no attempt to slow her speed, and at the next landing, she wrapped her hand around the cold brass doorknob and hit the metal door with her left shoulder. All at once, she was in an area filled with people.

She glanced around quickly and saw rows of tables piled with books and magazines. People were wandering between rows, stopping at a table for a moment, then moving on to the next one. She took a deep breath and moved away from the door and down the aisle nearest the elevators.

She joined a group of six or eight people gathered around a table covered with books laid out flat. Even at a glance, it was obvious the books were old. The colors and designs came from another age.

She stood next to a middle-aged man who was bent over looking down at the books. She pretended to be doing the same, but although she bowed her head, she kept her eyes on the fire door. The door began to open, and Jill stepped closer to the man next to her. She turned so she was partially shielded from sight by his bulk. She felt as though she would like to shrink down and make herself disappear. She was tired of trying to stay alert, but most of all, she was tired of feeling scared.

She forced herself to peer around the man beside her. She had to see who came out the door; she had to see who had been behind her on the stairs. She wasn't sure who it would be, but she was more than half expecting the Jaguar to come through the door. She felt her legs tremble as she craned her neck to look.

The door opened wide, and a short, husky Asian woman in a denim skirt walked into the room. The woman seemed confused, and she looked around quickly, as though trying to find someone. She kept a hand on the doorknob, and the quick, nervous way her eyes swept the room made her appear desperate. Jill wondered for a moment whether the woman might be a scout for the Jaguar, but she told herself she was being too suspicious. Everything the Jaguar did, he did alone. She took a deep breath and felt the pressure ease.

Then she heard the door open and close, and her heart began to race again. She turned quickly toward the stairway entrance, but she saw no one. Maybe the Asian woman had decided to walk down to the next floor to continue her search. Or maybe somebody else was using the stairs instead of the elevator.

Jill told herself to calm down; she was safe. But the whole experience reminded her it was possible that the Jaguar could be looking for her. She would have to stay alert, and she should definitely not go anyplace alone, not even down the stairs.

She shifted on one foot to move out of the way of the man screening her and inadvertently brushed her left arm against the transmitter attached to her waistband.

She had forgotten all about it! It was just as well she hadn't activated the transmitter when she had panicked on the stairs. She had just freaked out then and not been in danger. But not even to have thought of the transmitter? That was genuinely frightening.

Within a few minutes, she was feeling normal again, and she let herself relax and focus on the books in front of her. Her eye was caught by a paperback with a cover showing a futuristic city of spires and ramps and windowless buildings shaped like slabs. She read the words: *The Pocket Book of Science-Fiction, edited by Donald A. Wollheim.* A slip of white paper identified the book as "First anthology with 'science fiction' in title (1943)." The architecture of the city now belonged more to the past than to the future, and the style of illustration was as dated as the yellowing cellophane that once added a high gloss to the cover.

As she looked at the faded book, she felt a wave of sadness pass through her. She had never before realized so vividly the extent to which time could transform even a dream of the distant future into dim and dated images. She had let her dreams die with Jeff, but she now saw her foolishness.

She looked up and forced a smile for the burly, red-bearded man behind the table. "I can give you a good price on the Wollheim," he said.

"I'm just looking," she said.

"That's fine," he said, without a trace of disappointment. "You can find plenty of reading-grade books at other stalls. If it's not mint or excellent, I won't touch it." He nodded toward the book she had been examining. "Of course, the Wollheim is special. Even just the cover would be valuable."

"I'm not really a fan," Jill said. "I'm here for *Boston Update* to write a story on the convention. If you're willing, I'd like to ask you some questions."

"Sure." The man shrugged. "But you'll just be getting the picture from the point of view of a huckster." He smiled. "That's what they call people who sell things at conventions. This whole place is called the Huckster Room." He made a broad gesture that took in the surrounding tables.

"What do fans buy? Is there anything in particular demand?"

"This year it's all Dune material," the man said. "Anything and everything connected with the novels, the movie, or Frank Herbert himself. Of course, Dune is part of the Boscon environmental theme, so that's not too surprising."

"I noticed that a lot of the scheduled talks are about Dune," Jill said. "But otherwise I haven't seen much connected with it."

"Then you have to go into the Dune Room," he said without hesitation. "It's filled with exhibits about living on Dune, conserving water, spice mining—all of it."

"Where is the Dune Room?"

"It's on the first floor," the man told her. "It takes up the entire Exhibit Hall." He shook his head in wonder. "Going through it is a real experience."

41

Wednesday 1:55 P.M.

Firecaster leaned his shoulder against the dirt-stained wall of the second-floor landing and looked up the stairs. Chase stood beside him, her hands crossed in front of her, as though she couldn't bear the idea of touching anything in the building.

Both were absorbed by the activity at the top of the stairs. Jim Mahare, a sergeant from Special Services, and his helper were working hard at breaking through the apartment's door.

The helper drilled a rectangular pattern of holes in the door panel, then stepped aside. Mahare picked up a cordless saber saw and began sawing lines to connect the holes. The saw made an angry snarling sound, and the heavy resinous odor of freshly cut wood perfumed the sour smell of the stairwell. In a few minutes, the high-pitched whine of the saw's motor abruptly ceased.

"It's all ready for you, Lieutenant," Mahare said.

"Come on, Karen," Firecaster said. "You can witness the entrance." He trotted up the stairs with Chase close behind him.

Mahare had left the panel attached to the door by not sawing all the way to the holes at two places. Firecaster shoved against the panel, and it hit the linoleum floor inside with a clattering sound. Only the metal bar of a police lock ran across the center of the opening.

"Have you got your gloves?" Firecaster asked.

"I've got them," Chase said, her voice strained. Firecaster was also beginning to feel the tension; the left side of his chest tightened with a dull aching grip.

They pulled on thin latex gloves. Taking the lead, Firecaster bent over and stepped crabwise through the narrow rectangle. Once in the room, he moved to the right of the door to get out of Chase's way.

"Jesus, it's putrid in here," Chase said. She held up a hand to her throat as though she could shut off the sickly sweetish odor. "It smells like mothballs and something dead."

"You've got the right combination," Firecaster said. "Let's get some fresh air."

He pushed aside the brown curtains, and dust particles swirled and floated in the sunlight streaming through the dirty glass. He gulped shallow swallows of air through clenched teeth and wished he didn't have to breathe at all. He struggled with the window, pushing it up as far as it would go. Chilly air flooded the room.

He stood in front of the window and surveyed the room. Even though the air was fresher, he was uncomfortable. Something about the room besides the odor was foul and unclean. He sensed he was encountering the spoor of some feral creature, and he didn't want to be contaminated by it. He had expected to feel elated at finally locating the Jaguar's lair, but the idea of going inside was repulsive. He felt like ducking through the hole in the door and trying to forget he had ever set foot in such a place.

Yet he knew he couldn't leave. He had his job to do, and with Jill involved, that was more important than ever. The pain along the left side of his chest became sharper, and he massaged it with his right hand.

"Let's start with the kitchen," Firecaster said. He turned away from the window and glanced at Chase. Her face was grave and her thoughts seemed elsewhere.

"Righty-ho," she said at once. The attempt at jauntiness failed; her tone was forced and artificial.

Firecaster crossed the room and shoved back one of the folding doors hiding the kitchen alcove. A dozen cockroaches scurried across the worn linoleum floor and disappeared into cracks along the wall and at the base of the cabinets. He pushed back the other door, and another wave of roaches ran from the light and slipped out of sight into the darkness.

Chase shone her flashlight around the area. "Disgusting hole," she said. The yellow beam picked out the hanging cord of the ceiling fixture. She tugged the string, and bright light mercilessly flooded the alcove. The dark grime around the handles of the metal cabinets and the orange rust of the sink drain stood out with clarity.

The fresh air from the window had not penetrated the closed alcove, and Firecaster felt his desire to leave intensify. The rancid sweetness and the acrid smell of naphthalene were mixed in a heavy, nauseating combination. He stepped out of the alcove, took a deep breath, then went back inside.

"I think we know what we're likely to find," Chase said softly. "We just don't want to believe it." She was holding a small and surprisingly dainty blue handkerchief over her nose.

"Let's do what we came to do and get out," Firecaster said.

"Do you want to do the notes?" Chase asked.

"You do them," Firecaster said. "You're good at dictating."

"I'd rather talk than touch anything in here," she said.

Chase reached into her canvas bag and took out a small recorder with a voice-activated microphone. Speaking in a level, official voice she identified herself and Firecaster, gave the date, time, and address. She mentioned the number of the search warrant and the name of the judge issuing it. She concluded the first entry by saying, "The next comments will refer to our search of the kitchen area."

Firecaster waited until Chase was through speaking, then he opened the cabinets on the right side of the sink. "Nothing but dishes," he said. "Plates, bowls, cups, several glasses." He ran his fingers along the upper inside edges of the metal cabinets. He found nothing but cobwebs and the brittle brown casings that were the remains of dead cockroaches.

He stepped to the left side of the sink, pulled open the rusted cabinet door, then jumped back as though a jolt of electricity had hurled him away. The white skull on the middle shelf seemed to shine in the brightness of the overhead light. The skull looked so clean and perfect it might have been an anatomical specimen.

"My God, it's one of the heads," Chase said. Her voice sounded strangled in her throat. She then dictated a quick description of what they were looking at. "But what's that above the skull? In those jars?"

"Brains," Firecaster said. His tone was flat. "Two of them." He made no effort to take down the glass containers.

"Shit," Chase said. "I don't believe it."

Firecaster kept quiet. He could feel a stress reaction begin to develop. The muscles in his left temple tightened until his head began to ache dully, and then Karen Chase's voice seemed to come from a long way off as she spoke into the recorder.

He told himself to remain calm, but he couldn't keep from thinking about what had almost happened the night before. If Jill had not been both intelligent and resourceful, her brain would now be in a glass jar lined up on the shelf with the others.

Impulsively, he shoved on the metal door, and the spring built into the hinge slammed it shut with a sharp clap. He had seen no need to touch anything in the cabinet, and he wanted to hide everything as quickly as possible. It was just one more sight his job forced him to witness that he wished he could avoid.

What he really wanted, he realized, was to keep away from death's corrupting power. It was unbearable to think how fragile the barrier was between life and death, between a person and a brain in a glass jar.

"Do you need to take a break?" Chase asked. She looked at him with concern.

"I'm all right," Firecaster said. He cleared his throat. He did feel better, because now he was certain they hadn't made a mistake. John Webb was the Jaguar.

"Then let's keep going," Chase said. "I want to get out of here." She used her flashlight to gesture toward the sheet-draped tank resting on the drainboard. "What the hell is that?"

"Let's find out," Firecaster said. He began unwinding the loose folds of the pale green sheet.

He let the sheet fall to the floor as he unwrapped it, and when it was finally unwound, they both stood and gazed at the glass tank. The fluffy white cotton batting filling it looked both peculiar and uninteresting. They glanced at each other and shook their heads.

Firecaster rapped on the tank sharply with his knuckles. The noise changed everything in the tank. The carpet beetles swarmed from their secret tunnels in the batting and began crawling on the cotton. With their iridescent heads and black bodies, they seemed decorated for some grotesque ritual.

Chase leaned forward. "What the hell are those things?" she wondered aloud. "They aren't like any roaches I ever saw."

"I don't know," Firecaster said. Then he saw the kitchen tongs on the drainboard and guessed the answer. "There's something beneath the cotton." He picked up the tongs. "This is going to be it."

He took off the screen and used the tongs to pull away the white cotton. The partially stripped and decomposed head of Anna Louise Hamilton emerged. The sickly sweet odor of putrefaction seemed stronger than ever in the small alcove. He felt his throat close up and fought back the need to gag.

"I always hated biology," Chase said. She stepped back from the countertop. "I've seen it, and that's enough." She walked into the living room.

Firecaster pulled the screen back into place, then spread the green sheet over the tank. Everything he did, he did fast. He jerked the cord to turn off the light and stepped out of the alcove. He pulled each of the doors back into place. The warped one scraped against the other, but he pushed it hard enough to jam it shut.

"Nobody lives here," Chase said. She was standing in the door of the bathroom. "Dirt an inch thick is on the bottom of the tub, and even the dirt on the washbasin is old. There's soap, a razor and shaving cream, but they don't look like they've been used for a year."

"Somebody has been here recently, though," Firecaster said. "Look at the top of the desk. The area in front of the chair is clean, even though the part further back has dust on it."

"Oh, yeah, the desk chair is the same," Chase said. "The part you sit on is clean, but the rest is as dusty as the desk." She shot a glance at Firecaster. "What do you think? Do we stake the place out?"

"Yes, but my guess is it won't help. This place is a cut-out. Whoever goes by the name John Webb lives somewhere else and uses the apartment as a base of operations."

"You think he'll learn we were asking about him?"

"I think John Webb is prepared to stop being John Webb, if he thinks we're on to him."

"But will he give up being the Jaguar?" Chase asked.

"That's one thing he can't do. He was defeated by Jill last night, and you can bet he's furious today."

"Do you think he's going to go after her again?"

"He's got to so he can prove to himself he can't be defeated," Firecaster said.

He reached under his jacket and touched the hard plastic of the receiver as though rubbing an amulet. He was glad to have a link with Jill, but he was even more reassured to know Helen Kim was keeping watch.

42

Wednesday 2:00 P.M.

The Jaguar was on the prowl. He was hunting, and he knew better than to hurry. Slowly and deliberately was the way to go.

Yet he could feel excitement building inside. He could feel his muscles tightening and his stomach growing tense. Like a drug, the hunt was changing him, altering his body and shaping his mind. He was alive, aware, and in tune with everything around him.

The elevator car was transparent on two sides. Directly to the east, he had a clear view of the Eastern General Hospital complex. Cars driving past the soot-stained buildings looked as small as toys.

He had once had a set of cars like them. When he was five, a man visiting his mother had brought them. "This is so you won't forget Jack Varr," the man told him. Jack Varr was tall and tanned, with white teeth that flashed when he smiled. He looked happy and spirited, but his mother had seemed even more angry and sullen than usual.

The cars were brightly painted cast metal and came in a red plastic box shaped like a racing car. Inside the box, each car nestled in a molded plastic rectangle. Putting the cars away, making sure each was in its right slot, gave him even more pleasure than sending them on trips down imaginary roads. Then two weeks after he got the cars, they disappeared from his room. "You're better off without them," his mother said. "Only trash comes from trash."

He got off on the twenty-seventh floor and walked across the corridor to the art gallery. The sign outside read *Sense of Wonder: Cover Art 1920s–1950s*. The slanted red letters progressively diminished in size so the words seemed to be rushing into the future.

Jill might be inside already. She could skip the award ceremonies and the lectures, but she couldn't write about Boscon without visiting the exhibition and without going to the Dune Room. If he shuttled between them, eventually he would score a hit. It was like going from a water hole to a salt lick.

He scanned the room. He was confident he would have no trouble locating her. He would feel her in the room, because his attraction for her was even stronger than before. The others were nothing compared to Jill.

The standing exhibit panels made it impossible to survey the room from one position, and he moved quickly past the first area, not bothering to examine the art. The crowd was relatively sparse. It was too early in the convention for fans to be concerned with anything but locating friends and spotting celebrities.

He made himself stop at the nearest display. Attached to the beige grasscloth of the panel were several framed science fiction magazines. The covers were frayed and nicked at the edges, and the faded paper along the spines was peeling off. Yet the colors on the enameled paper remained vivid and bright.

He stared with fascination at the first cover. The magazine was *Science Wonder Stories* of 1929, and the artist was Frank R. Paul. Two figures, one with white skin and the other with green, were sitting in futuristic chairs. Both were wearing what looked like diving helmets with wires and glass tubes attached to the outside. Instead of face plates, though, the helmets had rectangular display screens.

The figure with white skin was manipulating dials and switches on the electronic console in front of him. The angle made it impossible to see what was on his screen, but the other screen was prominent. A reptilian creature with scaly green skin, slitted yellow eyes, and curving claws stood erect on its hind legs, its lipless mouth opened to show rows of knifelike teeth.

For a moment, he had the feeling he was being drawn into the picture. He wondered what such a machine would show of his subconscious: Would his hard dream appear on the screen? Would he see himself lying in the jungle, paralyzed, waiting for the two masked figures coming to steal his brain?

After his encounter with Jill, the dream had come again the night before. He had wakened out of breath, with his heart pounding. She had surprised him on the porch. He had intended to demonstrate his power to her and the police lieutenant; he hadn't expected her to trick him and hurt him.

Jill was supposed to be the quarry, and she wasn't playing the game properly. She was too much a hunter herself. If only she realized the closeness they could experience by allowing death to blend their feelings together, she would stop resisting him. But then how could she know? It was beyond her experience.

He had to admit that the trouble she caused not only added to the excitement of the chase, it made her more desirable. He touched the crysknife in the scabbard at his side. She would be a worthy tribute. He would make her his first heart sacrifice, and only after he offered her heart to the sky gods would he add her head to the wall of skulls.

Thinking about Jill excited him and made it hard to maintain his slow, deliberate pace. He moved rapidly toward the next panel of covers, and a woman wearing a black sweatshirt with *It's Not Too Late To Have A Happy Childhood* printed across the front stopped to watch him. She stood with her hands on her hips and looked at him with an assessing, critical stare. "You've got it down," she told him as he walked past her. "I'd follow you anywhere."

"Thanks," he said and forced a smile. She was attractive, but she didn't appeal to him the way Jill did. Would a deer hunter want to stalk a tame doe?

He began to examine another cover, but he couldn't make himself pay attention to the ocean-liner-length spaceship. The more he thought about Jill, the more he was aware that his patience was at an end. A mixture of desire and anger stirred inside and made him eager to find her. He picked up his pace, but still he scanned the room carefully. By the time he reached the gallery exit, he was sure she wasn't there.

The elevator came to a halt in an area of the lower level filled with a profusion of green plants. Ferns, banana trees, and broad-leaf bushes grew so thick and close they formed a miniature rain forest. He found it easy to imagine he was in a genuine South American jungle as he peered through the foliage. The wide leaves of a banana tree blocked his line of sight, and he crouched low to see under them. He had a clear view of the large public area on the other side of the plantings.

He immediately spotted Jill. He smiled at her, but he was so well hidden by the foliage she couldn't have seen him, even if she had been looking.

43

Wednesday 2:15 P.M.

Jill carefully surveyed the entrance to the Dune Room. It was obviously designed to look like the opening of a cave on Arrakis. Layers of weathered gray shale formed a ragged outcropping, and the small, dark passage leading inside might have been the result of a geological shift's tearing open the rocks. White sand from a thick layer on top of the shale trickled down through cracks and formed small piles along the sides.

She found it easy to imagine the feelings of awe and fear that must have come over Paul Atreides as he stood friendless in the glaring heat of the desert and gazed into the darkness of the cave. Despite his fear, it must have seemed the only place he could hope to find refuge on such an alien and inhospitable planet. She quickly scribbled down a few phrases to help her recapture her experiences when she started to write.

The inside of the room was both dark and light. Brilliant white illumination streamed from overhead tracks, but the bulbs shone only on the glass-fronted cases running along three sides of the room. Near the cases, reflection produced a watery gray light almost too pale to see by, and the rest of the hall was in utter darkness.

The lighting made her think of the reptile house at the zoo. She usually avoided the place, because just going inside made her skin crawl. There, too, bright lights were focused on glass cases, but in spite of that, the snakes often hid themselves so well you couldn't find them. You would stare at an empty case, then with a feeling of horror, you would suddenly realize you were looking at a deadly viper.

The images that filled her mind were too close to her own recent encounter with a snake not to disturb her. She could feel her arms and legs tremble as though she were chilled. Then she felt a stirring of anger with herself. She was letting her imagination influence her too much. She should just do things, not let her mind roam so freely. Action was what she needed. She took a few steps toward the middle of the dim room.

She was momentarily blinded by the darkness, then when she could see a little, she moved to the left and stood by the first exhibit. It was a diorama showing an immense stretch of white sand that was featureless, except where the wind had made whorls and stripes of almost geometrical exactness.

She could see no person or creature in the scene, but as she watched, the situation suddenly altered. The ground seemed to fall away into a circular pit that opened beneath it. Then there was a deep roaring sound, and without warning, a rounded shape shot from beneath the sand of the pit. Its blue-white color gave its skin the appearance of dead flesh.

Jill was startled by the noise and the abruptness with which the creature appeared from nowhere. A ripple of fear ran through her, and she took a step backward, away from the glass case.

Once the sand had fallen back, she could see that the mouth of the creature was a ring of razor-sharp teeth at the end of its blunt body. It was eyeless, but it twisted in the air in a deliberate fashion, then thrust its head into the sand on the opposite side of the diorama. The roaring noise became louder, then the cylindrical body began to disappear beneath the sand, slithering into an invisible opening.

"Shai-Hulud," a man said from behind her.

His voice was not loud, but she had no trouble hearing what he said, because the word was spoken close to her ear. She turned quickly and realized at once he must be the kwisatz haderach Susan had told her about at lunch. She had to admit he was a dramatic sight in his black, tight-fitting clothes, black mask, and cloak.

"That's the name we use on Dune," he continued. He was looking into the case, then he switched his gaze to her. "You may know it as a sandworm."

"Shai-Hulud sounds better," Jill said.

He smiled at her. The gray light of the room made it difficult to see exactly what he looked like, but she could tell he was attractive. She felt flattered he had picked her out of the crowd as someone worth talking to. Since she had planned to interview him before she left the convention, she was also pleased to be spared the effort of trying to find him.

"We also call it the Old Man of the Desert," he said. "The one on display here is very young. Most are several hundred meters long, and they live to a great age." He smiled again. "Unless they encounter someone like me who takes their water and their teeth."

She found herself listening closely to his voice. It was cultured and precise, and his intonation sounded more British than American. It was a studied actor's voice, and something about it seemed vaguely familiar.

"Their teeth?" she said, realizing what he had said.

"We use them to make our crysknives."

He reached to his side, pulled out a knife, and held it up for her to see. She barely had the opportunity to glimpse the wedge-shaped blade with its dagger point, when in a lightning-fast movement of his hand, he clicked the knife back into its scabbard.

"I assume you must be the son of Duke Leto," Jill said. She wanted to show she could play the Dune game.

"The Duke was my father," he said. "Alas, he is now buried in the Skull Tomb on Arrakis." His voice dropped, then it rose and became stronger as he introduced himself. "I am Paul Muuad-'Dib, the Umma Regent." He then smiled once more, and now she could see his teeth in the watery light.

"I'm honored to meet you, Muuad-'Dib," she said.

"Please call me Paul," he said in a more relaxed and friendly tone. "Now, who are you?"

"I'm Jill Brenner." Before she could say anything else, the sandworm roared again. She turned to look at the dead-white figure as it rose from the sand. Although she told herself the creature was purely mechanical, she couldn't escape feeling a little scared by it. She moved a step closer to Paul.

While they waited for the noise of the sandworm to die away, she decided she might as well approach him with her request for an interview immediately. If she waited until later, he might think she was being friendly to trick him into talking.

She said, "I'm a writer, and I'm doing an article on Boscon for *Boston Update*. Could I interview you for it? I would just ask about yourself and your involvement in science fiction. Nothing embarrassing."

The dim light and the mask covering the area around his eyes made it impossible for her to judge his reaction. He said nothing for a moment, and she thought he must be about to refuse.

"I would be delighted," he said suddenly. "I can tell you're an easy person to talk to."

"Wonderful," Jill said. "But let's find a place to get coffee or a drink. It's too noisy to talk in here."

"I know a perfect place," Paul said. "It's just a few blocks from here. Are you up for walking?"

Jill hesitated a moment. She had promised herself she would stay with the crowds, but that didn't mean she couldn't leave the hotel. She would just make sure she was always in a public place. "No problem," she said. "We can talk on the way."

After they passed under the shale arch, Jill cut sharply to the right to get them out of the main flow of traffic. As she did, she suddenly caught sight of the heavy-set Asian woman in the cluster of people gathered to enter the exhibition hall. The woman was scanning the crowd with an anxious look on her face.

Jill felt a tremor run through her. Could her first suspicion have been right? Was it possible that the woman might scout out victims for the Jaguar? Maybe he only seemed to work alone. The idea was probably foolish, but right now she would just play it safe and make sure the woman didn't see her.

"Let's go through the fire exit," Jill said. She didn't bother to look around at Paul to see if he agreed. Instead, she cut a diagonal line through the crowd and shoved on the bar attached to the gray steel door.

The door swung open easily, and she walked through without

looking back. Paul caught the door to keep it from slamming, and she was aware of his large form looming behind her. She found it comforting to be with him. If the Asian woman caught up with them, Paul would be able to scare her off.

The air in the space between the fire door and the outside door was chill, and the exit sign cast a reddish glow over the concrete floor and walls. Without pausing, Jill walked straight across the area and pushed through the door to the outside.

Paul was close behind her, then he was beside her. As soon as she heard the dull thud of the heavy door automatically closing behind them, she felt a sense of safety and security.

Now no one knew where they were.

44

Wednesday 2:30 P.M.

Jill stopped and glanced left, then right. They were on an unpopulated sidewalk half a block from the main entrance, and the hotel wall at that point was a windowless expanse of cream brick. Low clouds made the sun pale and feeble, and a slight wind from the east was cold after the heat of the hotel. The sudden change in temperature made her sweater feel too thin.

"Go to the right," Paul said.

"Toward Eastern General Hospital?" Jill said. "I used to know the area around it pretty well." She shivered and wrapped her arms around her chest to ward off the breeze. "Where are you taking us?" she asked.

"I can't remember the name of the place, but I'll know it when I see it. It's right by the hospital."

"Do you mind if I ask you some questions on the way?" Jill asked. "I'm curious about how you got interested in science fiction. Can you tell me about it?"

"It's the usual kind of beginning for fans," Paul said. "When I was about twelve, I read a story in school called *In Hiding*. It was about mutant kids so intelligent they couldn't let adults find out or scientists would lock them up for study."

"Did the kids know one another?"

"Not at first. Then they did things like publish poetry and mathematical proofs under pseudonyms, and some of the kids figured out from that there were others like them."

"And did any adults ever find out?"

"One kid told his psychologist," Paul said. "Then he agreed to help them all get in touch."

Jill could hear excitement in his voice, and he slowed his walking almost to a stop as he told the story. He might have been twelve years old again. She decided she was going to feature him in her Boscon piece.

"It was so easy to imagine being one of those kids," Paul said. A wistful tone replaced the excitement. "You knew you were special, even though nobody else did. And you knew that despite whatever adults tried to do to stop you, eventually you would take over the world." He fell silent for a moment.

"And you found there were more stories like that one," Jill prompted.

"Oh, yes," he said. "I found there were magazines like *Astounding* that had been published since the 1930s, and I started to collect them. Then there were movies and TV shows like *Star Trek*." He gave a short laugh. "You could say Mr. Spock taught me how to think. He made me logical."

They strolled along in silence for a moment, then she said, "You sound like you've gotten a lot from science fiction."

"It saved my life," Paul said. His voice became somber. "It gave me a place to live when I realized that where I was living was intolerable."

"Could you tell me more about that?" Jill asked. "You sound like you also got some emotional comfort from those stories." If Paul could tell her how science fiction was a way of life for him, a kind of religion, then she could contrast his view with somebody for whom it was just a hobby.

"Emotional comfort?" he said, sounding scornful. "What I got out of science fiction was that giving in to emotion leads to destruction; and that hate, anger, self-pity, and even love can be controlled by the mind. That's the lesson." Then he added in a harsh voice, "I don't want to say anything more about the topic."

She realized she had upset him, and without thinking, she touched his arm. "I didn't mean to pry," she said.

He turned toward her, then jerked his head back quickly. "I know you want to find out more about me," he said. "Don't worry, because I'm going to let you. It's going to be on my terms, though." He spoke without looking at her.

Jill didn't like the direction the conversation was taking. She wasn't sure what Paul meant by his last remark. Yet it made her uncomfortable, and she decided to shift her line of questioning.

"Do you mind if I ask what made you decide to come here dressed as Paul Atreides?" she asked.

"Because Paul Atreides was the kwisatz haderach of Dune," he said.

Jill waited for him to go on. When he didn't, she said, "I understand that, but why are you dressed like him?"

"Because I am the kwisatz haderach of this planet," he said. He spoke without any particular inflection, as though stating an obvious fact.

Jill was beginning to feel frustrated. Paul was playing games with her. Maybe deciding to interview him had been a mistake. Yet he had been interesting when he was talking about how he got started reading science fiction. She decided it was too soon to give up.

"Let's stop talking about science fiction and talk about you for a minute," she said. "What's your real name?"

"People know me by lots of names," he said. "You call me Paul, and that's good enough."

Jill took a deep breath. "All right, Paul," she said. "Where are you from?"

"I was born on earth," he said. "But my real home is beyond the stars."

Jill waited a moment before speaking. "I really do want to know about you," she said gently. "I wish you would tell me the truth."

"I can't," he said. His voice was as gentle as hers, but it had a finality in its tone.

She started to ask him why, then all at once something about the way he had said "can't" caught her attention. His way of pronouncing it made it clear he wasn't British.

At first she thought he was just acting, playing the role he was dressed for. That seemed natural enough, and even genuine actors often let their accents slip. But just that change in a single word made his voice seem more familiar than before. She turned and for the first time looked at him closely in the brighter light.

She felt her heart stop, skip a beat, then resume beating at a rapid rate. The blond hair, the handsome face, the build, the height . . . it was the Jaguar. She seemed to forget to breathe, even though her mouth was open. She was staring at him, trying to see past the mask, trying to accept what was obvious.

She felt her muscles tense and heard her own involuntary gasp. He turned and looked at her, and for the first time she could see him full face. She saw the fine, strong line of his jaw and chin and the flat planes of his cheekbones. His catlike eyes peered out of the slits in the black mask.

He smiled and she could see the even, white teeth and, below the mask, the edge of the wound on his left cheek that she had made with the Mace can. Her eyes sought his left hand, but it was hidden by his leg.

She then realized why he was smiling; he was mocking her, playing with her.

He lunged for her, but only the tips of his fingers grazed the fabric of her sweater.

Jill was running now, running down the sidewalk. She was trying to run straight, trying to put as much distance between the two of them as possible.

She could feel the stinging in the bottom of her feet as her shoes hit the pavement. Her legs were pistons that mechanically worked without her direction. They functioned without effort, driving her body forward, faster and faster. Fear made her breath come in ragged, jerky gasps.

She was scared, but she also felt curiously exultant. She had broken free. He had waited too long and been too slow. She was out of reach, and she had to stay that way long enough to get to someone who could help her. She was on the street in public during the day, and it was just a matter of time before someone saw what was happening.

Yet the street was deserted; the only cars she could see were in the distance. The sidewalk was a windswept plain, a concrete desert devoid of people.

Now he was closer behind her. The distance she had gained by surprise was being lost to his longer legs and greater power. The blank wall of the hotel seemed an endless length. No matter how hard her legs pumped, nothing seemed to change. The featureless brick continued to mock her progress and belie her speed.

The end of the hotel was at the corner of a cross street, and she made the street her target. She willed herself to reach it. She could hear his feet hit the concrete, hear the dull percussion of his boots.

As she neared the corner, she could see a gray, old-fashioned humped-back Pontiac coming toward her. The car pulled into the left lane to make a turn into the cross street. Before it completed the turn, while it paused, Jill began to wave her arms above her head.

"Stop! Stop!" she yelled in the direction of the car. "Help me! Help me!" A pain in her left side, below her ribs, was so sharp she could hardly get her breath. She wasn't sure she could run anymore. She might not be able to shout again.

Miraculously, the car pulled over to the curb and stopped.

Jill was only a few feet away now, close enough to see the white-powdered face of an elderly woman looking out at her with alarm. The woman herself was obviously afraid, but she rolled down her window a narrow crack.

"I need help," Jill gasped. Her chest heaved, and the pain in her side was so severe she thought something inside her must have ruptured. She leaned against the car and bent over so the woman could hear her.

"Unlock the door, and let me in the car," Jill said.

She was about to explain when she instantaneously lost touch with everything around her. A gray-white light flashed inside her brain, and her arms, legs, and entire body jerked together.

Without support, her body fell to the pavement.

45

Wednesday 2:45 P.M.

Haack looked at Jill's crumpled body lying at his feet. He was breathing hard, but his lips pulled away from his teeth in a mocking smile. He slid the stun gun into its holster and snapped the flap closed.

"What's going on?" the old woman asked. Her voice was thin and hesitant. She craned her neck to look out the car window.

"Keep quiet," Haack commanded.

He unwound his long, black sash, then knelt on the sidewalk beside Jill. Working swiftly, he bent her arms behind her back and tied her wrists together. He tore off the loose end of the cloth and used it to secure her feet. From a zippered pocket, he took a folded rectangle of red cloth, unfolded it, then twirled the cloth by the ends to make a soft roll. He forced the roll between Jill's teeth, and tied the ends at the nape of her neck.

He stood up and leaned over Jill's body so he could talk through the partly opened car window. The old woman drew back. Her bony hands gripped the steering wheel tightly, and her watery blue eyes were open wide. She seemed puzzled and frightened.

"Sorry for being so abrupt," he said. "I didn't have time to explain. I'm Dr. Wilson, and this is my wife." He tried to sound calm and reassuring. "She's had an epileptic seizure."

"Will she be all right?" the woman asked. Her voice sounded choked.

"We were on our way to the hospital so I could put on a magic show in the children's ward. That's why I've got this costume on." He talked rapidly, not giving the woman an opportunity to think. "What's your name?" he asked her.

"Mrs. Cabell," she said faintly.

"Mrs. Cabell, Jill felt a seizure coming on, and that's why she was running and waving her arms. She wanted to ask you to take her to the hospital, but the seizure hit just as I caught up with her."

"Should we do something now?" the woman asked.

"She needs to get help," he said. "Unlock the door, and I'll put her in the car."

"I don't know," the woman said. She looked confused and uneasy. "I thought she was running away from you."

"I can see why it would look like that to you," Haack said calmly.

"Why did you tie her up?"

"So she wouldn't chew her tongue or thrash around and hurt herself," he said. "Now, Mrs. Cabell, I've got to insist you unlock the door. We need to get her to the hospital before she has another seizure." He spoke in his command voice, using the low, powerful tones that would compel obedience.

But instead of obeying, the old woman turned her head away from him and began to roll up the window as fast as she could. As soon as he realized what was happening, he thrust his fingers through the opening and held the window in position. She turned to look at him, and the white powder made her face appear bloodless.

Realizing she couldn't budge the window crank, she groped for the key to start the car. She twisted the key in the ignition and the engine turned over once but failed to catch. She tried again, hunched forward over the steering wheel. Haack thrust his hand through the narrow opening. She leaned to the right to escape his grasping fingers, but he grabbed her by her white hair and jerked her head toward him.

She fought to pull away, but he was much too strong. Her head hit the window with a sharp crack, and a thin red line of blood sprang out on her temple.

"Open the door, Mrs. Cabell," Haack said. "If you don't, I'll smash the window open with your skull." He jerked her toward the window but abruptly stopped before her head hit the glass. "See how easy it would be," he said.

The old woman was leaning to the left, giving in to the pain in her head. She said nothing but reached across with her right hand. Her fingers fumbled on the slick chrome of the latch, but she finally managed to grasp it firmly enough to pull it up.

Haack jerked the door open. With his right hand, he reached across his body and pulled the survival knife from its scabbard with one smooth arcing motion. He paused at the apex of the arc and gazed at the knife's gleaming needle point. Then as though demonstrating a move in fencing, he leaned forward and jabbed the knife through Mrs. Cabell's throat.

As he pulled out the blade, he flicked his wrist slightly to be sure he had severed her vocal cords. Blood shot from the narrow wound and splashed in a webbed pattern against the glass. Mrs. Cabell gasped loudly, then made a wet, choking noise.

Haack put down his knife, opened the back door, and picked up Jill under her arms. He leaned her shoulders against the seat, then pushed her forward so she slid across. Unfastening the clasp at his neck, he pulled off the red cape and draped it over her. It covered her from the top of her head to her ankles.

Mrs. Cabell was slumped across the steering wheel. Her powder blue suit and frilly blouse were drenched dark with blood. Her breathing was ragged. At times it stopped altogether, then afterward she would take several breaths in rapid succession.

Haack picked up his knife, wiped off its blade on the back of Mrs. Cabell's suit, and slid it into its scabbard. He grabbed Mrs. Cabell by her hair and pulled her out of the car. She fell by the front door, a foot or so from where Jill had lain. She lay face up with one arm thrown out to the side.

It was only when Mrs. Cabell lay on the pavement that he realized how much she reminded him of his mother's sister. Aunt Emily had the same powdered, pale white face as she lay in her coffin at the funeral home. Her eyelids were closed, but he knew what her eyes looked like. They had been blue also, and he could remember the way she would focus them on him with disgust she didn't bother to hide. She might have been looking at a stray dog someone had carelessly allowed to wander into the house.

"Do you have to keep the boy here?" she had asked his mother when he was about twelve. "Can't he be sent away to school?"

"We must live with our mistakes," his mother said firmly. "I know my duty." By repeating her two favorite sayings, she was declaring the topic closed.

Haack rolled down the window to hide the pattern of blood splashed on the glass. Mrs. Cabell's blue raincoat was folded neatly on the passenger seat. He shook out the coat and used it to cover the patches of blood on the driver's seat. He decided there was nothing he could do about the blood on the floor. The mat had soaked up most of it, so at worst he would get the bottoms of his boots stained.

He climbed behind the steering wheel, slammed the door, and started the engine. As he pulled away from the curb, he could feel a small bump. It was the front wheel running over Mrs. Cabell's outstretched arm.

46

Wednesday 2:50 P.M.

Don Renuzi was waiting for them at the Mt. Zion Deli. He was smiling and fingering the gold-link chain stretched across his vest.

"You look like Eliot Ness sitting there," Chase told him. She put down her bottle of beer and sat beside him.

"I feel more like Sherlock Holmes," Renuzi said.

Firecaster sat across from them with nothing but a cup of coffee. He couldn't imagine eating anything, and Chase seemed to feel the same. Except now that they were out of the apartment, she was in a surprisingly good mood. Firecaster suspected her reaction was due to a release of tension, and he could only envy her. He rubbed the left side of his face, trying to make the muscles relax.

"You couldn't have found out more than we did," Chase said. "Eric and I know who the Jaguar is."

"That's interesting," Renuzi said. Neither his face nor his voice expressed surprise. "I do too."

"You can't," Chase said. She sounded as disappointed as a child.

Firecaster was beginning to find their banter annoying. "Tell us what you and Ted Castle learned," he said abruptly. "Karen can fill you in on our morning while you two go back to Prospect Street with Ed Murphy."

"Prospect Street?" Renuzi said with surprise. "That's about a block away from City Hall."

"It's very convenient for investigation," Firecaster said sharply. "Now let's hear what you've got."

Renuzi's face became serious. "The Allen Agency was happy to cooperate. Their files aren't computerized, but they gave us a couple of people."

"So you really did find him," Chase said.

"I think so," Renuzi said. "We started a search for ex-employees going back for two years, and once we took into account sex, age, race, approximate height, blood type, and residence in the Boston area, we came up with only five names."

Firecaster hid his impatience with a question. "Was Ted Castle any help ranking them in terms of probability?"

Renuzi smiled. "How about down to one?"

"Sounds fishy," Chase said.

"Listen to this," Renuzi said. He held up an index finger. "How about somebody who was sent to work at Eastern General Hospital primarily because he was a trained locksmith? A big hospital is always having lock problems, and this guy made an ideal security officer."

Firecaster put down his coffee cup and nodded. "That would account for his ease with locks, as well as for the knowledge of the hospital Klore's killer must have had."

"Anybody who has worked security at the hospital is going to be familiar with its layout," Chase said.

"Then let me tell you something else," Renuzi said. He held up two fingers to indicate his second point. "This is a guy who used to hang around the autopsy suites watching the pathologists at work. At least he did until one of them suspected him of stealing some postmortem photographs of a woman and reported him to the administration."

"That's awful," Chase said. She curled her upper lip in disgust. "They didn't fire him for that?"

"No real evidence," Renuzi said. "The Allen Agency reassigned him to the emergency room for a while."

"Was he fired?" Firecaster asked. Renuzi's information was getting more interesting.

"Eventually," Renuzi said. "One of the morgue attendants reported a set of autopsy instruments missing. It was a special set used to do postmortems in the field. The Allen Agency had a description. It was a heavy plastic folder that contained knives, a bone saw, several scalpels, scissors, and the like."

"No direct link with your suspect?" Chase asked.

241

"Only indirect," Renuzi said. "Our suspect was working the night before the theft. He had access to every key and could go wherever he wanted to in the hospital."

"Even to places like the basement room with the power grinder," Firecaster said.

"What's his name?" Chase asked.

"John Horace Haack," Renuzi said.

Chase whistled. "Sounds very much like John Charles Webb," she said. "Give me a description."

"Twenty-nine, six-foot, blue eyes, blond hair, one-seventy."

"Bingo," Chase said in a loud voice.

Firecaster looked at Chase, but he was no longer paying attention. Something felt wrong. When he thought about Webb, Jill didn't seem to be in any special danger, and the same was true when he thought about Haack. She was in danger from the Jaguar, not Webb or Haack. But now he had to rethink everything.

"I've got a photo, prints, and blood type," Renuzi was saying. "The blood type matches, and I'll bet dollars to doughnuts Brenner can ID the picture."

"We've converged," Chase said. She held out her hands with the palms up. "We've got to be right, because we've identified the same person under two different names."

Chase's use of "converged" triggered the reconfiguration he had been trying for.

The Jaguar didn't know where Jill would be, but Webb might. Jill could have told him about doing a story on Boscon when she asked for *Dune* at Bookkeepers. Now Jill was at a hotel near the hospital where Haack had worked and had killed Richard Klore. A new picture emerged from the pieces—*the Jaguar would be at Boscon hunting Jill.*

"Let's go," Firecaster said. He jumped up from the table and headed for the door at a rapid pace. Renuzi was right behind him. Chase looked at her unfinished beer with regret, but she immediately followed Renuzi.

"Tell us what's going on," Chase said outside.

"I need to get patched through to Helen Kim," Firecaster said. "Jill is in more trouble than we suspected."

"But we knew the Jaguar might go after her," Chase said. "That's why we've got her watched and wired. If your beeper doesn't go off, everything is okay."

"I wish I could believe that," Firecaster said.

47

Wednesday 2:55 P.M.

The slamming of the Pontiac's door jarred her and made her dimly aware of her own existence. She could see nothing but faint gray light, and as she changed position slightly, she felt something covering her head.

She remembered the sickening feeling that had come over her when she realized that the person walking beside her was the Jaguar. She remembered how hard she had run and the sound of pounding boots and labored breathing so close behind her. She remembered the old lady. Then she remembered nothing else. The Jaguar had done something to her.

Her body was uncomfortable, but she wasn't in pain. Her shoulders were twisted, and because her wrists were tied, she couldn't move her arms. She tried to move her legs and found her ankles were also tied. Even though she couldn't use her hands to explore her body, she couldn't feel any wet places that might be blood. He must have knocked her out, but how could he have done it? Her head wasn't sore.

The more she became aware of herself and her predicament, the angrier she was at her own stupidity. She hadn't been on her guard. Otherwise she wouldn't have let herself be taken in by a psychopath she knew was a slick actor. She had actually asked the Jaguar to sneak out of the hotel with her. If it weren't so serious, it would be funny.

The worst was that she hadn't activated the transmitter. She had panicked, just the way she did in the stairwell of the hotel. Now with her hands tied behind her, she had no chance of reaching the button. Instead of being sure Eric would be looking for her, all she could be sure of was that she was in terrible danger.

Her feelings of anger made her fully alert, and she promised herself she wouldn't let the Jaguar make her head a trophy without a struggle. Even if she died, she would die fighting.

She made herself concentrate on the present. She knew they were in a car. Not only did the cushion under her feel like a car seat, but the sound of the engine was easy to hear. A window was open and

243

a chill breeze blew on her. She had read of kidnapped people who had been blindfolded and yet were able to tell where they were going by listening to street sounds.

The only sounds she heard were the noises of traffic. Apparently that meant they were still in a city, but beyond that she could tell nothing.

The car suddenly turned left. Odors of exhaust fumes and gasoline began drifting through the window. Then three jolts in rapid succession rattled the car as they ran over what had to be speed bumps. The only place she could remember speed bumps was the driveway into Eastern General. Jeff complained that they were so high they smashed his muffler.

The car made another sharp turn to the left, then slowed and stopped. She heard the click of a latch and then a long creaking sound as the driver's door opened. Almost at once, she heard the back door open, and she felt a rush of cool air as the cloth covering her was pulled off. She blinked her eyes, half-blinded by the daylight. She twisted her head and strained her neck as far as she was able to look past her shoulder.

The Jaguar had taken off his mask, and she could see his face clearly. His blond hair was tousled, and the cut beneath his eye was a dark red line. He looked completely calm, as though they were just out for a drive.

She closed her eyes and lowered her head as she noticed him leaning over to look inside. She tried to relax the muscles in her body. She could do nothing but pretend to be unconscious and hope she might be able to take him by surprise later. If he left her alone long enough, maybe she could work the knots off her wrists or ankles.

She felt him grab her legs. She fought down her impulse to jerk free and concentrated on making herself limp. She could tell from his grip that he was immensely strong. She realized then that if she expected to get away from him, she would have to avoid direct physical struggle.

As he was pulling her across the seat, she opened her eyelids barely enough to be able to see. She glimpsed a line of empty wheelchairs arranged in an orderly row in front of a steel and plate-glass wall. She knew where she was and why he had brought her there.

He relaxed his grip. Her legs now stuck out over the end of the seat, and he began tugging at the fastenings that bound her ankles together. In a moment, he was unwrapping the bindings. Her legs were free.

She felt the thrill of hope come alive. Surely he was going to untie her hands next. He couldn't take her into the hospital bound and gagged. That would attract the attention of Security, and they would stop and question him. He had to untie her for his own safety. Then she could at least activate the transmitter.

She could sense him bending over her. "I know you're awake," he said. He spoke softly in her ear, and she could feel his warm breath against her skin. She kept her eyes closed and gave no sign of hearing him. "The stun gun doesn't knock anybody out for a long time. So don't think you're fooling me with your little game." A stun gun! What he had done to her was clear.

She felt two cold points on her neck.

Then she experienced nothing at all.

48

Wednesday 3:00 P.M.

Haack used the piece of black sash that had tied Jill's hands to wipe down the steering wheel, window crank, turn signal, and door handles. His cloak and the other pieces of fabric were on the floor in the back of the Pontiac. The possibility of tracing any of them to him or to Charles Webb was too remote to worry about.

He was stuffing the wiping cloth into a zippered pocket when he saw a security officer coming toward him. The officer was a tall black woman, and she was walking rapidly and purposefully. She wore a dark blue uniform jacket with a red and white Allen Agency badge sewn on the left shoulder.

He felt a jolt of fear, then he realized she wasn't someone he knew. Calmly, he took out an Eastern General ID badge he had brought with him and clipped it to the collar of his stillsuit. The badge identified him as *Richard Wilson, M.D./Emergency Medicine*.

"There's no stopping here, sir," the officer said.

"I'm Dr. Wilson," he said. He tapped the plastic ID card with a fingertip. "I've got a lady with seizures in the car, and I need help getting her to the ER." He looked straight at the woman. "Please get me a wheelchair," he told her. He nodded toward the line of chairs near the hospital entrance.

The security officer glanced at the ID badge, then looked down at Jill stretched out on the back seat. She turned back to Haack. "Doctor, we're not supposed to let people go through the main doors to the emergency room," she said. "Just drive her around back to the ambulance entrance."

"I don't have time to argue with you about some goddamned stupid rule," Haack told her heatedly. He gave the woman a contemptuous look. "This patient needs help right now, so you go ahead and report me to Director Burns." He slammed the car door. "I'll get the chair myself."

Leaving the woman looking angry, he ran toward the row of wheelchairs. He pulled one out of the line and raced back with it.

The security officer was standing by the car writing in her notebook when he returned. "Brace the chair so it doesn't roll," Haack ordered her. She stared at him for a tense moment, then to his relief, she stuck the notebook into a belt holster and did as she was told. He grabbed Jill by the knees and pulled her across the seat until she was resting on her shoulders. He grabbed her under the arms, swung her around, and dropped her into the chair. He placed her feet on top of the footrests.

"I'll take it from here," Haack told the officer.

"Doctor, you can't leave this car parked here," the security officer insisted. "It's blocking traffic."

Haack glared at her, knowing he now had the upper hand. "If you want it moved, you'll have to do it yourself," he said. "Put it in the staff lot and leave the keys at the security office."

Haack then turned abruptly and pushed the chair rapidly toward the entrance. Jill's head lolled to the side. Her cheek pressed against one of the metal handles, and her hands rested uselessly in her lap. Her lips were open slightly, and saliva wet the skin at the corner of her mouth.

As Haack approached the doors, electronic sensors opened them, and he pushed the wheelchair inside without hesitating. Now that he was on a smoothly carpeted floor, he increased his speed until he was almost running.

Although patients and their friends and families filled the hospital lobby, those who noticed the wheelchair rushing toward them quickly moved out of the way and gave it room to pass.

He turned the corner into the elevator corridor and inserted his key into the staff elevator. The elevator doors rolled open, and two women with badges identifying them as nurse's aides stepped off. They glanced at Jill, then moved quickly out of the way.

Haack inserted his key into the control panel and pushed the button marked *SB*. He glanced down at Jill. He hadn't been able to pay much attention to her since she had forced him to run her down and subdue her. He didn't hold that against her. That she was full of fight added to the excitement.

Not that she didn't have other characteristics. He liked the smooth curve of her cheeks and the lean, almost boyish lines of her body. She was so beautiful and so helpless.

He wanted to spend time with her, talk to her. She would see how they could become closer than even sex could make them. First, though, they would talk. She was intelligent, and that gave them something in common. He would leave time for conversation, because he wanted her to get to know him.

He wouldn't have to worry about other people disturbing them. No one would be looking for her yet; no one knew where she was. The two of them formed their own small universe. He had planned carefully for this moment, and he would stretch it out as long as possible.

The elevator stopped at the subbasement, and he pulled the wheelchair backward onto the white vinyl floor. Beyond the vinyl, floors of dusty and unpainted concrete began.

He swiveled the chair to the right and wheeled it rapidly down the gray concrete path leading toward the old medical school building. The corridor was smooth and dry, and the halogen fixtures overhead provided white light that eliminated shadows. After five minutes of rapid walking, he passed beyond the whitewashed wall that marked the end of modern construction. Light fixtures then became infrequent, and the pale yellow glow of low-wattage incandescent bulbs deepened the shadows and accentuated the darkness.

In some places great doorless rooms, like vast empty caverns, opened off the main hall. Once they had been used for storage, and some contained remnants of their contents—a rusty operating table not used since the 1930s, abandoned instrument cabinets, broken suction machines, and tall, white-enameled light stands with missing reflectors.

Once the corridor had run straight, but it no longer did. New plumbing stacks and air-conditioning blowers interrupted it, and collateral corridors had been constructed to replace parts of the blocked original. These cut across the building at unpredictable angles, and narrow passages leading to special rooms shot off them like capillaries branching from a main artery. A turn down the wrong one would lead to a dead end, an unsuspected room, or a puzzling maze of intersecting passageways.

When he first explored the labyrinth, he had been sufficiently worried about getting lost that he tied the end of a ball of string on a doorknob near the entrance.

He glanced at Jill occasionally, but she showed no signs of re-covering consciousness. With luck, he could get her to the vat room and into his private chamber before she woke up. He would prefer not to zap her again, because he wanted to be able to talk to her as soon as they reached his room.

The vat room's heavy oak door was unlocked, just as he had left it. He tugged open the door, then turned the wheelchair around and pulled it backward across the threshold.

He was starting to suspect Jill was already conscious and just playing possum. Yet it didn't really make any difference, so long as she sat slumped in the chair. He would explain to her later that everything would be better for both of them if she cooperated.

He left Jill just inside the small room and squeezed past the chair to close the door. He twisted the porcelain wall switch, and the overhead light came on. He knelt on the floor by the end of the rusting vat. He could smell the harsh, sweetish odor of formalin coming from the tank. It gave him a thrill to know he was in a place thousands of corpses had passed through and been preserved for a time. Death had hallowed the room.

He found the recessed handle of the steel plate covering the access hole. He worked the handle loose, then stood in a crouch to get enough leverage to pull off the cover. He was standing directly behind the wheelchair, and he bumped against it slightly as he jerked the plate free and pushed it to the side. The metal cover made a harsh scraping sound on the concrete.

Suddenly two hands pushed against his back. The shove was surprisingly strong, and he was caught off guard. He staggered forward, and as he did so he half turned to look behind him.

Jill was conscious. She was still in the wheelchair, but she had twisted backward to be able to reach him. He felt a flash of anger.

Then a sickening fear drove out the anger. His right foot came down in the open air above the access hole.

He was falling.

49

Wednesday 3:15 P.M.

As soon as Jill was out the door, she grabbed for the pin at her waistband. Without slackening her pace, she held the silver octagon with her left hand and reached across with her right. She grasped the edge of the circle and gave it a quick jerk. Her fingertips slipped uselessly off the smooth metal. Her hands were too sweaty for her to get a good grip.

She tried once more with the same result, and then panic and frustration overtook her. Her heart began to pound even harder, and she began to think she was going to faint. She couldn't stop, because while she was struggling with the pin the Jaguar might catch up with her.

Fear pushed her onward, and she increased her speed as she hurtled down the dim passageway. She wasn't paying attention to where she was going. She was just running.

Then with a sudden clarity of mind she saw that sending the signal to Eric might be even more important than a temporary escape. Realizing that also made her see that it was essential to resist giving in to fear. Her only hope lay in outmaneuvering the Jaguar.

Ahead of her on the left, she could see a break in the wall that suggested an intersecting corridor. When she reached the spot, she turned down the passage and put on an extra burst of speed.

She then stopped abruptly. Still breathing heavily, she rubbed the fingers of her right hand against her corduroy pants until she was sure all the sweat was wiped off. She once more grabbed the edge of the green enameled ring and tugged on it. This time she felt some hidden mechanism click into position.

The lack of any noise when she pulled up the ring, though, made her doubt whether the signal was activated. What if the batteries were low or the silicon chip was defective? Of course, it made sense for the device to be silent. If you were an undercover cop, a buzz or beep might get you killed. Still, as she began to run again, she couldn't help wondering if Eric would get her message.

When she had leaped out of the wheelchair and run from the room, she thought help would be easy to get. She would only have to locate a security officer or meet up with some people. She was completely surprised when the corridor turned out to be deserted.

She had been in Eastern General many times but always in the public areas or the labs. The large corridor and the area around her were completely unfamiliar. She must be in a basement of one of the hospital buildings. Eventually she would run into somebody. She just had to avoid the Jaguar until that happened.

The passage she had turned into was even darker than the main one. At intervals of twenty or thirty feet, bare twenty-five-watt bulbs hung from frayed cords, but the long stretches between the small pools of gray light seemed blacker than a moonless night. She could see little, but even so she continued to run heedlessly down the hall.

The farther she ran, the more she realized she actually welcomed the darkness. It made her feel safer, as though she were partially invisible. She was far enough from the main corridor to make it unlikely anyone glancing down the passage could see her through the gloom. Also, the first rush of fear that had threatened to overwhelm her had dissipated. She felt secure enough to slow her pace to no more than a fast walk.

She might actually be safer walking, because the rapid pounding of her shoes on the concrete floor would give her away. Eventually, too, she would be so out of breath that her gasping would become noisy. She had to start thinking about details like these if she was going to elude the Jaguar. *Think like the hunter, not like the prey*, she told herself.

Haack thought his hip was broken. When he fell he had collapsed to the right, and the upper part of his thigh hit the sharp iron rim of the access hole. Pain so sharp it seemed unendurable drove everything else from his mind.

His fingers had then clawed at the rough concrete floor to gain enough hold to keep him from sliding into the open shaft and falling twenty feet to the bottom. Pounding the air desperately with his left foot, he had finally made contact with a rung of the slippery iron ladder.

Then he was safe.

He now shoved himself away from the access hole and rolled over on his back. He lay on the dirty floor with his arms at his sides, staring up at the yellowed plaster ceiling and trying to will away the red waves of pain.

He might have passed out. He wasn't sure, but it couldn't have been for long. After a while the sharpness of the pain was gone, but it was replaced by a throbbing hurt so intense he had to clench his jaw to avoid screaming when he first moved his leg.

He lay on his back and waited for the pain to subside. He would have liked to stay there for a long time, but he didn't want to let Jill get too much of a head start. He rolled onto his stomach and got to his knees. The pain in his leg was dull and throbbing, but it wasn't so severe he couldn't stand it.

He grabbed the side of the vat, and by pulling with his arms and pushing with his left leg, he got himself into an erect position. He tested his right leg by taking a step forward. The pain was sharper, and he smiled as though he were enjoying it. He would still get to celebrate the changing of the Maya month with a heart sacrifice.

He turned to leave, then he remembered the flashlight in the drawer of his desk below. Having a flashlight would greatly simplify the search. He walked over to the lift.

When he first oiled the cable and restored the electrical connections, he had thought about using the device to transport himself. He never liked climbing the rusty, wet ladder into the darkness that lay so heavily at the bottom of the shaft. He had rejected the idea, though, because the lift produced so much noise.

The drum always made a high-pitched squeal as it wound up the wire rope. Even worse, the cable holding the counterweight supporting the cargo compartment constantly sawed back and forth against some piece of metal. This produced a rough rasping sound that vibrated throughout the basement. But since these were special circumstances, he was willing to take some risk.

The cargo compartment was nothing more than a rectangular iron box open on both sides. The bottom was a flat shelf barely seven feet long and less than three feet wide, with a three-inch lip. The lip was high enough to keep a load from sliding off while the lift was operating, but not so high as to make it awkward to load or unload a rigid cadaver when transporting it to the charnel room below.

The lift's opening was three feet above the floor, and he had no difficulty sitting on the shelf and swinging his legs into position. Pain and stiffness forced him to grasp his right leg with his hand to help raise it onto the shelf. Because the platform was a little below the opening, the sharp edge of the metal plate forming the lift's housing bit into the back of his thighs.

Once he settled himself, he leaned out of the cargo compartment to turn on the motor. The process was awkward. The lift hadn't been designed to be operated from the inside, and the switch was on the wall two feet from the opening. He grasped the black wooden handle of the knife-switch, closed the circuit with a sharp downward push, then quickly jerked his arm back inside the compartment.

As the electric motor engaged, it began to unreel the cable that lowered the compartment and to raise the counterweight that would lift it again. The cable drum squealed, and the counterweight cable gave off a tortured rasping noise.

When he returned with the flashlight, the real hunt would begin.

50

Wednesday 3:20 P.M.

Firecaster stood in the vestibule outside Communications and looked at Chase and Renuzi without really seeing them. His face was a tight mask of anxiety.

"Don," Firecaster said. "I want everybody from the Task Force on duty and at the Cambridge Plaza."

"You've got it," Renuzi said.

"Order the call-up, then go to Patrol and talk to Captain Petersen directly. Tell him I need forty people to search the hotel. If he can spare more, I want them too."

"I'm on the way," Renuzi said, turning toward the door.

"Karen," Firecaster said. "I want you to take the ID photo of Jill and have Photography make a hundred copies." He held up his hand to stop her as she was leaving. "Tell them to do color photocopies. Time is crucial."

"Got it," Chase said. "I'll give them a description to put on the same sheet."

"Good idea," Firecaster said. "Wait and bring them over yourself."

Chase nodded but said nothing. She started to leave, then came back and patted Firecaster on the shoulder. "Don't let yourself believe the worst," she told him. She hurried through the door without looking behind her.

Firecaster had no real reason to believe Jill was in trouble. Helen Kim's losing sight of her didn't mean anything in itself, and he was just being cautious in sending people out to search for her. Would he do the same for somebody else? Probably, but that didn't really matter. He wasn't going to lose Jill, and he didn't care if he had to turn out the whole department to look for her.

He stood alone at the side of the hallway for a moment. He unclipped the black box of the receiver from his belt and examined it. He checked the red slide switch to make sure it was in the "on" position, then opened the battery compartment to see if the two nickel-cadmium cells were installed properly. So far as he could tell, they were.

Following his impulse to double-check everything, he turned toward the Communication offices once more. He walked through the padded soundproof door, and in the background he could hear the drone of dispatchers as they sat in their partitioned cubicles and relayed messages. He rapped his knuckles on the pebbled glass of the first door on the right, then walked in without waiting for a response.

Mary Weinthaler was sitting behind a desk cluttered with stacks of cassette tapes. Earphones with foam pads covered her ears, and she was making notes on a lined yellow pad. As soon as she saw Firecaster, she pulled off the earphones and punched a button to turn off the multihead tape deck.

"Is this thing set to work properly?" Firecaster asked. He held the black receiver so she could see it.

Mary Weinthaler peered at the receiver, then took it from his hand and began to examine it. She checked the things he had checked, then clicked open a panel on the back and looked at the wiring inside. She used the tip of a metal probe to test a few connections.

"Looks okay," she said. She slid the panel into place and handed the device back to Firecaster. "Have you got a bee out?"

"A bee?"

"The keyed-frequency transmitter," Mary Weinthaler said. "You're waiting for a bee to give you a buzz."

"I'm hoping I don't get one," Firecaster said. "But if one comes, I want to be sure I can receive it."

"How far away is the bee?"

"About three miles."

"That should be okay," she said. "You've got a variable-pitch Doppler receiver, so the higher and more often it beeps, the closer you are to the transmitter."

"Thanks for checking it out," Firecaster said. "Sorry to be rude, but I've got to get to the Cambridge Plaza Hotel in a hurry." He turned away and put his hand on the doorknob.

"Is that where the bee is?" Mary Weinthaler asked.

"Yes." He looked around but kept his hand on the doorknob.

"I wouldn't count on getting a buzz from anybody inside there."

"What the hell?" He took his hand off the doorknob. "John Barks told me it would receive for up to five miles. I asked him if it would work if there were buildings in the way, and he assured me it would."

"It will if the transmitter is outside or in a regular house," Mary said. "But if it's inside a big building, the signal may not carry so well. Large masses of concrete and steel tend to disrupt radio waves." She paused, then added, "I'm not saying you can't get a signal this far away, but I am saying don't count on it."

"Goddamn it!" Firecaster said. He jerked open the door and began pounding down the hall.

51

Wednesday 3:30 P.M.

A wavering, high-pitched squeal rose and fell above the steady background of a rough, wearing sound. The noise was not loud, but it filled the corridor and masked the soft scraping made by the soles of her shoes.

The noise startled her, and she stood with her back pressed against the wall. She leaned forward and carefully peered right, then left, but she saw nothing in either direction. Obviously, some sort of machinery was at work. She suddenly realized she should head in the direction of the sound to find the people who must be operating the equipment. The idea of being with people cheered her at once.

Yet in an instant her cheer evaporated. The sound seemed to be coming from the area she had just left, and she might go hurrying back that way only to run right into the waiting jaws of the Jaguar. The noise might even be a trap to lure her out of the darkness.

The noise abruptly stopped. She strained her ears to try to catch the sound of voices, but she could hear only machines. Somewhere close to her, a sharp click was followed by the whirring of a blower fan. The fan started with a strain, then turned faster and faster, until it was running with a steady hum.

She took a deep breath and exhaled slowly, feeling her muscles lose some of their tension. She hadn't stopped running since breaking away from the Jaguar, and the few moments of leaning against the wall made her realize how tired she was. But safety demanded she keep moving and stay wary.

She was just pushing herself away from the wall to start walking, when the noise started again. The squeal was high-pitched but thin, as though it were far away. She could tell nothing at all about the scraping, wearing sound. Probably some machine part dragging against another.

Once more, after a brief time, the noise ended suddenly. Chances were it was caused by some automatic system like the blower fan and had nothing to do with the Jaguar.

Moving more slowly than before, she started walking in the same direction. The few minutes she had stopped seemed to have given exhaustion a chance to catch up, and she thought how nice it would feel to curl up on the floor and sleep.

When she first escaped, she had thought her ordeal was virtually over. Instead, she was now trapped in semidarkness, alone, unarmed, and hunted by a killer. But it was dangerous to let herself think that way. She pushed away the feelings of panic and hopelessness that hovered on the edge of her awareness. She would do better if she concentrated on practical matters connected with survival. *Think like a hunter.*

Resting was practical. She would have a better chance of eluding the Jaguar if she weren't exhausted. If she could find a place to hide, a hole to crawl into, she could recuperate a little. Her walking slowed until she was barely shuffling forward. She stopped in one of the black spaces between the pools of feeble yellow light, but she didn't notice. She just might have hit on the only reasonable strategy, and she felt an urgent need to think it through.

Although this part of the hospital was unknown to her, the Jaguar must be familiar with it. Otherwise, he would have killed her on the street and not brought her here. Realistically, then, her capture was inevitable—unless she did something he didn't anticipate. He would expect her to run from place to place trying to find a way out of this dark maze. In fact, he would expect her to do exactly what she had been doing.

Her best bet, then, would be to break the pattern. To do that, she had to find a place to conceal herself. If she just disappeared, that would get her out of immediate danger. And if she could hide long enough, Eric would arrive.

No matter how she looked at it, her best strategy was to keep away from the Jaguar, and the best way to keep away was to find a place to hide.

She started walking again, this time with more energy and purpose. She reached another junction of hallways and after hesitating a moment, turned to the right. The intersecting corridor was even narrower and darker.

She had to move slowly now, for the only light was the one that shone at the intersection. The illumination in the passage changed rapidly from pale gray to deep blackness. The darkness seemed to affect her mind, and she lost all sense of direction. Left and right, backward and forward, felt arbitrary and puzzling. The darkness seemed to swirl around her like opaque water, and she had the feeling she was being swallowed up by it.

In panic, she flailed out and scraped her fingers against the rough plaster of the wall. She pressed her face against it until the feeling of drowning in the darkness subsided. She moved forward, but she now walked with her fingertips trailing lightly against the wall.

She walked for what seemed a great distance. She moved slowly, raising each foot and putting it down carefully, trying to avoid making noise. Her fingers encountered nothing but coarse plaster and ragged holes broken down to the lath.

Then her fingers brushed against a wooden board. A door frame! That meant a possible hiding place. She ran her hands over the door, then put her ear to the panel and listened. She heard nothing inside. Very slowly she turned the metal knob, and the latch slid back smoothly.

She pushed gently on the door, but its rusty hinges creaked sharply. When she pushed more slowly, the hinges merely produced longer, more lingering creaks. She was advertising her location, but since she had gone this far, it was probably safer to keep going. No longer trying to be quiet, she shoved the door open enough to slip inside.

She leaned her head into the corridor and listened. In the far distance, she was almost sure that she heard the hollow sounds of footsteps. But she might have imagined them. That would be easy to do, because the throbbing of ventilating fans, water pumps, and other machines would easily mimic the echoing sounds of someone walking along the hall.

She eased the door closed, then quickly began running her fingers over its surface. She explored the doorknob, then examined the areas above and below it, searching for a lock. She found none, and the disappointment brought her to the verge of tears. The fears she had felt as a child at night in the woods came flooding back to her, and she was possessed by an overwhelming conviction that she was going to die in the darkness. It seemed suffocating and horrible, as if it were a black liquid that filled her throat and her lungs and made it impossible to breathe.

Then she made herself stop searching and stand quietly for a moment. She hadn't realized how much she had been counting on locking herself away, but if she let herself panic, she was as good as dead.

Telling herself to work slowly and carefully, she ran her hand along the door facing to search for a hasp or slide fastener. Her fingers brushed against something on the wall that puzzled her—a device like a wing nut attached to a round smooth base. Then she realized it was an old-fashioned light switch. She twisted the top.

Blinding light flooded out of a single naked bulb hanging from the ceiling. Needles of pain shot through her eyes, and she covered them with her hands. Only gradually did she move her fingers aside.

She was in a storeroom. Broken chairs, rusty filing cabinets, and peculiar medical machines with dials and dangling electrical cords were scattered around. The equipment was in no particular order, and it looked as though it had been dumped in the closest empty space. White dust lay in a thick layer on every surface.

As she swiftly scanned the room, her eyes were drawn to the left back corner. A small enameled sign attached to the rough plaster read *Fire Department: Electrical Access*. Directly below the sign, flush with the wall, was a rectangular gray metal panel. Presumably the panel opened onto the tunnel carrying the building's electrical cables. She felt her spirits lighten. If she could get into the tunnel, not only would she be out of sight, but the tunnel was sure to have other exits.

She hurried across the room and knelt by the panel. Then she saw that getting into the cable tunnel was impossible. The panel was fastened with a setscrew requiring a screwdriver to turn. She pounded her clenched fist on the wall in anger.

But she wasn't ready to give up the possibility yet. She stood up and looked around at the equipment in the room. She noticed a large wooden desk standing on its end just inside the door. Was it possible one of the drawers might contain some forgotten screwdriver? Possible, but not likely.

She glanced at the setscrew again. The top was wide and the slot rather deep. Then she suddenly remembered what she used to do when she went fishing and had to tighten her reel on the rod—she had used a coin.

She jammed her hand into the side pocket of her black corduroys and found she had change of all sorts. She chose a quarter, then knelt back down by the metal panel and fit the coin into the slot. Putting as much pressure against the quarter as she could, she simultaneously twisted it to the left. The muscles in the back of her hand hurt with the strain. The screw moved a fraction of an inch before the pain forced her to stop.

She glanced over her shoulder to make sure the door was still closed. She rubbed the back of her right hand vigorously with her left, and as soon as the ache disappeared, she put the quarter back into the slot. She leaned forward, and once again, she pushed and turned. This time the screw moved as easily as if it had been oiled. She grabbed the edge of the metal panel with her fingernails, and when she pulled, the panel swung silently toward her on its hinges.

She got down on her hands and knees and peered into the tunnel. She had expected it to intersect with the wall at a right angle, but it actually paralleled the wall. A group of wires bundled together by plastic fasteners hung on the back wall, and several lines of metal conduit hung below the wires. Otherwise, the tunnel seemed empty.

She put her head inside and looked right and left. The tunnel was narrow and dark, but the blackness wasn't total. To the right, she could see a distant patch of light so bright it was like the glare of a searchlight. She guessed the light came from some other access opening. It would have to be one that had its cover off, so it should provide her a back-door exit.

She pulled her head out of the tunnel and crossed the room to turn off the light. She stood for a moment and carefully surveyed the location of objects so she wouldn't stumble over them as she made her way back to the tunnel in the dark.

With her hand on the switch, she again noticed the wooden desk balanced on its end by the door. The stubby legs were turned away from her, but the top was a smooth slab of dark wood. The desk was close to seven feet long and probably had been dumped just inside the door because it was so heavy. She would have to be careful. Standing on its end, the desk might easily fall on someone.

It might easily fall on someone!

The thought triggered a memory. When she was twelve and in the sixth grade, she asked her father to help her catch a few wild quail to take to school for the science fair. He had shown her how to rig up a box with a prop and a string and bait it with chicken feed. When the quail came up to get the feed, all she had to do was jerk out the prop and the box would fall over the quail.

She had followed his directions and caught three quail on her second try. "If you want to go after bigger game, you can build a deadfall trap the same way," her father told her. "Just prop up a log, instead of a box, and bait it with something juicy. If you get a log heavy enough, you can put a big animal out of commission."

She began to walk rapidly around the storage room to find the things she needed. If the Jaguar was familiar with the basement, sooner or later he would come into the room. To have a chance of success, she would have to work fast.

She would need a rope or something like it. Her hopes rose when she saw the drawers of a filing cabinet tied shut with a piece of twine. But when she jerked on it, it broke. It was rotten and much too weak for what she needed.

Then she saw a machine with a thick coil of brown electrical cord wrapped around the prongs of the holder jutting out from the back. The double-stranded wire was perfect for her purpose. In a flurry of action, she started unwrapping the cord from the holder. As the cord piled up at her feet, the white dust flying into the air made her eyes water.

When she reached the end of the cord, she gave it a sharp, sudden jerk. Nothing happened. She wrapped the cord around her right wrist, held the last part of it in her hand, and jerked once more. Again nothing happened.

She stood with the cord wrapped around her hand and made herself look around the room. She saw no other cord nearly as long. She clamped down her teeth in exasperation, and the frustration began to turn into the first stirrings of panic. As she fought to control her feelings, she thought she heard a faint scraping noise from somewhere down the corridor.

She quickly turned back to the machine in front of her. She stood on her left foot, raised her right foot and planted it against the gray box. She then simultaneously shoved forward with her foot and jerked back on the cord. The cord popped loose from the machine. But the machine lurched forward, bumped a broken armchair, then rocked back into place with a metallic clatter.

She winced at the noise but continued to work at a rapid pace. Starting with the end she jerked free, she began to peel the two wires apart. The thin plastic coating between them tore easily. She stopped when she reached the plug, and tied the strands together at that point. She now had a cord half as thick and twice as long as the one she started with.

She had noticed a small pile of lumber against the front wall, and she turned over boards until she found a long piece of two-by-four. She measured the two-by-four against the desk and decided it would do the job.

Now came the tricky part of the undertaking. She leaned the

board against the door and used both hands to grab the desk at the top. She had to reach above her head, and in that position, she had little leverage.

She locked her fingers around the lip between the top and the base and leaned backward with all her weight. She lifted her right foot off the floor, held it suspended behind her, and tugged. She grunted with the exertion. The desk moved toward her, reached its center of gravity, and hung poised.

She balanced the desk on its pivot point with her left hand, and with her right she grabbed the two-by-four. She held it in position and tugged on the desk. It started falling toward her, but it fell only a few inches before the top hit the timber.

The desk was now checked in its fall, though barely. The slightest disturbance would cause the prop to slip. Then the weight of two or three hundred pounds would come crashing to the floor, smashing anybody who happened to be in the way.

Kneeling in front of the door, she put her ear to the panel and listened for the footsteps. She was sure she had heard them earlier, but now she could hear nothing at all.

Working faster than ever, she wrapped three turns of wire around the two-by-four at a spot a few inches off the floor. She then tied the wire to itself, being careful not to put any pressure on the support.

A few feet away, she looped the wire around the back of a chair. She laid the wire in a straight line to the access hole and placed the coil inside the tunnel.

She walked back to the door to turn out the light. As she paused to survey her work, she heard a slight scraping noise, maybe the sound of a boot dragging on concrete. With a quick twist, she turned the switch and plunged the room into absolute darkness. The noise came from down the corridor, and when she heard it again, it was closer.

52

Wednesday 3:40 P.M.

Jill lay stretched on her stomach in the tunnel, her head toward the distant light. The tops of her toes pushed against the concrete floor, and her leg muscles were already beginning to cramp. The metal panel was opened just enough for her to see the door, and the electrical cord was wrapped around her right hand. Sweat from her hand made the cord slick.

She remembered how Eric had said he wanted to keep her safe in his hip pocket, and the sense of loss she felt made her eyes burn with tears. She should at least have let him send someone to watch over her. Had he even gotten her signal? So much time had passed. And she seemed so remote, so much out of sight, that it was hard to believe he was trying to find her. It felt as if she existed only for the Jaguar.

As she lay in the dark, hours seemed to pass. She tried to keep perfectly still and to make herself breathe regularly and slowly. Her back muscles ached, and she half turned to lie on her left hip. She was careful not to tug on the trip wire.

She peered into the darkness, looking toward the door. All she could see was a faint line of light shining between the edge of the door and the jamb. The room itself was too dark even for shadows. The desks, broken chairs, and cast-off machines were all invisible.

The only sounds she could detect were the noises of her own breathing and the soft rustle of her clothes. Then she sensed another sound. She strained her ears to catch it—a faint click. She held her breath and froze in position.

The thin line of light between the door and the jamb slowly widened as the door swung open with a barely audible creak. The absolute blackness gave way as more light broke in and transformed the room into a place of gray shadows and hulking shapes.

She had no doubt about the identity of the shadowy figure standing in the opening. What surprised her was that he could be so quiet, so cautious. She gently pulled on the electrical cord, taking up the slack until she could feel tension develop. The Jaguar hadn't moved, but she wanted to be ready.

Time crawled by, but he stood as unmoving as a statue. *Turn on the goddamned light,* she shouted in her mind. The frustration was almost unendurable, and she shook her head and squeezed her left hand into a tight fist.

Suddenly, she had a disconcerting thought. What if he came into the room without turning on the light? She wouldn't be able to tell when to jerk the trip wire, and she might do it too soon or too late. Everything had to work just right or it wouldn't work at all. She had to do something.

She relaxed the tension on the cord and turned back onto her stomach. She pushed gently on the panel covering the access hole. The hinge produced a faint metallic squeak that shattered the silence with the force of an explosion.

The naked bulb in the center of the room blazed into brilliance. She blinked and squinted her eyes, until she could see the Jaguar standing in the doorway.

In his black suit, he looked like an executioner in a Renaissance play. His handsome face was fixed in a twisted expression, and he moved his head from side to side as his eyes rapidly swept the room. They stopped at the metal panel that hid her. He looked away, then back again. This time he smiled slightly.

She felt he knew exactly where she was hiding. The feeling unnerved her, and she almost failed to notice when he took a step into the room. The step put him exactly in line with the desk. If he looked to his right, he would see it.

While her luck was still good, she gave a sharp jerk on the trip line. A raw scraping sound filled the room. The chair! She forgot she had tied the trip cord to the chair.

The Jaguar stopped where he was and turned his head warily to the left to look for the cause of the noise. Panic threatened to engulf her. With desperation, she jerked the trip wire again, pulling it hard enough to overturn the chair and tear loose the support.

The first sound she heard was the noise of the timber smacking the concrete floor. Then she saw the Jaguar jump to the side with his right arm extended, attempting to ward off the broad expanse of wood hurtling down on him. But the door was in his way. He stumbled against it, slamming it back into the wall.

The desk hit him on the top of the shoulder, and he stood upright for a long moment, as though he were going to support the massive weight. Then his right leg seemed to collapse under him. He staggered to the side and fell.

When he fell, the desk went with him. The crash shook the concrete floor and sent up clouds of dust as thick as smoke. Jill heard him give a deep-throated gasp of shock or pain, and in the confusion, she was sure the desk had knocked him unconscious or hurt him so badly he would be unable to move.

Nevertheless, she remained perfectly still and waited to see if she could come out of hiding. A moment later, she watched in horror as he sat up and rubbed his shoulder with his left hand. He explored the area carefully, pressing and poking himself.

She lay silent, frozen into immobility by disappointment. Then the chill of fear began to spread from deep inside her. If he didn't already know exactly where she was, all he had to do now was follow the wire. *Why was Eric taking so long?* She fingered the octagon to make sure the button was pulled out.

The Jaguar braced himself against the fallen desk and stood up, clearly favoring his right leg. He tried to move his arm forward, tracing the beginning of a circle, but he abruptly stopped and rubbed his shoulder again. When he took a step forward, he seemed to avoid putting weight on his right leg. He staggered slightly.

She needed to get moving while he was still dazed. She inched forward toward the distant light. As she drew close to the access hole, the Jaguar spoke.

"Congratulations," she heard him say. She had no doubt he was addressing her. "I didn't expect to get a scratch." He paused, then in a louder voice said, "But the hunt's not over yet." She could no longer see him, but she could hear him clearly.

Behind her, she heard a rustle, then a sharp clank. It was the cord, she realized. He had jerked the cord, and the coil in the tunnel hit the metal panel and slammed it against its frame. Now he knew exactly where she was.

She glanced backward, but the light in front made it impossible to see anything in the darkness behind her. Yet it was easy to imagine he was already crossing the room to reach the entrance to the tunnel, and she made herself hurry even more. She no longer worried about being quiet.

She stopped to listen, but she could hear nothing but her own gasping. She held her breath, and behind her she heard the faint scraping of boots on concrete.

She raised herself to a low crouch and rushed forward down the tunnel. Her head struck the rough concrete above her, forcing her to bend lower. Within a short distance the muscles of her thighs began to burn and ache.

She bit her lip in pain and continued as far as she could, then she dropped to her knees and began to crawl. The light ahead was much brighter, and the opening couldn't be more than fifteen feet away. Yet the noises behind her were even louder than before. He was gaining on her.

The rough concrete of the floor tore at her hands. Her knees felt bruised and skinned. But despite her pains, she had gained some distance. The opening was only half a dozen feet in front of her. She was going to make it!

The noises from behind her were not as close as they had been. She hurled herself the last few inches forward and at last was even with the light coming from the tunnel opening.

Then she saw that she was trapped. A metal grating covered the opening. A grid of small squares let the bright light flow into the tunnel but kept her from getting out.

For a moment, her heart stopped, then it beat faster than ever. "Oh, my God," she said aloud. She put her fingers through the grillwork and shook it. The metal was thin, but not so thin that she could rip it apart with her fingers.

The sounds behind her were growing louder.

She pounded on the center of the grille with her fist. The metal bent slightly but showed no sign of breaking. She hit it again and again. A small rounded pouch formed, but the grating held firm.

In desperation, she twisted her body around in the tunnel and put both feet against the grille. She was almost too doubled up to move, but she did have some leverage. With her back propped against the wall and the bundle of cables pressing against her spine she shoved outward with both feet.

Nothing happened, but she kept up the pressure. She shoved, then slacked off, then did the same thing again and again. Finally she felt something break loose. Yet the grate still didn't fall out.

Now she could hear the labored breathing of the Jaguar as he hauled himself along the tunnel after her. The sounds were so clear he had to be just a few feet from her.

She shoved once more, harder than ever before. She strained her back against the concrete, pushing as though she wanted to force herself into the wall.

The grating gave way at last, popping out of the opening and clattering to the floor outside. Both her feet jutted through the access hole, and she made no attempt to turn around. She gave a shove with her hands and shot out of the tunnel and into the full brightness of the room.

She hit the floor sitting down, but she was immediately on her feet. With relief, she saw that the metal panel of the access hole hadn't been removed. She swiped at it with her hand and slammed it shut.

She took a quarter from her side pocket and tried to fit it into the setscrew on the panel. Her hands were trembling so much the coin rattled on the metal, but she managed to get it into the slot, then quickly turned the screw to fasten the latch.

A loud hammering noise made her jump away from the tunnel entrance. She turned to run, but then looked back.

A bulge was already forming in the center of the metal panel.

53

Wednesday 3:50 P.M.

Jill knew the thin metal wouldn't be strong enough to keep the Jaguar inside. He could be out of the tunnel and running after her before she could cross the room. Even if she made it out the door, she couldn't count on finding another place to hide. With his greater speed, he would run her down.

Then the pounding stopped. Perhaps he was gathering his strength or perhaps he wanted to catch her unprepared. Whatever the reason, the delay gave her a chance to think.

She looked around quickly for a weapon.

The room was brightly lighted, and the floor was a cream-colored vinyl polished to a high gloss. Yet what she noticed most was the musty animal smell filling the air.

To her right she saw a stainless steel animal cage a good five feet tall and eight feet wide. Her initial impression was that something large and white was inside. When she took a few steps closer, she saw the cage was filled with a writhing mass of hundreds of white rats. The rats were packed together into an almost solid body, and as they jostled against one another, the composite body rippled like the skin of a giant animal.

A printed sign hung above the cage door: *Project Futureworld.* Below, a message said in smaller letters: *No food or water without OK from Dr. Polk. Keep door latched!*

The rats immediately became aware of her. They threw themselves against the heavy wire rods of the cage and crawled on top of one another. All seemed to be trying to escape at once. The bright overhead light glinted from dozens of beadlike eyes, and a strange combination of chattering and squealing rose in pitch until she could hear nothing else.

She turned away from the cage with revulsion, but she had no time to dwell on what she saw. The practical matter of finding a weapon was much too pressing.

Then she saw it. Leaning against the wall opposite the rat cage was a round wooden pole, two inches in diameter and five feet long, with a metal hook screwed into the end. Apparently the pole was used to adjust the flow of air coming through the register above the rat cage.

She snatched up the rod and hurried back to stand by the opening. She could still hear nothing from behind the panel, but she knew the reprieve wouldn't last much longer.

Her plan was simple. The panel couldn't keep him from getting out, but he would have to crawl through the opening. During that time she would have the advantage. When his head came through, she would hit it with the pole.

She took up a position to the left of the opening. She would have to make it hard for the Jaguar to grab her or take away her pole. She stood with her right shoulder to the front. That way she could bring the pole down parallel to the wall and deliver the blow without putting herself in danger.

She made a practice pass. With a single, smooth chopping motion, she swung it past the opening, then pulled up short just as its tip hit the vinyl floor. Everything worked just the way she wanted it to.

Suddenly the rats seemed disturbed again. Their chattering squeals rose in volume until they became so loud she was sure she wouldn't be able to hear any noises from the tunnel. She wanted to look around to see why the rats were agitated, but she dared not take her eyes off the panel.

Then she heard what could only be the click of a key in a lock. She turned toward the front of the room.

The Jaguar was standing just inside the doorway. His black stillsuit was now covered with splotches of white dust, and his blond hair was disheveled. A long scratch still oozing blood ran down one cheek from his temple to his chin.

She realized he must not even have tried to get out of the opening she was guarding. He must have known about another opening farther on. Or maybe he just worked his way back to the storage room.

Time seemed to have come to a stop and rendered everything unreal. She felt as if she were not part of the scene but an onlooker.

She was not frightened. She wasn't even particularly interested. She had become as unreal as everything around her.

The Jaguar smiled at what she realized must be the stunned, stupid expression on her face. But the smile had the effect of breaking the spell his appearance had cast over her. She was angry now, angry and determined that he wasn't going to get her without a fight.

Still smiling, he took two steps toward her. Although he limped slightly, he moved warily, ready to change his direction if she should suddenly bolt and run. She stayed where she was until he was about four feet from the rat cage.

"Yaaahaaa!" she shouted and ran at him with the pole lowered like a lance. The Jaguar was startled enough to jump backward, and while he was off balance, she tore open the latch on the rat cage. She dropped the heavy steel wire door, and it hit the floor with a sharp clang.

Hardly pausing to see what was happening, she moved sharply to the right and away from the front. She then swung the pole against the side of the cage.

Rats by the hundreds came streaming out of the cage, running directly toward the Jaguar. Their red eyes glittered in the bright light, and their pink hairless tails whipped back and forth across the vinyl. The scratchings of their claws as they scrabbled across the slick floor mixed with thousands of high-pitched squeaks.

The Jaguar stared in surprise, but before he could do anything, a dozen rats were crawling all over him. They dug their nails into the black fabric of his clothes and clawed their way toward his face. Their small sharp teeth were bared in anticipation of feeding.

He knocked rats off with his hands, brushing them to the floor. Some he tore off and threw down at the moving stream that continued to come toward him. He began to kick at the rats, and their thin high-pitched squeals of pain filled the air like smoke.

Jill worked her way around the back of the cage to the opposite side and prepared to run out the door. She waited a few seconds, until the Jaguar seemed completely engaged in fighting off the rats that still climbed over him.

Then she stopped thinking and allowed her body to take over. She gripped the pole in her right hand, then running on her toes, she left the cover of the cage and rushed for the door. She was halfway there when a rat scurried in front of her. She was moving too fast to avoid stepping on it, and she came down hard with all her weight. The rat screamed as her foot crushed its back, and she looked down in horror.

She jerked up her foot, throwing herself off stride. She lost her balance and fell to the floor. As she fell, she flung out her right hand to catch herself and lost her grip on the pole. It rattled across the floor and landed far out of her reach.

Rats immediately swarmed over her, and she felt razor-sharp bites on her arms and the backs of her hands. She jumped to her feet and began flailing at the rats with both hands.

The blow that hit her on the side of the head caught her totally by surprise.

54

Wednesday 3:55 P.M.

Firecaster raced down Massachusetts Avenue toward Boston, then turned north at the first cross street. To make the turn, he had to cut in front of two lanes of oncoming cars. Brakes screeched and drivers cursed him, but he was already around the corner and speeding down Compton Street.

The Saab had neither red lights nor sirens to clear the traffic, and as Firecaster dodged past slow cars, he wished he had an escort to make traffic stop altogether. But he didn't have time.

Compton was a narrow street with more stop signs than traffic lights, but he didn't stop for either. As he reached each intersection, he slowed to make sure a car wasn't going to ram him. Then with his horn blowing he sped across and immediately increased his speed again.

He unclipped the beeper from his belt and put it on the seat beside him. As soon as he reached a straight stretch of road, he picked it up and waved it out the window.

Nothing happened.

He dropped the beeper back onto the seat so he could pay attention to his driving. Four cars were lined up taking their turns at a stop sign. He began pushing on his horn repeatedly to create a series of annoying beeps, then he turned the Saab into the left lane and rushed past the waiting cars.

Suddenly a black Ford Towncar was coming down the left lane toward him. The driver was wearing a blue chauffeur's cap and paying no attention to the road.

Firecaster squeezed tight on the steering wheel and made his horn blare constantly. The driver looked up in sudden fear and pulled the wheel to his right. Firecaster pulled hard to his right, and the two cars shot past one another just as they reached the center of the intersection.

Firecaster cut back into the right lane and slowed slightly. He snatched up the receiver again, held it out the window, and waved it around. The speaker emitted a faint, thin electronic noise, but as he moved his arm, the signal died away.

He pointed the receiver in what he thought was the direction of the hotel. The tone sounded again. It was wavering and intermittent, but when he held his hand in place, it became constant.

The signal confirmed his fear—Jill was in trouble and needed help. A rush of dread smothered him for an instant. Could he find her in time to do any goddamned good? The hotel was a huge place.

He dropped the beeper onto the seat. The muscles around his left eye were pulled tight, and his vision on that side was distorted. The cars on the street and the small brick business buildings all looked slightly twisted and out of focus.

A yellow flash of lightning turned the dark sky purple, and in seconds a clash of thunder rattled the windows of the Saab. The windshield was dry, but in only a matter of minutes the rain would come. Driving would be even more hazardous, but what worried him most was what rain might do to the signal from Jill's transmitter.

All at once, the receiver came to life, and the speaker began to emit faint, slow beeps. The signal was weak, but at least it could now be picked up inside the car. He smiled wildly and pushed harder on the accelerator. He blew his horn in a series of rapid beeps and dodged one car after another.

The Cambridge Plaza Hotel was on Locust Street, and when he reached the intersection of Compton and Locust, he took the corner on two wheels. The rear of the car skewed to the left, and he simultaneously applied the brake and turned the steering wheel to try to keep from flipping over.

As soon as he felt sure the Saab wasn't going to roll, he sped up again. Locust was four wide lanes and had little traffic. He was within a mile of the hotel, and the beeps from the receiver were becoming stronger and more frequent.

The semicircular driveway in front of the hotel was crowded with cars. One lane was filled with six Cambridge patrol cars and four light-colored Dodges and Plymouths used by the Detective Division. Two other patrol cars were parked on the street, and a dozen uniformed officers were headed toward the hotel's entrances.

Firecaster stopped the Saab on the street in front of a patrol car. He jumped out with the beeper in his hand, and as he passed the patrol car, he could hear its radio crackling out information and instructions. He walked rapidly across the concrete driveway and into the carpeted lobby of the hotel.

He stopped suddenly just inside the door. He held up the beeper over his head, then moved it around. He expected the strength and frequency of its beeps to increase.

But they weren't. The beeps actually sounded slightly slower and weaker. Moving the receiver around didn't help.

"Eric!" someone shouted.

He looked across the lobby and saw Renuzi coming toward him. He was pushing his way through knots of people and walking so fast he was almost running.

"We're doing a floor-by-floor search," Renuzi told him. He sounded breathless. "We don't have good news, but we don't have bad news either."

"No news is still good right now," Firecaster said.

"Brady told me something you should know," Renuzi said. He leaned closer to Firecaster to exclude people standing near them. "Right before you got here, an old lady was found stabbed to death at the end of the block. She had also been run over with a car."

Firecaster grasped the picture at once. "So it's possible she was driving, the Jaguar stopped her, killed her, and took her car."

"Right," Renuzi said. "And of course it's possible he took Jill with him."

"Which corner was it?" Firecaster asked.

"The east one," Renuzi said. He nodded his head in the direction. "The one toward Eastern General."

Firecaster sensed that Renuzi had just handed him the final piece to a puzzle. He stood silent for a moment, staring out at the crowd with fixed eyes. Then all at once, without any effort, the pattern emerged.

The receiver wasn't beeping the way it was supposed to, because Jill wasn't at the Cambridge Plaza Hotel at all.

"Follow me," he ordered Renuzi.

Firecaster shoved open the plate-glass door with such force it thudded against the rubber stop. Renuzi raised his left hand and caught the door on the rebound.

Firecaster was running and already halfway to his car.

55

Wednesday 4:00 P.M.

Jill was aware of a luminous gray darkness swirling around her like heavy smoke. She felt that something terrible had happened, but exactly what it was eluded her.

Her nose was clogged with dust, and her throat was intolerably dry. Her arms and hands burned from the many scrapes and bites, and the back of her head hurt where it rested on the floor. As her eyes slowly came into focus, she could see someone standing above her. She thought Eric had finally arrived, and she started to smile. He would take her in his arms and lift her up, and all the bad things would be forgotten.

Then she saw it wasn't Eric.

"Sit up," the Jaguar commanded. His voice was harsh.

She pushed against the gritty concrete floor and managed to struggle to a sitting position. Her legs were stretched in front of her, and she put her right hand behind her to prop herself up. She rubbed the back of her head, then winced with pain as her fingers touched a large, tender lump on the left side.

She glanced around and saw they were in the hallway again. A metal door with a light above it was opposite her. Two white rats lay curled up outside. One looked dead, but the other was still moving slightly, a front paw feebly clawing the air.

The Jaguar was leaning against the wall with his right foot extended in front of him, and his right arm held close to his body. His face looked drawn and tired, but his eyes were as hard and unsympathetic as steel.

"Why are you doing this to me?" she asked. Her voice broke, and tears ran down her cheeks. She looked away, then wiped her eyes with her fingertips.

"I want us to know one another," he said. The harshness was gone, and he sounded reassuring, as if he were speaking to a worried child. "We'll be closer than you ever imagined possible."

"Just go ahead and kill me," she said impulsively. Her voice was harsh and angry, with no hint of pleading in it. She didn't want to give him the satisfaction of knowing how frightened she was.

271

"We can't stay out here in the hall," he said, ignoring what she said. Then in an almost conspiratorial tone he added, "I know a place where we can be private." He spoke like a lover planning a rendezvous.

"I'll do whatever you tell me to," she said, trying to sound resigned. Something was keeping Eric away, and playing along would gain her time and maybe another chance to escape. If she could break away and run, he might not be able to catch her. His right leg was obviously painful.

"I'm glad you're so agreeable," he said. "You've hurt me worse than I've hurt you." He patted his leg and held out his arm. "I can't zap you with the stun gun, because I can't carry you. You're going to have to go under your own steam."

He spoke as if she had done him a great wrong, and she realized he was looking for sympathy. He sounded very sorry for himself.

"Your leg must be very painful," she said gently. Could she make him trust her?

"My shoulder is, too," he said, sounding like a small child seeking his mother's reassurance. "My collarbone may be broken."

"I'm sorry you got hurt."

"I didn't *get* hurt," he said. "You hurt me." He sounded more surprised and petulant than angry.

"I'm very sorry," she said soothingly.

"You've been a good opponent, but in the end you had to lose. You simply don't have the same mental abilities I do." He shrugged his left shoulder. Looking squarely at her, he said, "You see, my ancestors really did come from beyond the stars."

Jill nodded but kept quiet. She was afraid if she said anything, he might construe it as doubting him.

"Tie this around your neck," he said. He pulled out the strip of black fabric he had used on her wrists and tossed it into her lap. "Fix it so a long piece hangs behind."

Jill folded the fabric into a narrow band and wrapped it around her neck one turn. Instead of tying a knot, she simply crossed the ends and pulled the band tight.

"Let's see what you've done," he said. He pushed himself off the wall and took two short steps toward her. He inserted a rigid finger between the fabric and her neck and jerked. The fabric pulled loose.

"Predictable," he said. "Now tie it again, and do it right or I'll have to punish you."

She tied the scarf with a knot that held when he tugged on it. "Excellent," he said. "I'm pleased you can do as you're told, but you must learn to do it the first time. I'm going to give you another chance to show me how well you behave."

"What do you want me to do?" Jill asked.

"I want you to lie back down on the floor and raise your left arm." He looked at her with a fixed smile.

Jill glanced up at him and hesitated. Seeing no alternative, she eased herself down onto the dusty concrete. The bump on her head hurt as she was forced to put weight on it.

"Excellent," he said again, as though she had done something particularly difficult. "Now raise your left arm."

She lifted her arm so it stuck straight up from her shoulder. The Jaguar wrapped his left hand around her wrist and held it. His grip was so powerful she could feel a tingling in her fingers as the pressure shut off the circulation. Her wrist might as well be locked into the jaws of a machine.

"Now pay attention," he said. "Notice what I'm doing."

As she looked up at his impassive face, she could feel fear begin to rise in her again. What was he planning to do?

With his right hand, he took hold of her ring finger and bent it backward a little toward her wrist. She felt a twinge of pain and jerked on her hand, but she couldn't move it. It was locked into the machine.

"Ow!" she said loudly, exaggerating the pain. "You're hurting me."

"I learned this trick from primitive tribes," he said. "If you want somebody to remember what you tell them, hurt them while you're telling them."

"I'll remember," Jill said. "Now please turn me loose."

He gazed down at her and smiled, then pushed farther back on her finger. As she began struggling to get off the floor, he put his right foot against her throat and shoved her back. She tried to scream, but he increased the pressure on her larynx. She could barely breathe.

"Hurts, doesn't it?" he said. He sounded pleased. "Maybe as much as where you stabbed me last night. Maybe as much as my leg and my arm . . . you fucking bitch." He spat out the last words. For a moment, his anger seemed to hover in the air, swirling around them like a disgusting odor.

"Please stop," she tried to say. The pressure on her throat made her voice strange and whispery.

Then with a single sharp jerk, he bent her finger all the way back toward her wrist. She could hear the bone snap.

Then agonizing pain ran through her whole hand like molten metal. She convulsively jerked her arm toward her, but the machine held it tight. She tried to scream, but he shoved down even harder with his foot. Her voice came out of her mouth as little more than a gargling, croaking noise.

He turned loose of her wrist and stepped away from her. She picked up her left hand in her right and stroked the damaged finger. The pain was so intense she could think of nothing else. It filled her mind with a turbulent red haze that blinded her to her surroundings.

"I am in control," the Jaguar said. His voice was calm and reasonable once more. "Do exactly what I tell you to, and don't make me tell you twice. Is that clear?"

Jill licked her lips and tried to speak. For a moment, she couldn't get her mouth to work. At last she was able to say softly, "Yes."

"You have nine more fingers, and you see how much it hurts to break one. Imagine how it would feel to have them all broken." He paused, then added, "One right after the other."

Jill said nothing. She rested her left hand against her chest. Keeping her hand immobile seemed to help. Her finger was throbbing, and each beat of her heart made the blood pulse painfully in the tip.

"Get up," he said. "That's your first command."

She used her right arm to help her sit up, then she pulled her legs under her and stood. She felt dizzy and nauseated. Her throat hurt where the Jaguar's foot had pressed against it. The Jaguar stood behind her, and she could feel him take hold of the black noose he had made her tie around her neck.

"I've got your tail now," he said. He gave the noose a sharp jerk. It threw her off balance, and she had to take a step backward to keep from falling. "If you try to wander off, I'll just give a little pull, and you'll come right back. Understand?"

"I understand," she said.

"Just to be sure, I have another little something to remind you," he said. He sounded like a small boy playing a game. She heard a movement behind her, then felt the sharp prick of a knife point through her sweater. She gasped and involuntarily stepped forward to escape the pain. As she did so, he jerked tight on the black noose.

"If you try to escape, you're dead," he told her. "Now walk straight ahead. I'll tell you where to turn."

She walked slowly, and except to tell her to go right or left, he said nothing. Now and then, he would give the noose a twitch, as if he were walking a dog and wanted to remind it who was master.

"Stop," he ordered. They were in front of a battered, black-painted wooden door. "Spread your legs, and lean against the wall."

She tried not to put any weight on her left hand. Her finger was swelling at an alarming rate, and it was still throbbing with every beat of her heart. He held onto the end of the noose while he unlocked the door. He pulled it open and stepped back.

When she stepped inside, she realized she was back where she had started. The wheelchair was pushed to the side, and in front of her was the giant galvanized tank.

"Walk to the left," he told her. "I'm going to give you the ride of your life."

"Where are we going?"

"To a place where we can get to know one another," he said. "A place where nobody will disturb us."

She halted at the rear wall and stood staring into an opening at a rusty metal platform attached to some sort of machinery. She wasn't sure what the device was, but it resembled a lidless iron coffin.

"Get in," the Jaguar told her.

56

Wednesday 4:15 P.M.

Twisting waves of rain high as telephone poles whipped in from the east and rushed down the street with the speed of an express train. The rain flattened itself on the windshield and spread out to form a thin sheet of gray water. The Saab's wipers whipped back and forth at their highest speed, but visibility was virtually nil.

"Goddamn it," Firecaster said. "It hasn't rained in a month and it has to rain now." He hunched over the steering wheel and thrust his head forward, as though a few extra inches would make it easier to see the road.

Directly in front of the Saab, a patrol car with flashing red lights and a howling siren cleared the way through the traffic. The car was traveling at barely forty miles an hour, but the curtain of rain hanging over the street made the speed seem reckless.

"It's raining too hard to last," Renuzi said. He wiped off his window to get a view of the street. Everything was at a virtual standstill. Pedestrians had disappeared from the sidewalk, and a large number of cars were stopped by the side of the road to wait out the storm.

The thunderstorm had broken while they were running the short distance from the hotel to the car. Firecaster escaped with only a few wet spots on the shoulders of his jacket, but Renuzi got drenched during the few extra seconds it took to order an escort. His wet hair hung in black strands over his forehead, and the front of his suit was dark with rainwater.

"Check the beeper," Firecaster said.

Renuzi picked up the receiver from the seat and slid the red switch on top to the "receive" position. Immediately, the box emitted a stream of rapid, high-pitched beeps.

"The rate is definitely faster," Renuzi said.

"It's got to be the hospital," Firecaster said.

Without signaling, the patrol car suddenly turned left in front of a brown and white Moxie delivery truck. Firecaster put on the brakes to reduce his speed for the turn, and the Saab began a slow skid sideways in front of the truck.

The truck driver had no time even to try to stop. The bumper of the truck caught the Saab on the left rear fender with a solid jolt and a dull crunch of metal. The rain-slick street offered little resistance to the force of the crash, and the car spun around in the opposite direction.

The truck slewed to the right side of the road, hurling cases of soda bottles out of the open-sided racks and onto the concrete. The breaking of the glass bottles produced a soft popping sound that seemed to go on for minutes, and gallons of caramel-colored soda mixed with gray rain in the gutter.

"Christ almighty," Renuzi said softly.

Firecaster fought the wheel to keep the car from running over the curb and smashing into the curved metal pole of a street light. The right wheel clipped the curb and the pole flashed past the fender. The car rocked from side to side, but Firecaster wrestled it back into the road.

Firecaster slowed almost to a stop, then completed a U-turn to follow the patrol car into the semicircular drive of Eastern General Hospital. The massive buildings were shrouded in curtains of rain, but the green glare of sodium vapor lights marked the way to the patients' entrance.

"Check the beeper," Firecaster said.

Renuzi slid the red switch into the "on" position, and beeps immediately came from the tiny speaker. "Same as last time," he said.

"We're still not close enough."

Firecaster pulled the Saab under the concrete canopy over the row of doors leading into the lobby. The patrol car was stopped in front of the closest door. The driver's window was rolled down, and as Firecaster drew parallel, the officer gave Renuzi a questioning look.

Renuzi turned to Firecaster and asked, "Should we go inside?"

"Not without a stronger signal," Firecaster said, holding up the transmitter. "Let's go around to the emergency entrance and see what we get."

Renuzi cranked down his window. "Emergency room!" he shouted to the patrol car driver. As he rolled up the window he said, "I thought we were going to be patients there ourselves a few minutes ago." He took a deep breath and exhaled. "Which wouldn't help Jill much."

Leaving the protection of the canopy and driving into the rain again was like running into a wall of water. Rain swept over the hood and roof in waves, and the constant pounding of rain on the windows produced a dull hammering noise.

"Should I turn off the beeper?" Renuzi asked.

"Leave it on," Firecaster said.

"Where is the emergency room?"

"At the rear," Firecaster said. He pulled onto the street, then at once turned left. At the end of the block, he turned left again and drove behind the older section of the hospital.

As soon as they rounded the corner, the beeper immediately began to change its frequency and pitch. The beeps came faster and faster, until they were almost a single high-pitched sound.

"We've got it!" Renuzi said. "Stop here!"

Firecaster stepped on the brakes and slowed to a virtual crawl. He and Renuzi leaned inward, hovering over the receiver on the seat between them. Within a few dozen feet, the beeper's tone dropped back to a rapid but discontinuous pattern. Firecaster stopped the car immediately, then backed up. Once more the beeper resumed its high-pitched constant wail.

"The other side of that wall," Firecaster said. He nodded toward the windowless expanse of red brick directly opposite them.

"I'm not sure that's even part of the hospital," Renuzi said. "It might be a research wing."

"I don't care what it is. We're going inside."

"How do we get in?" Renuzi asked. "There aren't even any windows, and it might take us an hour to find our way back to this spot." He shook his head. "The hospital's a goddamned maze, you know that."

"Look right there," Firecaster said. He pointed to the long, rectangular door set flush with the brick wall. Where the black paint had flaked off the metal, rust spots showed through. In the rain, the spots looked dark and gritty.

Firecaster got out of the car. With the wind whipping rain into his face, he jumped the torrent of water rushing down the gutter and crossed the few feet of sidewalk. Renuzi followed right behind him.

"That's steel or cast-iron," Renuzi said. He raised his voice to be heard above the rain. "And I can see the places where it's been welded shut." He touched two flat scarred places on the metal door. "It would take too long to get tools."

"But look at this," Firecaster said. He tapped a heavy metal ring that had once been part of the door's latch. Then turning to Renuzi he said, "Get the patrol car over here. Tell them to back up and jump the curb. I want the rear end right where we are now."

Renuzi opened his mouth to say something, but Firecaster was already running back toward the Saab.

57

Wednesday 4:20 P.M.

For the second time, Jill listened to the wavering, high-pitched squeal and the dull rubbing sound. Only now the noises were louder and she knew exactly what was producing them.

She lay on the cold iron shelf of the lift, and as the platform moved down the dark shaft, the noises made by the cables blocked out all other sounds. The screeching and rubbing made her wonder if the cables were going to snap and kill her by dropping her to the bottom of the shaft. Then she wondered if she wouldn't be better off if they did.

The only light was the feeble gray glow coming from the rectangular slot directly above her. Her hands and feet were lashed together with the black sash, and she felt completely helpless, adrift in the darkness, suspended between living and dying. She was frightened, but she no longer experienced the sharp edge of fear.

She was caught, and her body was no longer preparing her for flight.

Her broken finger still throbbed, but the intense agony that made her cry out at first was gone. Strangely, what upset her most was that her father could never know she died so young. As she realized that, tears filmed her eyes.

The strength of her reaction was unexpected. If her father had a dream for her, he never told her about it. Yet she still felt as if she were dying before she had done what he wanted her to. Maybe it was because his dream was no more specific than that she live a full life, and she had been on the threshold of that.

Thoughts of her father blended with thoughts of Eric. She wasn't sure she remembered what he looked like, because the face of the Jaguar kept forcing its way into her awareness.

With a single sharp jerk, the iron platform came to a halt. The squeaking and rubbing of the lift cables ceased, producing a silence made more profound by the darkness surrounding her. She had no idea where she might be. She could tell from a current of air that an opening was on her left. She turned her head to look out, but in the total absence of light, she could see nothing.

The blackness seemed as vast and endless as an ocean at night. She was almost glad to feel the tug of the bonds on her hands and ankles and the pressure of the iron platform against her body.

Time was beginning to feel as endless as the silence and the darkness. Then she heard muffled noises, the sharp snap of a key turning in a lock, and a door opening. Suddenly a flood of light washed over her. The brightness made her eyes hurt, and she automatically squeezed them shut. But she opened them quickly and blinked against the glare as she heard the slow steps of the Jaguar coming toward her. One foot dragged on the floor.

Then he was standing in front of her, looking down. His broad torso blocked the light, and his face was partly hidden by his own shadow. She could see his eyes, though. They stared at her with an unblinking intensity that made her want to turn away.

"I hope you enjoyed your ride," the Jaguar said. "Thanks to you, I had a painful climb down the ladder." His tone was gently scolding, like a teacher chiding a pupil for some minor rudeness.

"I'm sorry," Jill said. She tried to sound contrite.

"Maybe you are," he said, nodding his head. Then suddenly he asked, "If I untie you, will you promise not to try to escape?"

"Yes," Jill said. She felt a thrill of elation; he seemed susceptible to some degree of manipulation.

He bent over her, and she could feel his fingers brushing against her ankles as he loosened the knot binding her feet. He unwound the black scarf, then stepped back and tugged on its loose end. Her wrists were still tied, and the pull raised her hands. He slackened the strain, and her hands fell back to a resting position. She was like a marionette.

"Slide your feet off first, then stand up," he ordered.

"Aren't you going to untie my hands?" she asked in genuine surprise.

"Maybe later," he said. "Now get out of there."

She slid her feet and legs off the edge, then grasped the top of the iron frame with her right hand. She gasped with pain as she bumped her left hand. She pushed her torso off the shelf, but before she could regain her balance, she fell to the floor.

She pulled herself into a kneeling position, then got to her feet. For the first time, she was able to get a view of the room. She noticed the large oak desk and the massive wooden table standing under the hanging light. The light illuminated only a small circular area at the front part of the room and left most of the cavernous space hidden in deep shadows.

The Jaguar reached toward her, and she involuntarily stepped backward. He had only been picking up the dangling end of the black scarf. "Don't be afraid," he said. "I want you to come over here where we can be more comfortable."

He tugged on the scarf, and she followed behind him. He didn't turn his back to her but walked almost sideways to keep her in sight. He avoided resting his weight on his right foot, and that made him walk with a slow, shuffling step.

He stopped in front of the heavy wooden table. "Climb up here," he ordered. He slapped his hand against the top with a loud crack.

Now that she was close to the table, she could see the thick leather straps and brass buckles. She could also see that the surface of the wood was marked with knife cuts and innumerable dark stains and splotches. She suspected she was looking at some sort of operating table.

"Just sit up here so we can talk," the Jaguar said. "You don't have to lie down." She noticed his hand was resting on the hilt of the knife at his left side.

"I can't climb up with my hands tied," Jill said. "The table is too tall."

He glanced at her, then at the table, apparently measuring her against it. He nodded at her and said, "Hold your hands out in front of you." When she did, he told her, "Push your wrists in opposite directions."

She pushed hard, watching her arms strain against each other.

She heard a soft click, then suddenly the wedge-shaped blade of the knife was flashing in front of her eyes. The blade cut through the black fabric with ease, and by the time she looked up, the knife was back in its scabbard.

"Up on the table now," the Jaguar said.

She backed up to the table and placed the palms of her hands on its rough wooden surface. Then she gave a small jump and landed on the edge of the table top. The pain in her left hand made her gasp.

"Now we can get to know one another," he said. "We'll play a game." He smiled at her, but the smile was such a parody of warmth and charm that she found it obscene. She had seen what he was capable of when he had broken her finger.

"You killed Marie Thomas and Anna Louise Hamilton, didn't you?" She couldn't keep the anger out of her voice.

"Among others," he said. He looked straight at her, and his dark blue eyes appeared surprisingly gentle.

"Why?" she asked.

"Lots of reasons," he said. "Basically, because I'm lonely." He spoke softly, as if talking only to himself.

"Why does that mean you have to kill someone?"

"Because it's the most perfect way of breaking down all the barriers between two people. No union is more complete than that of hunter and prey, killer and victim."

He looked away from her into the darkness, and his expression was thoughtful. "When I kill someone, I incorporate her life into mine and take on her power. We are joined together." He nodded his head. "It's a wonderful feeling you have to experience to understand."

"That doesn't explain why you have to mutilate them." She didn't try to hide her disgust.

"Don't say that," he said sharply. He was no longer smiling. His face had turned hard, and his eyes were narrowed into slits. "My ancestors demand sacrifices, and I perform them in the proper way. Don't talk about it."

"I thought you wanted us to talk."

"I want you to understand me," he said. "But I'm not going to let you stray into areas you know nothing about."

"I didn't mean to make you angry," Jill said. She hesitated, then asked, "Do you really believe you're Paul Atreides?"

The signs of anger disappeared, and he gave a loud laugh that seemed to echo in the darkness. "Paul is a fictional character, and I'm quite real. But we're a lot alike. I've got many of the same powers, and I'm also destined for greatness." He smiled at her again. "You probably think that shows I'm a lunatic, but you're wrong—dead wrong."

Jill looked straight into his eyes and said, "You're going to kill me, aren't you?"

His face registered surprise. "I'm playing a game with you. That's what it's been all along, and whether I kill you depends on you."

"Really?"

"Just behave yourself, and you've got a good chance of coming through this alive." His face took on a knowing look.

"I can identify you," Jill said flatly.

"That doesn't matter," he said, shaking his head. "I'm leaving Boston and taking up a new identity. By the time somebody finds you, I'll be long gone."

"Okay, I won't cause any trouble," Jill said. She believed nothing he had told her.

He abruptly turned away and walked the few steps to the head of the table. He stopped at the white-enameled instrument stand and picked up a black leather case.

"I want to show you some of the props in our game," he said.

He unzipped the case and opened it flat on the stand so she could get a clear view. Nickel-plated surgical instruments gleamed in the brightness of the overhead light. The one that immediately grabbed her attention was a long, curved knife with a knurled grip that looked like something a butcher would use. Above the knife was a short-bladed bone saw and a brace with a variety of bits. Below was a row of various-sized scalpels, a large syringe, and several small glass jars fitted under elastic bands.

"They're autopsy instruments," he said. He studied her closely to catch her response. She tried to keep her face wooden, but an icy lump was forming in her stomach.

"We're going to pretend you're dead," he said. He gave her a smile of professional friendliness, a smile doctors give their patients. "I'm going to pretend to remove your heart, and then I'll offer it up to the sky gods. You'll like the ritual."

"And my head?" Jill asked. Her voice was level, but her throat was so tight she could hardly breathe.

"That's next," the Jaguar said. He slipped the curved knife from under its elastic band and held it up so she could see it. "I used this on Marie and Anna. But of course, I'm only going to pretend to use it on you."

"I don't like this game," Jill said. Her hands were trembling, and her voice was dry and choked.

The Jaguar put down the knife and turned away from the head of the table to come stand beside her.

"We're all a little shy doing something for the first time," he said. "I'm going to make it a lot easier for you. Just turn your head a little to the right."

Jill glanced down and saw he had taken the stun gun out of its holster and was holding it in his right hand.

58

Wednesday 4:30 P.M.

"Over the curb!" Firecaster yelled at the patrol car driver. "Get over the curb, goddamn it!"

The car's back wheels bumped against the curb and came to a stop. As the driver raced the engine, the tires made a high-pitched whine and slung up water from the gutter in a dense spray. Firecaster wiped his hand over his face to get the water out of his eyes. The rain showed no sign of slackening, and he was soaked to the skin. He was very cold.

"The curb is too high!" the other officer shouted to Firecaster. He was at the rear of the car wearing a yellow slicker and a hat with a hood. "He's not going to make it over, Lieutenant. We need to call for assistance."

"Fuck that!" Firecaster shouted at him. "We're in a hurry." He jerked his head at the car. "Come on, let's push."

Renuzi was leaning against the left front fender. The officer in the raincoat stationed himself in the middle, and Firecaster took the right fender. The driver looked through the windshield at them.

"Rock it!" Firecaster yelled. He made a back-and-forth gesture with his hand so the driver could see it.

The driver nodded and pulled the car forward a foot or so. Then he put it in reverse and rammed into the curb. The car slipped down, then hit the curb again. In two more tries, they got the rhythm.

"Now shove!" Firecaster shouted.

The three strained together, and Firecaster could feel the sharp, wet metal of the fender's edge cut into his hand. The rim of the headlight hurt his chest, but he kept up the pressure.

All at once, the combined effort worked, and the car's back wheels were up on the sidewalk. The car jerked backward so quickly the three of them were thrown off balance and had to scramble to keep from falling onto the rain-swept street.

Firecaster walked to the driver's door and pulled it open. The uniformed driver was alert and ready. He gave Firecaster an inquiring look.

"I dropped my tow-chain on the sidewalk," Firecaster said. "Loop it around your axle and attach it to the ring in that iron door." He gestured toward the rectangular plate.

"Yes, sir," the driver said.

"When I give the order, pull forward. Don't go slow. Just jump ahead, because we need to hit it with a jerk."

The driver nodded. "I got you," he said.

The driver got out of the car and hurried around to the back. The rain immediately soaked his blue uniform. He picked up the yellow plastic reel wrapped with the heavy tow-chain and unwound the first few feet.

He looped the loose end of the chain through the welded ring, doubled the chain on itself, and snapped on the clasp to keep the loop in place. He then payed out the chain to the bumper of the car, put down the reel, and without hesitating, climbed under the car to wrap the chain around the axle.

Firecaster turned to the officer in the yellow slicker who had come up to stand by the opened door. Renuzi was beside him, his dark suit so completely soaked it hardly looked wet.

"Get your shotgun and stand by," Firecaster told the officer. "I'm going in first, but I don't want you shooting unless I give the order."

"But don't you want me to cover you?" the officer asked.

"Just do what I say," Firecaster said sharply. "It's going to be close quarters, and I don't want to have to worry about you blowing me away or shooting the hostage. Don't do anything until I tell you to. Got it?"

"Yes, sir," the officer said.

"How about me?" Renuzi asked.

"You come right behind me," Firecaster told him. "Keep on my right so I'll know where you are."

"That's it?" the officer in the slicker asked incredulously. "That's the whole plan?"

"The main idea is for you to stay out of the way," Firecaster said coldly. "Now let's go."

The driver shut the car door, and the other three took up stations by the brick wall. Firecaster stood next to the tow line, with Renuzi on his right.

Firecaster wiped his right hand on his pants to get off as much water as possible. He then took his .38 Police Special out of its holster, raised his left hand and glanced at the driver. The driver's head was sticking out the window, and he was peering through the gray curtain of rain.

Firecaster raised his hand above his head, and the driver raced the engine.

59

Wednesday 4:35 P.M.

As the stun gun came nearer to her neck, every detail of its structure stood out with clarity. The device became more real than the person holding it, and she was transfixed, as though she were studying a textbook illustration.

She told herself to keep focusing on the two prongs at the front. She would have to sit still for only a moment longer. Her plan was desperate, and if it didn't work, she would be dead. But she wasn't going to go down without a fight.

The Jaguar leaned toward her, and she could smell the rank acrid scent of sweat coming from his body. The gray dust from the concrete tunnel powdered his hair and streaked his face with barbaric markings. The dust sticking to the sweat around his eyes formed an irregular dark mask. The blue eyes peering from the mask were as cold and unblinking as ovals of polished lapis.

The tips of the metal prongs touched the soft skin below her jaw. She looked into the stony eyes of the Jaguar and saw no warmth or recognition. Even as she watched, a transformation took place. The person behind the eyes ceased to be human even in facsimile.

She looked down at the Jaguar's hand wrapped around the black plastic grip of the stun gun. His fingers were dirty, and the blond hair that curled in wisps across his knuckles was matted with sweat and dust.

She could not move yet. She dared not move yet.

Then she saw the skin of his fingers grow taut as his muscles began to contract to squeeze the trigger.

At that moment, she leaped forward and grabbed him around the throat with both hands. His eyes opened wide in surprise, and he took a step backward. His neck was huge and slick with sweat, and she didn't think she would be able to hold on. Her broken finger caused agony, but she squeezed tighter as she felt her grip loosen.

The voltage must have surged through her body, but she felt no more than a sharp sting on her neck and a slight tingling in her hands. Most of the charge hit the Jaguar.

The voltage lifted him into the air, spun him around, and flung him out of her grip. The stun gun fell from his hand and hit the concrete with a metallic clatter. Almost simultaneously, he crashed to the floor. In the space of a second, he drew up into a tight ball with his head bowed down and pushed into his chest. His arms jerked in to clasp his sides, his back curved inward, and his knees doubled up to his stomach.

His body flopped once, then suddenly went limp. It was as though his clenched muscles had been clipped like a string. His arms and legs simply let go and fell into a loose sprawl. His neck lost its tension, and his head rolled to the side.

Jill felt an immediate surge of relief. She took a deep breath, and tears began to run down her cheeks, blurring her vision. Almost angry with herself, she wiped her eyes with her fingertips and jumped down from the table. Her plan had worked, but she couldn't afford the luxury of giving in to emotion.

The Jaguar was down, but she wouldn't be safe until he was locked up or dead. She hurried to the instrument stand at the head of the table and snatched up the long, curved autopsy knife. She stood over the Jaguar's curled body with the knife in her hand. She had seen farmers in St. Francisville hoist pigs with chains around their hind legs and slit their throats while they squealed in terror. If she pulled back the Jaguar's head, she could stick the knife through his throat.

She hesitated, glancing from the nickel-plated blade to the black-clothed figure. Killing an animal with your hands was hard, and even when the farmers kept sawing at the pigs' throats, they always kicked and struggled for several minutes.

She couldn't risk merely injuring the Jaguar, and she wasn't sure she could stick the knife in him at all. He wasn't like a snake. He was human. She could use the knife to protect herself, but she couldn't stab him while he was unconscious.

The important thing was to get away from him. If she could reach safety, Eric and the whole police force could hunt him down. But how could she get out?

The lift! If it brought her down, it should be capable of taking her up. She felt a tremor of excitement. The rectangular opening was no more than forty feet away. Holding the knife in her right hand, she crossed the distance at a run.

She thrust her head inside the opening and quickly examined the walls of the shaft and the metal shelf where she had been forced to stretch out like a corpse. She could find no buttons or switches, and she stepped back and scanned the wall on both sides. *She was taking too long. The Jaguar wasn't going to stay unconscious much longer.* Her heart was pounding with anxiety. Then she saw the knife-switch three feet from the rectangular opening and on the left.

She stood for a moment, looking at the switch in puzzlement. She couldn't see how it would be possible to be inside the lift and throw the switch. It seemed too far to reach. Yet the Jaguar must have used the lift earlier, because she had heard the cables squealing. Maybe he just had longer arms. She lacked time to experiment.

She could feel desperation beginning to build inside. Her hands were shaking and her teeth chattering. Her eyes searched the wall for the door the Jaguar had used. When she saw it, she rushed to it. He said he had climbed down, so there must be a ladder behind the door. She twisted the doorknob and tugged at the door. It was locked.

She fought down the panic that threatened to engulf her. Where was the key? He came through the door, so he must have locked it behind him. He must have done that before getting her out of the lift. Probably the key was in his pocket, then.

"Oh, shit," she said. She would have to search his pockets.

She picked up the black scarf the Jaguar had used on her, then stood by his collapsed body. His eyes were closed, and his face was more relaxed than she had ever seen it.

Her own hands were trembling as she knelt down, put the knife on the floor, and picked up his right hand. It felt very heavy, as though it were made of something denser than ordinary flesh. She put both hands on top of his chest and draped the black scarf over his wrists. Then just as she was starting to wrap the cloth around, his chest heaved and a rush of air escaped from his mouth in a moan.

She jumped back as if his flesh had seared her hand. Almost simultaneously, she picked up the knife and pointed it toward him. She waited a moment, her heart fluttering and her breathing ragged, but nothing happened. She began to feel sure his movements were nothing more than an involuntary muscle tremor, but they frightened her. She gave up the idea of tying his hands and stood up. Her eyes swept the floor.

Where was the stun gun? Could he have thrown it somewhere during the convulsion? She turned and looked toward the dark rear of the room, then toward the brighter front. Suddenly she realized what must have happened. He must have fallen on it. It must be under his body.

If she had the stun gun, he could be controlled. She could just squeeze the trigger and put him out. Then she could search for the key without worrying about his waking up. She would have to turn him over.

She put down the knife again, and with a jerky movement, she snatched up his left arm and braced her feet against his right hip. Her broken finger throbbed, but she pulled with a steady strain and raised his left shoulder off the floor. He was heavy, but she was doing it.

Encouraged by her success, she pulled harder, trying to move the body forward to reach its center of gravity so it would roll over with only a slight effort. Her breathing was heavy, and her heart pounded with fear.

She kept her eyes on his face, searching for any sign to show he was returning to consciousness. Once she thought she saw his eyelids flutter, but when she looked closely, they were shut and unmoving. She kept up the strain, and his body rolled onto its side. She felt a sense of relief and tugged on his arm again.

Then without warning, the arm rotated in her grasp and his large hand grabbed her around her left wrist. The grip was powerful, and she could feel the strength leaving her wrist as he crushed the muscles with his fingers. The pain in her broken finger was so sharp she thought she might pass out.

She automatically jumped back, attempting to jerk free. But he hung on to her wrist, and as she bent her knees to try to pull herself loose, he used the pressure she was exerting to help raise himself into a standing position. As he got to his feet, he scooped up the stun gun.

She glanced toward the spot where she had put down the autopsy knife. She saw it was hardly two feet away, but it was on the floor behind the Jaguar. Reaching it was her only chance.

She suddenly let her body sag to the floor. The Jaguar staggered, thrown off balance by the sudden strain on his injured leg. She then lunged toward him, reaching between his legs with her right hand to grab for the knife.

His right knee smashed against her head, and for a moment she felt too dazed and confused to know what was happening. She collapsed onto the floor. Without loosening his grip on her left wrist, the Jaguar turned and and saw what she was trying to reach. He kicked the autopsy knife, sending it skittering across the concrete into the darkness.

He used both arms to jerk her to her feet. His lips were drawn away from his teeth, and his eyes had a wild triumphant look. Her chest seemed paralyzed, and she couldn't scream or even breathe.

The shock lasted for only a moment, then she began desperately to flail at him with her right hand, hitting at him with her fist. She aimed at his head, trying to strike him in the eye or to break his nose.

Her efforts were useless. He was too large and too strong. He kept looking straight at her as he raised his right arm to ward off the blows.

"I keep underestimating you," he said through clenched teeth. He shook his head, then smiled at her. He wasn't even breathing hard.

He pulled her toward him with a steady and unrelenting pressure. She braced her feet and leaned her whole body away from him, pushing in the opposite direction. But her effort did no good. He pulled her so close their shoulders were touching.

"I'm going to cut out your heart," he said. He spoke in a harsh whisper, as though letting her in on a dark secret he wanted no one else to hear.

She ignored the pain of her broken finger and tried to jerk loose, but he was holding her too tight. She turned her face away from him, but he released his grip on her arm and grabbed her head. The fingers digging into her scalp felt like steel talons, and he turned her head around so she had to look directly at him.

"I'm going to cut out your heart . . . then eat it," he said. He spoke the last words brutally, almost spitting them into her face. He pulled his fingers together, gathering up her hair. She almost cried out with the pain as he twisted her head away from him, then back again.

"There will be no more tricks," he said. "I'm not giving you a chance to touch me this time." He twisted her head so she was facing away from him, but she could see him bring up his right hand. He was still holding the stun gun.

At that moment, the dark end of the room seemed to explode. The wall fell outward with a crash of collapsing bricks, and harsh light poured into the darkness. She could smell the odor of rain, then she could actually hear it. That was her last memory before she felt the cold prongs of the stun gun against the back of her neck.

Firecaster was standing on the sidewalk, looking into the ragged hole made by ripping out the iron door. Directly in front of him he could see the Jaguar with his fingers twisted in Jill's hair and the stun gun pressed against her neck. They were under the bare, hanging bulb, spotlit as though they were on the stage in an amateur play.

Without hesitating, Firecaster clambered up the pile of collapsed bricks. Rain from behind him was blowing into the hole, and the wet, loose bricks skidded under his feet. His head seemed to swim, and he felt almost separate from his body.

He ignored everything he was feeling, except for the anger that had taken hold of him. He crouched low, bowed at the waist, and used the fingertips of his left hand to push against the bricks and maintain his balance. He held his right hand raised to keep his drawn weapon from hitting against a brick and accidentally discharging.

Firecaster was over the rubble and onto the concrete floor when he saw the Jaguar pull a knife out of the holster at his left side and kneel down beside Jill.

"John!" Firecaster yelled. "John Haack!" With Jill and Haack so close together, using a gun was out of the question.

"Police!" Firecaster shouted. "Put down that knife right now." He made his tone authoritative and firm, almost paternal. Then he began to run.

The Jaguar hesitated at the sound of Firecaster's voice, then looked up at him. Haack appeared confused and uncertain, and for a moment he seemed about to do as he was told.

Then he shook his head, as though to clear away his confusion. He looked down at Jill again, tugged on her arm and rolled her body over so she was lying on her back. He used the tip of the wedge-shaped blade to slice through the neckband of her black sweater.

He grabbed the fabric and ripped it. It tore in a straight line, and he pulled the material to the sides, as though he were peeling back skin. The torn fabric exposed the rounded mounds of Jill's breasts and the flat plane of her stomach. She was breathing softly, and her skin shone with a pale rose color.

Half-naked and lying on her back under the hanging light, she was totally vulnerable. She could have been an anesthetized patient waiting for the surgeon to make the first incision. The smooth softness of her bare skin seemed to invite the hard sharp edge of the knife blade.

Haack was raising the knife to strike when Firecaster kicked him in the face.

Firecaster's foot caught him on the left side of the jaw with a loud crack. Haack spun backward and to one side. He caught himself before he fell, still clutching the survival knife. Before Firecaster could gain back the balance the kick had cost him, Haack hurled himself forward. His right shoulder hit Firecaster in the chest.

Firecaster gave an involuntary grunt, then gasped for air with a long wheezing sound. He tried to bring up his revolver to get a shot, but Haack was too quick for him. Haack struck out with the knife, jabbing its point toward Firecaster.

Its blade hit Firecaster's wrist, knocking the gun out of his hand and slicing through the flesh. Firecaster jerked his arm back, and the action caused Haack to loose his grip on the survival knife. The pistol and the knife both clattered to the floor.

The room suddenly filled with a hollow booming sound, and chips of concrete flew into the air near Haack. A burning odor permeated the air.

"Hands up! Hands up!" Renuzi shouted, his voice made high by tension. He was running toward them from Firecaster's right.

Haack was bending over beside the pistol. He reached out to pick it up, when Firecaster stepped on his hand. Firecaster put all his weight on his foot and twisted it around, trying to crush Haack's fingers.

Haack let out a loud cry of pain, then bowled into Firecaster. Firecaster fell to the floor, and as he fell, his foot kicked the pistol, sending it skittering across the floor out of reach. Haack kicked at Firecaster's head, but Firecaster managed to dodge so that the edge of the boot merely grazed his cheek.

The chamber was once again filled with a deafening roar and a burning odor. Haack staggered backward and almost fell. He looked toward Renuzi, who was pointing his pistol at him, ready to squeeze off another shot.

Without looking toward Firecaster, Haack began to run the forty feet to the lift. He moved fast, even though he was hampered by his right leg. He ran with a lurching, jerky motion.

Firecaster was taken by surprise and stood puzzled for a moment. Then he saw the oak door Haack was running toward and took off after him, trailing blood from his gashed wrist. He wrapped his left hand around his wrist to stanch the flow.

Haack looked over his shoulder and saw he was maintaining his lead. When he reached the lift, he threw himself into the rectangular opening. He slid his feet down the platform, then leaned his head out the opening. He stretched out his left arm until the tips of his fingers located the black handle of the knife-switch.

He glanced at Firecaster, then shoved down on the switch, bringing the two parallel strips of metal into contact. The electric motor immediately began to unwind the cable to lower the counterweight and raise the lift.

The cable squealed and the brake began to make its usual rough rubbing sound. Haack watched Firecaster coming and saw he could never reach the lift in time to stop him. He gave Firecaster a contemptuous smile and waved at him.

Haack was pulling his arm back inside when a sharp clean crack like a coal popping in a fire made him look up.

A sudden windy rushing noise roared down the shaft as the brake broke and the counterweight began its plunge to the bottom of the shaft. Almost simultaneously, the cable attached to the counterweight rattled over the control pulley and jerked on the lift.

The lift shot straight up, and Haack's contemptuous expression changed to one of absolute terror as he realized what was happening. The sharp raised edge of the iron bed rushed past the metal frame of the opening, and Haack's head was instantly sheared from his neck a few inches below his chin.

A fine mist of blood sprayed the wall, forming a semicircular pattern on the crumbling plaster. A heavier rush of blood splashed to the floor under the opening of the lift.

Haack's head fell onto the concrete floor with a muffled thud. The head hit face down, bounced once, then rolled away from the wall for a few feet.

Firecaster pulled himself up short and jumped to the side to keep from stepping on the head. He turned back and, breathing heavily, stood looking down at it. The blond hair was drenched in blood, and the face was mottled with red streaks. Yet the eyelids blinked, the blue eyes were open and seemed to flicker in recognition. The mouth and lips moved, apparently forming words.

Then the eyes closed and the whole face went slack. Blood spilled from the opened mouth and joined blood from the mangled flesh of the neck that was spreading out into a widening pool.

Firecaster stood transfixed. Had Haack actually tried to say something?

Firecaster turned away as Renuzi ran up.

What could a person like Haack have wanted to say?

PART FIVE

EPILOGUE

April 29
Friday

60

Friday 4:00 P.M.

Jill sat behind her desk sorting through her papers, arranging some in stacks and throwing others into the wastebasket. The aluminum splint and layers of surgical tape on her finger made the process awkward.

She had already copied her files and prepared the computer for packing, and she was tempted to dump all her papers into a large box and sort them out after the move. But it was better to sort through the accumulations of her life now.

While she was at work, Firecaster was in the hall talking on the telephone. He was facing away from her, leaning with his knee on a chair pulled out from the small table. She could hear part of his conversation, but nothing he said meant much to her.

He had been on the phone a number of times during the day. Sometimes he spent more time listening than talking, then he would make a suggestion or authorize a request. This time he had been doing more listening, but eventually he hung up and returned to the living room. He sat down on the love seat and propped his feet up on the coffee table. He laid his bandaged hand across his lap, as though to protect it from accidental bumps.

She thought he looked exhausted. The lines between his nose and mouth were deep crevices, and the skin beneath his eyes had a bruised purple appearance. Still, when he smiled at her, his eyes were lively, and they lit up his whole face.

"Have you ever thought about getting out of the detective business?" she asked. "You're very good at it, but the hours are terrible and people are always trying to kill you."

"They don't succeed as often as they would like, and that makes the job interesting. Actually, I never even thought of doing anything else until I met you."

"What did I do?" she asked in surprise.

"Made me want to live a different kind of life. I'm tired of my mind making my body feel bad."

297

"Have you thought about what else you might do?"

"Maybe go back to teaching," he said. He shook his head. "I don't know."

The telephone rang again, and Firecaster answered it. He was gone for what seemed a long time. When he returned to his place on the love seat, he didn't resume their conversation. Instead, he sat for several minutes without talking, apparently thinking about what he had been told.

"I want to know everything," Jill finally said. She leaned her elbows on her desk and looked over at him.

Firecaster shot her a glance. "You sound like Doctor Faustus. Are you willing to surrender your soul?"

"No, but I'm prepared to make a substitute offer," she said. "Who were you talking to for such a long time?"

"Karen Chase. She and Don are going to be coming over in a few minutes."

"Any particular reason?"

"I asked them to," Firecaster said. "I wanted to know what their people have been finding out." He gave her a sly smile. "I could have met them at the office, but I suspected you might like to eavesdrop."

"Let's make some coffee," she said, getting up from her desk. "I hope everybody likes the taste of fingerprint powder, or whatever it's called. It's on everything."

Don Renuzi and Karen Chase sat at opposite ends of the dining table with their coffee cups in front of them. By Chase's cup was a small, red ceramic bowl Jill had offered her as an ashtray. Jill sat by Firecaster on the love seat.

"We couldn't have been luckier tracing Haack's history," Renuzi said. "We got in touch with a woman named Rosie Sanders through the lawyer for his mother's estate. She worked for the family as a cook and housekeeper for thirty-five years, and even though she's over seventy, her memory is perfect. She knows names of relatives, friends, dates, everything. She's like a family encyclopedia."

"I assume his mother's dead," Firecaster said.

"She died a year ago April," Renuzi said. "So far as we can determine, Haack killed his first victim within five months."

"Dr. Castle said that once his mother was dead, Haack was free to kill substitutes," Chase said.

"Tell me more about his mother," Firecaster said to Renuzi.

"Her name was Helen Horace Haack, and she was a neurosurgeon and clinical professor at New York Medical College. She was well-known and very respected. When she died, she left all her money to the medical school to endow a professorship named after her."

"All her money?" Jill asked with surprise.

"Except for a bequest setting up a pension for Rosie Sanders," Renuzi said. "She had quite a lot, too. Her father was a millionaire, and when he died, his estate was split between Helen Haack and her sister Emily. Even before that, though, the sisters inherited independent incomes from their mother, who died before they were in their teens."

"John Haack must have had more than his salary from Book-keepers," Firecaster said. "He couldn't have bought the condo-minium at Cambridge Court, paid rent on the Prospect Street apartment, and owned an expensive car without a lot of cash behind him."

"He had a fortune of his own," Renuzi said. "His Aunt Emily died five years ago and left her money to her husband, Richard. Then when he died three years later, he left everything to Haack. Apparently, the uncle liked Haack, or at least felt sorry for the way he was treated by his mother. He knew Helen wasn't going to leave Haack anything, and since Richard didn't have any kids himself, he felt Haack deserved to have a share of the family money."

"What about Haack's father?" Jill asked. "How does he figure in this?"

"Not at all, in one sense," Renuzi said. "In another, he's the key to everything. Helen Haack never married the boy's father. He was a medical technician at Colton Hospital, and she met him while she was a resident there. He was much below her educationally and socially, but she fell in love with him, and fell very hard. She got pregnant, maybe deliberately, but in the end he dumped her."

"She wanted him to marry her," Chase said.

"She couldn't believe he wouldn't," Renuzi said. "Here she was a beautiful woman, a surgeon, and very wealthy. She was a spoiled rich kid accustomed to having everything she wanted. How could somebody without money or family or even a profession possibly refuse to marry her?"

"Why did he?" Firecaster asked.

"No one knows for sure," Renuzi said. "Rosie Sanders steered me to a woman named Maude Leister, who knew both the sisters from the time they were all children. Her story is the guy told Helen life was too short to spend being bossed around, even by somebody rich and beautiful."

"But Helen still didn't have an abortion," Jill said.

"She kept hoping she could use the child as a bargaining chip,"

Renuzi said. "This guy continued to work at the hospital until after the baby was born." Renuzi shrugged. "Maybe he couldn't make up his own mind about what he wanted, but Maude Leister thinks he stuck around because Helen was providing him with lots of spending money. Anyway, before the kid was a month old, he got a job with an archaeological party as a medical corpsman. He left for the Yucatan."

"What happened to Helen Haack then?" Jill asked.

"Maude Leister says she went crazy," Renuzi said. "But she did it in such a way nobody could tell anything was wrong. She spent all her time at the hospital doing surgery, and people just regarded her as totally dedicated."

"None of that made her the ideal mother either," Chase said. "She blamed Haack for what his father had done to her. She seemed to confuse the two of them in her thinking, and she believed Haack ruined her life just by being born."

"Did you ever find Haack's father?" Firecaster asked.

"Nobody knows where he is," Renuzi said. "Rosie Sanders says he did come to visit Helen once. He brought the boy a present, but Helen wouldn't let them spend any time together." Renuzi shook his head. "That was at least twenty years ago, though, and so far as Rosie knows, he never came back. Helen would get cards or letters from time to time, but she would throw them away without reading them. Then they stopped about five years ago. Rosie thinks he may be dead."

"What was his name?" Firecaster asked.

"This is interesting," Renuzi said. He glanced down the table at Karen, then looked back at Firecaster and Jill. "His name was Jack Varr," Renuzi said.

"Jack Varr," Jill said. "That sounds very much like *jaguar*." She glanced at Chase.

"Bull's-eye on the first shot," Chase said. "So far as we can tell, though, Haack never knew Jack Varr was his father. His mother told him his father didn't exist anymore. Not that he was dead, but he just didn't exist. The few others who knew never told him either, maybe because Helen ordered them not to. Still, Haack must have sensed a conspiracy of silence."

"I'm sure that at some level he knew his father left his mother," Firecaster said. "But he didn't want to admit to himself that both his parents wanted nothing to do with him."

"That makes sense in terms of his dreams," Chase said. "We got into his computer's locked files and found out a lot about his inner life."

"Was cracking his code difficult?" Firecaster asked.

"It was so easy it makes you wonder if he didn't design it that way," Chase said.

"He wanted people to know about him," Firecaster said. "Look at *The Book of the Jaguar*. He needed the attention and admiration he didn't get as a child." He shook his head.

"We found over twenty conversations between Haack and the computer program he called FRIEND," Chase said. "That's how we learned about his dreams and connected them with his parents."

"Dr. Castle was in hog heaven," Renuzi said. "But he also warned us that the dreams only show how a kid's mind tries to make sense out of experiences he doesn't understand."

Chase broke in. "Dr. Castle's point was that we can learn a lot about Haack from his dreams, but we still can't explain why he turned out the way he did. Other people with similar experiences don't."

"Tell us about the dreams," Firecaster prompted Chase.

"He had two kinds," she said. "He called one soft and the other hard. In the soft one, he comes awake in the middle of a jungle and is terrified by a shadowy shape approaching him, then a bright sphere of light appears. An animal he knows is a jaguar suddenly appears, snarls, and frightens off the shape coming toward him."

"So the jaguar is Jack Varr protecting the boy from his mother," Jill said. "It's a fantasy by a kid who needed to have somebody care about him."

"That's what Dr. Castle thinks," Chase said. "The hard dream had him puzzled, until he saw the autopsy report. In the hard dream, two figures come toward Haack while he's asleep. Their faces are too blurred for him to recognize them, and he can't wake up to fight. He hears *jaguar* repeated several times. Then they do something to him that hurts, something in his groin."

"I think I'm getting the picture," Firecaster said. "I remember that Murphy found semen stains, but no sperm cells."

Chase nodded. "When you also remember his mother was a surgeon, you can put that together with the fact that she apparently told him he wasn't going to be able to treat anybody the way his father treated her."

"She didn't castrate him, did she?" Jill asked.

"No," Chase said. "But she did the next thing to it. Dr. Benson says Haack had a vasectomy so long ago that whatever the tube is called never completed its development. Haack could never have had children."

"So you think his mother did the surgery?" Firecaster asked.

"Right," Renuzi said. "We think that about the time the boy was hitting puberty, his mother operated on him, and her sister, Emily, helped her. They gave him a general anesthetic, then probably kept him doped up for a couple of days. Maybe they talked about Jack Varr while they worked."

"At that age, he wouldn't have known what was going on," Jill said. "What he later thought was just a dream may have been a real memory, except it would be hazy and distorted and he would hear *Jack Varr* as *jaguar.*"

"That's right," Chase said. "The dreams tell us a little about the life Haack had growing up. They certainly show the source of the psychological pain that led him to develop his fantasies about killing women."

"Ted Castle thinks he turned everything into a game to protect himself from fully realizing what he was doing," Renuzi said. "If he thought of himself as a hunter, then he could concentrate on being a good one. All he had to face were technical problems."

"Do we know now how many women he killed?" Firecaster asked.

"We only have his records to go on," Renuzi said. "We checked out the woman in Washington and the one in New York with the local people and found both are still listed as uncleared crimes. Thomas and Hamilton make four, but it's clear that he didn't plan on stopping with Jill."

Firecaster put his hand on top of hers. "Whatever he planned, we can be happy we stopped him *at* Jill."

"Absolutely," Renuzi said. "I'll have to hand it to you for guessing there might be a pattern in the twenty-day gap between Thomas and Hamilton."

"It wasn't totally a guess," Firecaster said. "I knew some calendars are based on twenty-day cycles, and if I had been clever, I would have remembered the Maya."

"I still don't get that connection," Jill said.

"We didn't either," Chase said. "Then Dr. Castle told us his view, and it made a certain amount of sense."

"Haack must have heard enough to suspect his father had gone to the Yucatan," Renuzi said. "That made him interested in everything about the Maya, and he identified his Jack Varr with the jaguar god. Then he mixed that up with the idea that the Maya were visited by aliens from outer space and the Maya gods were really ancient astronauts."

"I understand," Jill said. "From there it was easy to fantasize that earth was just like Dune and he was like Paul Atreides. Since Paul was destined to become a powerful leader and a cult figure, then so was he."

"He was wrong," Renuzi said firmly. He glanced at Chase. She nodded, and they both got up from the table. "We've got a lot of reports to write," Renuzi said.

Firecaster closed the front door behind Renuzi and Chase and returned to the living room. He sat on the love seat beside Jill. He said nothing, but stared off into the distance.

"What are you thinking about?" Jill asked.

"What you said about Haack's idea of his destiny," Firecaster said. "Destiny is just what he couldn't escape. He looked like somebody in control, but he had no more freedom than a roulette ball bouncing around on a rigged wheel."

"Do any of us?" Jill asked. "Has the past already determined our future, or can we control it?"

"That depends," Firecaster said. He spoke slowly, choosing his words. "We move along the grooves carved by the past. When a groove is shallow, we can change our course, but when it's deep, we have to go where it takes us. The problem is, we don't have any way of knowing the depths of the grooves. We're never sure what we can change and what we can't."

"Then the most we can know is what we want," Jill said.

"I know exactly what I want," Firecaster said. He turned and smiled at her.

She raised her eyes to meet his. Then she kissed him.